E. C. Davis

# KEZIAH COFFIN

# THE WORKS OF JOSEPH C. LINCOLN

---

CY WHITTAKER'S PLACE

MR. PRATT        "CAP'N ERI"

PARTNERS OF THE TIDE

THE "OLD HOME HOUSE"

CAPE COD BALLADS

"'All right,' she said; 'then I suppose I shall have to take it.'"

[Page 88.]

# KEZIAH COFFIN

BY

JOSEPH C. LINCOLN

AUTHOR OF "CY WHITTAKER'S PLACE,"
"CAP'N ERI," ETC.

WITH ILLUSTRATIONS BY

WALLACE MORGAN

D. APPLETON AND COMPANY
NEW YORK AND LONDON: MCMIX

# CONTENTS

# CONTENTS

vi

# LIST OF ILLUSTRATIONS

# KEZIAH COFFIN

## CHAPTER I

IN WHICH KEZIAH HEARS TWO PROPOSALS AND THE
BEGINNING OF A THIRD

TRUMET in a fog; a fog blown in during
the night by the wind from the wide Atlantic. So wet and heavy that one might taste
the salt in it. So thick that houses along the main
road were but dim shapes behind its gray drapery,
and only the gates and fences of the front yards were
plainly in evidence to the passers-by. The beach
plum and bayberry bushes on the dunes were spangled with beady drops. The pole on Cannon Hill,
where the beacon was hoisted when the packet from
Boston dropped anchor in the bay, was shiny and
slippery. The new weathervane, a gilded whale, presented to the " Regular " church by Captain Zebedee Mayo, retired whaler, swam in a sea of cloud.
The lichened eaves of the little " Come-Outer "
chapel dripped at sedate intervals. The brick walk
leading to the door of Captain Elkanah Daniels's fine
residence held undignified puddles in its hollows.
And, through the damp stillness, the muttered growl
of the surf, three miles away at the foot of the sandy
bluffs by the lighthouse, sounded ominously.

Directly opposite Captain Elkanah's front gate,
on the other side of the main road, stood the little

I

story-and-a-half house, also the captain's property, which for fourteen years had been tenanted by Mrs. Keziah Coffin and her brother, Solomon Hall, the shoemaker. But Solomon had, the month before, given up his fight with debt and illness and was sleeping quietly in Trumet's most populous center, the graveyard. And Keziah, left alone, had decided that the rent and living expenses were more than her precarious earnings as a seamstress would warrant, and, having bargained with the furniture dealer in Wellmouth for the sale of her household effects, was now busy getting them ready for the morrow, when the dealer's wagon was to call. She was going to Boston, where a distant and condescending rich relative had interested himself to the extent of finding her a place as sewing woman in a large tailoring establishment.

The fog hung like a wet blanket over the house and its small yard, where a few venerable pear trees, too conservative in their old age to venture a bud even though it was almost May, stood bare and forlorn. The day was dismal. The dismantled dining room, its tables and chairs pushed into a corner, and its faded ingrain carpet partially stripped from the floor, was dismal, likewise. Considering all things, one might have expected Keziah herself to be even more dismal. But, to all outward appearances, she was not. A large portion of her thirty-nine years of life had been passed under a wet blanket, so to speak, and she had not permitted the depressing covering to shut out more sunshine than was absolutely necessary. "If you can't get cream, you might as well learn to love your sasser of skim milk," said practical Keziah.

2

She was on her knees, her calico dress sleeves, patched and darned, but absolutely clean, rolled back, uncovering a pair of plump, strong arms, a saucer of tacks before her, and a tack hammer with a claw head in her hand. She was taking up the carpet. Grace Van Horne, Captain Eben Hammond's ward, who had called to see if there was anything she might do to help, was removing towels, tablecloths, and the like from the drawers in a tall " high-boy," folding them and placing them in an old and battered trunk. The pair had been discussing the subject which all Trumet had discussed for three weeks, namely, the " calling" to the pastorate of the " Regular " church of the Rev. John Ellery, the young divinity student, who was to take the place of old Parson Langley, minister in the parish for over thirty years. Discussion in the village had now reached a critical point, for the Reverend John was expected by almost any coach. In those days, the days of the late fifties, the railroad down the Cape extended only as far as Sandwich; passengers made the rest of their journey by stage. Many came direct from the city by the packet, the little schooner, but Mr. Ellery had written that he should probably come on the coach.

" They say he's very nice-looking," remarked Miss Van Horne soberly, but with a *mischievous* glance under her dark lashes at Keziah. The lady addressed paused long enough to transfer several tacks from the floor to the saucer, and then made answer.

" Humph ! " she observed. " A good many years ago I saw a theater show up to Boston. Don't be shocked; those circumstances we hear so much

3

tell of—the kind you can't control—have kept me from goin' to theaters much, even if I wanted to. But I did see this entertainment, and a fool one 'twas, too, all singin' instead of talkin'—op'ra, I believe they called it. Well, as I started to say, one of the leadin' folks in it was the Old Harry himself, and *he* was pretty good-lookin'."

Grace laughed, even though she had been somewhat shocked.

"Why, Aunt Keziah!" she exclaimed—those who knew Keziah Coffin best usually called her aunt, though real nephews and nieces she had none—"why, Aunt Keziah! What do you mean by comparing the—the person you just mentioned with a *minister!*"

"Oh, I wasn't comparin' 'em; I'll leave that for you Come-Outers to do. Drat this carpet! Seems's if I never saw such long tacks; I do believe whoever put 'em down drove 'em clean through the center of the earth and let the Chinymen clinch 'em on t'other side. I haul up a chunk of the cellar floor with every one. Ah, hum!" with a sigh, "I cal'late they ain't any more anxious to leave home than I am. But, far's the minister's concerned, didn't I hear of your Uncle Eben sayin' in prayer meetin' only a fortni't or so ago that all hands who wa'n't Come-Outers were own children to Satan? Mr. Ellery must take after his father some. Surprisin', ain't it, what a family the old critter's got."

The girl laughed again. For one brought up, since her seventh year, in the strictest of Come-Outer families, she laughed a good deal. Many Come-Outers considered it wicked to laugh. Yet Grace did it, and hers was a laugh pleasant to hear and distinctly pleasant to see. It made her prettier than ever, a fact which, if she was aware of it, should have been an additional preventive, for to be pretty smacks of vanity. Perhaps she wasn't aware of it.

"What do you think Uncle Eben would say if he heard that?" she asked.

"Say *I* took after my father, too, I presume likely. Does your uncle know you come here to see me so often? And call me 'aunt' and all that?"

"Of course he does. Aunt Keziah, you mustn't think Uncle Eben doesn't see the good in people simply because they don't believe as he does. He's as sweet and kind as——"

"Who? Eben Hammond? Land sakes, child, don't I know it? Cap'n Eben's the salt of the earth. I'm a Regular and always have been, but I'd be glad if my own society was seasoned with a few like him. 'Twould taste better to me of a Sunday." She paused, and then added quizzically: "What d'you s'pose Cap'n Elkanah and the rest of our parish committee would say if they heard *that?*"

"Goodness knows! Still, I'm glad to hear you say it. And uncle says you are as good a woman as ever lived. He thinks you're misled, of course, but that some day you'll see the error of your ways."

"Humph! I'll have to hurry up if I want to see 'em without spectacles. See my errors! Land sakes! much as I can do to see the heads of these tacks. Takin' up carpets is as hard a test of a body's eyesight as 'tis of their religion."

Her companion put down the tablecloth she was folding and looked earnestly at the other woman. To an undiscerning eye the latter would have looked much as she always did—plump and matronly, with brown hair drawn back from the forehead and parted in the middle; keen brown eyes with a humorous twinkle in them—this was the Keziah Coffin the later generation of Trumet knew so well.

But Grace Van Horne, who called her aunt and came to see her so frequently, while her brother was alive and during the month following his death, could see the changes which the month had wrought. She saw the little wrinkles about the eyes and the lines of care about the mouth, the tired look of the whole plucky, workaday New England figure. She shook her head.

" Religion ! " she repeated. " I do believe, Aunt Keziah, that you've got the very best religion of anybody I know. I don't care if you don't belong to our church. When I see how patient you've been and how cheerful through all your troubles, it——"

Mrs. Coffin waved the hammer deprecatingly. " There ! there ! " she interrupted. " I guess it's a good thing I'm goin' away. Here's you and I prais- in' up each other's beliefs, just as if that wasn't a crime here in Trumet. Sometimes when I see how the two societies in this little one-horse place row with each other, I declare if it doesn't look as if they'd crossed out the first word of ' Love your neighbor ' and wrote in ' Fight,' instead. Yet I'm a pretty good Regular, too, and when it comes to whoopin' and carryin' on like the Come-Outers, I— Well! well! never mind; don't begin to bristle up. I won't say another word about religion. Let's pick the new minister to pieces. *Any* kind of a Christian can do that."

But the new minister was destined to remain un- dissected that morning, in that house at least. Grace

6

was serious now and she voiced the matter which had been uppermost in her mind since she left home.

"Aunt Keziah," she said, "why do you go away? What makes you? Is it absolutely necessary?"

"Why do I go? Why, for the same reason that the feller that was hove overboard left the ship— 'cause I can't stay. You've got to have vittles and clothes, even in Trumet, and a place to put your head in nights. Long's Sol was alive and could do his cobblin' we managed to get along somehow. What I could earn sewin' helped, and we lived simple. But when he was taken down and died, the doctor's bills and the undertaker's used up what little money I had put by, and the sewin' alone wouldn't keep a healthy canary in bird seed. Dear land knows I hate to leave the old house I've lived in for fourteen years and the town I was born in, but I've got to, for all I see. Thank mercy, I can pay Cap'n Elkanah his last month's rent and go with a clear conscience. I won't owe anybody, that's a comfort, and nobody will owe me; though I could stand that, I guess," she added, prying at the carpet edge.

"I don't care!" The girl's dark eyes flashed indignantly. "I think it's too bad of Cap'n Elkanah to turn you out when——"

"Don't talk that way. He ain't turnin' me out. He ain't lettin' houses for his health and he'll need the money to buy his daughter's summer rigs. She ain't had a new dress for a month, pretty near, and here's a young and good-lookin' parson heavin' in sight. Maybe Cap'n Elkanah would think a minister was high-toned enough even for Annabel to marry."

"He's only twenty-three, they say," remarked

7

Grace, a trifle maliciously. "Perhaps she'll adopt him."

Annabel was the only child of Captain Elkanah Daniels, who owned the finest house in town. She was the belle of Trumet, and had been for a good many years.

Keziah laughed.

"Well," she said, "anyhow I've got to go. Maybe I'll like Boston first rate, you can't tell. Or maybe I won't. Ah, hum! 'twouldn't be the first thing I've had to do that I didn't like."

Her friend looked at her.

"Aunt," she said, "I want to make a proposal to you, and you mustn't be cross about it."

"A proposal! Sakes alive! What'll I say? 'This is so sudden!' That's what Becky Ryder, up to the west part of the town, said when Jim Baker, the tin peddler, happened to ask her if she'd ever thought of gettin' married. 'O James! this is so sudden!' says Becky. Jim said afterwards that the suddenest thing about it was the way he cleared out of that house. And he never called there afterwards."

Grace smiled, but quickly grew grave.

"Now, auntie," she said, "please listen. I'm in earnest. It seems to me that you might do quite well at dressmaking here in town, if you had a little —well, ready money to help you at the start. I've got a few hundred dollars in the bank, presents from uncle, and my father's insurance money. I should love to lend it to you, and I know uncle would——"

Mrs. Coffin interrupted her.

"Cat's foot!" she exclaimed. "I hope I haven't got where I need to borrow money yet a while. Thank

8

you just as much, deary, but long's I've got two hands and a mouth, I'll make the two keep t'other reasonably full, I wouldn't wonder. No, I shan't think of it, so don't say another word. *No.*"

The negative was so decided that Grace was silenced. Her disappointment showed in her face, however, and Keziah hastened to change the subject.

"How do you know," she observed, "but what my goin' to Boston may be the best thing that ever happened to me? You can't tell. No use despairin', Annabel ain't given up hope yet; why should I? Hey? Ain't that somebody comin'?"

Her companion sprang to her feet and ran to the window. Then she broke into a smothered laugh.

"Why, it's Kyan Pepper!" she exclaimed. "He must be coming to see you, Aunt Keziah. And he's got on his very best Sunday clothes. Gracious! I must be going. I didn't know you expected callers."

Keziah dropped the tack hammer and stood up.

"Kyan!" she repeated. "What in the world is that old idiot comin' here for? To talk about the minister, I s'pose. How on earth did Laviny ever come to let him out alone?"

Mr. Pepper, Mr. Abishai Pepper, locally called "Kyan" (Cayenne) Pepper because of his red hair and thin red side whiskers, was one of Trumet's "characters," and in his case the character was weak. He was born in the village and, when a youngster, had, like every other boy of good family in the community, cherished ambitions for a seafaring life. His sister, Lavinia, ten years older than he, who, after the death of their parents, had undertaken the job of "bringing up" her brother, did not sympathize with these ambitions. Consequently, when Kyan ran away she followed him to Boston, stalked aboard the vessel where he had shipped, and collared him, literally and figuratively. One of the mates venturing to offer objection, Lavinia turned upon him and gave him a piece of her mind, to the immense delight of the crew and the loungers on the wharf. Then she returned with the vagrant to Trumet. Old Captain Higgins, who skippered the packet in those days, swore that Lavinia never stopped lecturing her brother from the time they left Boston until they dropped anchor behind the breakwater.

"I give you my word that 'twas pretty nigh a stark calm, but there was such a steady stream of language pourin' out of the Pepper stateroom that the draught kept the sails filled all the way home," asserted Captain Higgins.

That was Kyan's sole venture, so far as sailoring was concerned, but he ran away again when he was twenty-five. This time he returned of his own accord, bringing a wife with him, one Evelyn Gott of Ostable. Evelyn could talk a bit herself, and her first interview with Lavinia ended with the latter's leaving the house in a rage, swearing never to set foot in it again. This oath she broke the day of her sister-in-law's funeral. Then she appeared, after the ceremony, her baggage on the wagon with her. The bereaved one, who was sitting on the front stoop of his dwelling with, so people say, a most resigned expression on his meek countenance, looked up and saw her.

"My land! Laviny," he exclaimed, turning pale. "Where'd you come from?"

"Never mind *where* I come from," observed his sister promptly. "You just be thankful I've come. If ever a body needed some one to take care of 'em, it's you. You can tote my things right in," she added, turning to her grinning driver, "and you, 'Bishy, go right in with 'em. The idea of your settin' outside takin' it easy when your poor wife ain't been buried more'n an hour!"

"But—but—Laviny," protested poor Kyan, speaking the truth unwittingly, "I couldn't take it easy *afore* she was buried, could I?"

"Go right in," was the answer. "March!"

Abishai marched, and had marched under his sister's orders ever since. She kept house for him, and did it well, but her one fear was that some female might again capture him, and she watched him with an eagle eye. He was the town assessor and tax collector, but when he visited dwellings containing single women or widows, Lavinia always accompanied him, "to help him in his figgerin'," she said.

Consequently, when he appeared, unchaperoned, on the walk leading to the side door of the Coffin homestead, Keziah and her friend were surprised.

"He's dressed to kill," whispered Grace, at the window. "Even his tall hat; and in this fog! I do believe he's coming courting, Aunt Keziah."

"Humph!" was the ungracious answer. "He's come to say good-by, I s'pose, and to find out where I'm goin' and how much pay I'm goin' to get and if my rent's settled, and a few other little things that ain't any of his business. Laviny put him up to it, you see. She'll be along pretty quick. Well, I'll fix him so he won't talk much. He can help us take down that stovepipe. I said 'twas a job for a man, and a half one's better than none— Why, how d'ye do, 'Bishy? Come right in. Pretty thick outside, isn't it?"

Mr. Pepper entered diffidently.

"Er—er—how d'ye do, Keziah?" he stammered. "I thought I'd just run in a minute and——"

"Yes, yes. Glad to see you. Take off your hat. My sakes! it's pretty wet. How did Laviny come to let you— I mean how'd you come to wear a beaver such a mornin's this?"

Kyan removed the silk hat and inspected its limp grandeur ruefully.

"I—I— " he began. "Well, the fact is, I come out by myself. You see, Laviny's gone up to Sarah B.'s to talk church doin's. I—I—well, I kind of wanted to speak with you about somethin', Keziah, so— Oh! I didn't see you, Gracie. Good mornin'."

He didn't seem overjoyed to see Miss Van Horne, as it was. In fact, he reddened perceptibly and backed toward the door. The girl, her eyes twinkling, took up her jacket and hat.

"Oh! I'm not going to stop, Mr. Pepper," she said. "I was only helping Aunt Keziah a little, that's all. I must run on now."

"Run on—nonsense!" declared Keziah decisively. "You're goin' to stay right here and help us get that stovepipe down. And 'Bishy'll help, too. Won't you, 'Bish?"

The stovepipe was attached to the "air-tight" in the dining room. It—the pipe—rose perpendicularly for a few feet and then extended horizontally,

12

over the high-boy, until it entered the wall. Kyan looked at it and then at his " Sunday clothes."

" Why, I'd be glad to, of course," he declared with dubious enthusiasm. " But I don't know's I'll have time. Perhaps I'd better come later and do it. Laviny, she——"

" Oh, Laviny can spare you for a few minutes, I guess; 'specially as she don't know you're out. Better take your coat off, hadn't you? Grace, fetch one of those chairs for Ky—for 'Bishy to stand in."

Grace obediently brought the chair. It happened to be the one with a rickety leg, but its owner was helping the reluctant Abishai remove the long-tailed blue coat which had been his wedding garment and had adorned his person on occasions of ceremony ever since. She did not notice the chair.

" It's real good of you to offer to help," she said. " Grace and I didn't hardly dast to try it alone. That pipe's been up so long that I wouldn't wonder if 'twas chock-full of soot. If you're careful, though, I don't believe you'll get any on you. Never mind the floor; I'm goin' to wash that before I leave."

Reluctantly, slowly, the unwilling Mr. Pepper suffered himself to be led to the chair. He mounted it and gingerly took hold of the pipe.

" Better loosen it at the stove hole first," advised Keziah. " What was it you wanted to see me about, 'Bish?"

" Oh, nothin', nothin'," was the hasty response. " Nothin' of any account—that is to say——"

He turned redder than ever and wrenched at the pipe. It loosened at its lower end and the wires holding it in suspension shook.

" I guess," observed the lady of the house,

13

" that you'd better move that chest of drawers out so's you can get behind it. Grace, you help me. There! that's better. Now move your chair."

Kyan stepped from the chair and moved the latter to a position between the high-boy and the wall. Then he remounted and gripped the pipe in the middle of its horizontal section.

" Seems to stick in the chimney there, don't it? " queried Keziah. " Wiggle it back and forth; that ought to loosen it. What was it you wanted to say, 'Bish? "

Apparently, Mr. Pepper had nothing to say. The crimson tide had reached his ears, which, always noticeable because of their size and spread, were now lit up like a schooner's sails at sunset. His hands trembled on the pipe.

" Nothin', nothin', I tell you," he faltered. " I —I just run in to say how d'ye do, that's all."

" Really, I think I'd better be going," said Grace, glancing from Kyan's embarrassed face to that of the unsuspecting Mrs. Coffin. " I'm afraid I'm in the way."

" No, no! " shouted the occupant of the chair. " No, no, you ain't! "

" But I'm afraid I am. And they'll be expecting me at home. Aunt Keziah, I——"

" Don't be in such a hurry," interrupted Keziah. " Does stick in the chimney, don't it? Tell you what you can do, Grace; you can go in the woodshed and fetch the hammer that's in the table drawer. Hurry up, that's a good girl."

Kyan protested that he did not need the hammer, but his protest was unheeded. With one more glance at the couple, Grace departed from the kitchen, biting her lips. She shut the door carefully behind her. Mr. Pepper labored frantically with the pipe.

"No use to shake it any more till you get the hammer," advised Keziah. "Might's well talk while you're waitin'. What was it you wanted to tell me?"

Abishai drew one hand across his forehead, leaving a decorative smooch of blacking on his perspiring countenance. He choked, swallowed, and then, with a look at the closed door, seemed to reach a desperate resolve.

"Keziah," he whispered hurriedly, "you've known me quite a spell, ain't you?"

"Known you? Known you ever since you were born, pretty nigh. What of it?"

"Yes, yes. And I've known you, you know. Fact is, we've known each other."

"Hear the man! Land sakes! don't everybody in Trumet know everybody else? What *are* you drivin' at?"

"Keziah, you're a single woman."

His companion let go of the chair, which she had been holding in place, and stepped back.

"I'm a single woman?" she repeated sharply. "What do you mean by that? Did—did anybody say I wasn't?"

"No, no! 'Course not. But you're a widow, so you *be* single, you know, and——"

"Well? Did you think I was twins? Get down off there this minute. You've gone crazy. I thought so when I saw that beaver. Either that or you've been drinkin'. Grace! What *does* make her so long gettin' that hammer?"

Finding the hammer did seem to take a long

time. There was no sound from the kitchen. Kyan, steadying himself with one hand on the pipe, waved the other wildly.

"S-s-sh! s-sh-h!" he hissed. "Hush! be still! Don't get her in here. Keziah, you're single and so am I. You ain't got nobody to take care of you and I ain't, neither—that is, I don't want to be took care of—I mean, I've been took care of too much."

Mrs. Coffin took another step in the direction of the kitchen.

"He *is* loony!" she exclaimed under her breath. "I——"

"No, no! I ain't loony. I want to make a proposal to you. I want to see if you won't marry me. I'm sick of Laviny. Let's you and me settle down together. I could have some peace then. And I think a whole lot of you, too," he added, apparently as an afterthought.

Keziah's face was red now, and growing redder every instant.

"Kyan Pepper!" she cried in amazed incredulity. "Kyan Pepper, do you——"

"Hurry up!" pleaded Abishai, in agitated impatience. "Say yes quick. She'll be back in a minute."

"Say *yes!* Why, you——"

"Don't stop to argue, Keziah. I've got 'most fifteen hundred dollars in the bank. Laviny keeps the pass book in her bureau, but you could get it from her. I own my house. I'm a man of good character. You're poor, but I don't let that stand in the way. Anyhow, you're a first-rate housekeeper. And I really do think an awful lot of you."

Mrs. Coffin stepped no farther in the direction

of the kitchen. Instead, she strode toward the rickety chair and its occupant. Kyan grasped the pipe with both hands.

"You poor—miserable—impudent—" began the lady.

"Why, Keziah, don't you *want* to?" He spoke as if the possibility of a refusal had never entered his mind. "I cal'lated you'd be glad. You wouldn't have to go away then, nor— My soul and body! some one's knockin' at the door! *And this dummed pipe's fetched loose!*"

The last sentence was a smothered shriek. Keziah heeded not. Neither did she heed the knock at the door. Her hands were opening and closing convulsively.

"Be glad!" she repeated. "Glad to marry a good-for-nothin' sand-peep like you! You sassy— *Get* down off that chair and out of this house! Get down this minute!"

"I can't! This stovepipe's loose, I tell you! Be reason'ble, Keziah. Do—don't you touch me! I'll fall if you do. Pl-e-ase, Keziah!— O Lordy! I knew it. *Laviny!*"

The door opened. On the threshold, arms akimbo and lips set tight, stood Lavinia Pepper. Her brother's knees gave way; in their collapse they struck the chair back; the rickety leg wabbled. Kyan grasped at the pipe to save himself and, the next moment, chair, sections of stovepipe, and Mr. Pepper disappeared with a mighty crash behind the high-boy. A cloud of soot arose and obscured the view.

Keziah, too indignant even to laugh, glared at the wreck. In the doorway of the kitchen Grace Van

Horne, hammer in hand, leaned against the jamb, her handkerchief at her mouth and tears in her eyes. Lavinia, majestic and rigid, dominated the scene. From behind the high-boy came coughs, sneezes, and emphatic ejaculations.

Miss Pepper was the first to speak.

"Abishai Pepper," she commanded, "come out of that this minute."

Her answer was a tremendous sneeze. Then from the dusky cloud by the wall sounded a voice feebly protesting.

"Now, Laviny," began poor Kyan, "I never in my life——"

"Do you hear me? Come out of that!"

There was a sound of scrambling. More soot floated in the air. Then around the corner of the high-boy appeared Mr. Pepper, crawling on his hands and knees. His hair was streaked with black; his shirt front and collar and shirt sleeves were spotted and smeared with black; and from his blackened cheeks his red whiskers flamed like the last glowing embers in a fire-scarred ruin.

"Laviny," he panted, "I never was so surprised and upsot in all my life afore."

This was too much for Grace. She collapsed in a chair and laughed hysterically. Even the wrathful Keziah smiled. But Lavinia did not smile. For that matter, neither did her brother.

"Hum!" sneered Miss Pepper. "Upsot! Yes, I see you're upsot. Get up, and try to look as much like a Christian as you can!"

Kyan rose from his knees to his feet and rubbed his back. He glanced reproachfully at Grace, then fearfully at his sister.

"'You sassy — *Get* down off that chair and out of this house!'"

" I was just tryin' to help Keziah take down her stovepipe," he explained. " You see, she didn't have no man to——"

" Yes, I see. Well, I judge you got it down. Now you go out to the sink and wash your face. Heavens and earth! Look at them clothes! "

" I do hope you didn't hurt yourself, Abishai," said the sympathetic Keziah. Then, as remembrance of what had led to the upset came to her, she added: " Though I will say 'twas your own fault and nobody else's."

Lavinia whirled on her.

" His own fault, was it? " she repeated, her voice shrill and trembling. " Thank you very much, marm. I cal'late 'twas his own fault comin' here, too, wa'n't it? Nobody led him on, I s'pose. Nobody put him up to riggin' out in his best bib and tucker and sneakin' here the minute I was out of the house. No, nobody did! Of *course* not! "

" No, nobody did," said Keziah briskly. " And you may know what you're hintin' at, but I don't."

" Dear me! Ain't we innocent! We've got plenty of money, *we* have. Widowers with property ain't no attraction to *us*. Everybody knows that— oh, yes! And they never talk of such a thing—oh, no! Folks don't say that—that— Well," with a snarl in the direction of the kitchen, " are you anywheres nigh clean yet? Get your coat and hat on and come home with me."

She jerked her brother into the blue coat, jammed the tall hat down upon his head, and, seizing him by the arm, stalked to the door.

" Good day, marm," she said. " I do hope the next widower you get to take down your stovepipe—

yes, indeed! ha! ha!—I hope you'll have better luck with him. Though I don't know who 'twould be; there ain't no more idiots in town that *I* know of. Good day, and thank you kindly for your attentions to our family."

She pulled the door open and was on the step; but Mrs. Coffin did not intend to let her go in just that way.

"Laviny Pepper," she declared, her eyes snapping, "I don't know what you're talkin' about, but if you dare to mean that I want any of your money, or your brother's money, you're mistaken—'cause I don't. And I don't want your brother either—Lord help him, poor thing! And I tell you right now that there's nobody that does; though some kind-hearted folks have said 'twould be a Christian act to poison him, so's to put him out of his misery. There! Good mornin' to you."

She slammed the door. Lavinia was speechless. As for her brother, but one remark of his reached Grace, who was watching from the window.

"Laviny," pleaded Kyan, "just let me explain."

At nine o'clock that night he was still "explaining."

Keziah turned from the door she had closed behind her visitor.

"Well!" she ejaculated. "*Well!*"

Her friend did not look at her. She was still gazing out of the window. Occasionally she seemed to choke.

Keziah eyed her suspiciously.

"Humph!" she mused. "'Twas funny, wasn't it?"

"Oh, dreadfully!" was the hurried answer.

"Yes. Seems to me you took an awful long time findin' that hammer."

"It was away back in the drawer. I didn't see it at first."

"Hum! Grace Van Horne, if I thought you heard what that—that *thing* said to me, I'd—I'd—Good land of mercy! somebody *else* is comin'."

Steps, measured, dignified steps, sounded on the walk. From without came a "Hum—ha!" a portentous combination of cough and grunt. Grace dodged back from the window and hastily began donning her hat and jacket.

"It's Cap'n Elkanah," she whispered. "I must go. This seems to be your busy morning, Aunt Keziah. I "—here she choked again—" really, I didn't know you were so popular."

Keziah opened the door. Captain Elkanah Daniels, prosperous, pompous, and unbending, crossed the threshold. Richest man in the village, retired shipowner, pillar of the Regular church and leading member of its parish committee, Captain Elkanah looked the part. He removed his hat, cleared his throat behind his black stock, and spoke with impressive deliberation.

"Good morning, Keziah. Ah—er—morning, Grace." Even in the tone given to a perfunctory salutation like this, the captain differentiated between Regular and Come-Outer. "Keziah, I—hum, ha!—rather expected to find you alone."

"I was just going, Cap'n Daniels," explained the girl. The captain bowed and continued.

"Keziah," he said, "Keziah, I came to see you on a somewhat important matter. I have a proposal I wish to make you."

He must have been surprised at the effect of his words. Keziah's face was a picture, a crimson picture of paralyzed amazement. As for Miss Van Horne, that young lady gave vent to what her friend described afterwards as a " squeal," and bolted out of the door and into the grateful seclusion of the fog.

# CHAPTER II

## IN WHICH KEZIAH UNEARTHS A PROWLER

THE fog was cruel to the gossips of Trumet that day. **Mrs.** Didama Rogers, who lived all alone, except for the society of three cats, a canary, and a white poodle named " Bunch," in the little house next to Captain Elkanah's establishment, never entirely recovered from the chagrin and disappointment caused by that provoking mist. When one habitually hurries through the morning's household duties in order to sit by the front window and note each passer-by, with various fascinating surmises as to his or her errand and the reasons for it, it is discouraging to be able to see only one's own front fence and a scant ten feet of sidewalk. And then to learn afterwards of a dozen most exciting events, each distinctly out of the ordinary, which might have been used as excuses for two dozen calls and as many sensations! As Captain Zeb Mayo, the irreverent ex-whaler, put it, " That fog shook Didama's faith in the judgment of Providence. 'Tain't the ' all wise,' but the ' all seein' ' kind she talks about in meetin' now."

The fog prevented **Mrs.** Rogers's noting the entrance of Mr. Pepper at the Coffin front gate. Also his exit, under sisterly arrest. It shut from her view the majestic approach of Captain Elkanah Daniels and Grace's flight, her face dimpled with smiles and breaking into laughter at frequent intervals. For a young lady, supposed to be a devout Come-Outer, to hurry along the main road, a handkerchief at her mouth and her eyes sparkling with fun, was a circumstance calculated to furnish material for enjoyable scandal. And Didama missed it.

Other happenings she missed, also. Not knowing of Captain Daniels's call upon Keziah, she was deprived of the pleasure of wonder at the length of his stay. She did not see him, in company with Mrs. Coffin, go down the road in the opposite direction from that taken by Grace. Nor their return and parting at the gate, two hours later. She did not see—but there! she saw nothing, absolutely nothing—except the scraggy spruce tree in her tiny front yard and the lonely ten feet of walk bordering it. No one traversed that section of walk except old Mrs. Tinker, who was collecting subscriptions for new hymn books for the Come-Outer chapel. And Didama was particularly anxious *not* to see her.

The dismal day dragged on. The silver-leaf trees dripped, the hedges were shining with moisture. Through the stillness the distant surf along the "ocean side" of the Cape growled and moaned and the fog bell at the lighthouse clanged miserably. Along the walk opposite Didama's—the more popular side of the road—shadowy figures passed at long intervals, children going to and from school, people on errands to the store, and the like. It was three o'clock in the afternoon before a visitor came again to the Coffin front gate, entered the yard and rapped at the side door.

Keziah opened the door.

"Halloa!" she exclaimed. "Back, are you? I begun to think you'd been scared away for good."

Grace laughed as she entered.

"Well, auntie," she said, "I don't wonder you thought I was scared. Truly, I didn't think it was proper for me to stay. First Kyan and then Cap'n Elkanah, and both of them expressing their wishes to see you alone so—er—pointedly. I thought it was time for me to go. Surely, you give me credit for a little delicacy."

Keziah eyed her grimly.

"Humph!" she sniffed. "If you'd been a little less delicate about fetchin' that hammer, we might have been spared at least one smash-up. I don't s'pose Laviny'll ever speak to me again. Oh, dear! I guess likely I'll never get the memory of that— that Kyan thing out of my mind. I never was so set back in my born days. Yes, you can laugh!"

She laughed herself as she said it. As for Grace, it was sometime before that young lady became coherent.

"He *did* look so funny!" she gasped. "Hopping up and down on that shaky chair and holding on to that pipe and—and— O Aunt Keziah, if you could have seen your face when I opened that door!"

"Yes; well, I will say you was sometime gettin' it open. And then, on top of the whole fool business, in parades Elkanah Daniels and——"

She paused. Her companion looked delightedly expectant.

"Yes," she cried eagerly. "Then Cap'n Elkanah came and the very first thing he said was— I almost laughed in his face."

25

"Almost! Humph! that's no exaggeration. The way you put out of that door was a caution."

"Yes, but what did the cap'n mean? Is it a secret? Ahem! shall I congratulate you, auntie?"

"Grace Van Horne! there's born fools enough in this town without your tryin' to be one. You know 'twa'n't *that*. Though what 'twas was surprise enough, I will say," she added. "Grace, I ain't goin' away to-morrow."

"You're not? Oh, splendid! Has the cap'n decided to let you stay here?"

"I guess his decidin' wouldn't influence me, if 'twas stayin' in his house he meant. The only way I could live here would be on his charity, and that would be as poor fodder as sawdust hasty puddin', even if I was fond of charity, which I ain't. He said to me— Well, you take your things off and I'll tell you about it. You can stay a little while, can't you?"

"Yes, I was going to stay all the afternoon and for supper, if you'd let me. I knew you had so much to do and I wanted to help. I told uncle and he said certainly I ought to come. He said he should try to see you and say good-by before you left to-morrow."

"You don't say! And me a Regular! Well, I'm much obliged, though I guess your Uncle Eben won't see me to-morrow—nor speak to me again, when he knows what I *am* going to do. Grace, I ain't goin' to leave Trumet, not for the present, anyhow. I've got a way of earnin' my livin' right here. I'm goin' to keep house for the new minister."

The girl turned, her hat in her hand.

"Oh!" she cried in utter astonishment.

Keziah nodded. "Yes," she affirmed. "That

was what Elkanah's proposal amounted to. Ha! ha! Deary me! When he said ' proposal,' I own up for a minute I didn't know *what* was comin'. After Kyan I was prepared for 'most anything. But he told me that Lurany Phelps, who the parish committee had counted on to keep house for Mr. Ellery, had sent word her sister was sick and couldn't be left, and that somebody must be hired right off 'cause the minister's expected by day after to-morrow's coach. And they'd gone over every likely candidate in town till it simmered down to Mehitable Burgess. And Cap'n Zeb Mayo spoke right up in the committee meetin' and gave out that if Mehitable kept house for Mr. Ellery he, for one, wouldn't come to church. Said he didn't want to hear sermons that was inspired by *her* cookin'. Seems she cooked for the Mayos one week when Mrs. Mayo had gone to Boston, and Cap'n Zeb declares his dreams that week was somethin' awful. ' And I'm a man with no nerves and mighty little imagination,' he says. ' Land knows what effect a dose of Mehitable's biscuits might have on a *minister*.'

"And so," continued Keziah, "they decided Mehitable wouldn't do, and finally somebody thought of me. I have a notion 'twas Zeb, although Cap'n Elkanah did his best to make me think 'twas himself. And the cap'n was made a delegate to come and see me about it. Come he did, and we settled it. I went down to the parsonage with him before dinner and looked the place over. There's an awful lot of sweepin' and dustin' to be done afore it's fit for a body to live in. I did think that when I'd finished with this house I could swear off on that kind of dissipation for a while, but I guess, judgin' by the looks of that parsonage, what I've done so far is only practice." She paused, glanced keenly at her friend and asked: "Why! what's the matter? You don't act nigh so glad as I thought you'd be."

Grace said of course she was glad; but she looked troubled, nevertheless.

"I can hardly make it seem possible," she said. "Is it really settled—your salary and everything? And what will you do about your position in Bos· ton?"

"Oh, I'll write Cousin Abner and tell him. Lord love you, *he* won't care. He'll feel that he did his duty in gettin' me the Boston chance and if I don't take it 'tain't his fault. *His* conscience'll be clear. Land sakes! if I could clean house as easy as some folks clear their consciences I wouldn't have a backache this minute. Yes, the wages are agreed on, too. And totin' them around won't make my back ache any worse, either," she added drily.

Grace extended her hand.

"Well, Aunt Keziah," she said, "I'm ever and ever so glad for you. I know you didn't want to leave Trumet and I'm sure everyone will be delighted when they learn that you're going to stay."

"Humph! that includes Laviny Pepper, of course. I cal'late Laviny's delight won't keep her up nights. But I guess I can stand it if she can. Now, Grace, what is it? You *ain't* real pleased? Why not?"

The girl hesitated.

"Auntie," she said, "I'm selfish, I guess. I'm glad for your sake; you mustn't think I'm not. But I almost wish you were going to do something else. You are going to live in the Regular parsonage and keep house for, of all persons, a Regular minister. Why, so far as my seeing you is concerned, you might as well be in China. You know Uncle Eben."

Keziah nodded understandingly.

"Yes," she said, "I know him. Eben Hammond thinks that parsonage is the presence chamber of the Evil One, I presume likely. But, Grace, you mustn't blame me, and if you don't call I'll know why and I shan't blame you. We'll see each other once in a while; I'll take care of that. And, deary, I *had* to do it—I just had to. If you knew what a load had been took off my mind by this, you'd sympathize with me and understand. I've been happier in Trumet than I ever was anywhere else, though I've seen some dark times here, too. I was born here; my folks used to live here. My brother Sol lived and died here. His death was a heavy trouble to me, but the heaviest came to me when I was somewheres else and—well, somehow I've had a feelin' that, if there was any real joys ever planned out for me while I'm on this earth, they'd come to me here. I don't know when they'll come. There's times when I can't believe they ever will come, but— There! there! everybody has to bear burdens in this life, I cal'late. It's a vale of tears, 'cordin' to you Come-Outer folks, though I've never seen much good in wearin' a long face and a crape bathin' suit on that account. Hey? What are you listenin' to?"

"I thought I heard a carriage stop, that was all."

Mrs. Coffin went to the window and peered into the fog.

"Can't see anything," she said. "'Tain't anybody for here, that's sure. I guess likely 'twas Cap'n Elkanah. He and Annabel were goin' to drive over to Denboro this afternoon. She had some trimmin' to buy. Takes more than fog to separate Annabel Daniels from dressmakin'. Well, there's a little more packin' to do; then I thought I'd go down to that parsonage and take a whack at the cobwebs. I never saw so many in my born days. You'd think all the spiders from here to Ostable had been holdin' camp meetin' in that shut-up house."

The packing took about an hour. When it was finished, the carpet rolled up, and the last piece of linen placed in the old trunk, Keziah turned to her guest.

" Now, Gracie," she said, " I feel as though I ought to go to the parsonage. I can't do much more'n look at the cobwebs to-night, but to-morrow those spiders had better put on their ascension robes. The end of the world's comin' for them, even though it missed fire for the Millerites when they had their doin's a few years ago. You can stay here and wait, if 'twon't be too lonesome. We'll have supper when I get back."

Grace looked tempted.

" I've a good mind to go with you," she said. " I want to be with you as much as I can, and *he* isn't there yet. I'm afraid uncle might not like it, but——"

" Sho! Come along. Eben Hammond may be a chronic sufferer from acute Come-Outiveness, but he ain't a ninny. Nobody'll see you, anyway. This fog's like charity, it'll cover a heap of sins. Do come right along. Wait till I get on my things."

She threw a shawl over her shoulders, draped a white knitted " cloud " over her head, and took from a nail a key, attached by a strong cord to a block of wood eight inches long.

" Elkanah left the key with me," she observed. " No danger of losin' it, is there. Might as well lose a lumber yard. Old Parson Langley tied it up this way, so he wouldn't miss his moorin's, I presume likely. The poor old thing was so nearsighted and absent-minded along toward the last that they say he used to hire Noah Myrick's boy to come in and look him over every Sunday mornin' before church, so's to be sure he hadn't got his wig on stern foremost. That's the way Zeb Mayo tells the yarn, anyhow."

They left the house and came out into the wet mist. Then, turning to the right, in the direction which Trumet, with unconscious irony, calls " downtown," they climbed the long slope where the main road mounts the outlying ridge of Cannon Hill, passed Captain Mayo's big house—the finest in Trumet, with the exception of the Daniels mansion— and descended into the hollow beyond. Here, at the corner where the " Lighthouse Lane " begins its winding way over the rolling knolls and dunes to the light and the fish shanties on the " ocean side," stood the plain, straight-up-and-down meeting house of the Regular society. Directly opposite was the little parsonage, also very straight up and down. Both were painted white with green blinds. This statement is superfluous to those who remember Cape architecture at this period; practically every building from Sandwich to Provincetown was white and green.

They entered the yard, through the gap in the white fence, and went around the house, past the

31

dripping evergreens and the bare, wet lilac bushes, to the side door, the lock of which Keziah's key fitted. There was a lock on the front door, of course, but no one thought of meddling with that. That door had been opened but once during the late pastor's thirty-year tenantry. On the occasion of his funeral the mourners came and went, as was proper, by that solemn portal.

Mrs. Coffin thrust the key into the keyhole of the side door and essayed to turn it.

" Humph! " she muttered, twisting to no purpose; " I don't see why— This must be the right key, because— Well, I declare, if it ain't unlocked already! That's some of Cap'n Elkanah's doin's. For a critter as fussy and particular about some things, he's careless enough about others. Mercy we ain't had any tramps around here lately. Come in."

She led the way into the dining room of the parsonage. Two of the blinds shading the windows of that apartment had been opened when she and Captain Daniels made their visit, and the dim gray light made the room more lonesome and forsaken in appearance than a deeper gloom could possibly have done. The black walnut extension table in the center, closed to its smallest dimensions because Parson Langley had eaten alone for so many years; the black walnut chairs set back against the wall at regular intervals; the rag carpet and braided mats— homemade donations from the ladies of the parish— on the green painted floor; the dolorous pictures on the walls; " Death of Washington," " Stoning of Stephen," and a still more deadly " fruit piece " committed in oils years ago by a now deceased boat painter; a black walnut sideboard with some blue-and-white crockery upon it; a gilt-framed mirror with another outrage in oils emphasizing its upper half; dust over everything and the cobwebs mentioned by Keziah draping the corners of the ceiling; this was the dining room of the Regular parsonage as Grace saw it upon this, her first visit. The dust and cobwebs were, in her eyes, the only novelties, however. Otherwise, the room was like many others in Trumet, and, if there had been one or two paintings of ships, would have been typical of the better class.

"Phew!" exclaimed Keziah, sniffing disgustedly. "Musty and shut up enough, ain't it? Down here in the dampness, and 'specially in the spring, it don't take any time for a house to get musty if it ain't aired out regular. Mr. Langley died only three months ago, but we've been candidatin' ever since and the candidates have been boarded round. There's been enough of 'em, too; we're awful hard to suit, I guess. That's it. Do open some more blinds and a window. Fresh air don't hurt anybody —unless it's spiders," with a glare at the loathed cobwebs.

The blinds and a window being opened, more light entered the room. Grace glanced about it curiously.

"So this is going to be your new home now, Aunt Keziah," she observed. "How queer that seems."

"Um—h'm. Does seem queer, don't it? Must seem queer to you to be so near the headquarters of everything your uncle thinks is wicked. Smell of brimstone any, does it?" she asked with a smile.

" No, I haven't noticed it. You've got a lot of cleaning to do. I wish I could help. Look at the mud on the floor."

Keziah looked.

" Mud? " she exclaimed. " Why, so 'tis! How in the world did that come here? Wet feet, sure's you're born. Man's foot, too. Cap'n Elkanah's, I guess likely; though the prints don't look hardly big enough for his. Elkanah's convinced that he's a great man and his boots bear him out in it, don't they? Those marks don't look broad enough for his understandin', but I guess he made 'em; nobody else could. Here's the settin' room."

She threw open another door. A room gloomy with black walnut and fragrant with camphor was dimly visible.

" Cheerful's a tomb, ain't it? " was Mrs. Coffin's comment. " Well, we'll get some light and air in here pretty soon. Here's the front hall and there's the front stairs. The parlor's off to the left. We won't bother with that yet a while. This little place in here is what Mr. Langley used to call his ' study.' Halloa! how this door sticks! "

The door did stick, and no amount of tugging could get it open, though Grace added her efforts to those of Keziah.

" 'Tain't locked," commented Mrs. Coffin, " 'cause there ain't any lock on it. I guess it's just swelled and stuck from the damp. Though it's odd, I don't remember— Oh, well! never mind. Let's sweeten up this settin' room a little. Open a window or two in here. We'll have to hurry if we want to do anything before it gets dark. I'm goin' into the kitchen to get a broom."

She hurried out, returning in a moment or two with a broom and a most disgusted expression.

" How's a body goin' to sweep with that? " she demanded, exhibiting the frayed utensil, the business end of which was worn to a stub. " More like a shovel, enough sight. Well, there's pretty nigh dust enough for a shovel, so maybe this'll take off the top layers. S'pose I'll ever get this house fit for Mr. Ellery to live in before he comes? I wonder if he's a particular man? "

Grace, who was struggling with a refractory window, paused for breath.

" I'm sure I don't know," she replied. " I've never seen him."

" Nor I either. Sol was so bad the Sunday he preached that I couldn't go to meetin'. They say his sermon was fine; all about those who go down to the sea in ships. That's what got the parish committee, I guess; they're all old salts. I wonder if he's as fine-lookin' as they say? "

Miss Van Horne tossed her head. She was resting, prior to making another assault on the window.

" I don't know," she said. " And I'm sure I don't care. I don't like good-looking ministers."

" Deary me! You're different from most females in this town, then. And you spoke of his good looks yourself this very mornin'. Why don't you like the good-lookin' ones? "

" Oh, because they're always conceited and patronizing and superior—and spoiled. I can just imagine this Mr. Ellery of yours strutting about in sewing circle or sociables, with Annabel and Georgianna Lothrop and the rest simpering and gushing and getting in his way: ' O Mr. Ellery, I did so enjoy that sermon of yours Sunday!' and 'O Mr. Ellery, it was *so* good of you to come this afternoon!' Pooh! I'm glad I'm a Come-Outer. Not that *I* would simper over him if I wasn't. He couldn't patronize me—not more than once, at any rate."

Keziah was greatly amused.

"Sakes alive!" she chuckled. "You're awfully high and mighty, seems to me. And changeable since mornin'. You was willin' enough to talk about him then. Now, Gracie, you mustn't take a spite against poor Mr. Ellery just because I've got to keep house for him. 'Tain't his fault; he don't even know it yet."

"I don't care. I know he'll be a conceited little snippet and I shall hate the sight of him. There! there! Auntie, you mustn't mind me. I told you I was a selfish pig. But don't you ask me to *like* this precious minister of yours, because I shan't do it. He has no business to come and separate me from the best friend I've got. I'd tell him so if he was here— What was that?"

Both women looked at each other with startled faces. They listened intently.

"Why, wa'n't that funny!" whispered Keziah. "I thought I heard——"

"You *did* hear. So did I. What do you suppose——"

"S-s-s-h-h! It sounded from the front room somewhere. And yet there can't be anybody in there, because— My soul! there 'tis again. I'm goin' to find out."

She grasped the stubby broom by the handle and moved determinedly toward the front hall. Grace seized her by the arm.

"Don't you do it, auntie!" she whispered frantically. "Don't you *do* it! It may be a tramp."

"I don't care. Whoever or whatever it is, it has no business in this house, and I'll make that plain in a hurry. Just like as not it's a cat got in when Elkanah was here this forenoon. Don't be scared, Grace. Come right along."

The girl came along, but not with enthusiasm. They tiptoed through the dark, narrow hall and peered into the parlor. This apartment was dim and still and gloomy, as all proper parlors should be, but there was no sign of life.

"Humph!" sniffed Keziah. "It might have been upstairs, but it didn't sound so. What did it sound like to you?"

"Like a footstep at first; and then like something falling—and rustling. Oh, what is the matter?"

Mrs. Coffin was glancing back down the hall with a strange expression on her face. Her grip upon the broom handle tightened.

"What *is* it?" pleaded the girl in an agonized whisper.

"Grace," was the low reply, "I've just remembered somethin'. That study door isn't stuck from the damp, because—well, because I remember now that it was open this mornin'."

Before her companion could fully grasp the import of this paralyzing fact, Keziah strode down the hall and seized the knob of the study door.

"Whoever you are in there," she commanded sternly, "open this door and come out this minute. Do you hear? I'm orderin' you to come out."

There was an instant of silence; then a voice from within made answer, a man's voice, and its tone indicated embarrassment.

"Madam," it said, "I—I am—I will be out in another minute. If you will just be patient——"

Grace interrupted with a smothered shriek. Keziah brandished the broom.

"Patient!" she repeated sharply. "Well, I like that! What do you mean by— Open that door! Grace, run out and get the—the constable."

This command was delivered entirely for effect. The office of constable in Trumet is, generally speaking, a purely honorary one. Its occupant had just departed for a week's cruise as mate of a mackerel schooner. However, the effect was instantaneous. From behind the door came sounds of hurry and commotion.

"Don't get the police on my account, please," said the voice. "If you will be patient until I get this—I'm just as anxious to come out as you can be to have me. Of all the ridiculous——"

"Come out then!" snapped Keziah. "Come out! If you're so everlastin' anxious, then come out. Patience! Of all the cheek! Why don't you come out *now?*"

The answer was brisk and to the point. Evidently, the unknown's stock of the virtue which he demanded of others was diminishing.

"Well, to be frank, since you insist," snapped the voice, "I'm not fully dressed."

This was a staggerer. For once Keziah did not have a reply ready. She looked at Grace and the latter at her. Then, without words, they retreated to the sitting room.

"'I'm—I'm sure I beg your pardon, ladies,' he stammered."

"Shall—shall I go for help?" whispered the girl. "Hadn't we better leave him here and— He doesn't sound like a tramp, does he. What *do* you suppose——"

"I hope you won't be alarmed," continued the voice, broken by panting pauses, as if the speaker was struggling into a garment. "I know this must seem strange. You see, I came on the coach as far as Bayport and then we lost a wheel in a rut. There was a—oh, dear! where *is* that—this is supremely idiotic!—I was saying there happened to be a man coming this way with a buggy and he offered to help me along. He was on his way to Wellmouth. So I left my trunk to come later and took my valise. It rained on the way and I was wet through. I stopped at Captain Daniels's house and the girl said he had gone with his daughter to the next town, but that they were to stop here at the parsonage on their way. So—there! that's right, at last!—so I came, hoping to find them. The door was open and I came in. The captain and his daughter were not here, but, as I was pretty wet, I thought I would seize the opportunity to change my clothes. I had some dry—er—things in my valise and I—well, then you came, you see, and—I assure you I—well, it was the most embarrassing—I'm coming now."

The door opened. The two in the sitting room huddled close together, Keziah holding the broom like a battle-ax, ready for whatsoever might develop. From the dimness of the tightly shuttered study stepped the owner of the voice, a stranger, a young man, his hair rumpled, his tie disarranged, and the buttons of his waistcoat filling the wrong buttonholes. Despite this evidence of a hasty toilet in semidarkness, he was not unprepossessing. Incidentally, he was blushing furiously.

" I'm——I'm sure I beg your pardon, ladies," he stammered. " I scarcely know what to say to you. I——"

His eyes becoming accustomed to the light in the sitting room, he was now able to see his captors more clearly. He looked at Keziah, then at Miss Van Horne, and another wave of blushes passed from his collar up into the roots of his hair. Grace blushed, too, though, as she perfectly well knew, there was no reason why she should.

Mrs. Coffin did not blush. This young fellow, although evidently not a tramp or a burglar, had caused her some moments of distinct uneasiness, and she resented the fact.

" Well," she observed rather tartly, " I'm sorry you don't know what to say, but perhaps you might begin by telling us who you are and what you mean by makin' a——er——dressin' room of a house that don't belong to you, just because you happened to find the door unlocked. After that you might explain why you didn't speak up when we first come, instead of keepin' so mighty quiet. That looks kind of suspicious to me, I must say."

The stranger's answer was prompt enough now. It was evident he resented the suspicion.

" I didn't speak," he said, " because you took me by surprise and I wasn't, as I explained——er——presentable. Besides, I was afraid of frightening you. I assure you I hurried as fast as I could, quietly, and when you began to talk "——his expression changed and there was a twitch at the corner of his mouth—— " I tried to hurry still faster, hoping you might not hear me and I could make my appearance—or my escape—sooner. As for entering the house—well, I considered it, in a way, my house; at least, I knew I should live in it for a time, and——"

"Live in it?" repeated Keziah. "*Live* in it? Why! mercy on us! you don't mean to say you're——"

She stopped to look at Grace. That young lady was looking at her with an expression which, as it expressed so very much, is beyond ordinary powers of description.

"My name is Ellery," said the stranger. "I am the minister — the new minister of the Regular society."

Then even Keziah blushed.

# CHAPTER III

### IN WHICH KEZIAH ASSUMES A GUARDIANSHIP

DIDAMA would have given her eyeteeth—and, for that matter, the entire upper set—to have been present in that parsonage sitting room when the Rev. John Ellery made his appearance. But the fates were against Didama that day and it was months afterwards before she, or any of what Captain Zeb Mayo called the "Trumet Daily Advertisers," picked up a hint concerning it. Keziah and Grace, acquainted with the possibilities of these volunteer news gatherers, were silent, and the Reverend John, being in some respects a discreet young man with a brand-new ministerial dignity to sustain, refrained from boasting of the sensation he had caused. He thought of it very often, usually at most inconvenient times, and when, by all the requirements of his high calling, his thought should have been busy with different and much less worldly matters.

"I declare!" said Mrs. Thankful Payne, after the new minister's first call at her residence, a week after his arrival at Trumet, "if Mr. Ellery ain't the most sympathetic man. I was readin' out loud to him the poem my cousin Huldy B.—her that married Hannibal Ellis over to Denboro—made up

42

when my second husband was lost to sea, and I'd just got to the p'int in the ninth verse where it says:

> 'The cruel billows crash and roar,
>   And the frail craft is tempest-tossed,
> But the bold mariner thinks not of life, but says,
>   "It is the fust schooner ever I lost." '

And 'twas, too, and the last, poor thing! Well, I just got fur as this when I looked up and there was the minister lookin' out of the window and his face was just as red, and he kept scowlin' and bitin' his lips. I do believe he was all but sheddin' tears. Sympathy like that I appreciate."

As a matter of fact, Mr. Ellery had just seen Grace Van Horne pass that window. She had not seen him, but for the moment he was back in that disgusting study, making a frenzied toilet in the dusk and obliged to overhear remarks pointedly personal to himself.

Grace left the parsonage soon after the supposed tramp disclosed his identity. Her farewells were hurried and she firmly refused Mrs. Coffin's not too-insistent appeal to return to the house "up street" and have supper. She said she was glad to meet Mr. Ellery. The young minister affirmed his delight in meeting her. Then she disappeared in the misty twilight and John Ellery surreptitiously wiped his perspiring forehead with his cuff, having in his late desire for the primal necessities forgotten such a trifling incidental as a handkerchief.

"Well, Mr. Ellery," observed Keziah, turning to her guest, or employer, or incumbrance—at present she was more inclined to consider him the latter

—" well, Mr. Ellery, this has been kind of unexpected for all hands, ain't it? If I'd known you was comin' to-day, I'd have done my best to have things ready, but Cap'n Elkanah said not before day after to-morrow and—but there, what's the use of talkin' that way? I didn't know I was goin' to keep house for you till this very forenoon. Mercy me, what a day this has been!"

The minister smiled rather one-sidedly.

" It's been something of a day for me," he admitted. " I am ahead of time and I've made a lot of trouble, I'm afraid. But yesterday afternoon I was ready and, to tell the truth, I was eager to come and see my new home and get at my work. So I started on the morning train. Then the stage broke down and I began to think I was stranded at Bayport. But this kind-hearted chap from Wellmouth—I believe that's where he lived—happened to pull up to watch us wrestling with the smashed wheel, and when he found I was in a hurry to get to Trumet, offered to give me a lift. His name was— was Bird. No, that wasn't it, but it was something like Bird, or some kind of a bird."

" Bird?" repeated Keziah thoughtfully. " There's no Birds that I know of in Wellmouth. Hum! Hey? 'Twa'n't Sparrow, was it?"

" That was it— Sparrow."

" Good land! Emulous Sparrow. Run consider'ble to whiskers and tongue, didn't he?"

" Why, yes; he did wear a beard. As for tongue —well, he was conversational, if that's what you mean."

" That's what I mean. If you rode twelve mile with Emulous, you must have had an earache for the last six. Did he ask a question or two about your personal affairs, here and there between times?"

Mr. Ellery laughed.

"Yes, one or two, between times," he admitted.

"I shan't die of surprise. Did you tell him who you was?"

"No-o, to be honest, I didn't. He was so very anxious to find out, that—well, I dodged. I think he believed I was going to visit Captain Daniels."

"Good enough! If I was governor of this state I wouldn't send any Thanksgivin' proclamations down this way. I'd just write Em Peters and Didama Rogers and a couple more like them and save myself the trouble. They'd have all I wanted to proclaim spread from one end of the county to the other in less'n a day, and a peck or two of extrys pitched in for good measure. I'm awful glad you didn't tell Emulous you was the minister. You see, Trumet's Trumet, and, considerin' everything, maybe it's just as well nobody knows about your bein' shut up in that study. Not but what 'twas all right, you know, but——"

"I understand. I'm not proud of it. Still, some one may have seen me come here."

"No, no, they didn't. This fog is as thick as Injun-meal puddin'. Nobody saw you."

"Well," with some hesitation, "the young lady who was here with you——"

"Oh, Grace Van Horne! She's all right. She won't tell. She ain't that kind."

"Van Horne? That doesn't sound like a New England name."

"'Tisn't. Her folks come from Jersey somewheres. But she was adopted by old Cap'n Ham-

45

mond, who keeps the tavern down on the bay shore by the packet wharf, and she's lived in Trumet since she was six years old. Her father was Teunis Van Horne, and he was mate on Cap'n Eben's coastin' schooner and was drowned off Hatteras. Eben was saved just by the skin of his teeth and got a broken hip and religion while it happened. His hip's better except that he's some lame; but his religion's been more and more feverish ever since. He's one of the head Come-Outers, and built their chapel with his own money. You mustn't think I'm speakin' lightly of religion, nor of Cap'n Eben, either. He's a dear good soul as ever was, but he is the narrowest kind of Come-Outer. His creed is just about as wide as the chapel door, and that's as narrow as the way leadin' to salvation; it *is* the way, too, so the Come-Outers think."

"What are Come-Outers? Some new sect?"

"Sakes alive! Haven't you heard of Come-Outers? Cat's foot! Well, you'll hear of 'em often enough from now on. They're folks who used to go to our church, the Regular, but left because the services was too worldly, with organs and choir singin', and the road to paradise too easy. No need for me to tell you any more. You'll learn."

Mr. Ellery was interested. He had been in Trumet but once before, on the occasion when he preached his trial sermon, and of that memorable visit remembered little except the sermon itself, the pews filled with captains and their families, and the awe-inspiring personality of Captain Elkanah Daniels, who had been his host. To a young man, the ink upon his diploma from the theological school still fresh, a trial sermon is a weighty matter, and the preaching of it weightier still. He had rehearsed it over and over in private, had delivered it almost through clinched teeth, and had returned to his room in the Boston boarding house with the conviction that it was an utter failure. Captain Elkanah and the gracious Miss Annabel, his daughter, had been kind enough to express gratification, and their praise alone saved him from despair. Then, to his amazement, the call had come. Of casual conversation at the church and about the Daniels's table he could recall nothing. So there was another religious organization in town and that made up of seceders from his own church. He was surprised.

"Er—this Miss Van Horne?" he asked. "Is she a—Come-Outer?"

Mrs. Coffin nodded.

"Yes," she said. "She's one. Couldn't be anything else and live with her Uncle Eben, as she calls him."

The minister experienced a curious feeling of disappointment and chagrin. This young person, already predisposed to regard a clergyman of his denomination with disapproval, had seen him for the first time under most humiliating circumstances. And he should never have the opportunity to regain her favor, or his own self-respect, by his efforts in the pulpit. No matter how well he might preach she would never hear him.

"Has this Captain Hammond no children of his own?" he asked.

Keziah's answer was short for her.

"Yes," she said. "One."

"Ah! another daughter?"

"No, a son. Name's Nathaniel, and he's a sea

47

captain. He's on his way from Surinam to New York now. They expect him to make port most any time, I believe. Now, Mr. Ellery, I s'pose we've got to arrange for your supper and stayin' overnight; and with this house the way 'tis and all, *I* don't see——"

But the minister was still interested in the Hammond household.

"This Nathaniel Hammond?" he asked. "You don't seem enthusiastic over him. Is he a black sheep?"

This reply also was short, but emphatic.

"No," said Keziah. "He's a fine man."

Then she resumed her semisoliloquy concerning her companion's entertainment.

"I guess," she said, "that the best thing for you to do will be to go to Cap'n Elkanah's. They'll be real glad to see you, I know, and you'll be in time for supper, for Elkanah and Annabel have been to Denboro and they'll be late home. They can keep you overnight, too, for it's a big house with lots of rooms. Then, after breakfast to-morrow you come right here. I'll have things somewhere near shipshape by then, I guess, though the cleanin'll have to be mainly a lick and a promise until I can really get at it. Your trunk'll be here on the coach, I s'pose, and that'll be through early in the forenoon. Get on your hat and coat and I'll go with you to Elkanah's."

The young man demurred a little at thrusting himself upon the hospitality of the Daniels's home, but Keziah assured him that his unexpected coming would cause no trouble. So he entered the now dark study and came out wearing his coat and carrying his hat and valise in his hand.

" I'm sure I'm ever so much obliged to you," he said. " And, as we are going to be more or less together—or at least I guess as much from what you say—would you mind if I suggest a mutual introduction. I'm John Ellery; you know that already. And you——"

Keziah stopped short on her way to the door.

" Well, I declare! " she exclaimed. " If I ain't the very worst! Fact is, you dropped in so ahead of time and in such a irregular sort of way, that I never once thought of introducin' anybody; and I'm sure Grace didn't. I'm Keziah Coffin, and Cap'n Elkanah and I signed articles, so to speak, this mornin', and I'm goin' to keep house for you."

She explained the reason upsetting the former arrangement by which Lurania Phelps was to have had the position.

" So I'm to keep house for you," she concluded. Adding: " For a spell, anyhow."

" Why do you say that? " asked the minister.

" Well, you might not like me. You may be particular, you know."

" I think I can run that risk."

" Yes; well, you can't tell. Or I might not like you. You see, I'm pretty particular myself," she added with a laugh.

At the Daniels's door Keziah turned her new charge over to Matilda Snow, the hired girl. It was an indication of the family's social position that they kept " hired help." This was unusual in Trumet in those days, even among the well to do.

" Good night," said the young man, extending his hand. " Good night, Miss—or is it Mrs.— Coffin? "

" Mrs. Good night."

" She's a widow," explained Matilda. " Husband died 'fore she come back here to live. Guess he didn't amount to much; she never mentions his name."

" There was one thing I meant to tell her," mused the minister, hesitating on the threshold. " I meant to tell her not to attempt any cleaning up at the parsonage to-night. To-morrow will do just as well."

" Heavens to Betsy! " sniffed the " hired help," speaking from the depths of personal conviction, " nobody but a born fool would clean house in the night, 'specially after the cleanin' she's been doin' at her own place. I guess you needn't worry."

So Mr. Ellery did not worry. And yet, until three o'clock of the following morning, the dull light of a whale-oil lantern illuminated the rooms of the parsonage as Keziah scrubbed and swept and washed, giving to the musty place the " lick and promise " she had prophesied. If the spiders had prepared those ascension robes, they could have used them that night.

After breakfast the wagons belonging to the Wellmouth furniture dealer drove in at the gate of the little house opposite Captain Elkanah's, and Keziah saw, with a feeling of homesickness which she hid beneath smiles and a rattle of conversation, the worn household treasures which had been hers, and her brother's before her, carried away out of her life. Then her trunks were loaded on the tailboards of the wagons, to be left at the parsonage, and with a sigh and a quick brush of her hand across her eyes, she locked the door for the last time and walked briskly down the road. Soon afterwards John Ellery, under the eminently respectable escort of Captain Elkanah and Miss Annabel, emerged from the Daniels's gate and followed her. Mrs. Didama Rogers, thankful for a clear atmosphere and an unobstructed view, saw them pass and recognized the stranger. And, within a quarter of an hour, she, arrayed in a hurried calling costume, was spreading the news along the main road. The "Trumet Daily Advertiser" had, so to speak, issued an extra.

Thus the new minister came to Trumet and thus Keziah Coffin became his housekeeper. She entered upon her duties with the whole-hearted energy peculiar to her. She was used to hard work, and, as she would have said, felt lonesome without it. She cleaned that parsonage from top to bottom. Every blind was thrown open and the spring sunshine poured in upon the braided mats and the rag carpets. Dust flew in clouds for the first day or two, but it flew out of windows and doors and was not allowed to settle within. The old black walnut furniture glistened with oil. The mirrors and the crockery sparkled from baths of hot water and soap. Even St. Stephen, in the engravings on the dining-room wall, was forced to a martyrdom of the fullest publicity, because the spots and smears on the glass covering his sufferings were violently removed. In the sleeping rooms upstairs the feather beds were beaten and aired, the sheets and blankets and patchwork comforters exposed to the light, and the window curtains dragged down and left to flap on the clothesline. The smell of musty dampness disappeared from the dining room and the wholesome odors of outdoors and of good things cooking took its place.

Keziah, in the midst of her labors, found time to coach her employer and companion in Trumet ways, and particularly in the ways which Trumet expected its clergymen to travel. On the morning following his first night in the parsonage, he expressed himself as feeling the need of exercise. He thought he should take a walk.

"Well," said his housekeeper from her station opposite him at the breakfast table, "if I was you I wouldn't take too long a one. You'd better be back here by ten, anyhow. Where was you thinkin' of goin'?"

Mr. Ellery had no particular destination in mind. He would like to see something of the village and, perhaps, if she could give him the names of a few of his parishioners, he might make a few calls. Keziah shook her head.

"Gracious goodness!" she exclaimed. "I wouldn't advise you to do that. You ain't been here long enough to make forenoon calls. If you should catch some of the women in this town with aprons and calico on, they'd never forgive you in this world. Wait till afternoon; they'll be expectin' you then and they'll be rigged out in their best bibs and tuckers. S'pose you found Annabel Daniels with her hair done up in curl papers; what do you think would happen? Mornin's are no time for ministers' calls. Even old Mr. Langley never made calls in the forenoon—and he'd been here thirty-odd years."

"All right, you know best. Much obliged for the advice. Then I'll simply take my walk and leave the calls until later."

"I'd be back by ten, though. Folks'll begin callin' on you by that time."

"They will? Doesn't the rule work both ways?"

"Not with new ministers it don't. Cat's foot! You don't s'pose Didama Rogers and Laviny Pepper and their kind'll wait any longer'n they can help afore they come to see what you look like, do you?"

"Well, they must have seen me when I preached here before. I remember——"

"Mercy on us! that was in meetin'. Meetin's diff'rent. All they could say to you then was how much they liked your sermon. They say that to every minister that comes, no matter how they may pick him to pieces afterwards. But here they can ask you questions; about how you came to come here and what you think of it far's you've got, and what your views are on certain points in the creed. Likewise, who your folks were and whether they was well off, and a few things like that. Then they'll want to see what kind of clothes you wear and——"

"Whew!" Ellery whistled. "You're unfolding a pleasant prospect for me, I must say. Am I supposed to be catechized on all of my private affairs?"

"Of course! A minister hasn't got any private affairs; he's a public character. There!" she laughed, as she poured the coffee, "I mustn't discourage you. But don't you see that every mother's son—and, for that matter, every daughter and children's child unto the third and fourth generation—feel that, so long as they pay pew rent or put a cent in the collection, they own a share in you. And we always keep a watch on our investments down this way. That's the Yankee shrewdness you read so much about, I guess."

53

The minister absently played with his spoon.

" I'm afraid you're a cynic," he said.

" No, no, I ain't. Though sometimes, considerin' everything, I feel as though I had excuse enough if I wanted to belong to that tribe. But you're young. You mustn't mind my sayin' that; if you was old, of course, I wouldn't talk about ages. But you are young and this is your first church. So you must start right. I'm no cynic, bless you. I've got trust in human nature left—most kinds of human nature. If I hadn't, I'd have more money, I s'pose. Perhaps you've noticed that those who trust a good deal are usually poor. It's all right, Mr. Ellery; you go and take your walk. And I'll walk into that pantry closet. It'll be a good deal like walkin' into the Slough of Despond, but Christian came out on the other side and I guess likely I will, if the supply of soapsuds holds out."

When, promptly at ten o'clock, the minister returned from his walk, he found Mrs. Rogers waiting in the sitting room. It is a prime qualification of an alert reporter to be first on the scene of sensation. Didama was seldom beaten. Mr. Ellery's catechism began. Before it was over Keziah opened the door to admit Miss Pepper and her brother. " Kyan " was nervous and embarrassed in the housekeeper's presence. Lavinia was a glacier, moving majestically and freezing as it moved. Keziah, however, was not even touched by the frost; she greeted the pair cordially, and begged them to " take off their things."

It was dinner time before the catechizers departed. The catechized came to the table with an impaired appetite. He looked troubled.

"Don't let it worry you, Mr. Ellery," observed Keziah calmly. "I think I can satisfy you. Honest and true, I ain't half as bad as you might think."

The minister looked more troubled than before; also surprised.

"Why, Mrs. Coffin!" he cried. "Could you hear——"

"No, no! I couldn't hear nothin' in that closet except my own opinion on dirt and dust. But if I was as deaf as the man that set on the powder keg and dropped his pipe ashes into it, it wouldn't have made any difference. The man said after they picked him up that they needn't have been so rough, he'd have moved without bein' pushed if they'd have made signs they wanted to use the keg. And if I was out in the next lot I'd have known what you was listenin' to in that sittin' room. They hinted that they were real sorry for you, but 'twasn't any of *their* doin's. The parish committee, bein' just men, was apt to make mistakes in certain matters. Of course everything *might* be well enough, and if you wa'n't *too* particular about cookin' and so on, why— Anyhow, you mustn't think that *they* were criticisin'. 'Twas only that they took an interest and— That was about it, wasn't it?"

"Mrs. Coffin, I—I hope you don't think I paid any attention to their remarks—of that kind, I mean. Honestly, I did my best to stop them. I said——"

"Man alive! I'm not worried. Why should you be? We were talkin' about trust just now—or I was. Well, you and I'll have to take each other on trust for a while, until we see whether we're goin' to suit. If you see anything that I'm goin' wrong in, I wish you'd tell me. And I'll do the same by you, if that's agreeable. You'll hear a lot of things said about me, but if they're very bad I give you my word they ain't true. And, to be real frank, I'll probably hear some about you, which I'll take for what they're worth and considerin' who said 'em. That's a good wholesome agreement, I think, for both of us. What do you think?"

John Ellery said, with emphasis, that he thought well of it. He began to realize that this woman, with her blunt common sense, was likely to be a pilot worth having in the difficult waters which he must navigate as skipper of the Regular church in Trumet. Also, he began to realize that, as such a skipper, he was most inexperienced. And Captain Daniels had spoken highly—condescendingly but highly—of his housekeeper's qualifications and personality. So the agreement was ratified, with relief on his part.

The first Sunday came and with it the first sermon. He read that sermon to Keziah on Saturday evening and she approved of it as a whole, though she criticised some of its details.

" Don't be afraid to put in plenty of salt," she said. "Where you've got the Christian life and spirit written down as bein' like a quiet, peaceful home, free from all distrust, and like that, why don't you change it to a good safe anchorage, where the soul can ride forever without fear of breakers or no'theasters or the dangers besettin' the mariner on a lee shore. They'll understand that; it gets right home to 'em. There's scarcely a man or a woman in your congregation that ain't been out of sight of land for weeks on a stretch."

The breakfast hour on Sunday would be at nine

o'clock, instead of seven, as on week days, she told him.

"Trumet lays to bed Sunday mornin's," she explained. "It's almost a part of its religion, as you might say, and lived up to more conscientious than some other parts, I'm afraid. Six days shalt thou labor and wear comfort'ble clothes; and on the seventh you must be lazy and dress up. Likewise you must have baked beans Saturday for supper, as we're havin' 'em, and more beans with fish balls next mornin'. That is, if you want to be orthodox."

The service began at eleven o'clock. At half past ten the sexton, old Mr. Jubal Knowles, rang the "first bell," a clanging five-minute reminder. Twenty minutes later he began on the second and final call. Mr. Ellery was ready—and nervous— before the first bell had finished ringing. But Keziah, entering the sitting room dressed in black alpaca and carrying the hymn book with her name in gilt letters on the cover, forbade his leaving the parsonage thus early.

"I shall go pretty soon," she said, "but you mustn't. The minister ain't expected until the last bell's 'most done. Parson Langley used to wait until the Winslows went in. Gaius Winslow is a widower man who lives up to the west end of the town and he's got nine children, all boys. You'll know 'em because they always drive down to meetin' in one carryall with a white horse. Gaius is as punctual as a boardin'-house dinner. The old parson used to wait until the last Winslow had toddled up the meetin'-house steps and then he'd come out of this side door with his sermon in his hand. It's a pretty good rule to remember and saves watchin' the clock.

Besides, it's what we've been used to, and that goes a good ways with some folks. Good-by, Mr. Ellery. You'll see me in the third pew from the back, on the right side, wishin' you luck just as hard as I can."

So, as in couples or family groups, afoot or in all sorts of vehicles, the members of Trumet's Regular society came to the church to hear their new minister, that functionary peeped under the parlor window shade of the parsonage and waited, fidgetting and apprehensive, for the Winslows. They arrived at last, and were not hard to recognize, for ten individuals packed into one carriage are hard to overlook anywhere. As Gaius, with the youngest in his arms, passed in at the church door, John Ellery passed out of the parsonage gate. The last bell clanged its final stroke, the vibrations ceased, the rustle of skirts and the sounds of decorous coughing subsided and were succeeded by the dry rattle of the hymn-book pages, the organ, presented by Captain Elkanah and played by his daughter, uttered its preliminary groan, the service began.

Outside the spring breeze stirred the budding silver-leafs, the distant breakers grumbled, the crows in the pines near Captain Eben Hammond's tavern cawed ribald answers to the screaming gulls perched along the top of the breakwater. And seated on one of the hard benches of the little Come-Outer chapel, Grace Van Horne heard her " Uncle Eben," who, as usual, was conducting the meeting, speak of " them who, in purple and fine linen, with organs and trumpets and vain shows, are gathered elsewhere in this community to hear a hired priest make a mock of the gospel." (A-*men!*)

58

But John Ellery, the "hired priest," knew nothing of this. He did know, however, that he was the center of interest for his own congregation, the people among whom he had been called to labor. Their praise or criticism meant everything to him; therefore he preached for dear life.

And Keziah Coffin, in the third pew from the back, watched him intently, her mind working in sympathetic unison with his. She was not one to be greatly influenced by first impressions, but she had been favorably impressed by this young fellow, and had already begun to feel that sense of guardianship and personal responsibility which, later on, was to make Captain Zebedee Mayo nickname the minister "Keziah's Parson."

The sermon was a success.

# CHAPTER IV

O N Monday afternoon the minister made a
few calls. Keziah made out a short list
for him to follow, a " sort of chart of the
main channel," she called it, " with the safe ports
marked and the shoals and risky places labeled dangerous."

"You see," she said, "Trumet ain't a course
you can navigate with your eyes shut. We divide
ourselves into about four sets—aristocrats, poor relations, town folks, and scum. The aristocrats are
the big bugs like Cap'n Elkanah and the other well-
off sea captains, afloat or ashore. They 'most all go
to the Regular church and the parish committee is
steered by 'em. The poor relations are mainly
widows and such, whose husbands died or were lost
at sea. Most of them are Regulars. The town
folks are those that stay ashore and keep store or
run salt works or somethin'. And the scum work
around on odd jobs or go fishin'. So, if you really
want to be safe, you must call on the aristocrats first,
after that on the poor relations, and so on down.
You won't be bothered with scum much; they're
mainly Come-Outers."

60

Ellery took the list from her hand and looked it over.

"Hum!" he said musingly. "Am I supposed to recognize these—er—class distinctions?"

"Yes. That is, not in meetin' or sewin' circle or anything like that, or not out and out and open anywhere. But you want to cultivate a sort of different handshake and how-dy-do for each set, so's to speak. Gush all you want to over an aristocrat. Be thankful for advice and always *so* glad to see 'em. With the poor relations you can ease up on the gush and maybe condescend some. Town folks expect condescension and superiority; give it to 'em. When it comes to scum, why—well, any short kind of a bow and a "'Mornin'" 'll do for them. 'Course the Lord, in His infinite mercy, made 'em, same as He did potato bugs, but it's necessary to keep both bugs and them down to their proper place."

She delivered this in the intervals between trips to the kitchen with the dinner dishes. The minister listened with a troubled expression on his face.

"Mrs. Coffin," he said, "I guess I'm dull. There was a Scotch professor at college and the fellows used to say his bump of humor was a dent. Maybe mine isn't much better. Are you joking?"

Keziah stacked the cups and saucers.

"I ain't jokin'," she declared. "I've been a poor relation in this village for a good while and my brother was a shoemaker and on the upper fringe of the town-folk class. My humor bump would have to stick up like Cannon Hill afore I could see any joke in that."

"But you're not seriously advising me to treat a rich man differently from a poor one?"

61

"Not openly different—no. But if you want to steer a perfectly *safe* course, one that'll keep deep water under your keel the whole voyage, why, there's your chart."

Mr. Ellery promptly tore the " chart " into small pieces.

"I'm going out," he said. "I shall be back by supper time."

Mrs. Coffin eyed him grimly.

"Goin' to run it blindfold, are you?" she asked.

"Yes, I am."

Her grimness disappeared and she smiled.

"I'll have your supper ready for you," she said. "Bring back a good appetite."

The young man hesitated on the threshold.

"Mrs. Coffin," he demanded, "would *you* have called only on the aristocrats at first?"

She shook her head, smiling still.

"No," she replied, "not me. I've always taken risks. But I didn't know but you might be a safe sailor. It saves a lot of trouble in this world."

"How about the next?"

"Oh, well, perhaps even the scum may count for somethin' over there." She turned to face him and her smile vanished. "Go on, Mr. Ellery," she said. "Go and call where you please. Far be it from me that I should tell you to do anything else. I suppose likely you hope some day to be a great preacher. I hope you will. But I'd enough sight rather you was a good man than the very greatest. No reason why you can't be both. There was a preacher over in Galilee once, so you told us yesterday, who was just good. 'Twa'n't till years afterwards that the crowd came to realize that he was great, too. And, if I recollect right, he chummed in with publicans and sinners. I'm glad you tore up that fool paper of mine. I hoped you might when I gave it to you. Now you run along, and I'll wash dishes. If cleanliness is next to godliness, then a parson ought to eat out of clean plates."

As a matter of fact, the minister's calls were in the nature of a compromise, although an unintentional one. He dropped in on Zebedee Mayo, owner of the big house on the slope of the hill. Captain Zeb took him up into what he called his "cupoler," the observatory on the top of the house, and showed him Trumet spread out like a map. The main road was north and south, winding and twisting its rutted, sandy way. Along it were clustered the principal houses and shops, shaded by silver-leaf poplars, a few elms, and some willows and spruces. Each tree bent slightly away from the northeast, the direction from which blew the heavy winter gales. Beyond the main road were green slopes and pastures, with swamps in the hollows, swamps which were to be cranberry bogs in the days to come. Then the lower road, with more houses, and, farther on, the beach, the flats—partially uncovered because it was high tide—and the bay.

Behind the Mayo house was the crest of Cannon Hill, more hills, pastures and swamps, scattered houses and pine groves. Then began the tumbled, humped waste of sand dunes, and, over their ragged fringes of beach plum and bayberry bushes, the deep blue of the wide Atlantic. The lighthouse was a white dot and the fish shanties a blotch of brown. Along the inner edge of the blue were scars of dancing white, the flashing teeth of hungry shoals which had torn to pieces and swallowed many a good ship. And, far out, dotted and sprinkled along the horizon, were sails.

"See?" said Captain Zeb, puffing still from the exertion of climbing the ladder to the "cupoler," for he was distinctly "fleshy." "See? The beacon's up. Packet come in this mornin'. There she is. See her down there by the breakwater?"

Sure enough, the empty barrel, painted red, was hoisted to the top of its pole on the crest of Cannon Hill. And, looking down at the bay and following the direction of the stubby pointing finger, Ellery saw a little schooner, with her sails lowered, lying, slightly on her side, in a shallow pool near a long ridge of piled stones—the breakwater. A small wharf made out from the shore and black figures moved briskly upon it. Carts were alongside the schooner and there more dots were busy.

"Eben's pennant's flyin'," said Captain Zeb. "He always sets colors when the packet's in. Keeps packet tavern, Eben does. That's it, that old-fashioned, gambrel-roofed house on the rise by the wharf. Call it 'Saints' Rest,' they do now, 'cause Eben's so mighty religious."

The minister saw the long, rambling house, with one lonely, twisted tree in its yard, a flag flying from a pole beside it. So that was where the Hammonds lived. And where the girl lived who was certain he was a "conceited snippet." Whatever he might be in reality he hoped it was not that. "Snippet" was not in his dictionary, but he didn't like the sound of it.

"Who owns the packet?" he asked, to make conversation.

"Zach Foster. Married Freewill Doane's daughter over to Harniss. She's dead now."

"A good sailor, is he?"

Captain Zeb spat in supreme disgust.

"Good farmer!" he snorted. "Zach took over the packet for a debt when the chap that used to run her died. His dad, old man Foster, raised garden truck at the same time mine went to sea. Both of us took after our fathers, I guess. Anyhow, my wife says that when I die 'twill be of salt water on the brain, and I'm sure Zach's head is part cabbage. Been better for him if he'd stuck to his garden. However, I s'pose he does his best."

"They say angels can do no more."

"Um-m. Well, Zach'll be an angel pretty soon if he keeps on cruisin' with that old hooker as she is. 'Bijah Perry, he's mate and the only good seaman aboard, tells me that most of the riggin's rotten and the main topmast ain't sound, by a good deal. The old man's put off havin' her overhauled for two reasons, one that repairs cost money, and t'other that puttin' off is the main sheet of his gospel. When there's no rain the roof don't leak and long's it don't blow too hard 'most any kind of gear'll hold. That's philosophy—cabbage philosophy."

Ellery decided that he should like Captain Zeb, although it was evident that the old whaler had decided opinions of his own which he did not hesitate to express. He judged that the Mayos were of the so-called aristocracy, but undoubtedly unique specimens. He visited four more households that afternoon. The last call was at Mrs. Thankful Payne's, and while there, listening to the wonderful "poem," he saw Miss Van Horne pass the window, as has already been told. He came home to a Cape Cod supper of scalloped clams, hot biscuits, and baked Indian pudding, and Keziah greeted him with a cheery smile which made him feel that it *was* home. His summary disposal of the " chart " had evidently raised him in his housekeeper's estimation. She did not ask a single question as to where he had been.

Next day he had a taste of Trumet's real aristocracy, the genuine article. Captain Elkanah Daniels and his daughter made their first formal call. The captain was majestic in high hat, fur-collared cape, tailed coat, and carrying a gold-headed cane. Miss Annabel wore her newest gown and bonnet and rustled as she walked. They entered the sitting room and the lady glanced superciliously about the apartment.

" Hum—ha ! " barked Captain Elkanah. " Ahem ! Mr. Ellery, I trust you're being made comfortable. The parish committee are—hum—ah —anxious that you should be. Yes ? "

The minister said that he was very comfortable indeed.

" It isn't what you've been used to, we know," observed Miss Annabel. " Mr. Langley, our former pastor, was a sweet old gentleman, but he was old-fashioned and his tastes were queer, especially in art. Have you noticed that ' fruit piece ' in the dining room ? Isn't it too ridiculous ? "

Ellery admitted that the fruit piece was rather funny; but no doubt it had been a gift and so——

" Yes, indeed. I guess it was a present, fast enough. Nobody would buy such a thing. It seems strange to pa and me that, although so many of our people have been abroad, they have such strange ideas of art. Do you remember the beautiful marbles in the palaces at Florence, Mr. Ellery? Of course you've seen them?"

The minister was obliged to admit that he had never been abroad.

"Oh, is that so? I've been so many times with pa that it seems almost as if everybody was as familiar with Yurrup as I am. You remember what I said about the marbles, pa?"

Her parent nodded.

"Hum—ha! Oh, yes, yes," he said. "That was when I was in the fruit-carrying trade and made a voyage to Valenchy."

"Valencia, pa," corrected Annabel. "And Valencia is in Spain."

"I know it. But we went to Leghorn afterwards. I sailed to Cronstadt for some years regular. Cronstadt is in Rooshy, Mr. Ellery."

"Russia, pa," snapped his daughter. Then she changed the subject to church and parish affairs. They spoke of the sewing circle and the reading society and the Friday-evening meetings.

"The Come-Outers are so vexed with us," tittered Miss Annabel, "that they won't even hold prayer meeting on the same night as ours. They have theirs on Thursday nights and it's as good as a play to hear them shout and sing and carry on. You'll enjoy the Come-Outers, Mr. Ellery. They're a perfect delight."

And as they rose to go Captain Elkanah asked: "Is there anything you'd like done about the parsonage, Mr. Ellery? If so, it shall be done immejitly. How are you satisfied with your housekeeper?"

67

"Very well, indeed, Captain Daniels," was the prompt reply.

"She's a character, isn't she?" giggled Annabel. "She was born here in Trumet, but went away to New Bedford when she was young and grew up there. Her maiden name was Hall, but while she was away she married a man named Ansel Coffin. They didn't live together very long and weren't happy, I guess. I don't know whose fault it was, nobody knows much of anything about it, for that's the one thing she won't talk about. Anyhow, the Coffin man was lost to sea, and after a while she came back to keep house for her brother Solomon. She's an awful odd stick, but she's a good cook, I believe; though I'm afraid you won't get the meals people such as ourselves, who've been so much in the city, are used to."

Ellery thought of the meals at his city boarding house and shuddered. He was an orphan and had boarded for years. Incidentally, he had worked his way through college. Captain Elkanah cleared his throat.

"Keziah," he commanded. "Hum—ha! Keziah, come in here a minute."

Keziah came in response to the call, her sewing in her hand. The renovation of the parsonage had so far progressed that she could now find time for a little sewing, after the dinner dishes were done.

"Keziah," said the captain pompously, "we expect you to look out for Mr. Ellery in every respect. The parish committee expects that—yes."

"I'll try," said Mrs. Coffin shortly.

"Yes. Well, that's all. You can go. We must be going, too, Mr. Ellery. Please consider our house at your disposal any time. Be neighborly—hum—ha!—be neighborly."

"Yes," purred Annabel. "*Do* come and see us often. Congenial society is very scarce in Trumet, for me especially. We can read together. Are you fond of Moore, Mr. Ellery? I just dote on him."

The last "hum—ha" was partially drowned by the click of the gate. Keziah closed the dining-room door.

"Mrs. Coffin," said the minister, "I shan't trouble the parish committee. Be sure of that. I'm perfectly satisfied."

Keziah sat down in the rocker and her needle moved very briskly for a moment. Then she said, without looking up:

"That's good. I own up I like to hear you say it. And I am glad there are some things I do like about this new place of mine. Because—well, because there's likely to be others that I shan't like at all."

On Friday evening the minister conducted his first prayer meeting. Before it, and afterwards, he heard a good deal concerning the Come-Outers. He learned that Captain Eben Hammond had preached against him in the chapel on Sunday. Most of his own parishioners seemed to think it a good joke.

"Stir 'em up, Mr. Ellery," counseled Lavinia Pepper. "Stir 'em up! Don't be afraid to answer 'em from the pulpit and set 'em where they belong. Ignorant, bigoted things!"

Others gave similar counsel. The result was that the young man became still more interested in these people who seemed to hate him and all he stood for so profoundly. He wished he might hear their side

69

of the case and judge it for himself. It may as well be acknowledged now that John Ellery had a habit of wishing to judge for himself. This is not always a politic habit in a country minister.

The sun of the following Thursday morning rose behind a curtain of fog as dense as that of the day upon which Ellery arrived. A flat calm in the forenoon, the wind changed about three o'clock and, beginning with a sharp and sudden squall from the northwest, blew hard and steady. Yet the fog still cloaked everything and refused to be blown away.

"There's rain astern," observed Captain Zeb, with the air of authority which belongs to seafaring men when speaking of the weather. "We'll get a hard, driving rain afore mornin', you see. Then, if she still holds from the northwest'ard, it'll fair off fine."

"Goin' out in this, Mr. Ellery!" exclaimed Keziah, in amazement, as the minister put on his hat and coat about seven that evening. "Sakes alive! you won't be able to see the way to the gate. It's as dark as a nigger's pocket and thicker than young ones in a poor man's family, as my father used to say. You'll be wet through. Where in the world are you bound for *this* night?"

The minister equivocated. He said he had been in the house all day and felt like a walk.

"Well, take an umbrella, then," was the housekeeper's advice. "You'll need it before you get back, I cal'late."

It was dark enough and thick enough, in all conscience. The main road was a black, wet void, through which gleams from lighted windows were

but vague, yellow blotches. The umbrella was useful in the same way that a blind man's cane is useful,
in feeling the way. The two or three stragglers
who met the minister carried lanterns. One of these
stragglers was Mr. Pepper. Kyan was astonished.

"Well, I snum!" cried Kyan, raising the lantern.
"If 'tain't Mr. Ellery. Where you bound this kind
of night?"

Before the minister could answer, a stately figure
appeared and joined the pair. Lavinia, of course.

"Well, Mr. Ellery," she said. "Ain't you lost,
out in this fog? Anybody sick?"

No, no one was sick.

"That's a mercy. Goin' callin', be you?"

"No."

"Hum! Queer weather for a walk, I call it.
Won't be many out to-night, except Come-Outers
goin' to holler their lungs loose at prayer meetin'.
He, he! You ain't turned Come-Outer, have you,
Mr. Ellery? You've headed right for the chapel."

Ellery's reply was hurried and a bit confused.
He said good night and went on.

"Laviny," whispered the shocked Kyan, "do
you think that was a—er—polite thing to say to a
parson? That about his turnin' Come-Outer? He
didn't make much answer, seemed to me. You don't
think he was mad, do ye?"

"I don't care if he was," snorted Miss Pepper.
"He could tell a body where he was goin' then.
Nobody can snub me, minister or not. *I* think he's
kind of stuck-up, if you want to know, and if he is,
he'll get took down in a hurry. Come along, don't
stand there with your mouth open like a flytrap. I'd
like to know what he was up to. I've a precious

good mind to follow him; would if 'twa'n't so much trouble."

She didn't. Yet, if she had, she would have deemed the trouble worth while. For John Ellery stumbled on through the mist till he reached the "Corners" where the store was located and the roads forked. There, he turned to the right, into the way called locally "Hammond's Turn-off." A short distance down the "Turn-off" stood a small, brown-shingled building, its windows alight. Opposite its door, on the other side of the road, grew a spreading hornbeam tree surrounded by a cluster of swamp blackberry bushes. In the black shadow of the hornbeam Mr. Ellery stood still. He was debating in his mind a question: should he or should he not enter that building?

As he stood there, groups of people emerged from the fog and darkness and passed in at the door. Some of them he had seen during his fortnight in Trumet. Others were strangers to him. A lantern danced and wabbled up the "Turn-off" from the direction of the bay shore and the packet wharf. It drew near, and he saw that it was carried by an old man with long white hair and chin beard, who walked with a slight limp. Beside him was a thin woman wearing a black poke bonnet and a shawl. In the rear of the pair came another woman, a young woman, judging by the way she was dressed and her lithe, vigorous step. The trio halted on the platform of the building. The old man blew out the lantern. Then he threw the door open and a stream of yellow light poured over the group.

The young woman was Grace Van Horne. The minister recognized her at once. Undoubtedly, the old man with the limp was her guardian, Captain Eben Hammond, who, by common report, had spoken of him, Ellery, as a "hired priest."

The door closed. A few moments thereafter the sound of a squeaky melodeon came from within the building. It wailed and quavered and groaned. Then, with a suddenness that was startling, came the first verse of a hymn, sung with tremendous enthusiasm:

> "Oh, who shall answer when the Lord shall call
> His ransomed sinners home?"

The hallelujah chorus was still ringing when the watcher across the street stepped out from the shadow of the hornbeam. Without a pause he strode over to the platform. Another moment and the door had shut behind him.

The minister of the Trumet Regular church had entered the Come-Outer chapel to attend a Come-Outer prayer meeting!

# CHAPTER V

## IN WHICH THE PARSON CRUISES IN STRANGE WATERS

THE Come-Outer chapel was as bare inside, almost, as it was without. Bare wooden walls, a beamed ceiling, a raised platform at one end with a table and chairs and the melodeon upon it, rows of wooden settees for the congregation —that was all. As the minister entered, the worshipers were standing up to sing. Three or four sputtering oil lamps but dimly illuminated the place and made recognition uncertain.

The second verse of the hymn was just beginning as Ellery came in. Most of the forty or more grown people in the chapel were too busy wrestling with the tune to turn and look at him. A child here and there in the back row twisted a curious neck but twisted back again as parental fingers tugged at its ear. The minister tiptoed to a dark corner and took his stand in front of a vacant settee.

The man whom Ellery had decided must be Captain Eben Hammond was standing on the low platform beside the table. A quaint figure, patriarchal with its flowing white hair and beard, puritanical with its set, smooth-shaven lips and tufted brows. Captain Eben held an open hymn book back in one hand and beat time with the other. He wore

74

brass-bowed spectacles well down toward the tip of his nose. Swinging a heavy, stubby finger and singing in a high, quavering voice of no particular register, he led off the third verse:

> "Oh, who shall weep when the roll is called
> And who shall shout for joy?"

The melodeon and the hymn book were in accord as to the tune, but Captain Eben and the various members of the congregation seemed to have a desire to improvise. They sang with spirit, however, and the rhythmic pat of feet grew louder and louder. Here and there men and women were swaying and rocking their bodies in time to the music. The chorus for each verse was louder than the one preceding it.

Another hymn was given out and sung. And another and still another. The windows rattled. The patting grew to a steady "thump! thump!" Momentary pauses between lines were punctuated by hallelujahs and amens. Standing directly in front of the minister was a six-foot, raw-boned individual whose clothes smelled strongly of fish, and whose hands, each swung at the end of an exposed five inches of hairy red wrist, looked like flippers. At the end of the third hymn this personage sprang straight up into the air, cracked the heels of a pair of red cowhide boots together, and whooped: "Glory be! Send the *paower!*" in a voice like the screech of a northeast gale. Mr. Ellery, whom this gymnastic feat had taken by surprise, jumped in sympathy, although not as high.

The singing over, the worshipers sat down. Captain Eben took a figured handkerchief from his pocket and wiped his forehead. The thin, near-sighted young woman who had been humped over the keyboard of the melodeon, straightened up. The worshipers relaxed a little and began to look about.

Then the captain adjusted his spectacles and opened a Bible, which he took from the table beside him. Clearing his throat, he announced that he would read from the Word, tenth chapter of Jeremiah:

" ' Thus saith the Lord. Learn not the way of the heathen, and be not dismayed at the signs of heaven; for the heathen are dismayed at them.

" ' For the customs of the people are vain: for one cutteth a tree out of the forest, the work of the hands of the workmen, with the ax.' "

He read in a measured singsong, stopping occasionally to hold the book in a better light and peering at the fine print through his spectacles. And as he read, there was a sudden rustle on one of the back benches. A child had turned, stared, and pulled at its mother's sleeve. The rustle grew and spread.

Captain Eben drawled on to the twentieth verse:

" ' My tabernacle is spoiled and all my cords are broken: my children are gone forth from me, and they are not: there is none to stretch forth my tent any more, and to set up my curtains!

" ' For the pastors are become brutish and have not sought the Lord: therefore they shall not prosper, and——' "

" A-*men!*"

The shout came from the second bench from the front, where Ezekiel Bassett, clam digger and fervent religionist, was always to be found on meeting nights. Ezekiel was the father of Susannah B. Bassett, "Sukey B." for short, who played the melodeon. He had been, by successive seizures, a Seventh Day Baptist, a Second Adventist, a Millerite, a Regular, and was now the most energetic of Come-Outers. Later he was to become a Spiritualist and preside at table-tipping séances.

Ezekiel's amen was so sudden and emphatic that it startled the reader into looking up. Instead of the faces of his congregation, he found himself treated to a view of their back hair. Nearly every head was turned toward the rear corner of the room, there was a buzz of whispering and, in front, many men and women were standing up to look. Captain Eben was scandalized.

"Well!" he exclaimed. "Is this a prayer meetin' or—or—what? Brethren and sisters, I must say——"

Ezekiel Bassett stepped forward and whispered in his ear. The captain's expression of righteous indignation changed to one of blank astonishment. He, too, gazed at the dark corner. Then his lips tightened and he rapped smartly on the table.

"Brethren and sisters," he thundered, in the voice which, of old, had enforced obedience aboard his coasting schooner, "remember this is the house of the Lord. Be reverent!"

He waited until every eye had swung about to meet his. Then he regarded his abashed but excited hearers with a steady and prolonged stare.

"My friends," he said, "let us bow in prayer."

John Ellery could have repeated that prayer, almost word for word, years after that night. The captain prayed for the few here gathered together: Let them be steadfast. Let them be constant in the

77

way. The path they were treading might be narrow and beset with thorns, but it was the path leading to glory.

"Scoffers may sneer," he declared, his voice rising; "they may make a mock of us, they may even come into Thy presence to laugh at us, but theirs is the laugh that turns to groanin'. O Lord, strengthen us to-night to speak what's in our hearts, without fear." ("A-men!") "To prophesy in Thy name! To bid the mockers and them that dare—dare to profane this sanctuary be careful. Hired singers and trumpets and vain shows we have not" ("Thank the Lord! Amen!"), "but the true faith and the joy of it we do have." ("Hallelujah! Hallelujah! Glory!")

And so on, his remarks becoming more personal and ever pointing like a compass needle to the occupant of that seat in the corner. The minister's determination to attend a Come-Outer meeting, though it had reached the sticking point only a half hour before, was the result of considerable deliberation. He had argued with himself and had made up his mind to find out for himself just what these people did. He was finding out, certainly. His motives were good and he had come with no desire to scoff, but, for the life of him, he could not help feeling like a criminal. Incidentally, it provoked him to feel that way.

"O Lord," prayed Captain Hammond, the perspiration in beads on his forehead, "Thou hast said that the pastors become brutish and have not sought Thee and that they shan't prosper. Help us to-night to labor with this one that he may see his error and repent in sackcloth and ashes."

They sang once more, a hymn that prophesied woe to the unbeliever. Then Ezekiel Bassett rose to " testify." The testimony was mainly to the effect that he was happy because he had fled to the ark of safety while there was yet time.

" I found out," he shouted, " that fancy music and—ah—and—ah—sot sermons and fine duds and suchlike wa'n't goin' to do *me* no good. I needed somethin' else. I needed good times in my religion " ("Hallelujah!") "and I've found 'em right here. Yes, sir! right here. And I say this out loud," turning to glare at the intruder, " and I don't care who comes to poke fun at me for sayin' it." ("Amen!")

A sharp-nosed female followed Mr. Bassett. She spoke with evident feeling and in a voice that trembled and shook when her emotion carried it aloft. *She'd* had enough of high-toned religion. Yes, and of them that upheld it. When her brother Simeon was took bad with phthisic, "wheezin' like a busted bellerses " and 'twas " up and down, trot, trot, trot," to fetch and carry for him day in and night out, did the folks from the Reg'lar church help her? She guessed *not.* The only one that came nigh her was Laviny Pepper, and she came only to gas and gabble and find out things that wa'n't none of her business. What help she got was from a Come-Outer, from Eben Hammond, bless his good soul! ("Amen!") That phthisic settled her for Reg'larism. Yes, and for them that preached it, too. So there!

Captain Eben called for more testimony. But the testifiers were, to use the old minstrel joke, backward in coming forward that evening. At an ordinary meeting, by this time, the shouts and enthusiasm would have been at their height and half a dozen Come-Outers on their feet at once, relating their experiences and proclaiming their happiness. But tonight there was a damper; the presence of the leader of the opposition cast a shadow over the gathering. Only the bravest attempted speech. The others sat silent, showing their resentment and contempt by frowning glances over their shoulders and portentous nods one to the other.

"Come, brethren," commanded the captain sharply; "we are waitin' to hear you. Are you afraid? If your faith is real, nothin' nor nobody should keep you from cryin' it out loud. Now, if ever, is the accepted time. Speak up for the spirit that's in you."

An elderly man, grave and quiet, arose and said a few words, dignified and solemn words of prayer and thankfulness for the comfort this little society of true believers had been to him. Ellery realized that here was another sort of Come-Outer, one of the Hammond type. Evidently, they were not all like Ezekiel and the shrill-voiced woman.

Then, from the settee in front of him, rose the lengthy and fishy person with the cowhide boots and enormous hands. His name was Josiah Badger and he was, according to Trumet's estimate, "a little mite lackin' in his top riggin'." He stuttered, and this infirmity became more and more apparent as he grew eloquent.

"I—I ain't afraid," he proclaimed. "They can call me a C-C-Come-Outer all they want to. I—I don't care if they do. Let 'em, I say; l-let 'em! They can p-p-poke their fun and p-p-p-pup-pup-poke it, but I tell 'em to h-heave ahead and p-pup-pup-

*poke*. When I used to g-go to their old Reg'lar
meetin' house, all I done was to go to sleep. But I
don't go to sleep here, glory hallelujah! No, sir!
There's too much b-b-blessed noise and we have too
g-good times to g-go to sleep here. That old K-Kyan
Pepper called me t-town f-fool t'other day. T-tut-
town fool's what he called me. Says I to him, says I:
' You-you-y-you ain't got spunk enough to be a fool,'
I says, ' unless Laviny says you c-can be. You old
Reg'lar p-p-pepper shaker, you! ' "

By this time tee-hees from the children and
chuckles from some of the older members interfered
with Mr. Badger's fervent but jerky discourse. Captain Eben struck the table smartly.

" Silence! " he thundered. " Silence! Brother
Badger, I beg your pardon for 'em. Go on! "

But Josiah's train of thought had evidently been
derailed by the interruption.

" I—I—I cal'late that's about all," he stammered and sat down.

The captain looked over the meeting.

" I'm ashamed," he said, " ashamed of the behavior of some of us in the Lord's house. This has
been a failure, this service of ours. We have kept
still when we should have justified our faith, and
allowed the presence of a stranger to interfere with
our duty to the Almighty. And I will say," he
added, his voice rising and trembling with indignation, " to him who came here uninvited and broke
up this meetin', that it would be well for him to
remember the words of Scriptur', ' Woe unto ye,
false prophets and workers of iniquity.' Let him
remember what the Divine wisdom put into my head
to read to-night: ' The pastors have become brutish

and have not sought the Lord; therefore they shall not prosper.'"

"Amen!" "Amen!" "Amen!" "So be it!" The cries came from all parts of the little room. They ceased abruptly, for John Ellery was on his feet.

"Captain Hammond," he said, "I realize that I have no right to speak in this building, but I must say one word. My coming here to-night may have been a mistake; I'm inclined to think it was. But I came not, as you seem to infer, to sneer or to scoff; certainly I had no wish to disturb your service. I came because I had heard repeatedly, since my arrival in this town, of this society and its meetings. I had heard, too, that there seemed to be a feeling of antagonism, almost hatred, against me among you here. I couldn't see why. Most of you have, I believe, been at one time members of the church where I preach. I wished to find out for myself how much of truth there was in the stories I had heard and to see if a better feeling between the two societies might not be brought about. Those were my reasons for coming here to-night. As for my being a false prophet and a worker of iniquity"— he smiled—"well, there is another verse of Scripture I would call to your attention: 'Judge not, that ye be not judged.'"

He sat down. There was silence for a moment and then a buzz of whispering. Captain Eben, who had heard him with a face of iron hardness, rapped the table.

"We will sing in closin'," he said, "the forty-second hymn. After which the benediction will be pronounced."

The Regular minister left the Come-Outers' meeting with the unpleasant conviction that he had blundered badly. His visit, instead of tending toward better understanding and more cordial relationship, had been regarded as an intrusion. He had been provoked into a public justification, and now he was quite sure that he would have been more politic to remain silent. He realized that the evening's performance would cause a sensation and be talked about all over town. The Come-Outers would glory in their leader's denunciation of him, and his own people would perhaps feel that it served him right. If he had only told Mrs. Coffin of what he intended to do. Yet he had not told her because he meant to do it anyhow. Altogether it was a rather humiliating business.

So that old bigot was the Van Horne girl's "uncle." It hardly seemed possible that she, who appeared so refined and ladylike when he met her at the parsonage, should be a member of that curious company. When he rose to speak he had seen her in the front row, beside the thin, middle-aged female who had entered the chapel with Captain Hammond and with her. She was looking at him intently. The lamp over the speaker's table had shone full on her face and the picture remained in his memory. He saw her eyes and the wavy shadows of her hair on her forehead.

He stepped off the platform, across the road, out of the way of homeward-bound Come-Outers, and stood there, thinking. The fog was as heavy and wet as ever; in fact, it was almost a rain. The wind was blowing hard from the northwest. The congregation dispersed in chattering groups, their lanterns dipping and swinging like fireflies. The chatter dealt entirely with one subject—himself. He heard his name mentioned at least twenty times. Out of the gusty, dripping blackness came Mr. Badger's voice.

"By time!" crowed Josiah, "he was took down a few p-p-pup-pegs, wa'n't he! My! how Eben did g-gi-gi-give it to him. He looked toler'ble white under the gills when he riz up to heave out his s-s-sus-sassy talk. And foolish, too. I cal'late I won't be the only town fuf-fuf-fool from now on. He! he!"

The noises died away in the distance. Within the chapel the tramp of heavy boots sounded as the lights were blown out, one by one. The minister frowned, sighed, and turned homeward. It is not pleasant to be called a fool, even by a recognized member of the fraternity.

He had taken but a few steps when there was a rustle in the wet grass behind him.

"Mr. Ellery," whispered a voice, "Mr. Ellery, may I speak to you just a moment?"

He wheeled in surprise.

"Why! why, Miss Van Horne!" he exclaimed. "Is it you?"

"Mr. Ellery," she began, speaking hurriedly and in a low voice, "I—I felt that I must say a word to you before——"

She paused and glanced back at the chapel. Ezekiel Bassett, the janitor, having extinguished the last lamp, had emerged from the door and was locking up. In another moment he clumped past them in the middle of the road, the circle of light from his lantern just missing them as they stood in the grass at the side under the hornbeam and black-

84

berry bushes. He was alone; Sukey B. had gone on before, other and younger masculine escort having been providentially provided.

Mr. Bassett was out of hearing before Grace finished her sentence. The minister was silent, waiting and wondering.

" I felt," she said, " that I must see you and— explain. I am *so* sorry you came here to-night. Oh, I wish you hadn't. What made you do it?"

" I came," began Ellery, somewhat stiffly, " because I—well, because I thought it might be a good thing to do. As I said——"

" Yes, I know. But it wasn't. It was so— so——"

" So foolish. Thank you, I'm aware of it. I've heard myself called a fool already since I left your church. Not that I needed to hear it. I realize the fact."

There was a bitterness in his tone, unmistakable. And a little laugh from his companion did not tend to soothe his feelings.

" Thank you," he said. " Perhaps it is funny. I did not find it so. Good evening."

This was priggish, but it must be borne in mind that John Ellery was very, very fresh from the theological school, where young divines are taught to take themselves seriously. He was ashamed of himself as soon as he said it, which proved that his case was not beyond hope.

The girl detained him as he was turning away.

" I wasn't laughing at that," she said. " I know who called you that—that name. It was Josiah Badger, and he really is one, you know. I was thinking of his testimony in meeting and how he called

Ky—Abishai—a pepper shaker. That was ridiculous enough, but it reminded me of something else about Mr. Pepper, and I *had* to laugh. It wasn't at you, truly."

So the minister begged her pardon; also he remained where he was, and heard the drops from the tree patter hollow on his hat.

" I came after you," went on Grace rapidly and with nervous haste, " because I felt that you ought not to misjudge my uncle for what he said to-night. He wouldn't have hurt your feelings for the world. He is a good man and does good to everybody. If you only knew the good he does do, you wouldn't— you wouldn't *dare* think hardly of him."

She stamped her foot in the wet grass as she said it. She was evidently in earnest. But Ellery was not in the mood to be greatly impressed by Eben Hammond's charity or innate goodness. The old tavern keeper's references to himself were too fresh in his mind. " False prophet " and " worker of iniquity! "

" I'm not judging your uncle," he declared. " It seemed to me that the boot was on the other leg."

" I know, but you do judge him, and you mustn't. You see, he thought you had come to make fun of him—and us. Some of the Regular people do, people who aren't fit to tie his shoes. And so he spoke against you. He'll be sorry when he thinks it over. That's what I came to tell you. I ask your pardon for—for him."

" Why—why, that's all right. I think I understood——"

" I'm not asking it because he's a Come-Outer and you're a Regular minister. He isn't ashamed of his religion. Neither am I. I'm a Come-Outer, too."

"Yes. I—I supposed you were."

"Yes, I am. There, good night, Mr. Ellery. All I ask is that you don't think too hardly of uncle. He didn't mean it."

She turned away now, and it was the minister who detained her.

"I've been thinking," he said slowly, for in his present state of mind it was a hard thing to say, "that perhaps I ought to apologize, too. I'm afraid I did disturb your service and I'm sorry. I meant well, but— What's that? Rain?"

There was no doubt about it; it was rain and plenty of it. It came in a swooping downpour that beat upon the trees and bushes and roared upon the roof of the chapel. The minister hurriedly raised his umbrella.

"Here!" he cried, "let me—Miss Van Horne! Where are you?"

The answer came from a short distance down the "Turn-off."

"Good night," called the girl. "I must run."

Evidently, she *was* running. Therefore the young man ran after her. He caught up with her in a moment, in spite of some stumbles over the rough road.

"Here!" he commanded, "you must take the umbrella. Really, you must. You haven't one and you'll be wet through."

She pushed the umbrella aside.

"No, no," she answered. "I don't need it; I'm used to wet weather; truly I am. And I don't care for this hat; it's an old one. You have a long way to go and I haven't. Please, Mr. Ellery, I can't take it."

" Very well," was the sternly self-sacrificing reply, " then I shall certainly go with you."

" But I don't wish you to."

" I can't help that. I'm not going to let you go unprotected through this flood. Especially as you might have been at home before this if you hadn't stopped to speak with me."

" But you mustn't."

" I shall."

Here was the irresistible force and the immovable object. They stood stock still in the middle of the road, while the rain drops jumped as they struck the umbrella top. The immovable object, being feminine, voiced the unexpected.

" All right," she said; " then I suppose I shall have to take it."

" What? "

" The umbrella. I'm sorry, and you'll get dreadfully wet, but it's your own fault."

He could feel her hand near his own on the handle. He did not relinquish his grasp.

" No," he said. " I think, on the whole, that that is unreasonable. I *should* get wet and, though I don't mind it when it is necessary, I——"

" Well? " rather sharply, " what are you going to do? "

" Go with you as far as your gate. I'm sorry, if my company is distasteful, but——"

He did not finish the sentence, thinking, it may be, that she might finish it for him. But she was silent, merely removing her hand from the handle. She took a step forward; he followed, holding the umbrella above her head. They plashed on, without speaking, through the rapidly forming puddles.

Presently she stumbled and he caught her arm to prevent her falling. To his surprise he felt that arm shake in his grasp.

"Why, Miss Van Horne!" he exclaimed in great concern, "are you crying? I beg your pardon. Of course I wouldn't think of going another step with you. I didn't mean to trouble you. I only— If you will please take this umbrella——"

Again he tried to transfer the umbrella and again she pushed it away.

"I—I'm not crying," she gasped; "but—oh, dear! this is *so* funny!"

Mr. Ellery gazed blankly at her through the rain-streaked dark. This was the most astonishing young person he had met in his twenty-three years of worldly experience.

"Funny!" he repeated. "Well, perhaps it is. Our ideas of fun seem to differ. I——"

"Oh, but it *is* so funny. You don't understand. What do you think your congregation would say if they knew you had been to a Come-Outers' meeting and then insisted on seeing a Come-Outer girl home?"

John Ellery swallowed hard. A vision of Captain Elkanah Daniels and the stately Miss Annabel rose before his mind's eye. He hadn't thought of his congregation in connection with this impromptu rescue of a damsel in distress.

"Ha, ha!" he laughed mournfully. "I guess it is rather funny, after all."

"It certainly is. Now will you leave me and go back to your parsonage?"

"Not unless you take the umbrella."

"Very well. It is a beautiful evening for a walk, don't you think so? Mr. Ellery, I'm afraid we shan't have you with us in Trumet very long."

"Why not?"

"Oh, because you're so very, very original. Are your sermons that way, too? Captain Elkanah doesn't like his ministers to be too original."

The minister set his teeth. At that moment he felt an intense desire to bid the Daniels family mind their own business. Then another thought struck him.

"Possibly your Uncle Eben might be somewhat —er—surprised if he knew you were with me. Perhaps he might have something to say on the subject."

"I guess he would. We shall know very soon. I ran away and left him with Mrs. Poundberry, our housekeeper. He doesn't know where I am. I wonder he hasn't turned back to look for me before this. We shall probably meet him at any moment."

She seemed to enjoy the prospect of the meeting. Ellery wondered what on earth he should say to Captain Hammond—that is, provided he was allowed to say anything.

Suddenly a heavier gust of rain and wind beat upon them. The minister struggled with the umbrella. The gust passed and with it the fog. An instant before it had been all about them, shutting them within inky walls. Now it was not. Through the rain he could see the shadowy silhouettes of bushes at the road side. Fifty yards away the lighted windows of the Hammond tavern gleamed yellow. Farther on, over a ragged, moving fringe of grass and weeds, was a black flat expanse —

the bay. And a little way out upon that expanse twinkled the lights of a vessel. A chain rattled. Voices shouting exultingly came to their ears.

"Why!" exclaimed Grace in excited wonder, "it's the packet! She was due this morning, but we didn't expect her in till to-morrow. How did she find her way in the fog? I must tell uncle."

She started to run toward the house. The minister would have followed with the umbrella, but she stopped him.

"No, Mr. Ellery," she urged earnestly. "No, please don't. I'm all right now. Thank you. Good night."

A few steps farther on she turned.

"I hope Cap'n Elkanah won't know," she whispered, the laugh returning to her voice. "Good night."

Ellery stood still in the rain and watched her. He saw her pass the lighted windows and open a door. Into the yellow radiance she flashed and disappeared. A minute more and the bulky form of Eben Hammond, lantern in hand, a sou'wester on his head and his shoulders working themselves into an oilskin coat, burst out of the door and hurriedly limped down toward the shore. On the threshold, framed in light, stood his ward, gazing after him. And the minister gazed at her.

From the bay came the sound of oars in rowlocks. A boat was approaching the wharf. And suddenly from the boat came a hail.

"Halloo! Ahoy, dad! Is that you?"

There was an answering shout from the wharf; a shout of joy. Then a rattle of oars and a clamor of talk. And Grace still stood in the doorway, waiting.

The lantern bobbed up the slope. As it reached the tavern gateway, the minister saw that it was now carried by a tall, active man, who walked with a seaman's stride and roll. Captain Eben was close beside him, talking excitedly.

They entered the yard.

"Grace! Grace!" screamed Captain Eben. "Gracie, girl, look who's come! Look!"

The tall man ran forward.

"Hi, Grace!" he cried in a deep, hearty voice. "Is that you? Ain't you got a word for your old messmate?"

The girl stepped out into the rain.

"Why! why, *Nat!*" she cried.

The big man picked her up bodily in his arms and carried her into the house. Captain Eben followed and the door closed.

John Ellery picked his way homeward through the puddles and the pouring rain.

He found Keziah in the sitting room, seated by the table, evidently writing a letter. She looked tired and grave—for her.

"Well!" she exclaimed as he entered. "I guess you're soppin' now, sartin sure. There's a light in your room. Take off your wet things and throw 'em down to me, and I'll dry 'em in the kitchen. Better leave your boots here now and stand that umbrella in the sink. The kettle's on the stove; you'd better have somethin' hot—ginger tea or somethin'. I told you not to go out such a night as this. Where in the world have you been?"

The minister said he would tell her all about it

in the morning. Just now he thought he had better go up and take off his wet clothes. He declined the ginger tea, and, after removing his boots, went upstairs to his room.

Keziah dipped her pen in the ink and went on with her letter.

"I inclose ten dollars," she wrote. "It is all I can send you now. More than I ought to afford. Goodness knows why I send anything. You don't deserve it. But while I live and you do I can't——"

The minister called from the landing.

"Here is my coat," he said. "The cuffs and lower part of the sleeves are pretty wet. By the way, the packet came in to-night. They didn't expect her so soon on account of the fog. There was a passenger aboard whom I think must be that Nathaniel Hammond you told me of."

Keziah's pen stopped. The wet coat struck the hall floor with a soft thump. The tick of the clock sounded loud in the room. A sheet of wind-driven rain lashed the windows.

"Did you hear?" called the minister. "I said that Nathaniel Hammond, Captain Eben's son, came on the packet. I didn't meet him, but I'm sure it was he. Er—Mrs. Coffin, are you there? Do you hear me?"

The housekeeper laid the pen down beside the unfinished letter.

"Yes," she said, "I hear you. Good night."

For minutes she sat there, leaning back in her chair and staring at the wall. Then she rose, went into the hall, picked up the coat, and took it out into the kitchen, where she hung it on the clotheshorse by the cook stove. After a while she returned to the table and took up the pen. Her face in the lamplight looked more tired and grave than ever.

It was a long time before John Ellery fell asleep. He had much to think of—of the morrow, of the talk his rash visit to the chapel would cause, of the explanation he must make to Captain Elkanah and the rest. But the picture that was before his closed eyes as he lay there was neither of Captain Elkanah nor the parish committee; it was that of a girl, with dark hair and a slim, graceful figure, standing in a lighted doorway and peering out into the rain.

# CHAPTER VI

## IN WHICH OLD FRIENDS MEET

WHEN Ellery came down to breakfast the rain was over, the wind had gone down, and the morning sunshine was pouring in at the dining-room windows. Outside the lilacs were in bud, the bluebirds were singing, and there was a sniff of real spring in the air. The storm was at an end and yet the young minister was conscious of a troublesome feeling that, for him, it was just beginning.

However, he had determined while dressing to make a clean breast of it to his housekeeper—a nominally clean breast, that is. There were some things he would not tell her, some that he would not speak of to anyone, the picture in the doorway for instance. True, it was only a picture and of no moment, but it was pleasant to remember. One of the very few pleasant things connected with the previous evening.

So, as they sat opposite each other at the table, he began his confession. The muffins scorched in the oven and the coffeepot boiled over as he told his story, for Keziah was too much interested to think of trifles. Interested and astounded, for, since Come-Outers had been Come-Outers and the split in the society took place, no Regular minister had crossed the threshold of a seceder's dwelling, much less attended their services and walked home with a member of their congregation. She knew what this amazing procedure was likely to mean, if her parson did not.

"Well!" she exclaimed when the recital was finished. "Well!"

"I—I'm afraid I was too hasty," observed Mr. Ellery thoughtfully. "Perhaps it would have been wiser not to have done it."

"Perhaps 'twould. Yes, I wouldn't wonder a mite."

"It will be talked about some, I suppose. Don't you think so?"

"Some, yes."

"I'm afraid some of my own people may think it queer."

"Queer! Say, Mr. Ellery, you remind me of a half-breed Portugee feller—half Portugee and a half Indian—that went to sea with my father, back in the old days. He hardly ever spoke a word, mainly grunted and made signs. One day he and another fo'mast hand went aloft in a calm to do somethin' to the tops'l. The half-breed—they called him Billy Peter and he always called himself that—was out on the end of the yard, with his foot on the rope underneath, I forget the name of it, when the tarred twine he had for a shoe string caught. Tryin' to get it loose it broke sudden, his shoe pulled off, he lost his balance and fell. He grabbed at the yard, saved himself for a second, fell again, grabbed the next yard, then a rope and so on down, grabbin' and pullin' all the way. First his shoe hit the deck, then his sheath knife, then a piece of rope, and finally him-

self, landin' right on top of the Irish cook who was
goin' aft from the galley with father's dinner.

"There was the greatest racket you ever heard,
pans fallin', dishes smashin', men yellin', and the
cook swearin'. Father run on deck, thinkin' the ship
was dismasted. He found the cook and Billy Peter
sittin' in the middle of the mess, lookin' at each
other. Neither was hurt a mite. The mates and
the crew, part of 'em, was standin' starin' at the pair.

"'For Heaven sakes!' says father; 'what happened?'

"The half-breed looked up and rubbed his head.
'Ugh!' says he, 'Billy Peter bust his shoe string.'

"The cook, his name was O'Neill, looked at him
disgusted. 'Well, begorra!' says he, 'Billy Peter,
you don't exaggerate none, do ye! It's a good thing
*both* of 'em didn't bust or we'd have foundered.'

"You remind me of Billy Peter, Mr. Ellery, you
don't exaggerate. Queer? Some folks think your
goin' to that meetin' last night *queer?* At this moment one half of Trumet is talkin' about it and runnin' out to tell the other half. I guess I'd better
hurry up with this breakfast. We're goin' to have
callers."

Strange to say, however, this prophecy of early
morning visitors did not prove true. Nine o'clock,
then ten, and no visitor came to the parsonage.
Mrs. Coffin affirmed that she did not understand it.
Where was Didama? Where Lavinia Pepper?
Had the "Trumet Daily Advertiser" suspended
publication?

At half past ten the gate slammed. Keziah
peered from the window.

"Humph!" she ejaculated. "Here comes Elkanah and he's got storm signals set, by the looks. He's comin' after you, Mr. Ellery."

"Very well," was the calm reply; "let him come."

"What are you goin' to say to him?"

"Nothing, except that I did what I considered right at the time. Show him into the study, Mrs. Coffin, please."

Captain Daniels marched to the dining-room door, his gold-headed cane marking time like a drumbeat. He nodded curtly to Keziah, who answered the knock, and stepped across the threshold.

"Hum—ha!" he barked. "Is the minister—hum—ha! is Mr. Ellery in?"

"Yes, he's in."

"Tell him I want to see him."

The housekeeper announced the visitor.

"He's as sour as a skimmin' of last week's milk," she whispered. "Don't be afraid of him, though."

"Oh, I'm not. Show him in."

"All right. Say, Mr. Ellery, it's none of my business, but I wouldn't say anything about your seein' Grace home. That's none of *his* business, either, or anybody else's."

The head of the parish committee stalked into the study and the door closed behind him. A rumble of voices in animated conversation succeeded.

Mrs. Coffin went out into the kitchen and resumed her business of making a dried-apple pie. There was a hot fire in the stove and she opened the back door to let in the fresh air. She worked briskly, rolling out the dough, filling the deep dish, and pinking the edges of the upper crust with a fork. She was thinking as she worked, but not of the minister or his visitor.

She put the pie in the oven and set the damper. And, as she knelt by the stove, something struck her lightly on the back of the neck. She looked up and about her, but there was no one in sight. Then she picked up the object which had struck her. It was a cranberry, withered and softened by the winter frosts.

She looked at the cranberry, then at the open door, and her eyes twinkled. Running quickly to the threshold she peered out. The back yard was, apparently, empty, save for a few hens belonging to near neighbors, and these had stopped scratching for a living and were huddled near the fence.

"Hum!" she mused. "You rascal! Eddie Snow, if it's you, I'll be after you in a minute. Just because you're big enough to quit school and drive store wagon is no reason why I can't— Hey? Oh!"

She was looking down below the door, which opened outward and was swung partly back on its hinges. From under the door projected a boot, a man's boot and one of ample size.

Keziah's cheeks, already red from the heat of the stove, reddened still more. Her lips twitched and her eyes sparkled.

"Hum!" she said again. "They say you can tell the Old Scratch by his footprints, even if you can't smell the sulphur. Anyhow, you can tell a Hammond by the size of his boots. Come out from behind that door this minute. Ain't you ashamed of yourself?"

The owner of the boot stepped forth from behind the door and seized her by both hands.

"Halloo, Keziah!" he cried joyfully. "My, but it's good to see you."

"Halloo, Nat!" said Keziah heartily. "It's kind of good to see you, too."

The rest of him was in keeping with his boots. He was big and broad-shouldered and bearded. His face, above the beard, was tanned to a deep reddish brown, and the corners of his eyes were marked with dozens of tiny wrinkles. He was dressed in blue cloth and wore a wide-brimmed, soft felt hat. He entered the kitchen and tossed the hat into a corner.

"Well!" he exclaimed. "Why don't you act surprised to see a feller? Here I've been cruisin' from the Horn to Barnegat and back again, and you act as if I'd just dropped in to fetch the cup of molasses I borrowed yesterday. What do you mean by it?"

"Oh, I heard you'd made port."

"Did, hey? That's Trumet, sure pop. You ain't the only one. I sneaked off acrost lots so's to dodge the gang of neighbors that I knew would be sailin' into our yard, the whole fleet loaded to the gunwale with questions. Wanted to see you first, Keziah."

"Yes. So, instead of callin' like a Christian, you crept up the back way and threw cranberries at me. Ain't you ashamed of yourself?"

"Not a mite." He took a handful of the frost-bitten berries from his coat pocket and inspected them lovingly. "Ain't they fine?" he asked, crunching two or three between his teeth. "I picked 'em up as I came along. I tell you, that's the home taste, all right."

"Don't eat those frozen things. They'll give you your never-get-over."

"What? Cape Cod cranberries! Never in the world. I'd rather eat sand down here than the finest mug my steward can cook. Tell you what I'll do, though; I'll swear off on the cranberries if you'll give me a four-inch slice of that pie I saw you put in the oven. Dried-apple, I'll bet my sou'wester. Think you might ask a feller to sit down. Ain't you glad to see me?"

Mrs. Coffin pulled forward one of the kitchen chairs. He seated himself on it and it groaned under his weight.

"Whew!" he whistled. "Never made to stand rough weather, was it? Well, *ain't* you glad?"

Keziah looked at him gravely.

"You know I'm glad, Nat," she said.

"So? I hoped you would be, but I did want to hear you say it. Now you come to anchor yourself and let's have a talk. I've been countin' on it ever since we set tops'ls off Surinam."

The housekeeper took the other chair.

"How are you—" she began. He stopped her.

"S-shh!" he interrupted. "Don't say anything for a minute. Let me look at you. Just as clean and wholesome and good-lookin' as ever. They don't make girls like that anywhere else but down on this old sand bar. Not a day older, by the jumpin'——"

She held up her hand.

"Hush, Nat," she protested; "don't talk foolish. Girl? Not a day older? Why, if feelin's count for anything, I'm as old as Methusaleh. Haven't I had enough to make me old?"

He was grave immediately.

"I beg your pardon, Keziah," he said. "I'm a dough head, that's a fact. I hadn't forgot about Sol, but I was so glad to be home again and to see dad and Grace and the old town and you that everything else flew out of my mind. Poor Sol! I liked him."

"He liked you, too. No wonder, considerin' what you did to——"

"Belay! Never mind that. Poor chap! Well, he's rid of his sufferin's at last. Tell me about it, if you can without bringin' all the trouble back too plain."

So she told him of her brother's sickness and death, of having to give up the old home, and, finally, of her acceptance of the housekeeper's position. He listened, at first with sympathy and then with suppressed indignation.

"By the jumpin' Moses!" he exclaimed. "And Elkanah was goin' to turn you out of house and home. The mean, pompous old——"

"Hush! hush! he's in there with Mr. Ellery."

"Who? Elkanah?"

"Yes; they're in the study."

"By the jumpin'—— Let me talk to him for a few minutes. *I'll* tell him what's good for his health. You just listen."

He rose from the chair, but she made him sit down again.

"No, no," she protested. "He wasn't to blame. He had to have his rent and I didn't feel that I could afford to keep up a whole house, just for myself. And, besides, I ought to be thankful to him, I suppose. He got me this place."

"He did?"

"Yes, he did. I rather guess Zeb Mayo or somebody may have suggested it to him first, but——"

"Humph! I rather guess so, too."

"Well, you can't always tell. Sometimes when you really get inside of a person you find a generous streak that——"

"Not in a Daniels. Anybody that got inside of Elkanah would find nothin' but Elkanah there, and 'twould be crowded at that. So he's talkin' to the new parson, hey? Bossin' him, too, I'll bet."

"I ain't so sure. Mr. Ellery's young, but he's got a mind of his own."

Captain Hammond chuckled and slapped his knee.

"Ho, ho!" he laughed. "I've been hearin' somethin' about that mind. Went to the chapel last night, I understand, and he and dad had a set-to. Oh, I heard about it! Wish I might have been there."

"How does your father act about it?"

"'Bout the way a red-hot stove acts when you spill water on it; every time he thinks of the minister he sizzles. Ho, ho! I do wish I could have been there."

"What does Grace say?"

"Oh, she doesn't say much. I wouldn't wonder if she felt the way I do, though we both keep quiet. I'll tell you, between ourselves and the ship's pump, that I sort of glory in the young chap's spunk."

"Good! So do I. I like him."

"See here, Keziah! I'm gettin' frightened. You ain't settin' your cap to be a parson's wife, are you? Because——"

"Don't be silly. I might adopt him, but that's all, I guess."

Her friend leaned forward.

"Keziah," he said earnestly, "there's no sense in your slavin' yourself to death here. I can think of a good deal pleasanter berth than that. Pleasanter for me, anyhow, and I'd do my best to make it pleasant for you. You've only got to say the word and— No? Well, then all I can do is hope through another voyage."

"Please don't, Nat. You know."

"No, I don't know."

"Well, perhaps you don't. But *I* know. I like you, Nat. I count on you as the straightest, truest friend I've got; and I want to keep on countin' on you just that way. Mayn't I?"

"'Course you can, Keziah. But——"

"Then don't say another word, please."

He sighed and looked out at the open door. The kitchen clock ticked loud in the silence.

"All right," he said at last. "All right, but I'm goin' to keep on hopin'."

"You mustn't, Nat."

"Keziah, when you set your foot down you're pretty stubborn; but I've got somethin' of a foot myself. You remember you said so a few minutes ago. Hi, hum! Well, speakin' of dad reminds me that I'm kind of worried about him."

"You are? Why? Isn't he well?"

"Pretty well, but he ain't strong, and he gets too excited over things like last night's foolishness. Grace tells me that the doctor says he must be careful or he'll drop off sudden some of these days. He had a shock five or six years ago, a little one, and I've been anxious about him ever since. I've got to go to New York off and on for the next month; after that I hope to be home for a spell and I can keep an eye on him. Keziah, if you'll listen I'll whisper somethin' to you—religion's a good thing and so's a mustard plaster, but both of 'em can be put on too strong. Dad is just a little mite crazy on Come-Outers, I'm afraid."

"Oh, no, I guess not! You mustn't worry. How did Grace look to you?"

"Like the harbor light on a stormy night. She's a brick, that girl, and gets prettier every minute. Wonder to me some of the young chaps down here don't carry her off by main strength. She'll make somebody a good wife."

"Um-hm. Have—have you ever thought of her that way yourself?"

"Keziah!"

"Well, don't get mad. I think a lot of Grace, and I don't know anyone I'd rather see you marry."

"I do. Keziah, that's enough of that. Are you and dad in partnership to get me spliced and out of the way? He was at me this mornin' along the same line. Don't say anything like that again, even in fun. *You* know why."

"All right, all right. Now tell me about yourself. Have you had a good voyage? How do you like your owners? How did Zach Foster ever get the packet in through yesterday's fog?"

"Voyage was all right. Some rugged weather on the trip out, but homeward bound we slid along like a slush bucket on a greased plank. Owners are all right. Good people as ever I sailed for. As for Zach and the packet— Ho, ho!"

He laughed, rocking back and forth on the chair, which creaked in sympathy.

"What's the joke?" demanded the housekeeper. "Don't do that! That chair wasn't made for elephants to use."

"Hey? 'Tis pretty weak in the knees, ain't it? Dad would say 'twas a piece with the creed of those that owned it. I— What's that? Somebody's comin'. I'm goin' to clear out. I don't want to be put through my catechism yet a while."

"No, you mustn't go. I want you to meet Mr. Ellery. You sit out on the wash bench by the back door till I get rid of whoever 'tis that's comin'. Scoot!"

Nat "scooted," stopping to snatch up his hat as he ran. Keziah went into the dining room and admitted Captain Zebedee Mayo, who was panting from the exertion of his walk.

"Whew!" puffed Captain Zeb, mopping his forehead. "How be you, Keziah? What? You ain't all alone! Thought you'd have a cabin full of gab machines by this time. Have they been and gone?"

"No, they haven't been. I— My land, my pie!"

She rushed into the kitchen and snatched the pastry from the oven. Her new caller followed her.

"So they ain't been, hey?" he said. "That's queer."

"Elkanah's here. He's in there with the minister now."

"He is? Givin' the young feller Hail Columby, I cal'late. Well, now, he shan't. He, he! When they told me how the minister passed old hop-and-go-fetch-it what was due him at the chapel last night I riz up and hoorayed till my wife shut the windows. She said the neighbors all thought I was loony, anyhow, and I needn't prove it to 'em. He, he! But Elkanah ain't got any funny bone. He's as solemn as a stuffed owl, and he'll—  Well, I'm goin' to put *my* oar in. I'm parish committee, too, I cal'late, and I've got somethin' to say, even if I wa'n't christened Daniels. Here goes!"

He headed for the study, but before he crossed the threshold of the kitchen Ellery and his visitor came out into the dining room. Captain Elkanah's face was flushed, and he fidgeted. The minister looked determined but calm.

" Ahoy there, Elkanah!" hailed Zebedee cheerfully. " 'Mornin', Mr. Ellery. Been havin' officers' counsel, have you?"

" Good morning, Captain Mayo," said the minister.

" 'Mornin', Zebedee," grunted Elkanah. " I have—hum—ha!—been discussing the regrettable affair of last night with Mr. Ellery. I have tried—hum—ha! to show him that respectable people of our society don't associate with Come-Outers, and that for a Regular minister to go to their meetings is something neither the congregation nor the parish committee approves of. No—er—hum—ha! no!"

" And I explained to Captain Daniels," observed the minister, " that I went there for what seemed to me good reasons, and, as they did seem to me good at the time, I'm not ashamed of having gone. It was an honest mistake on my part and I may make more."

"But the society——" began Elkanah. Captain Zeb interrupted him.

"Don't worry about the society, Mr. Ellery," he said with emphasis. "Nor about the parish committee, either. Great fishhooks! the most of us are tickled to death over what you said to Eben Hammond. We think it's a mighty good joke. *You* didn't know, of course, and what you did was done innocent. He! he! he! Did you lay him out, hey?"

"Zebedee," began Captain Daniels, "I must say I can't see anything to laugh at."

"You never could, Elkanah. I remember that time when you and me and some of the fellers home from sea went out sailin' and the boom knocked you overboard with your Sunday clothes on. Lordy, how the rest of us did holler! but you never cracked a smile. If you'd seen yourself when we hauled you in! whiskers runnin' salt water; beaver hat lookin' like a drownded kitten——"

"There! There! Never mind that. I think you'll find a good many of the society feel as I do, shocked and—hum—ha!—sorry. I'm surprised they haven't been here to say so."

"I expected them," remarked the minister.

"So did I," chimed in Captain Zeb. "But I cal'late to know why they ain't been. They're all too busy crowin' over the way Nat Hammond fetched the packet home last night. *What?* You ain't heard? Great fishhooks! it's the best thing ever——"

"I've heard about it," snapped Elkanah impatiently. "Mr. Ellery, I'm glad you realize that your action was a mistake and I will take pains to have that immejitly made plain to——"

" *You* ain't heard, Keziah, have you? " broke in Zebedee. " Nor you, Mr. Ellery? Well, I must tell you. Here's where I gain a lap on Didama Rogers. Seems the *Deborah S.*—that's the packet's name, Mr. Ellery—she hauled out of Boston night afore last on the ebb, with a fair wind and sky clear as a bell. But they hadn't much more'n got outside of Minot's 'fore the fog shut down, thicker'n gruel for a sick rich man. The wind held till 'long toward mornin'; then she flattened to a dead calm. 'Bije Perry, the mate, he spun the yarn to me, and he said 'twas thick and flat as ever he see and kept gettin' no better fast.

" They drifted along till noon time and then they was somewheres out in the bay, but that's about all you could say. Zach, he was stewin' and sputterin' like a pair of fried eels, and Lafayette Gage and Emulous Peters—they're Denboro folks, Mr. Ellery, and about sixteen p'ints t'other side of no account— they was the only passengers aboard except Nat Hammond, and they put in their time playin' high low jack in the cabin. The lookout was for'ard tootin' a tin horn and his bellerin' was the most ex- citin' thing goin' on. After dinner—corned beef and cabbage—trust Zach for that, though it's next door to cannibalism to put cabbage in *his* mouth —after dinner all hands was on deck when Nat says: 'Hush!' he says. 'Don't I hear some- thin'? '

" They listened, and then they all heard it—all 'cept Zach, who's deef in his larboard ear.

" ' Stand by! ' roars Nat. ' It's a squall, dead astern and comin' abilin'! I'll take her, 'Bije. You look out for them tops'ls.'

" So Nat grabs the wheel and 'Bije tears for'ard and sends the two fo'mast hands aloft on the jump. Zach was skipper, but all he done was race around and holler and trip over his own feet. Oh, he's a prize sailor, he is! Don't talk to me about them Fosters! I——"

" Nobody is talkin' about 'em but you, Zeb," observed Keziah drily. " Go on. How about the squall? "

" It hit 'em 'fore they got even one tops'l clewed down. That one, the foretops'l 'twas, split to rags. The main tops'l was set, and when the squall struck, the rotten old topmast went by the board ' Kerrash-o! ' 'Course splinters flew like all possessed, and one of 'em, about a foot long, sailed past Nat's head, where he stood heavin' his whole weight on the wheel, and lit right on the binnacle, smashin' it to matches.

" They say Nat never paid the least attention, no more'n if the chunk of wood had been a June bug buzzin' past. He just held that wheel hard down and that saved the packet. She come around and put her nose dead in the wind just in time. As 'twas, 'Bije says there was a second when the water by her lee rail looked right underneath him as he hung onto the deck with finger nails and teeth.

" Well, there they was, afloat, but with their upper riggin' gone and the compass smashed flat. A howlin' no'thwester blowin' and fog thick as ever. Zach was a whimperin', fidgetin' old woman, Lafayette and Emulous was prayin' in the scuppers—and that ain't an exercise they're used to, neither—and even 'Bije was mighty shook up and worried—he says he was himself. But Nat Hammond was as cool and refreshin' as the bottom of my well up home.

" 'Better clear away that mess aloft, hadn't you?' he says to the skipper.

"Zach said he guessed so; he wa'n't sure of nothin'. However, they cleared it away, and incidentally 'Bije yanked the prayer meetin' out of the scuppers and set 'em to work. Then Nat suggests gettin' the spare compass and, lo and behold you! there wa'n't any. Compasses cost money and money's made to keep, so Zach thinks.

" So there they was. Wind was fair, or ought to be, but 'twas blowin' hard and so thick you couldn't hardly see the jib boom. Zach he wanted to anchor, then he didn't, then he did, and so on. Nobody paid much attention to him.

" 'What'll we do, Nat?' says 'Bije. He knew who was the real seaman aboard.

" 'Keep her as she is, dead afore it, if you ask me,' says Nat. 'Guess we'll hit the broadside of the cape somewheres if this gale holds.'

" So they kept her as she was. And it got to be night and they knew they'd ought to be 'most onto the edge of the flats off here, if their reck'nin' was nigh right. They hove the lead and got five fathom. No flats about that.

"Zach was for anchorin' again. 'What do you think, Nat?' asks 'Bije.

" 'Anchor, of course, if you want to,' Nat says. 'You're runnin' this craft. I'm only passenger.'

" 'But what do you *think?*' whines Zach. 'Can't you tell us what you do think?'

" 'Well, if 'twas me, I wouldn't anchor till I had to. Prob'ly 'twill fair off to-morrow, but if it shouldn't, we might have to lay out here all day. Anyhow, we'd have to wait for a full tide.'

" ' I'm afraid we're off the course,' says 'Bije, ' else we'd been acrost the bar by this time.'

" ' Well,' Nat tells him, ' if we are off the course and too far inshore, we would have made the bar— the Bayport bar—if not the Trumet one. And if we're off the course and too far out, we'd ought to have deeper water than five fathom, hadn't we? 'Course I'm not sure, but— What's that, landsman?'

" ' Three and a half, sir,' says the feller with the lead. That showed they was edgin' in somewheres. Nat he sniffed, for all the world like a dog catchin' a scent, so 'Bije declares.

" ' I can smell home,' he says.

" Three fathom the lead give 'em, then two and a half, then a scant two. They was drawin' six feet. Zach couldn't stand it.

" ' I'm goin' to anchor,' he squeals, frantic. ' I believe we're plumb over to Wellmouth and drivin' right onto Horsefoot Shoal.'

" ' It's either that or the bar,' chimes in 'Bije. ' And whichever 'tis, we can't anchor in the middle of it.'

" ' But what'll we do?' shouts Zach. ' Can't nobody say somethin' to *do?*'

" ' Tell you I smell home,' says Nat, calm and chipper, ' and I'd know that smell if I met it in Jericho. Ha! there she deepens again. That was the bar and we're over it.'

" The wind had gone down to a stiff sailin' breeze, and the old *Debby S.* slapped along afore it. Sometimes there was twelve foot under her keel and sometimes eight or nine. Once 'twas only seven and a half. Zach and 'Bije both looked at each other, but Nat only smiled.

"'Oh, you can laugh!' hollers Zach. ''Tain't your vessel you're runnin' into danger. *You* ain't paid out your good money——'

"Nat never answered; but he stopped smilin'.

"And all to once the water deepened. Hammond swung her up into the wind.

"'*Now* you can anchor,' says he.

"'And 'bout time, too, I guess,' says 'Bije. 'I cal'late the skipper's right. This *is* Horsefoot and we're right between the shoals. Yes, sir, and I hear breakers. Lively there!'

"They hove over the mudhook and dropped the sails. Nat shook his head.

"'Breakers or not,' says he, 'I tell you I've smelt home for the last half hour. Now, by the jumpin' Moses, I can *taste* it!'

"And inside of a couple of shakes come the rain. It poured for a while and then the fog cleared. Right acrost their bows was Trumet, with the town clock strikin' ten. Over the flat place between the hills they could see the light on the ocean side. And they was anchored right in the deep hole inside the breakwater, as sure as I'm knee high to a marlin spike!

"'Bije just stared at Hammond with his mouth open.

"'Nat,' says he, 'you're a seaman, if I do say it. I thought I was a pretty good bay pilot, but I can't steer a vessel without a compass through a night as black as Pharaoh's Egypt, and in a thick fog besides, and land her square on top of her moorin's.

If my hat wa'n't sloshin' around thirty mile astern, I snum if I wouldn't take it off to you this minute!'

"'Nat,' stammers Zach, 'I must say I——'

"Nat snapped him shut like a tobacco box. 'You needn't,' says he. 'But I'll say this to you, Zach Foster. When I undertake to handle a vessel I handle her best I know how, and the fact that I don't own her makes no difference to me. You just put that down somewheres so you won't forget it.'

"And this mornin'," crowed Captain Zebedee, concluding his long yarn, "after that, mind you, that lubber Zach Foster is around town tellin' folks that his schooner had been over the course so often she *couldn't* get lost. She found her way home herself. *What* do you think of that?"

The two members of the parish committee left the parsonage soon after Captain Mayo had finished his story. Elkanah had listened with growing irritation and impatience. Zebedee lingered a moment behind his companions.

"Don't you fret yourself about what happened last night, Mr. Ellery," he whispered. "It'll be all right. 'Course nobody'd want you to keep up chummin' in with Come-Outers, but what you said to old Eben'll square you this time. So long."

The minister shut the door behind his departing guests. Then he went out into the kitchen, whither the housekeeper had preceded him. He found her standing on the back step, looking across the fields. The wash bench was untenanted.

"Hum!" mused Ellery thoughtfully, "that was a good story of Captain Mayo's. This man Hammond must be a fine chap. I should like to meet him."

Keziah still looked away over the fields. She did not wish her employer to see her face—just then.

"I thought you would meet him," she said. "He was here a little while ago and I asked him to wait. I guess Zeb's yarn was too much for him; he doesn't like to be praised."

"So? Was he here? At the Regular parsonage? I'm surprised."

"He and I have known each other for a long while."

"Well, I'm sorry he's gone. I think I should like him."

Keziah turned from the door.

"I know you would," she said.

# CHAPTER VII

IT is probable that John Ellery never fully realized the debt of gratitude he owed to the fog and the squall and to Captain Nat Hammond. Trumet, always hungry for a sensation, would have thoroughly enjoyed arguing and quarreling over the minister's visit to Come-Outer meeting, and, during the fracas, Keziah's parson might have been more or less battered. But Captain Nat's brilliant piloting of the old packet was a bit of seamanship which every man and woman on that foam-bordered stretch of sand could understand and appreciate, and the minister's indiscretion was all but forgotten in consequence. The "Daily Advertisers" gloated over it, of course, and Captain Elkanah brought it up at the meeting of the parish committee, but there Captain Zeb Mayo championed the young man's course and proclaimed that, fur's he was concerned, he was for Mr. Ellery more'n ever. "A young greenhorn with the spunk to cruise single-handed right into the middle of the Come-Outer school and give an old bull whale like Eben the gaff is the man for my money," declared Zebedee. Most of his fellow-committee agreed with him. "Not guilty, but don't do it again," was the general verdict.

As for the Come-Outers, they professed to believe

that their leader had much the best of the encounter, so they were satisfied. There was a note of triumph and exultation in the "testimony" given on the following Thursday night, and Captain Eben divided his own discourse between thankfulness for his son's safe return and glorification at the discomfiture of the false prophets. Practically, then, the result of Ellery's peace overture was an increased bitterness in the feeling between the two societies and a polishing of weapons on both sides.

Keziah watched anxiously for a hint concerning her parson's walk in the rain with Grace, but she heard nothing, so congratulated herself that the secret had been kept. Ellery did not again mention it to her, nor she to him. A fortnight later he preached his great sermon on "The Voyage of Life," and its reference to gales and calms and lee shores and breakers made a hit. His popularity took a big jump.

He met Nat Hammond during that fortnight. The first meeting was accompanied by unusual circumstances, which might have been serious, but were actually only funny.

The tide at Trumet, on the bay side, goes out for a long way, leaving uncovered a mile and a half of flats, bare and sandy, or carpeted with seaweed. Between these flats are the channels, varying at low water from two to four feet in depth, but deepening rapidly as the tide flows.

The flats fascinated the young minister, as they have many another visitor to the Cape, before or since. On cloudy days they lowered with a dull, leaden luster and the weed-grown portions were like the dark squares on a checkerboard, while the deep water beyond the outer bar was steely gray and angry. When the sun shone and the wind blew clear from the northwest the whole expanse flashed into fire and color, sapphire blue, emerald green, topaz yellow, dotted with white shells and ablaze with diamond sparkles where the reflected light leaped from the flint crystals of the wet, coarse sand.

The best time to visit the flats—tide serving, of course—is the early morning at sunrise. Then there is an inspiration in the wide expanse, a snap and tang and joy in the air. Ellery had made up his mind to take a before-breakfast tramp to the outer bar and so arose at five, tucked a borrowed pair of fisherman's boots beneath his arm, and, without saying anything to his housekeeper, walked down the lawn behind the parsonage, climbed the rail fence, and "cut across lots" to the pine grove on the bluff. There he removed his shoes, put on the boots, wallowed through the mealy yellow sand forming the slope of the bluff, and came out on the white beach and the inner edge of the flats. Then he plashed on, bound out to where the fish weirs stood, like webby fences, in the distance.

It was a wonderful walk on a wonderful day. The minister enjoyed every minute of it. Out here he could forget the petty trials of life, the Didamas and Elkanahs. The wind blew his hat off and dropped it in a shallow channel, but he splashed to the rescue and laughed aloud as he fished it out. It was not much wetter than it had been that night of the rain, when he tried to lend his umbrella and didn't succeed. This reflection caused him to halt in his walk and look backward toward the shore. The brown roof of the old tavern was blushing red in the first rays of the sun.

A cart, drawn by a plodding horse and with a single individual on its high seat, was moving out from behind the breakwater. Some fisherman driving out his weir, probably.

The sand of the outer bar was dimpled and mottled like watered silk by the action of the waves. It sloped gradually down to meet the miniature breakers that rolled over and slid in ripples along its edge. Ellery wandered up and down, picking up shells and sea clams, and peering through the nets of the nearest weir at the " horsefoot crabs " and squid and flounders imprisoned in the pound. There were a few bluefish there, also, and a small school of mackerel.

The minister had been on the bar a considerable time before he began to think of returning to the shore. He was hungry, but was enjoying himself too well to mind. The flats were all his that morning. Only the cart and its driver were in sight and they were half a mile off. He looked at his watch, sighed, and reluctantly started to walk toward the town; he mustn't keep Mrs. Coffin's breakfast waiting *too* long.

The first channel he came to was considerably deeper than when he forded it on the way out. He noticed this, but only vaguely. The next, however, was so deep that the water splashed in at the top of one of his boots. He did notice that, because though he was not wearing his best clothes, he was not anxious to wet his " other ones." The extent of his wardrobe was in keeping with the size of his salary.

And the third channel was so wide and deep that he saw at once it could not be forded, unless he was willing to plunge above his waist. This was provoking. Now he realized that he had waited too long. The tide had been flowing for almost an hour; it had flowed fast and, as he should have remembered, having been told, the principal channels were eight feet deep before the highest flats were covered.

He hurried along the edge, looking for a shallower place, but found none. At last he reached the point of the flat he was on and saw, to his dismay, that here was the deepest spot yet, a hole, scoured out by a current like a mill race. Turning, he saw, creeping rapidly and steadily together over the flat behind him, two lines of foam, one from each channel. His retreat was cut off.

He was in for a wetting, that was sure. However, there was no help for it, so he waded in. The water filled his boots there, it gurgled about his hips, and beyond, as he could see, it seemed to grow deeper and deeper. The current was surprisingly strong; he found it difficult to keep his footing in the soft sand. It looked as though he must swim for it, and to swim in that tide would be no joke.

Then, from behind him, came a hail. He turned and saw moving toward him through the shallow water now covering the flat beyond the next channel, the cart he had seen leave the shore by the packet wharf, and, later, on the outer bar. The horse was jogging along, miniature geysers spouting beneath its hoofs. The driver waved to him.

" Hold on, mate," he called. " Belay there.

"'Say,' he cried, 'I'm cruisin' your way; better get aboard, hadn't you?'"

Stay where you are. I'll be alongside in a shake. Git dap, January!"

Ellery waded back to meet this welcome arrival. The horse plunged into the next channel, surged through it, and emerged dripping. The driver pulled the animal into a walk.

"Say," he cried, "I'm cruisin' your way; better get aboard, hadn't you? There's kind of a heavy dew this mornin'. Whoa, Bill!"

"Bill" or "January" stopped with apparent willingness. The driver leaned down and extended a hand. The minister took it and was pulled up to the seat.

"Whew!" he panted. "I'm much obliged to you. I guess you saved me from a ducking, if nothing worse."

"Yes," was the answer, "I wouldn't wonder if I did. This ain't Saturday night and 'twould be against Trumet principles to take a bath any other time. All taut, are you? Good enough! then we'll get under way." He flapped the reins and added, "G'long, Julius Cæsar!"

The horse, a sturdy, sedate beast to whom all names seemed to be alike, picked up his feet and pounded them down again. Showers of spray flew about the heads of the pair on the seat.

"I ain't so sure about that duckin'," commented the rescuer. "Hum! I guess likely we'll be out of soundin's if we tackle that sink hole you was undertakin' to navigate. Let's try it a little further down."

Ellery looked his companion over.

"Well," he observed with a smile, "from what I've heard of you, Captain Hammond, I rather guess you could navigate almost any water in this locality and in all sorts of weather."

The driver turned in surprise.

"So?" he exclaimed. "You know me, do you? That's funny. I was tryin' to locate you, but I ain't been able to. You ain't a Trumetite, I'll bet on that."

"Yes, I am."

"Tut! tut! tut! you don't tell me. Say, shipmate, you hurt my pride. I did think there wa'n't a soul that ever trod sand in this village that I couldn't name on sight, and give the port they hailed from and the names of their owners. But you've got me on my beam ends. And yet you knew *me*."

"Of course I did. Everybody knows the man that brought the packet home."

Nat Hammond sniffed impatiently.

"Um—hm!" he grunted. "I cal'late everybody does, and knows a lot more about that foolishness than I do myself. If ever a craft was steered by guess and by godfrey, 'twas that old hooker of Zach's t'other night. Well— Humph! here's another piece of pilotin' that bids fair to be a mighty sight harder. Heave ahead, Hannibal! hope you've got your web feet with you."

They had moved along the edge of the flat a short distance and now turned into the channel. The horse was wading above its knees; soon the water reached its belly and began to flow into the body of the cart.

"Pick up your feet, shipmate," commanded Nat. "You may get rheumatiz if you don't. This'll be a treat for those sea clams back in that bucket amidships. They'll think I've repented and have decided to turn 'em loose again. They don't know how long I've been countin' on a sea-clam pie. I'll fetch those clams ashore if I have to lug 'em with my teeth. Steady, all hands! we're off the ways."

The cart was afloat. The horse, finding wading more difficult than swimming, began to swim.

"Now I'm skipper again, sure enough," remarked Hammond. "Ain't gettin' seasick, are you?"

The minister laughed.

"No," he said.

"Good! she keeps on a fairly even keel, considerin' her build. *There* she strikes! That'll do, January; you needn't try for a record voyage. Walkin's more in your line than playin' steamboat. We're over the worst of it now. Say! you and I didn't head for port any too soon, did we?"

"No, I should say not. I ought to have known better than to wait out there so long. I've been warned about this tide. I——"

"S-sh-sh! *You* ought to have known better! What do you think of me? Born and brought up within sight and smell of this salt puddle and let myself in for a scrape like this! But it was so mighty fine off there on the bar I couldn't bear to leave it. I always said that goin' to sea on land would be the ideal way, and now I've tried it. But you took bigger chances than I did. Are you a good swimmer?"

"Not too good. I hardly know what might have happened if you hadn't——"

"S-sh-sh! that's all right. Always glad to pick up a derelict, may be a chance for salvage, you know. Here's the last channel and it's an easy one. There! now it's plain sailin' for dry ground."

The old horse, breathing heavily from his exertions, trotted over the stretch of yet uncovered flats and soon mounted the slope of the beach. The minister prepared to alight.

"Captain Hammond," he said, "you haven't asked me my name."

"No, I seldom do more'n once. There have been times when *I'd* just as soon cruise without too big letters alongside my figurehead."

"Well, my name is Ellery."

"Hey? *What?* Oh, ho! ho! ho!"

He rocked back and forth on the seat. The minister's feelings were a bit hurt, though he tried not to show it.

"You mustn't mind my laughin'," explained Nat, still chuckling. "It ain't at you. It's just because I was wonderin' what you'd look like if I should meet you and now— Ho! ho! You see, Mr. Ellery, I've heard of you, same as you said you'd heard of me."

Ellery smiled, but not too broadly.

"Yes," he admitted, "I imagined you had."

"Yes, seems to me dad mentioned your name once or twice. As much as that, anyhow. Wonder what he'd say if he knew his son had been takin' you for a mornin' ride?"

"Probably that it would have been much better to have left me where you found me."

The captain's jolly face grew serious.

"No, no!" he protested. "Not so bad as that. Dad wouldn't drown anybody, not even a Regular minister. He's a pretty square-built old craft, even though his spiritual chart may be laid out different from yours—and mine."

" From yours? Why, I supposed——"

" Yes, I know. Well, *when* I go to meetin', I generally go to the chapel to please father. But when it comes right down to a confession of faith, I'm pretty broad in the beam. Maybe I'd be too broad even for you, Mr. Ellery."

The minister, who had jumped to the ground, looked up.

" Captain Hammond," he said, " I'm very glad indeed that I met you. Not alone because you helped me out of a bad scrape; I realize how bad it might have been and that——"

" Shsh! shh! Nothin' at all. Don't be foolish."

" But I'm glad, too, because I've heard so many good things about you that I was sure you must be worth knowing. I hope you won't believe I went to your father's meeting with any——"

" No, no! Jumpin' Moses, man! *I* don't find fault with you for that. I understand, I guess."

" Well, if you don't mind the fact that I am what I am, I'd like to shake hands with you."

Nat reached down a big brown hand.

" Same here," he said. " Always glad to shake with a chap as well recommended as you are. Yes, indeed, I mean it. You see, you've got a friend that's a friend of mine, and when she guarantees a man to be A. B., I'll ship him without any more questions."

" Well, then, good-by. I hope we shall meet again and often. And I certainly thank you for——"

" That's all right. Maybe you'll fish *me* out of the drink some day; you never can tell. So long! Git dap, Gen'ral Scott! "

He drove off up the beach, but before he turned the corner of the nearest dune he called back over his shoulder:

"Say, Mr. Ellery, if you think of it you might give my regards to—to—er—the lady that's keepin' house for you."

Breakfast had waited nearly an hour when the minister reached home. Keziah, also, was waiting and evidently much relieved at his safe arrival.

"Sakes alive!" she exclaimed, as she met him at the back door. "Where in the world have you been, Mr. Ellery? Soakin' wet again, too!"

Ellery replied that he had been for a walk out to the bar. He sat down on the step to remove the borrowed boots. A small rivulet of salt water poured from each as he pulled them off.

"For a walk! A swim, you mean. How could you get in up to your waist if you just walked? Did you fall down?"

"No, not exactly. But I waited too long and the tide headed me off."

"Mercy on us! you mustn't take chances on that tide. If you'd told me you was goin', I'd have warned you to hurry back."

"Oh, I've been warned often enough. It was my own fault, as usual. I'm not sure that I don't need a guardian."

"Humph! well, I ain't sure either. Was the channels very deep?"

"Deep enough. The fact is, that I might have got into serious trouble if I hadn't been picked up."

He told briefly the story of his morning's adventure. The housekeeper listened with growing excitement.

"Heavens to Betsy!" she interrupted. "Was the channel you planned to swim the one at the end of the flat by the longest weir leader?"

"Yes."

"My soul! there's been two men drowned in that very place at half tide. And they were good swimmers. After this I shan't dare let you out of my sight."

"So? Was it as risky as that? Why, Captain Hammond didn't tell me so. I must owe him more even than I thought."

"Yes, I guess you do. He wouldn't tell you, though; that ain't his way. Deary me! for what we've received let us be thankful. And that reminds me that biscuits ought to be et when they're first made, not after they've been dried up on the back of the stove forever and ever amen. Go on and change those wet things of yours and then we'll eat. Tryin' to swim the main channel on the flood! My soul and body!"

"Captain Nat sent his regards to you, Mrs. Coffin," said the minister, moving toward the stairs.

"Did, hey?" was the housekeeper's reply. "Want to know!"

# CHAPTER VIII

## IN WHICH THE PARSON AND MR. PEPPER DECLARE THEIR INDEPENDENCE

THAT afternoon, when dinner was over, the Reverend John decided to make a few duty calls. The first of these he determined should be on the Peppers. Lavinia and her brother had called at the parsonage several times, but as yet he had not paid them a visit. It was not a ceremony to which he looked forward with delight, but it must be performed. Miss Pepper had hinted several times, at sewing circle and after prayer meeting, of "partiality" and "only stoppin' in where they had fancy curtains up to the windows." So, as it could not be put off longer, without causing trouble, he determined to go through with it.

The Pepper house was situated just off the main road on the lane leading over the dunes to the ocean and the light. It was a small building, its white paint dingy and storm beaten, and its little fenced-in front yard dotted thickly with clumps of silver-leaf saplings. A sign, nailed crookedly on a post, informed those seeking such information that within was to be found "Abishai G. W. Pepper, Tax Collector, Assessor, Boots and Shoes Repaired." And beneath this was fastened a shingle with the chalked notice, "Salt Hay for sale."

# THE PARSON AND MR. PEPPER

The boot and shoe portion of the first sign was a relic of other days. Kyan had been a cobbler once, but it is discouraging to wait three or four weeks while the pair of boots one has left to be resoled are forgotten in a corner. Captain Zeb Mayo's pointed comment, " I want my shoe leather to wear while I'm alive, not to be laid out in after I die of old age," expressed the general feeling of the village and explained why custom had left Mr. Pepper and flown to the more enterprising shoemaker at " The Corners." The tax collectorship might have followed it, but here Lavinia kept her brother up to the mark. She went with him on his rounds and it gave her opportunity to visit, and afterwards comment upon, every family in town.

The minister walked up the dusty lane, lifted the Pepper gate and swung it back on its one hinge, shooed away the three or four languid and discouraged-looking fowls that were taking a sun bath on the clam-shell walk, and knocked at the front door. No one coming in answer to the knock, he tried again. Then he discovered a rusty bell pull and gave it a sharp tug. The knob came off in his hand and he hurriedly thrust it back again into its place. Evidently, that bell was solely for ornament.

He came to the conclusion that no one was at home and felt a guilty sense of relief in consequence. But his conscience would not let him depart without another try, so he clenched his fist and gave the cracked door panel a series of tremendous thumps. A thin black cat, which had evidently been asleep beneath the step, burst from its concealment and fled in frantic terror. Then from somewhere in the rear of the house came the sound of a human voice.

"Hi!" it called faintly. "Whoever you be, don't bust that door down. Come round here."

Ellery walked around the corner of the building. The voice came again.

"Say!" it wailed, "why don't you answer? Be you comin'? If you're a peddler, you needn't."

"I'm not a peddler," was the minister's amused reply.

"Oh, ain't ye? All right. Come along, then."

Ellery "came along" as far as the angle where the ell joined the main body of the house. So far as he could see every door and window was closed and there were no signs of life. However, he stepped to the door, a green-painted affair of boards, and ventured another knock.

"Don't start that poundin' again!" protested the voice. "Come round to t'other side where I be."

So around went the Reverend John, smiling broadly. But even on "t'other side" there was no one to be seen. And no door, for that matter.

"Why!" exclaimed the voice, "if 'tain't Mr. Ellery! How d'ye do? Glad to see you, Mr. Ellery. Fine day, ain't it? Here I be at this window."

Sure enough; one of the windows on this side of the house was raised about six inches at the bottom, the shade was up, and peering beneath the sash the minister discerned the expressive features of Abishai Pepper—or as much of those features as the size of the opening permitted to be seen.

"Oh!" exclaimed the visitor, "is that you, Mr. Pepper? Well, I'm glad to see you, at last. You are rather hard to see, even now."

Kyan was plainly embarrassed. He stammered as he answered.

"Yes," he agreed, " I—I shouldn't wonder if I be. How be you? Pretty smart?"

"Yes, thank you. I'm well."

"Er—er—come to call, did you?"

"Why, yes, that was my intention."

"Hum! Er—er—Laviny, she's gone over to Thankful Payne's. She heard that Thankful's cousin up to Middleboro had died—passed away, I mean—and she thought she'd run over and find out if Thankful was willed anything. She said she'd be back pretty soon."

"Very well. Then, as she won't be gone long, perhaps I'll come in and wait."

He was moving away toward the corner when a shout from beneath the window sash brought him to a halt.

"Hi!" called Abishai. "Hi, Mr. Ellery! don't go to that door. 'Tain't no use; it's locked."

"Locked? Well, you can unlock it, can't you?"

"No, not very well. That is, I—Mr. Ellery, come back here, won't ye? I don't want anybody to hear."

The house of the nearest neighbor being several hundred yards away, the likelihood of being over-heard was improbable; but the minister came back, nevertheless.

"You see, Mr. Ellery," stammered Kyan, " I—I'd like to have you come in fust rate, but—er—Laviny she's got the key."

Ellery was surprised.

"She has!" he exclaimed.

"Um—hm, she's got it. She took it with her."

"But there are other doors. She didn't take them all, did she?"

"No—o, but— Well, the fact is, Mr. Ellery, I—I—I'm locked in."

"Locked in?"

"Yes, locked in this room. She—she— Oh, consarn it all, Mr. Ellery, she's locked me in this room a-purpose, so's I won't get out and go somewheres without her knowin' it."

"What?"

"Um—h'm; that's what she's done. Did you ever hear of anything like that in your born days?"

This surprising disclosure was funny enough, but the tone of grieved indignation in which Mr. Pepper told of his imprisonment was funnier still. The minister coughed violently and looked the other way.

"She done it a-purpose," continued Kyan, in a burst of confidence. "She had me put one of them new-fangled spring locks on the door of this room t'other day, 'cause she said she was afraid of tramps and wanted some place to shut herself up in if one of 'em come. And—and after dinner to-day she sent me in here for somethin' and then slammed the door on me. Said she cal'lated I'd stay put till she got back from Thankful's. She knew mighty well I couldn't get out of the window, 'cause it won't open no further'n 'tis now. I wa'n't never so provoked in my life. 'Tain't no way to treat your own brother, lockin' him up like a young one; now, is it?"

Ellery's reply was not made immediately. He had heard numerous stories concerning this odd household, some of which seemed too absurd for belief. But this performance was more ridiculous than anything he had heard.

" 'Tain't right, is it, Mr. Ellery? " demanded Kyan.

" Why," answered the caller chokingly, " I—I —it is rather unusual, that's a fact. May I ask what you've done to——"

" Done? I ain't done nothin'. She's so darned scared some other woman'll get my money that— you see, a month or so ago I—I—well, she thought I done somethin', or was plannin' to do somethin' that— Keziah Coffin never told you anything about me, did she? "

" No, indeed. What could Mrs. Coffin tell me about you? "

" All right. Nothin', nothin'. Only if she did, 'tain't so. But I ain't goin' to stand it no more, Mr. Ellery. Bein' shut up in a darned old—excuse my swearin', I didn't mean to, though I got reason enough, land knows—bein' shut up in a room full of trunks and odds and ends is goin' too fur. I never want to smell old clothes ag'in long's I live. Would you stand it if you was me, Mr. Ellery? "

" Why, of course I mustn't interfere in your family matters, Mr. Pepper. Perhaps I'd better call some other time. Good afternoon."

" Hold on! hold on! you ain't answered me yet. You're a minister and I go to your meetin' house. Tell me what you'd do if you was me. Would you stand it? "

Ellery laughed aloud.

" No," he said, " I suppose I shouldn't."

" I bet you wouldn't! What would you do? "

" I don't know. You're of age, Mr. Pepper, and

you must decide for yourself. I think I should declare my independence. Really, I must go. I——"

"Don't be in such a hurry. I want advice. I need it. And, so fur's *declarin'* goes, that don't do me no good. She can declare more things in a minute than I can think of in a week. Tongue! I never heard— No, no! Never mind the declarin'. What would you *do?* S'posin' you wanted to go outdoor without havin' her tagged to your coat tails, how'd you stop the taggin'?"

The absurdity of the affair was too much for the visitor. He roared a "Ha, ha!" that caused Abishai to wave a warning hand beneath the sash.

"Ss-h-h! sshh!" he hissed. "Folks'll hear ye, and I'd be so ashamed if they did that I wouldn't dast to show my head. Can't show much of it, anyhow, just now. By gum! I'll do somethin' desperate. I—I dunno as I won't pizen her. I——"

"Hush! hush! you mustn't talk that way. I'm afraid you must be very fascinating, Mr. Pepper. If your sister is so very fearful of your meeting other women, it must be because she has good reason to fear."

"Stop your foolishness! Oh!—I—I ask your pardon, Mr. Ellery. That ain't no way to talk to a minister. But I'm goin' to go out when I want to if I bust a hole through the clapboards. I *ain't* fascinatin'. You ask any woman—except her—if I be, and see what they say. What'll I *do?*"

"Ha, ha! I don't know, I'm sure. You might lock *her* up, I suppose, just for a change.

"Hey!" There was a sound from behind the pane as if the imprisoned one had slapped his knee. "By gum! I never thought of that. Would you now,

Mr. Ellery? Would you? Sshh! sshh! somebody's comin'. Maybe it's her. Run around to the door, Mr. Ellery, quick. And don't tell her I've seen you, for mercy sakes! Don't now, will ye? Please! Run!"

The minister did not run, but he walked briskly around the corner. Sure enough, Lavinia was there, just unlocking the door. She expressed herself as very glad to see the caller, ushered him into the sitting room and disappeared, returning in another moment with her brother, whom she unblushingly said had been taking a nap. Abishai did not contradict her; instead, he merely looked apprehensively at the minister.

The call was a short one. Lavinia did seven eighths of the talking and Ellery the rest. Kyan was silent. When the visit was over, Miss Pepper escorted her guest to the door and bade him a voluble good-by. Over her shoulder the minister saw Kyan making frantic signs to him; he interpreted the signals as a request for secrecy concerning the interview by the window.

Several times during the remainder of that week he surprised his housekeeper by suddenly laughing aloud when there was, apparently, nothing to laugh at. He explained these outbursts by saying that he had thought of something funny. Keziah suggested that it must be mighty funny to make him laugh in the middle of sermon writing.

"I've heard sermons that were funny," she said, "though they wasn't intended to be; but what I've heard of yours ain't that kind. I wish you'd let me in on the joke. I haven't been feelin' like laughin' for the last fortni't."

She had been rather grave and preoccupied, for her, of late. Bustling and busy she always was, never sitting down to " rest," as she called it, without a lap full of sewing. The minister's clothes were mended and his socks darned as they had not been since his mother's day. And with him, at meal times, or after supper in the sitting room, she was always cheerful and good-humored. But he had heard her sigh at her work, and once, when she thought herself unobserved, he saw her wipe her eyes with her apron.

" No, no," she protested, when he asked if anything had gone wrong. " I'm all right. Got a little cold or somethin', I guess, that's all."

She would not give any other explanation and absolutely refused to see the doctor. Ellery did not press the matter. He believed the " cold " to be but an excuse and wondered what the real trouble might be. It seemed to him to date from the evening of his chapel experience.

He told no one, not even her, of Kyan's confidential disclosure, and, after some speculation as to whether or not there might be a sequel, put the whole ludicrous affair out of his mind. He worked hard in his study and at his pastoral duties, and was conscious of a pleasant feeling that he was gaining his people's confidence and esteem.

A week from the following Sunday he dined in state at the Daniels's table. Captain Elkanah was gracious and condescending. Annabel was more than that. She was dressed in her newest gown and was so very gushing and affable that the minister felt rather embarrassed. When, after the meal was over, Captain Elkanah excused himself and went upstairs for his Sabbath nap, the embarrassment redoubled. Miss Annabel spoke very confidentially of her loneliness, without "congenial society," of how *very* much she did enjoy Mr. Ellery's intellectual sermons, and especially what a treat it had been to have him as a guest.

"You must dine here every Sunday," she said. "It will be no trouble at all, and if you say no, I shall feel that it is because you don't want to see me—*father* and me, of course, I mean."

The minister didn't accept this pressing invitation; on the other hand, he could not refuse it absolutely. He did not like Miss Daniels overmuch, but she was the daughter of his leading parishioner and she and her parent did seem to like him. So he dodged the issue and said she was very kind.

He left the big house as soon as he could without giving offense, and started back toward the parsonage. But the afternoon was so fine and the early summer air so delightful that he changed his mind and, jumping the fence at the foot of Cannon Hill, set off across the fields toward the bluffs and the bay shore.

The sun was low in the west as he entered the grove of pines on the bluff. The red light between the boughs made brilliant carpet patterns on the thick pine needles and the smell was balsamy and sweet. Between the tree trunks he caught glimpses of the flats, now partially covered, and they reminded him of his narrow escape and of Nat Hammond, his rescuer. He had met the captain twice since then, once at the store and again on the main road, and had chatted with him. He liked him immensely and wished he might count him as an intimate friend.

But intimacy between a Regular clergyman and the son of the leader of the Come-Outers was out of the question. Partisans on both sides would shriek at the idea.

Thinking of the Hammond family reminded him of another member of it. Not that he needed to be reminded; he had thought of her often enough since she ran away from him in the rain that night. And the picture in the doorway was not one that he could forget—or wanted to. If she were not a Come-Outer, he could meet her occasionally and they might become friends. She was a disconcerting young person, who lacked proper respect for one of his profession and laughed when she shouldn't—but she was interesting, he admitted that.

And then he saw her. She was standing just at the outer edge of the grove, leaning against a tree and looking toward the sunset. She wore a simple white dress and her hat hung upon her shoulders by its ribbons. The rosy light edged the white gown with pink and the fringes of her dark hair were crinkly lines of fire. Her face was grave, almost sad.

John Ellery stood still, with one foot uplifted for a step. The girl looked out over the water and he looked at her. Then a crow, one of several whirling above the pines, spied the intruder and screamed a warning. The minister was startled and stepped back. A dead limb beneath his foot cracked sharply. Grace turned and saw him.

" Oh! " she cried. " Who is it? "

Ellery emerged from the shadow.

" Don't be frightened, Miss Van Horne," he said. " It is—er—I."

This statement was neither brilliant nor original; even as an identification it lacked considerable.

"I?" repeated the girl. "Who? Oh! Why——"

The minister came forward.

"Good afternoon, Miss Van Horne," he stammered. "I'm afraid I frightened you."

She was looking at him with a queer expression, almost as if she scarcely believed him real.

"I hope——" he began again. She interrupted him.

"No," she said confusedly, "you didn't frighten me. I was a little startled when I saw you there behind me. It seemed so odd, because I was just thinking—— No, I wasn't frightened. What is there to be frightened of—in Trumet?"

He had extended his hand, but partially withdrew it, not sure how even such a perfunctory act of friendliness might be received. She saved him embarrassment by frankly offering her own.

"Not much, that's a fact," he said, in answer to her question. He would have liked to ask what she had been thinking that made his sudden appearance seem so odd.

"You came to see the sunset, I suppose?" she said hurriedly, as if to head off a question. "So did I. It is a beautiful evening for a walk, isn't it?"

She had said precisely the same thing on that other evening, when they stood in the middle of "Hammond's Turn-off" in the driving rain. He remembered it, and so, evidently, did she, for she colored slightly and smiled.

"I mean it this time," she said. "I'm glad you didn't get cold from your wetting the other day."

"Oh! I wasn't very wet. You wouldn't let me lend you the umbrella, so I had that to protect me on the way home."

"Not then; I meant the other morning when Nat—Cap'n Hammond—met you out on the flats. He said you were wading the main channel and it was over your boots."

"Over my boots! Is that all he said? Over my head would be the plain truth. To cross it I should have had to swim and, if what I've heard since is true, I doubt if I could swim that channel. Captain Hammond helped me out of a bad scrape."

"Oh, no! I guess not. He said you were cruising without a pilot and he towed you into port; that's the way he expressed it."

"It was worse than that, a good deal worse. It might have been my last cruise. I'm pretty certain that I owe the captain my life."

She looked at him uncomprehendingly.

"Your life?" she repeated.

"I believe it. That part of the channel I proposed swimming was exactly where two men have been drowned, so people say. I'm not a very strong swimmer, and they were. So, you see."

Grace cried out in astonishment.

"Oh!" she exclaimed. Then pointing toward the bay, she asked: "Out there, by the end of that leader, was it?"

"Yes, that was it."

She drew a long breath. Then, after a moment: "And Nat spoke as if it was all a joke," she said.

"No doubt he did. From what I hear of your brother, he generally refers to his own plucky, capable actions as jokes. Other people call them something else."

She did not answer, but continued to gaze at the half-submerged "leader," with the pine bough tied at its landward end to mark the edge of deep water, and the tide foaming through its lath gratings.

" Your brother——" went on the minister.

" He isn't my brother," she interrupted absently. " I wish he was."

She sighed as she uttered the last sentence.

" No, of course he isn't your real brother; I forgot. But he must seem like one."

" Yes," rather doubtfully.

" You must be proud of him."

" I am." There was nothing doubtful this time.

" Well, he saved me from drowning. I'm almost certain of that."

" I'm so glad."

She seemed to mean it. He looked at her.

" Thank you," he said drily. " I'm rather glad myself."

" Oh! I didn't mean it exactly that way. Of course I'm glad you weren't drowned, but I'm especially glad that—that one of our family saved you. Now you won't believe that Come-Outers are all bad."

" I never believed it."

She shook her head.

" Oh, yes, you did," she affirmed stubbornly. " You've heard nothing good of us since you came here. Don't tell fibs, Mr. Ellery."

" But I assure you——"

" Nonsense! Does—well, does Cap'n Daniels,

or his daughter, say anything good of us? Be honest, do they?"

"I hardly think—that is, I shouldn't call their opinions unprejudiced. And, Miss Van Horne, perhaps the prejudice isn't all on one side. What did your uncle say about Cap'n Nat's meeting me the other day?"

"Uncle Eben doesn't know. Nat didn't tell anyone but me. He doesn't boast. And uncle would be glad he helped you. As I told you before, Mr. Ellery, I'm not ashamed of my uncle. He has been so good to me that I never can repay him, never! When my own father was drowned he took me in, a little orphan that would probably have been sent to a home, and no father could be kinder or more indulgent than he has been. Anything I asked for I got, and at last I learned not to ask for too much. No self-denial on his part was too great, if he could please me. When he needed money most he said nothing to me, but insisted that I should be educated. I didn't know until afterwards of the self-sacrifice my four years at the Middleboro Academy meant to him."

The minister had listened eagerly to this defense of the man whom he had been led to consider his arch enemy. It was given with spirit and the girl's head was uplifted and her eyes flashed as she spoke. Ellery's next remark was uttered without premeditation. Really, he was thinking aloud.

"So you went away to school?" he mused. "That is why——"

"That is why I don't say 'never done nothin'' and 'be you' and 'hain't neither.' Yes, thank you, that's why. I don't wonder you were surprised."

The young man blushed.

"You misunderstand me," he protested. "I didn't mean——"

"Oh! yes, you did. Not precisely that, perhaps, but pretty near it. I suppose you expected me to speak like Josiah Badger or Kyan Pepper. I try not to. And I try not to say 'immejitly,' too," she added, with a mischievous twinkle.

Ellery recognized the "immejitly" quotation and laughed.

"I never heard but one person say that," he observed. "And he isn't a Come-Outer."

"No, he isn't. Well, this lesson in English can't be very interesting to you, Mr. Ellery, and I must go. But I'm very glad Nat helped you the other day and that you realize the sort of man he is. And I'm glad I have had the opportunity to tell you more about Uncle Eben. I owe him so much that I ought to be glad—yes, glad and proud and happy, too, to gratify his least wish. I must! I know I must, no matter how I— What am I talking about? Yes, Mr. Ellery, I'm glad if I have helped you to understand my uncle better and why I love and respect him. If you knew him as I do, you would respect him, too. Good-by."

She was going, but the minister had something to say. He stepped forward and walked beside her.

"Just a minute, please," he urged. "Miss Van Horne, I do understand. I do respect your uncle. We have a mutual friend, you and I, and through her I have come to understand many things."

Grace turned and looked at him.

"A mutual friend?" she repeated. "Oh! I know. Mrs. Coffin?"

"Yes; Mrs. Coffin. She's a good woman and a wise one."

"She's a dear! Do you like her, too?"

"Indeed, I do."

"Has she told you about me—about uncle, I mean?"

"Yes. Why, she told me——"

He began to enumerate some of the things Keziah had told concerning the Hammond family. They were all good things, and he couldn't help seeing that the recital pleased her. So he went on to tell how his housekeeper had helped him, of her advice, of her many acts of kindness, of what he owed to her. The girl listened eagerly, asking questions, nodding confirmation, and, in her delight at hearing Keziah praised, quite forgetting her previous eagerness to end the interview. And, as he talked, he looked at her, at the red light on her hair, the shine of her eyes, like phosphorus in the curl of a wave at night, at her long lashes, and——

"Yes," said Miss Van Horne, "you were saying——"

The minister awoke with a guilty start. He realized that his sentence had broken off in the middle.

"Why! why—er—yes," he stammered. "I was saying that — that I don't know what I should have done without Mrs. Coffin. She's a treasure. Frankly, she is the only real friend I have found in Trumet."

"I know. I feel the same way about her. She means so much to me. I love her more than anyone else in the world, except uncle, of course—and Nat. I miss her very much since—since——"

"Since I came, you mean. I'm sorry. I wish—

I hate to think I am the cause which separates you two. It isn't my fault, as you know."

" Oh! I know that."

" Yes, and I object to having others choose my friends for me, people who, because of a fanatical prejudice, stand in the way of— If it wasn't for that, you might call and see Mrs. Coffin, just as you used to do."

Grace shook her head. They had moved on to the bend of the bluff, beyond the fringe of pines, and were now standing at the very edge of the high bank.

" If it wasn't for that, you would come," asserted the minister.

" Yes, I suppose so. I should like to come. I miss my talks with Aunt Keziah more than you can imagine—now especially. But, somehow, what we want to do most seems to be what we mustn't, and what we don't like is our duty."

She said this without looking at him, and the expression on her face was the same sad, grave one he had noticed when he first saw her standing alone by the pine.

" Why don't you come? " he persisted.

" I can't, of course. You know I can't."

" Why not? If my company is objectionable I can go away when you come. If you dislike me I——"

" You know I don't dislike you personally."

" I'm awfully glad of that."

" But it's impossible. Uncle respects and is fond of Aunt Keziah, but he wouldn't hear of my visiting the parsonage."

" But don't you think your uncle might be persuaded? I'm sure he misunderstands me, just as I should him if it weren't for Mrs. Coffin—and what you've said. Don't you think if I called on him and he knew me better it might help matters? I'll do it gladly. I will!"

"No, no. He wouldn't listen. And think of your own congregation."

"Confound my congregation!"

"Why, Mr. Ellery!"

She looked at him in amazement; then her lips began to curl.

"Why, Mr. Ellery!" she repeated.

The minister turned very red and drew his hand across his forehead.

"I—I don't mean that exactly," he stammered. "But I'm not a child. I have the right to exercise a man's discretion. My parish committee must understand that. They shall! If I choose to see you— Look out!"

She was close to the overhanging edge of the bluff and the sod upon which she stood was bending beneath her feet. He sprang forward, caught her about the waist, and pulled her back. The sod broke and rattled down the sandy slope. She would have had a slight tumble, nothing worse, had she gone with it. There was no danger; and yet the minister was very white as he released her.

She, too, was pale for a moment, and then crimson.

"Thank you," she gasped. "I—I must go. It is late. I didn't realize how late it was. I—I must go."

He did not answer, though he tried to.

"I must go," she said hurriedly, speaking at random. "Good afternoon. Good-by. I hope you will enjoy your walk."

"I have enjoyed it." His answer was unstudied but emphatic. She recognized the emphasis.

"Will you come to see Mrs. Coffin?" he asked.

"No, no. You know I can't. Good-by. The sunset is beautiful, isn't it?"

"Beautiful, indeed."

"Yes. I—I think the sunsets from this point are the finest I have ever seen. I come here every Sunday afternoon to see them."

This remark was given merely to cover embarrassment, but it had an unexpected effect.

"You *do?*" cried the minister. The next moment he was alone. Grace Van Horne had vanished in the gloom of the pine thickets.

It was a strange John Ellery who walked slowly back along the path, one that Keziah herself would not have recognized, to say nothing of Captain Elkanah and the parish committee. The dignified parson, with the dignified walk and calm, untroubled brow, was gone, and here was an absent-minded young fellow who stumbled blindly along, tripping over roots and dead limbs, and caring nothing, apparently, for the damage to his Sunday boots and trousers which might result from the stumbles. He saw nothing real, and heard nothing, not even the excited person who, hidden behind the bayberry bush, hailed him as he passed. It was not until this person rushed forth and seized him by the arm that he came back to the unimportant affairs of this material earth.

"Why! Why, Mr. Pepper!" he gasped. "Are you here? What do you want?"

"Am I here?" panted Kyan. "Ain't I been here for the last twenty minutes waitin' to get a chance at you? Ain't I been chasin' you from Dan to Beersheby all this dummed—excuse me—afternoon? Oh, my godfreys mighty!"

"Why, what's the matter?"

"Matter? Matter enough! It's all your fault. You got me into the mess, now you git me out of it."

Usually, when Abishai addressed his clergyman, it was in a tone of humble respect far different from his present frantic assault. The Reverend John was astounded.

"What *is* the trouble, Mr. Pepper?" he demanded. "Behave yourself, man. What *is* it?"

"You—you made me do it," gurgled Kyan. "Yes, sir, 'twas you put me up to it. When you was at our house t'other day, after Laviny locked me up, you told me the way to get square was to lock her up, too. And I done it! Yes, sir, I done it when she got back from meetin' this noon. I run off and left her locked in. And—and "—he wailed, wringing his hands— "I—I ain't dast to go home sence. *What*'ll I do?"

# CHAPTER IX

THE hysterical Mr. Pepper doubtless expected his clergyman to be almost as much upset as he was by the news of his action. But John Ellery was provokingly calm. As a matter of fact he scarcely grasped the purport of the little man's disjointed story. He had been wandering in dreamland, his head among the clouds, and the explosion of Keziah's bomb disturbed, but did not clear the air.

"What will you do?" he repeated. "Why—er—I don't know, I'm sure."

Kyan was staggered.

"You don't know?" he shouted. "*You* don't? Then who does, for the land sakes? Didn't you tell me to lock her up? Didn't I do it *'cause* you told me? Didn't—didn't——"

He seemed to be on the verge of apoplexy. Also he had raised his voice to a yell. The minister seized him by the arm and shook him into silence.

"Hush! hush!" he commanded. "Wait a minute. Let me understand this thing. Some one is locked up, you say. Who is it? Where——"

"*Who* is it? Ain't I tellin' you. It's Laviny. She went into that spare room where I was t'other day and I slammed the spring lock to on her. Then I grabbed the key and run. That was afore three

149

this afternoon; now it's 'most night and I ain't dast to go home. What'll she say when I let her out? I got to let her out, ain't I? She can't starve to death in there, can she? And *you* told me to do it! *You* did! Oh——"

The apoplectic attack was once more imminent.

"Stop it, Mr. Pepper," ordered Ellery. "I don't remember telling you to lock your sister up, though— Why, yes, I may have said something or other, as a joke, but I didn't expect you would seriously consider doing such a thing. Ha, ha! This is the most idiotic piece of business that I ever——"

"Be you laughin'?" demanded the shocked Abishai. "*Laughin'?* Why, my godfreys mighty! Idiotic? Well, who's the idiot? 'Tain't me! *I'd* never have thought of such a fool trick. But you said——"

"Hush! Let me think. Have you told anybody?"

"*Told* anybody! I guess *not*. And nobody'll never know if they wait for me to tell 'em."

"Well, then, I don't see why you can't go home and—hum—I don't like to advise your telling a lie, but you might let her infer that it was an accident. *Or*, if you really mean to be your own master, you can tell her you did it purposely and will do it again if she ever tries the trick on you."

"*I* tell her that! *I* tell her! O Mr. Ellery, *don't* talk so. You don't know Laviny; she ain't like most women. If I should tell her that she'd—I don't know's she wouldn't take and horsewhip me. Or commit suicide. She's said she would afore now if— if——"

"Nonsense! She won't do that, you needn't worry." He burst into another laugh, but checked himself, as he saw the look of absolute distress on poor Kyan's face.

"Never mind, Mr. Pepper," he said. "We'll think of some plan to smooth matters over. I'll go home with you now and we'll let her out together."

"Will you, Mr. Ellery? Will you, honest? Say, by godfreys mighty, I'd get down on my knees and thank you this minute if—if I wa'n't in such a hurry. Come right on; come quick!"

It was a silent procession of two that wended its way out of the pines and across the fields, by the brook and the pond, where the evening mists were rising and the frogs chanting their good-night song, through the gathering twilight shades, across the main road and up the lighthouse lane. Kyan, his mind filled with fearful forebodings, was busily trying to think of a reasonable excuse for the "accidental" imprisonment of his sister. John Ellery was thinking, also, but his thoughts were not of the Peppers.

The little house was dark and still as they approached it. No welcoming light in the dining-room windows, no open door, no shrill voice demanding to know where the wandering brother had been "all this everlastin' time." Even the hens had gone to roost. Abishai groaned.

"Oh, dear!" he wailed. "I'm scart to death. Where is she? You don't cal'late she's done it, do ye?"

"Done it? Done what?"

"Done the suicidin'. She said she would if— O Laviny!"

"Hush! Be quiet. She's all right. She's in the room where you left her, of course. She couldn't get out, could she? You've got the key. Come in."

They entered the house. The dining room was dark and quiet. So was the sitting room. The clock ticked, solemn and slow. Kyan clutched at his companion's arm.

"I don't hear her," he whispered. "You don't s'pose she *has* done it? Godfreys mighty!"

The gloom and mystery were having their effect, even on Mr. Ellery's nerves. His answer also was given in a tense whisper, but with some irritation.

"Hush!" he murmured. "Let go of my wrist. You've pinched it black and blue. Which room did you leave her in? Show me at once."

Kyan's trembling knees managed to carry him to the little hall leading from the sitting room toward the ell at the side of the house. This hall was almost pitch black. The minister felt his guide's chin whisker brush his ear as the following sentence was literally breathed into it:

"Here—here 'tis," panted Kyan. "Here's the door. I don't hear nothin', do you? Listen!"

They listened. Not a sound, save the dismal tick of the clock in the room they had left. Ellery knocked on the door.

"Miss Pepper," he said; "Miss Pepper, are you there?"

Kyan caught his breath. No answer.

"Miss Pepper," repeated the minister. "Miss Pepper!"

Silence, absolute. Abishai could stand it no longer. He groaned and collapsed on his knees.

"She has!" he moaned. "She's done it and

there ain't nothin' in there but her remains. Oh, my soul!"

Ellery, now rather frightened himself, shook him violently.

"Be quiet, you idiot!" he commanded. "We must go in. Give me the key."

After repeated orders and accompanying shakings, Kyan produced a key. The minister snatched it from his trembling fingers, felt for the keyhole and threw the door open. The little room was almost as dark as the hall and quite as still. There was a distinct smell of old clothes and camphor.

"A match," demanded Ellery. "Quick!"

"I ain't got none," quavered Mr. Pepper. "They're all in the box in the settin' room. Oh, my godfreys mighty! What'll I do? What undertaker'll I have? Solon Tripp's the reg'lar one, but Laviny and he had a row and she said she'd come back and ha'nt me if I ever let him touch her rema— Where you goin'? *Don't leave me here!*"

The minister was going after a match, and said so. In a moment he returned with several. One of these he lit. The brimstone sputtered, burned blue and fragrant, then burst into a yellow flame.

The little room was empty.

John Ellery drew a breath of relief. Then he laughed.

"Humph!" he exclaimed. "She's gone."

"*Gone?* Why, she ain't nuther! Where could she go?"

"I don't know, but she has gone—somewhere. At any rate, she's not here."

Kyan rose to his feet. His alarm had changed to paralyzed astonishment.

"How could she go?" he repeated. "That window won't open more'n six inches. Laviny ain't what you'd call fleshy, but she never could squeeze through that in this world. And I locked the door, 'cause I heard the click. I—I—I—do you b'lieve in spirits, Mr. Ellery?"

"Nonsense! Come into the sitting room, light a lamp, and let's talk it over."

The lamp was found and lighted at last. Its radiance brightened the dingy sitting room.

"Do you b'lieve in spirits?" repeated Kyan. "I've heard yarns about folks bein' spirited away, but I never took much stock in 'em. "And," he added with conviction, "'twould take a pretty husky spirit to handle Laviny if she had her mad up. She— Hush! hear that!"

The sound of wheels was heard in the lane by the front gate. A vehicle stopped. Then some one called a hurried good night. Mr. Pepper's fear returned.

"It's her!" he cried. "She's been ahuntin' for me. *Now* I'll get it! You stand by me, Mr. Ellery. You got to. You said you would. But how on earth did she get——"

The minister motioned him to silence.

"I'll stand by you," he whispered. "Don't speak. Leave it to me."

A step sounded on the back step. The dining-room door was hurriedly thrown open.

"'Bishy" called Miss Pepper eagerly. "'Bish, where are you?"

"Here—here I be, Laviny," faltered Kyan.

His sister appeared on the threshold. She was dressed in her Sunday best, flowered poke bonnet, mitts, imitation India shawl, rustling black bombazine gown. She looked at Mr. Pepper, then at the minister.

"O Mr. Ellery!" she exclaimed, "be you here?"

The Reverend John admitted his presence. Miss Pepper's demeanor surprised him. She did not seem angry; indeed, she acted embarrassed and confused, as if she, and not her brother, were the guilty party.

"I'm afraid I'm awful late, 'Bishy," she said. "Have you had your supper?"

Kyan was too perturbed to venture a reply. The sword above his head was quivering on its single hair and he was preparing to dodge the fall. But it did not fall.

"You haven't had any supper, have you?" purred Miss Pepper pityingly. "It's too bad. You poor thing! you must be awful hungry."

She moved across the room and kissed him. Abishai, who had prepared himself for a different sort of greeting, clutched his chair with both hands. He looked as if he might faint. The minister gazed open-mouthed.

"I'm awful sorry, Mr. Ellery," gushed Lavinia, removing the bonnet. "You see, I was invited out to ride this afternoon and—and—I went."

She glanced at her brother, reddened—yes, almost blushed—and continued.

"You know, 'Bishy," she said, "Thankful Payne's cousin's home avisitin' her. He come about that cousin's will—the other cousin that's just died. He's a reel nice man—her live cousin is—keeps a shoe store up to Sandwich, and I used to know him years ago. When I was over to Thankful's t'other day, him and me had quite a talk. We got speakin' of what nice drives there was around Trumet and—and—er—well, he asked me if I wouldn't like to go to ride next Sunday afternoon—that's to-day. And a ride bein' a good deal of a treat to me, I said I would. Thankful was goin', too, but—er—er—she couldn't very well. So Caleb—that's his name, you remember, 'Bishy—he come round with his horse and team about ha'f past three and we started. But I'd no *idee* 'twas so late. I—I—meant to tell you I was goin', 'Bish, but I forgot."

Kyan had listened to this recital, or explanation, or apology, with a curious succession of expressions passing over his face. He swallowed two or three times, but did not interrupt.

" I'm so sorry I kept you waitin' supper," gushed Lavinia. " I'll get you a good one now. Oh, well, deary me! I must be gettin' absent-minded. I ain't asked you where you've been all the afternoon."

Abishai's eyes turned beseechingly toward his promised backer. Ellery could not resist that mute appeal.

" Your brother has been with me for some time, Miss Pepper," he volunteered.

" Oh, has he? Ain't that nice! He couldn't have been in better comp'ny, I'm sure. But, oh, say, 'Bishy! I ain't told you how nigh I come to not gettin' out at all. Just afore Mr. Payne come, I was in that spare room and—you remember I put a spring lock on that door?"

It was here at last. The long-dreaded explosion was imminent. Kyan's chin shook. He braced himself for the blow. The minister prepared to come to the rescue.

" Yes," went on Lavinia. " I—I put a lock on that door so's I—I could shut the room up when I wanted to. Well, when I was in there this afternoon the wind blew the door shut and— Hey?"

" I—I never said nothin'," panted Kyan.

" Yes, it blew to, the lock clicked, and there I was. If I hadn't had the other key in my pocket I don't know's I wouldn't have been in there yet. That would have been a pretty mess, wouldn't it! He! he! he!"

She laughed shrilly. The minister looked at her, then at her brother, and he, too, burst into a shout of laughter. Kyan did not laugh; yet his grip upon the chair relaxed, and over his countenance was spreading a look of relief, of hope and peace, like a clear sunrise after a stormy night.

" Well, I must go and get supper," declared Lavinia. " You'll forgive me for leavin' you so, won't you, 'Bishy?"

Mr. Pepper sighed.

" Yes," he said slowly. " I'll forgive you, Laviny."

" I knew you would. I hope you ain't been too lonesome. Did you miss me? Was you worried?"

" Hey? Yes, I—I missed you consider'ble. I *was* gettin' sort of worried. I didn't s'pose you'd go off to ride with—with a feller and leave me all alone. But I forgive you." He stopped, drew his hand across his forehead, and then added, " I s'pose I hadn't ought to complain. Maybe I'd better get used to it; I guess likely this is only the beginnin'."

Lavinia blushed furiously.

" Why, 'Bish!" she exclaimed. " How you do talk! Ain't he awful, Mr. Ellery?"

The Reverend John did not answer. He could not trust himself to speak just then. When he did it was to announce that he must be getting toward home. No, he couldn't stay for supper.

Miss Pepper went into the kitchen, and Abishai saw the visitor to the door. Ellery extended his hand and Kyan shook it with enthusiasm.

"Wa'n't it fine?" he whispered. "Talk about your miracles! Godfreys mighty! Say, Mr. Ellery, don't you ever tell a soul how it really was, will you?"

"No, of course not."

"No, I know you won't. You won't tell on me and I won't tell on you. That's a trade, hey?"

The minister stopped in the middle of his step.

"What?" he said, turning.

Mr. Pepper merely smiled, winked, and shut the door. John Ellery reflected much during his homeward walk.

The summer in Trumet drowsed on, as Trumet summers did in those days, when there were no boarders from the city, no automobiles or telephones or "antique" collectors. In June the Sunday school had its annual picnic. On the morning of the Fourth of July some desperate spirits among the younger set climbed in at the church window and rang the bell, in spite of the warning threats of the selectmen, who had gone on record as prepared to prosecute all disturbers of the peace to the "full extent of the law." One of the leading citizens, his name was Daniels, awoke to find the sleigh, which had been stored in his carriage house, hoisted to the roof of his barn, and a section of his front fence tastefully draped about it like a garland. The widow Rogers noticed groups of people looking up at her house and laughing. Coming out to see what they were laughing at, she was provoked beyond measure to find a sign over the front door, announcing " Man Wanted Imediate. inquire Within." The door of the Come-Outer chapel was nailed fast and Captain Zeb Mayo's old white horse wandered loose along the main road ringed with painted black stripes like a zebra. Captain Zeb was an angry man, for he venerated that horse.

The storm caused by these outbreaks subsided and Trumet settled into its jog trot. The stages rattled through daily, the packet came and went every little while, occasionally a captain returned home from a long voyage, and another left for one equally long. Old Mrs. Prince, up at the west end of the town, was very anxious concerning her son, whose ship was overdue at Calcutta and had not been heard from. The minister went often to see her and tried to console, but what consolation is there when one's only child and sole support is nobody knows where, drowned and dead perhaps, perhaps a castaway on a desert island, or adrift with a desperate crew in an open boat? And Mrs. Prince would say, over and over again:

"Yes, yes, Mr. Ellery. Thank you. I'm sure you mean to encourage me, but oh, you don't know the things that happen to seafarin' men. I do. I went to sea with my husband for fourteen year. He died on a voyage and they buried him over the vessel's side. I can't even go to his grave. The sea got him, and now if it's taken my Ed-die——"

The young clergyman came away from these calls feeling very young, indeed, and woefully inadequate. What *did* he know of the great sorrows of life?

The Sunday dinners with the Daniels family were almost regular weekly functions now. He dodged them when he could, but he could not do so often without telling an absolute lie, and this he would not do. And, regularly, when the solemn meal was eaten, Captain Elkanah went upstairs for his nap and the Reverend John was left alone with Annabel. Miss Daniels did her best to be entertaining, was, in fact, embarrassingly confidential and cordial. It was hard work to get away, and yet, somehow or other, at the stroke of four, the minister always said good-by and took his departure.

"What is your hurry, Mr. Ellery?" begged Annabel on one occasion when the reading of Moore's poems had been interrupted in the middle by the guest's sudden rising and reaching for his hat. "I don't see why you always go so early. It's so every time you're here. Do you call at any other house on Sunday afternoons?"

"No," was the prompt reply. "Oh, no."

"Then why can't you stay? You know I—that is, pa and I—would *love* to have you."

"Thank you. Thank you. You're very kind. But I really must go. Good afternoon, Miss Daniels."

"Mrs. Rogers said she saw you going across the fields after you left here last Sunday. Did you go for a walk?"

"Er—er—yes, I did."

"I wish you had mentioned it. I love to walk,

and there are *so* few people that I find congenial company. Are you going for a walk now?"

"Why, no—er—not exactly."

"I'm sorry. *Good*-by. Will you come again next Sunday? Of *course* you will. You know how dreadfully disappointed I—we—shall be if you don't."

"Thank you, Miss Daniels. I enjoyed the dinner very much. Good afternoon."

He hurried down the path. Annabel watched him go. Then she did an odd thing. She passed through the sitting room, entered the front hall, went up the stairs, tiptoed by the door of her father's room, and then up another flight to the attic. From here a steep set of steps led to the cupola on the roof. In that cupola was a spyglass.

Annabel opened a window a few inches, took the spyglass from its rack, adjusted it, laid it on the sill of the open window and knelt, the glass at her eye. The floor of the cupola was very dusty and she was wearing her newest and best gown, but she did not seem to mind.

Through the glass she saw the long slope of Cannon Hill, with the beacon at the top and Captain Mayo's house near it. The main road was deserted save for one figure, that of her late caller. He was mounting the hill in long strides.

She watched him gain the crest and pass over it out of sight. Then she shifted the glass so that it pointed toward the spot beyond the curve of the hill, where the top of a thick group of silver-leafs hid the parsonage. Above the tree tops glistened the white steeple of the Regular church. If the minister went straight home she could not see him. But under those silver-leafs was the beginning of the short cut across the fields where Didama had seen Mr. Ellery walking on the previous Sunday.

So Annabel watched and waited. Five minutes, then ten. He must have reached the clump of trees before this, yet she could not see him. Evidently, he had gone straight home. She drew a breath of relief.

Then, being in a happier frame of mind, and the afternoon clear and beautiful, she moved the glass along the horizon, watching the distant white specks across the bay on the Wellmouth bluffs—houses and buildings they were—the water, the shore, the fish weirs, the pine groves. She became interested in a sloop, beating into Wellmouth harbor, and watched that. After a time she heard, in the house below, her father shouting her name.

She gave the glass one more comprehensive sweep preparatory to closing it and going downstairs. As she did this a moving speck came into view and vanished.

Slowly she moved the big end of the spyglass back along the arc it had traveled. She found the speck and watched it. It was a man, striding across the meadow land, a half mile beyond the parsonage, and hurrying in the direction of the beach. She saw him climb a high dune, jump a fence, cross another field and finally vanish in the grove of pines on the edge of the bluff by the shore.

The man was John Ellery, the minister. Evidently, he had not gone home, nor had he taken the short cut. Instead he had walked downtown a long way and *then* turned in to cross the fields and work his way back.

Annabel put down the glass and, heedless of her father's calls, sat thinking. The minister had deliberately deceived her. More than that, he had gone to considerable trouble to avoid observation. Why had he done it? Had he done the same thing on other Sunday afternoons? Was there any real reason why he insisted on leaving the house regularly at four o'clock?

Annabel did not know. Her eyes snapped and her sharp features looked sharper yet as she descended the steps to the attic. She did not know; but she intended to find out.

# CHAPTER X

KEZIAH was getting worried about her parson. Not concerning his popularity with his congregation. She had long since ceased to worry about that. The young minister's place in his people's regard was now assured, the attendance was increasing, and the Regular church was now on a firmer footing, financially and socially, than it had been in years. Even Mrs. Rogers and Lavinia Pepper had ceased to criticise, except as pertained to unimportant incidentals, and were now among the loudest of the praise chanters. And as Captain Zeb Mayo said: " When Didama and Laviny stops fault-findin', the millennium's so nigh port a feller ought to be overhaulin' his saint uniform."

But what worried Mrs. Coffin was John Ellery's personal appearance and behavior. He had grown perceptibly thinner during the past month, his manner was distrait, and, worst of all in the housekeeper's eyes, his appetite had fallen off. She tried all sorts of tempting dishes, but the result was discouraging.

" What! " she exclaimed. " Don't want but one piece of huckleberry pie? Why, a week ago you ate three and looked kind of disappointed 'cause the dish was empty. What is the matter? Are you sick?"

"No, Mrs. Coffin," replied the Reverend John. "No, I'm not sick. I just don't feel hungry, that's all."

"Hum! Well, I've usually noticed that when a healthy man don't feel hungry at dinner time, 'specially in the huckleberry season, his healthiness is pretty shaky. What does ail you, Mr. Ellery? Got somethin' on your mind? If you have, I'd heave it overboard. Or you might unload it onto me and let me prescribe. I've had consider'ble experience in that kind of doctorin'."

But the answer was unsatisfactory. Mr. Ellery laughed, changed the subject, and wandered out into the garden, where Keziah saw him, shortly afterwards, intently regarding nothing in particular with a rapt stare. She watched him for a few moments and then, with a puzzled shake of the head, returned to her work. She believed that he was troubled about something and was herself troubled in consequence.

His absent-mindedness was most acute on Sunday evenings, before prayer meeting, and after he had returned from the afternoon at Captain Elkanah's.

"Say, Mr. Ellery," she said, on one of these Sunday evenings, "do you know, it seems to me that Elkanah's meals must go to your head. Don't have any of his granddad's New England rum, do you? They tell me he's got some of that down cellar that he doles out occasional to his very particular friends. That's the common yarn around town, though I couldn't swear 'twas gospel."

The minister smiled and denied acquaintanceship with the New England beverage.

"Humph! Then it must be the other thing. You ain't in love, are you?"

The young man started, colored, and was plainly embarrassed.

"In love?" he repeated. "In love, Mrs. Coffin?"

"Yes, in love. Annabel hasn't landed a male at last, has she? She's a line over the side for a long time."

The hearty laugh with which this was received settled the question of Annabel's success. Keziah was relieved.

"Well, I'm glad of that," she said. "I ain't got any grudge against Annabel, but neither have I got one against you. Another man in that family would have an easy time in one way, he wouldn't have to do any thinkin' for himself—Elkanah and his daughter would do all that was necessary. So you're not in love. Then I don't know what does ail you. I'll say this, though, for a body that ain't in love you certainly stay with the Danielses a long time. You went there right after meetin' this noon and now it's seven o'clock and you've just got home. And 'twas the same last Sunday and the one before. Been there all the time, have you?"

She knew he had not, because she had seen him pass the parsonage, on the opposite side of the road, two hours before. But she was curious to learn what his reply would be. It was noncommittal.

"No," he said slowly. "Not all the time. I—er—went for a short walk."

Before she could inquire concerning that walk

he had entered the study and closed the door after him.

During the week which followed this particular conversation he was more absent-minded than ever. There were evenings when he spoke scarcely a word, but sat silent in his chair, while Keziah, looking up from her mending, watched him and guessed and wondered. After he had gone to his room for the night, she would hear him pacing the floor, back and forth, back and forth. She asked no more questions, however; minding her own business was a specialty of Keziah's, and it was a rare quality in Trumet.

Sunday was a cloudy, warm day, "muggy," so Captain Zeb described it. After the morning service Mr. Ellery, as usual, went home with Captain Daniels and Annabel. Keziah returned to the parsonage, ate a lonely dinner, washed the dishes, and sat down to read a library book. She read for an hour and then, finding it difficult to keep her mind on the story, gave it up, closed the book and, rising, walked to the window. But the misty, hot loneliness of the afternoon, was neither interesting nor cheerful, so she turned away and went upstairs to her own room. Her trunk was in one corner of this room and she unlocked it, taking from a compartment of the tray a rosewood writing case, inlaid with mother-of-pearl, a present from her father, who had brought it home from sea when she was a girl.

From the case she took a packet of letters and a daguerreotype. The latter was the portrait of a young man, in high-collared coat, stock, and fancy waistcoat. His hair, worn long over the ears, was smooth with a shine that suggested oil, and in his shirt front was a large pin, which might possibly have been mistaken by a credulous observer for a diamond. Mrs. Coffin looked at the daguerreotype, sighed, shuddered, and laid it aside. Then she opened the packet of letters. Selecting one from the top of the pile, she read it slowly. And, as she read, she sighed again.

She did not hear the back door of the parsonage open and close softly. Nor did she hear the cautious footsteps in the rooms below. What aroused her from her reading was her own name, spoken at the foot of the stairs.

"Keziah! Keziah, are you there?"

She started, sprang up, and ran out into the hall, the letter still in her hand.

"Who is it?" she asked sharply. "Mr. Ellery, is that you?"

"No," was the answer. "It's me—Nat. Are you busy, Keziah? I want to see you for a minute."

The housekeeper hurriedly thrust the letter into her waist.

"I'll be right down, Nat," she answered. "I'm comin'."

He was in the sitting room when she entered. He was wearing his Sunday suit of blue and his soft felt hat was on the center table. She held out her hand and he shook it heartily.

"Well!" she observed, smiling, "I declare if I don't believe you've got the tiptoe habit. This is the second time you've sneaked into the house and scared me 'most to death. I asked you before if you wa'n't ashamed of yourself and now I ask it again."

Before he could reply she caught a glimpse of his face.

"What is it?" she asked. "What is the matter? Is anybody sick? Is your father——"

"No, he's all right. That is, he's as well as he has been lately, though that isn't sayin' much."

"Is Grace——"

"No, she's all right, too, I guess. Been sort of quiet and sorrowful for the last few weeks—or I've seemed to notice that she has—but I cal'late it's nothin' serious. I wouldn't wonder if the same thing that's troublin' her is what ails me."

"But what is it? Why don't you tell me?"

"I'm goin' to tell you, Keziah. That's what I come here for. I——"

"Sit down, can't you? Don't stand up there like a lighthouse, shuttin' out the whole broadside of the room. You are the *biggest* thing!"

Captain Hammond selected the most substantial chair in the apartment and sat down upon it. He looked at his friend and shook his head.

"No use, Keziah," he said. "If I was as deep down in the blues as the bottom of the Whale Deep, a look at that face of yours would pull me to the top again. You're a good woman!"

"Thanks! When I have spare time on my hands I'll practice tryin' to believe that. But what is the trouble, Nat? Out with it."

"Well, Keziah, it's trouble enough. Dad and I have had a fallin' out."

Mrs. Coffin's mouth and eyes opened.

"What?" she cried, in utter astonishment.

"Yes. It's true. We had what was next door to a real quarrel after dinner to-day. It would have been a real one if I hadn't walked off and left him. He's as set as the rock of Gibraltar, and——"

" And your foundations ain't given to slippin' much. Nat Hammond, I'm surprised at you! What was it all about? Religion? "

" No, not a sliver of religion in it. If 'twas that, I could dodge, or haul down my colors, if I had to. But it's somethin' worse, enough sight worse. Somethin' I can't do—even for dad—and won't either. Keziah, he's dead set on my marryin' Grace. Says if I don't he'll know that I don't really care a tin nickel for him, or for his wishes, or what becomes of the girl after he's gone."

" Nat! "

" It's a fact. You see, dad realizes, better'n I thought he did, that his health is pretty shaky and that he is likely to founder 'most any time. He says that don't worry him; if he knew Grace and I were provided for he'd slip his cable with a clean manifest. But the dream of his life, he says, has been that we should marry. And he wants to see it done."

Keziah was silent for a moment. Then she said slowly:

" And Grace herself? How does she feel about it? Has he spoken to her? "

" I don't know. I guess likely he has. Perhaps that's why she's been so sort of mournful lately. But never mind whether he has or not; I won't do it and I told him so. He got red hot in a jiffy. I was ungrateful and stubborn and all sorts of things. And I, bein' a Hammond, with some of the Hammond balkiness in me, I set my foot down as hard as his. And we had it until—until—well, until I saw him stagger and tremble so that I actually got scared and feared he was goin' to keel over where he stood.

" ' Why can't you?' he kept sayin'. ' But *why* can't you? Ain't she a girl anyone would be proud to have for a wife?' 'Course there was no answer to that but yes. Then back he comes again with ' Then why can't you?' At last, bein' frightened, as I said, that he might have another shock or somethin', I said I'd think it over and come away and left him. And I come straight to you. Keziah, what shall I do? What can you say to help me?"

Keziah was silent. She was looking, not at her companion, but at the carpet center of one of the braided rugs on the floor. Her face was very grave and the lines about her mouth seemed to deepen. Her hands, clasped in her lap, tightened one upon the other. But her voice was calm when, at last, she spoke.

"Nat," she said, "there's only one thing I can say. And that's what your father said: Why can't you?"

The captain sprang from his chair.

"What?" he cried incredulously. "What are you sayin'?"

"Just what your father said, Nat. Why can't you marry Grace? She's a dear, good girl and——"

"That be—keelhauled! Keziah Coffin, you sit there and ask me why I can't marry her! *You* do?"

"Yes, Nat."

"Keziah, you're crazy! Don't talk to me like that. We're not jokin' now. You know why I can't marry her, nor anyone else in this round world but you."

"Nat, I can't marry you."

"I know, I know. You're always sayin' that. But you don't mean it. You can't mean it. Why, you and me have been picked out for each other by the Almighty, Keziah. I swear I believe just that. We went together when we were boy and girl, to parties and such. We was promised when I first went to sea. If it hadn't been for that fool row we had—and 'twas all my fault and I know it— you never would have let that da—that miserable Anse Coffin come near you. And when 'twas too late and you'd married him, the mean, drunken, cruel——"

"Hush, Nat! hush! Stop it!"

"He was, and you know he was. Yes, and worse besides. Runnin' off and leavin' a wife like you to— Oh, my God! when I think *I* might have been your husband to look out for you and take care of you! That you might have been with me on board my ships. That, when I come down the companion on stormy nights I might have found you there to comfort me and— O Keziah! we aren't young any more. What's the use of foolin'? I want you. I'm goin' to have you. Coffin is dead these ten years. When I heard he was drowned off there in Singapore, all I could say was: 'Serve him right!' And I say it now. I come home then more determined to get you. Say yes, and let's be happy. Do!"

"I can't, Nat."

"Why not? For Heaven sakes! why not? Don't you care for me? You've let me think—well, at any rate, I have thought you did. You used to. Don't you?"

"Nat, I—I care for you more than anybody else on earth. But I can't marry you. Oh, don't keep askin' it! Please don't. I can't marry you, Nat. No!"

"Well, not now, maybe. Not this month, or even this year, perhaps, but some day——"

"No, Nat. You must listen. There's no use of this goin' on any longer. I mean it. I can't marry you."

"You won't, you mean."

"Well, if you wish to think so. Then I won't."

"But by and by——"

"No, not by and by. Never, Nat. Never."

He drew his hand across his forehead.

"Never!" he repeated, more to himself than to her.

"Never. Yes, Nat."

"Then, by the everlastin'! I'll do somethin'——"

"No, no, you won't. Nat Hammond, I know you. You're a great big, brave-hearted, sensible man. You won't be foolish. You'll do—yes, I think you'd better do just what your father asks you to do. Marry Grace, if she wants you and will have you. She'll make you a good wife; you'll learn to care for her, and I know she'll have the best husband that a girl could hope for. And you and I will be friends, just as we've always been, and——"

"Keziah, stop that! Stop it, do you hear! I don't want to listen to such stuff. I tell you I'm past soft soap, and I didn't think you'd give it to me."

"Nat!"

"Oh, yes, 'Nat'! A lot you care for 'Nat'! Not a reason on God's footstool why you won't have me—except one, and that one that you don't want me."

"Please, Nat! I can hardly believe this is you. This trouble with your father has upset you. You don't mean what you say. You're not talkin' like yourself and——"

"Stop it, I tell you. I don't feel like myself. I banked on you, Keziah. I've lived for you. And now—— O Keziah, take it back! Give me a little hope, just enough to keep my head above water."

"I'd like to, Nat. I only wish I could. But 'twouldn't be any use. I can't do it."

He snatched his hat from the table and strode to the door. Turning, he looked at her.

"All right," he said chokingly. "All right. Good-by."

His steps sounded on the oilcloth of the kitchen. Then the back door slammed. He was gone.

Keziah started, as if the slam of the door had been an electric shock. During the interview she had been pale and grave but outwardly calm. Now she sank wearily down in the chair from which she had risen and her head dropped forward upon her arms on the table. The letter she had been reading before Captain Nat's arrival fell from her waist to the floor and lay there, its badly spelled and blotted lines showing black and fateful against the white paper. And she cried, tears of utter loneliness and despair.

The clouds thickened as the afternoon passed. The setting sun was hidden behind them; over the horizon of ocean and bay the fog banks were rolling in tumbled, crumpled masses. The shadows in the lonely sitting room deepened. There came a knock at the dining-room door.

Keziah sprang from her chair, smoothed her hair, hastily wiped her eyes, picked up the dropped letter and went to admit the visitor, whoever he or she might be. She was glad of the shadows, they prevented her face from being seen too plainly.

"Good afternoon," she said, opening the door. "Oh! it's you, is it?"

"Yes," admitted Abishai Pepper, standing on the stone step, and shifting uneasily from one foot to the other. "Yes, Keziah, it's—it's me, thank you."

"Don't mention it. Well, is Laviny with you?"

"No—o, she ain't. She—she didn't come."

"Hum! Did she know you was comin'?"

"No—o, I don't cal'late she did."

"I see. Well, what do you want?"

Mrs. Coffin's welcome was not too cordial. She had laughed many times over Abishai's proposal of marriage, but she had never quite forgiven him for making her ridiculous on that occasion. Incidentally, she did not feel like laughing.

"What do you want?" she repeated.

Kyan was plainly nervous.

"I only wanted to see Mr. Ellery," he announced. "It's all right, Keziah. You needn't be afraid."

"Afraid! What on earth should I be afraid of?"

"Why—why, I didn't know but you might be afraid I was goin' to—to talk about what we talked about when I—I talked to you that day up at——"

"There! that'll do. It ain't me that would have reason to be afraid if *that* was what you come for. What do you want? Don't stand there dancin' a jig."

"I only wanted to see Mr. Ellery."

"He's out. Good day."

"But I won't keep him but a minute."

"He's out, I tell you. Do you want to leave a message?"

"No—o. No, I guess not."

"Was it important?"

"Oh! I don't know. Kind of, maybe. I wanted to ask his advice about somethin'. It's a secret. Only him and me know about it. Good-by."

"Shall I tell him you'll call again? Or ask him to come up to your house?"

Mr. Pepper, who had started to go, now hurried back to the steps.

"No, no," he protested, in alarm. "Don't you tell him that. I wouldn't have him come there for no money. Why, Laviny, she——"

"Oh, Laviny isn't in the secret, then?" Keziah smiled in spite of herself.

"Not exactly. That is, not much. Don't you tell her I come here, will you? I'll find Mr. Ellery. I know where he is."

"I wouldn't go to the Danielses', if I was you. Elkanah might not like to have you chasin' after his visitors."

"Oh, the minister ain't at the Danielses', not as late's this, he ain't. I know where he is."

"You do?" The housekeeper looked at him keenly.

"Yes, sir, I do. *I* know where he goes Sunday afternoons—and why he goes, too. Mr. Ellery and me's good friends. We understand each other."

"Look here, Kyan Pepper! What are you talkin' about?"

"Nothin', nothin'. Good day."

"Stop! Stand still! Come in the house here. I want you to."

"No, no, Keziah. Really, I'd love to, but I can't stop."

"Come in, I tell you."

Reluctantly, but lacking the strength of mind to refuse, Mr. Pepper entered the dining room. Then Mrs. Coffin turned upon him.

"What do you mean," she demanded, "by throwin' out hints that the minister and you are in some sort of secret? How dare you go round tellin' people such yarns as that?"

"They ain't yarns. And I never told nobody afore, anyhow. I got to move along. I'll——"

"Stay where you are. I guess I'll run right up and ask your sister about this. Perhaps she might——"

"Ss-sh! ss-sh! don't talk that way, Keziah. Don't! Laviny don't know what I mean. Don't go askin' *her* things."

"But you said——"

"I just said I knew where Mr. Ellery goes every Sunday afternoon. He don't know anybody knows, but I do. That's all there is to it. I shan't tell. So——"

"Tell? Do you mean there's somethin' Mr. Ellery wouldn't want told? Don't you dare—I *will* see Laviny!"

"No, no, no, no! 'Tain't nothin' much. I just know where he goes after he leaves Elkanah's and who he goes to meet. I— Lordy! I hadn't ought to said that! I— Keziah Coffin, don't you ever tell I told you. I've said more'n I meant to. If it comes out there'd be the biggest row in the church that ever was. And I'd be responsible! *I* would! I'd have to go on the witness stand and then Laviny'd find out how I— Oh, oh, oh! what *shall* I do?"

The poor frightened creature's "jig" had, by this time, become a distracted fandango. But the housekeeper had no mercy on him. She was beginning to fear for her parson and, for the time, everything else, her own trouble and the recent interview with Nat, was pushed aside.

"What is it?" she persisted. "*What* would bring on the row in the church? *Who* does Mr. Ellery meet? Out with it! What do you mean?"

"I mean that the minister meets that Van Horne girl every Sunday afternoon after he leaves Elkanah's. There, now! It's out, and I don't give a darn if they hang me for it."

Keziah turned white. She seized Mr. Pepper by the lapel of his Sunday coat and shook him.

"Grace Van Horne!" she cried. "Mr. Ellery meets Grace Van Horne on Sunday afternoons? Where?"

"Down in them pines back of Peters's pastur', on the aidge of the bank over the beach. He's met her there every Sunday for the last six weeks— longer, for what I know. I've watched 'em."

"You *have? You* have! You've dared to spy on— I think you're lyin' to me. I don't believe it."

"I ain't lyin'! It's so. I'll bet you anything they're there now, walkin' up and down and talkin'. What would I want to lie for? You come with me this minute and I'll show 'em to you."

In the desire to prove his veracity he was on his

"Rising to peer over the bushes at the minister and Grace."

way to the door. But Keziah stepped in front of him.

"'Bish Pepper," she said slowly and fiercely, shaking a forefinger in his face, "you go straight home and stay there. Don't you breathe a word to a livin' soul of what you say you've seen. Don't you even think it, or—or dream it. If you do I'll—I'll march straight to Laviny and tell her that you asked me to marry you. I will, as sure as you're shakin' in front of me this minute. Now you swear to me to keep still. Swear!"

"How—how'll I swear?" begged Kyan. "What do you say when you swear? I'll say it, Keziah! I'll say anything! I'll——"

"All right. Then mind you remember. Now clear out quick. I want to think. I *must* think. *Go!* Get out of my sight!"

Kyan went, glad to escape, but frightened to the soul of him. Keziah watched him until he turned from the main road into the lighthouse lane. Then, certain that he really was going straight home, she reëntered the parsonage and sat down in the nearest chair. For ten minutes she sat there, striving to grasp the situation. Then she rose and, putting on her bonnet and shawl, locked the dining-room door, and went out through the kitchen. On the step she looked cautiously back to see if any of the neighbors were at their windows. But this was Sunday, the one day when Trumet people sat in their front parlors. The coast was clear. She hurried through the back yard, and down the path leading across the fields. She was going to the pine grove by the shore, going to find out for herself if Kyan's astonishing story was true.

For if it was true, if the Rev. John Ellery was meeting clandestinely the adopted daughter of Eben Hammond, it meant—what might it not mean, in Trumet? If he had fallen in love with a Come-Outer, with Grace Van Horne of all people, if he should dare think of marrying her, it would mean the utter wreck of his career as a Regular clergyman. His own society would turn him out instantly. All sorts of things would be said, lies and scandal would be invented and believed. His character would be riddled by the Trumet gossips and the papers would publish the result broadcast.

And Grace! If she loved a Regular minister, what would happen to her? Captain Eben would turn her from his door, that was certain. Although he idolized the girl, Keziah knew that he would never countenance such a marriage. And if Nat stood by Grace, as he would be almost sure to do, the breach between father and son would widen beyond healing. If it were merely a matter of personal selection, Mrs. Coffin would rather have seen her parson marry Grace than anyone else on earth. As it was, such a match must not be. It meant ruin for both. She must prevent the affair going further. She must break off the intimacy. She must save those two young people from making a mistake which would— She wrung her hands as she thought of it. Of her own sorrow and trouble she characteristically thought nothing now. Sacrifice of self was a part of Keziah's nature.

The pines were a deep-green blotch against the cloudy sky and the gloomy waters of the bay. She skirted the outlying clumps of bayberry and beach plum bushes and entered the grove. The pine needles made a soft carpet which deadened her footfalls, and the shadows beneath the boughs were thick and black. She tiptoed on until she reached the clearing by the brink of the bluff. No one was in sight. She drew a breath of relief. Kyan might be mistaken, after all.

Then she heard low voices. As she crouched at the edge of the grove, two figures passed slowly across the clearing, along the bush-bordered path and into the shrubbery beyond. John Ellery was walking with Grace Van Horne. He was holding her hand in his and they were talking very earnestly.

Keziah did not follow. What would have been the use? This was not the time to speak. She *knew* now and she knew, also, that the responsibility was hers. She must go home at once, go home to be alone and to think. She tiptoed back through the grove and across the fields.

Yet, if she had waited, she might have seen something else which would have been, at least, interesting. She had scarcely reached the outer edge of the grove when another figure passed stealthily along that narrow path by the bluff edge. A female figure treading very carefully, rising to peer over the bushes at the minister and Grace. The figure of Miss Annabel Daniels, the " belle " of Trumet. And Annabel's face was not pleasant to look upon.

# CHAPTER XI

IN WHICH CAPTAIN EBEN RECEIVES A CALLER

AT the edge of the bluff, just where the pines and the bayberry bushes were thickest, where the narrow, crooked little footpath dipped over the rise and down to the pasture land and the salt meadow, John Ellery and Grace had halted in their walk. It was full tide and the miniature breakers plashed amid the seaweed on the beach. The mist was drifting in over the bay and the gulls were calling sleepily from their perch along the breakwater. A night hawk swooped and circled above the tall " feather grass " by the margin of the creek. The minister's face was pale, but set and determined, and he was speaking rapidly.

" I can't help it," he said. " I can't help it. I have made up my mind and nothing can change it, nothing but you. It rests with you. If you say yes, then nothing else matters. Will you say it? "

He was holding both her hands now, and though she tried to withdraw them, he would not let her.

" Will you? " he pleaded.

" I can't," she answered brokenly. " I can't. Think of your church and of your people. What would they say if——"

" I don't care what they say."

" Oh! yes, you do. Not now, perhaps, but later

you will. You don't know Trumet as I know it. No, it's impossible."

"I tell you there is only one impossible thing. That is that I give you up. I won't do it. I *can't* do it! Grace, this is life and death for me. My church——"

He paused in spite of himself. His church, his first church! He had accepted the call with pride and a determination to do his best, the very best that was in him, for the society and for the people whom he was to lead. Some of those people he had learned to love; many of them, he felt sure, loved him. His success, his popularity, the growth of the organization and the praise which had come to him because of it, all these had meant, and still meant, very much to him. No wonder he paused, but the pause was momentary.

"My church," he went on, "is my work and I like it. I believe I've done some good here and I hope to do more. But no church shall say whom I shall marry. If you care for me, Grace, as I think and hope you do, we'll face the church and the town together and they will respect us for it."

She shook her head.

"Some of them might respect you," she said. "They would say you had been led into this by me and were not so much to blame. But I——"

"They shall respect my wife," he interrupted, snapping his teeth together, "or I'll know the reason why."

She smiled mournfully.

"I think they'll tell you the reason," she answered. "No, John, no! we mustn't think of it.

You can see we mustn't. This has all been a mistake, a dreadful mistake, and I am to blame for it."

"The only mistake has been our meeting in this way. We should have met openly; I realize it, and have felt it for sometime. It was my fault, not yours. I was afraid, I guess. But I'll not be a coward any longer. Come, dear, let's not be afraid another day. Only say you'll marry me and I'll proclaim it openly, to-night— Yes, from the pulpit, if you say so."

She hesitated and he took courage from her hesitation.

"Say it," he pleaded. "You *will* say it?"

"I can't! I can't! My uncle——"

"Your uncle shall hear it from me. We'll go to him together. I'll tell him myself. He worships you."

"Yes, I know. He does worship me. That's why I am sure he had rather see me dead than married to you, a Regular, and a Regular minister."

"I don't believe it. He can't be so unreasonable. If he is, then you shouldn't humor such bigotry."

"He has been my father for years, and a dear, kind father."

"I know. That's why I'm so certain we can make him understand. Come, dear! come! Why should you consider everyone else? Consider your own happiness. Consider mine."

She looked at him.

"I am considering yours," she said. "That is what I consider most of all. And, as for uncle, I know—I *know* he would never consent. His heart is set on something else. Nat——"

"Nat? Are you considering him, too? Is *he* to stand between us? What right has he to say——"

"Hush! hush! He hasn't said anything. But —but he and uncle have quarreled, just a little. I didn't tell you, but they have. And I think I know the reason. Nat is Uncle Eben's idol. If the quarrel should grow more serious, I believe it would break his heart. I couldn't bear to be the cause of that; I should never forgive myself."

"You the cause? How could you be the cause of a quarrel between those two? Grace, think of me."

Here was the selfishness of man and the unselfishness of woman answered.

"John," she said, "it is of you I am thinking. Everything else could—might be overcome, perhaps. But I must think of your future and your life. I *must*. That is why——"

He did not wait to hear more. He seized her in his arms and kissed her.

"Then you *do* care!" he cried joyfully. "You will marry me?"

For an instant she lay quiet in his embrace, receiving, if not responding to his caresses. Then she gently but firmly freed herself. He saw that there were tears in her eyes.

"Grace," he urged, "don't—don't hesitate any longer. You were meant to be my wife. We were brought together for just that. I know it. Come."

She was crying softly.

"Won't you?" he begged.

"I don't know," she sobbed. "Oh, I don't know! I must think—I *must*! Wait, please wait, John. Perhaps by to-morrow I can answer. I'll try

—I'll try. Don't ask me again, now. Let me think. Oh, do!"

Doubtless he would have asked her again. He looked as if he meant to. But just then, drifting through the twilight and the mist, came the sound of a bell, the bell of the Regular church, ringing for the Sunday evening meeting. They both heard it.

"Oh!" exclaimed Grace, "that is your bell. You will be late. You must go, and so must I. Good night."

She started down the path. He hesitated, then ran after her.

"To-morrow?" he questioned eagerly. "To-morrow, then, you'll say that you will?"

"Oh, perhaps, perhaps! I mustn't promise. Good night."

It was after seven when Grace reached the old tavern. The housekeeper, Mrs. Poundberry, was anxiously awaiting her. She wore her bonnet and Sunday gown and was evidently ready to go out.

"Land sakes alive!" she sputtered. "Where in the name of goodness have you been to? I was gettin' scairt. Didn't know but you'd run off and got married, or sunthin' dreadful."

Grace was thankful that the cloudy twilight made it impossible to see her face distinctly. The housekeeper rattled on without waiting for an answer.

"Supper's on the table and the kittle's abilin'. You better eat in a hurry, 'cause it's meetin' time now. Your uncle, he started ten minutes ago. I'm agoin' right along, too, but I ain't goin' to meetin'; I'm agoin' up to Betsy E.'s to stay all night. She's got a spine in her back, as the feller said, and ain't feelin' good, so I told her I'd come and stay a little spell. S'pose you can get along to-morrow without me?"

"Betsy E." was Mrs. Poundberry's second cousin, an elderly spinster living alone in a little house near the salt works. Grace assured her questioner that she could attend to the house and the meals during the following day, longer if the troublesome "spine" needed company. Mrs. Poundberry sighed, groaned, and shook her head.

"I shan't stay no longer," she affirmed; "not if Betsy's all over spines, like one of them Mexican cactus plants. No, marm, my place is right here and I know it. Your Uncle Eben's mighty feeble and peaked lately. He ain't long for this world, I'm afraid. You'd ought to be awful good to him, Gracie."

"I know it," was the hurried reply. "Where's Nat?"

"I don't know. Can't keep track of *him*. Might's well try to put your finger on a flea. He's here to-day and gone yesterday, as the Scriptur' says. He ate a little mite of supper, but not much, and then off he puts. Says he's goin' to walk the fog out'n his head. I told him, s' I, 'You'll walk a plaguey sight more in than you do out, *this* night,' but he went just the same. He was dreadful kind of dumpy and blue this evenin'. Seemed to be sort of soggy in his mind. And why he never went to meetin' with his dad and why his dad never asked him *to* go is more'n I can tell. Land of livin', how I do gabble! My grandmarm used to say my tongue was loose at both ends and hung in the middle, and I guess she wa'n't fur off the course. Good-by. Take care of yourself.

You can put what's left of that mock mince pie on the top shelf in the butt'ry and you'd better heave a dish towel or sunthin' over it to keep the ants out. There's more ants in this house than there is dollars, a good sight. Betsy E., she's got a plan for keepin' of 'em out by puttin' sassers of brimstone round the shelves, but I told her, s' I, ' *Them* ants don't care for no brimstone. They're used to it. Sometimes I b'lieve they're sent by the everlastin' father of brimstone,' and she——''

She had reached the gate by this time, and Grace shut off the flow of conversation by closing the door. Then she took a candle from the row on the dining-room mantel, lighted it, and went up to her own room. Standing before the old-fashioned bureau with its little oval mirror, she hastily arranged her hair. She did not wish to go to the prayer meeting at the chapel, but she felt that she must. The Come-Outer gatherings, with their noisy singing and shouting, had grown more and more repugnant to her.

And to-night, of all nights! How could she meet those people who had known her since she was a child, who boasted of her as one of their staunchest adherents, who believed in her and trusted her? How could she meet them and talk with them, knowing what she knew and realizing that they, too, would know it on the morrow? But her uncle would miss her and be worried about her if she did not come. She could not bear to trouble him now; she never loved him so dearly, was never so anxious to humor his every wish as on this, perhaps the last evening they would spend together. For, though she would not yet admit it, even to herself, her decision was made, had really been made the first time John Ellery asked her weeks before. Only the thought of what might happen to him if she consented had caused her to hesitate so long.

She blew out the candle and came out into the hall at the head of the stairs. She was about to descend when she heard voices. The door of the dining room opened and closed. She felt certain that Nat had returned and wondered who was with him. Then she heard her uncle's voice, speaking sharply and with unwonted sternness.

" I don't know what 'tis you want to see me about," said Captain Eben. " You say it's important; well, it's got to be to keep me from my meetin'. I ought to be on the Lord's business this minute and nothin' worldly's goin' to keep me from servin' Him. So speak quick. What is it? "

The voice that answered was one that Grace recognized, though she had never before heard in it the note of agitation and undignified excitement. There were no ponderous pauses and " Hum—ha's " now.

" Don't be a fool, Hammond! " it said. " And don't stand there preaching. Lock that door! Get a lamp! Are you sure there's nobody but us in the house? "

Captain Elkanah Daniels! Captain Elkanah visiting a Come-Outer! and the leader of the Come-Outers! ! Grace caught her breath. What in the world— She started to descend and then a thought flashed to her mind. She stopped short.

" *I* ain't the fool, Elkanah," she heard her uncle retort sternly. " The fools are them who are deef to the call from on high. My foot was on the threshold of His house when you led me astray. It's never halted there afore. I warn you——"

"Hush! Shut up! Can't you forget that—that Come-Outer circus of yours for a minute?"

"Elkanah Daniels, I'll have no blasphemy here. Another word like that and——"

"*Will* you be still and hear me? The Lord's business! I guess you'll think it's the Lord's business when you understand what I'm going to tell you! The Lord's business! The devil's business, you better say! Will you lock that door?"

"My church is waitin' for me and——"

"Let it wait. What's a parcel of yelling Come-Outers compared to the decency of this town? Stop! Shut up! Eben Hammond, I tell you that your precious church—yes and mine, the Regular church of Trumet—will go to rack and ruin if you and me don't pull together this night."

"And I tell you, Elkanah Daniels, I'll have no blasphemy here. That little sanctuary up the road is founded on a rock and neither you nor any of your Phariseein' priest-worshipin' crew can shake it. The Almighty'll protect His own. As for the Reg'lar church, that's no concern of mine."

"But I tell you 'tis your concern. Or if the church isn't, your own family is."

"My—my family?"

"Yes, your own family. Huh! that makes you listen, don't it?"

There was an instant of silence. Grace, crouching on the stairs, noticed the change in her uncle's voice as he answered.

"My own family?" he repeated slowly. "My

own— And the Reg'lar church— What do you mean? Has Nat——"

"No, he ain't. But that cussed girl of yours——"

"Stop!" Eben's shout rang through the house. The listener heard it, rose, and then sank slowly to her knees.

"Stop!" shouted Captain Hammond. "Elkanah Daniels, for your own sake now, be careful. If you dast to say a word, another word like that, I'll——"

"If I dast! The hussy! But there's no use talkin' to you. You're as crazy as a Bedlamite. Either that, or you're in the game with her. If you are, I warn you——"

"Stop! What game? What do you mean? Gracie! My Grace! What is it? For mercy sakes, Elkanah——"

"Humph! I wondered if I couldn't get some sense into you, finally. Lock that door!"

"I will! I will! But Elkanah——"

"Lock it! Give me the key!"

The click of the lock sounded sharply.

"Where's the lamp?" demanded Daniels. "And the matches? Don't stand there shaking."

A smell of sulphur floated out into the hall. Then the sickly glow of the "fluid" lamp shone through the doorway.

"What ails you?" asked Elkanah. "Are you struck dumb? Now go and see if there's anybody else in the house."

"But—but there ain't. I know there ain't. Hannah's gone and Gracie's at meetin' by this time."

"She? Humph! Well, maybe she's at meeting

and maybe she isn't. Maybe she's over in Peters's pines, hugging and kissing that man she's met there every Sunday for I don't know how long— Here! let go, you old fool! Let go, I tell you!"

A chair fell to the floor with a bang. There was the sound of hard breathing and rapid footsteps.

"Let go!" panted Daniels. "Are you crazy? Take your hands off me!"

"You liar!" snarled Captain Eben. "You low-lived liar! By the Almighty, Elkanah Daniels! I'll— You take that back or I'll choke the ever-lastin' soul out of you. I will——"

"Let go, you lunatic! You'll kill yourself. Listen! I'm not lying. It's the truth. She's met a man, I tell you. Been meeting him for months, I guess. There! now will you listen?"

The footsteps had ceased, but the heavy breathing continued.

"A man!" gasped Eben. "A man! Gracie! It's a— Who is he? What's his name?"

"His name's John Ellery, and he's minister of the Regular church in this town; that's who he is! Here! hold up! Good Lord! are you dying? Hold up!"

The girl on the stairs sprang to her feet. Her head was reeling and she could scarcely stand, but she blindly began the descent. She must go to her uncle. She must. But Captain Daniels's voice caused her to halt once more.

"There! there!" it said in a tone of relief. "That's better. Set still now. Be quiet, that's it. Shall I get some water?"

"No, no! let me be. Just let me be. I ain't what I used to be and this— I'm all right, I tell you. Grace! And—and— What was it you just said? I—I don't b'lieve I heard it right."

"I said that daughter of yours, or niece, or whatever she is, this Grace Van Horne, has been meeting young Ellery, our minister, in Peters's grove. Been meeting him and walking with him, and kissing him, and——"

"It's a lie! It ain't so, Elkanah! Prove it or— It—it *can't* be so, can it? Please——"

"It is so. She's met him in those pines every Sunday afternoon for a long time. She was seen there with him this afternoon."

"Who—who saw her?"

"Never mind. The one that did'll never tell— unless it's necessary. They're fixing to be married, and——"

"*Married!* She marry a Reg'lar minister! Oh——"

"Hush! Listen! They ain't married yet. We can stop 'em, you and I, if we get right to work. It isn't too late. Will you help?"

"Will I—I— Go on! tell me more."

"We can stop 'em. I know it would be a good catch for her, the sneaking, designing— Well, never mind. But it can't be. It shan't be. You've got to tell her so, Hammond. We folks of the Regular church have pride in our society; we won't have it disgraced. And we have been proud of our minister, the young, rattle-headed fool! We'll save him if we can. If we can't"—the speaker's teeth grated—"then we'll send him to eternal smash or die trying."

"But I can't believe it's true. It's a mistake; some other girl and not Gracie. Why, she don't even know him. She wouldn't— But she *has* been out every Sunday afternoon for weeks. If it *should* be!"

"It is. I tell you it is. Don't waste time rolling your eyes and talking stuff. We've got to work and you've got to work first. I don't know whether you're only making believe or not. I realize that 'twould be a good thing for your girl to marry a promising young chap like him, but— Hush! let me go on. I tell you, Hammond, it can't be. We won't let her. *I* won't let her. I'm a man of influence in this town, and outside of it, too. I'm head of the parish committee and a member of the National Regular Society. I can't reach your precious ward, maybe, but I can reach the fellow she's after, and if he marries her, I'll drive 'em both to the poorhouse.

"Here's where you come in, Hammond. It may be she does really care for him. Or maybe she's after position and money. Well, you talk to her. You tell her that if she keeps on going with him, if she doesn't break off this damnable business now, to-morrow, I'll ruin John Ellery as sure as I'm a living man. He'll be ruined in Trumet, anyhow. He'll be thrown out by the parish committee. I'm not sure that his church people won't tar and feather him. Marrying a low-down Come-Outer hussy! As if there wa'n't decent girls of good families he might have had! But losing this church won't be the only thing that'll happen to him. The committee'll see that he doesn't get another one. I'll use my influence and have him thrown out of the Regular ministry. Think I can't? What sort of yarns do you suppose will be told about him and her, meeting the way they did? Won't the county papers print some fine tales? Won't the Boston ones enjoy such a scandal? I tell you, Eben Hammond, that young chap's name will be dragged so deep in the mud it'll never get clean again."

He stopped for breath. His companion was silent. After a moment, he continued:

"You tell her that, Hammond," he went on. "If she really cares for him, it'll be enough. She won't let him ruin his life. And I'll keep quiet till I hear from you. If she's sensible and really decent, then she can give him his clearance papers without his knowing why she did it and everything will be a secret and kept so. Nobody else'll ever know. If she won't do that, then you tell me and I'll have a session with *him*. If *that's* no good, then out he goes and she with him; and it's ruination for both of 'em, reputations and all. Why am I doing this? I'll tell you. I like him. He isn't orthodox enough to suit me, but I have liked him mighty well. And Annab— Humph! that's neither here nor there. What I'm fighting for is the Trumet Regular church. That's *my* church and I'll have no dirty scandal with Come-Outers dragging it down. Now you understand. Will you tell her what I've said?"

The chair creaked. Evidently, Captain Eben was rising slowly to his feet.

"Well?" repeated Elkanah.

"Elkanah Daniels," said Eben slowly, his voice shaking from nervous exhaustion and weakness, but with a fine ring of determination in every word, "Elkanah Daniels, you listen to me. I've heard you through. If your yarn is true, then my heart is broke, and I wish I might have died afore I heard it. But I didn't die and I have heard it. Now listen to me.

I love that girl of mine better'n the whole wide world and yet I'd ruther see her dead afore me than married to a Reg'lar minister. Disgrace to *him!* Disgrace to your miser'ble church! What about the disgrace to *mine?* And the disgrace to *her?* Ruin to your minister! Ruin to my girl here and hereafter is what I'm thinkin' of; that and my people who worship God with me. I'll talk to Grace. I'll talk to her. But not of what'll happen to him or you—or any of your cantin', lip-servin' crew. I'll tell her to choose between him and me. And if she chooses him, I'll send her out of that door. I'll do my duty and read her out of my congregation. And I'll know she's gone to everlastin' hell, and that's worse'n the poorhouse. That's all to-night, Elkanah. Now you better go."

"Humph! Well, I declare! you *are* a bigoted——"

"Stop it! I've kept my hands off you so fur, because I'm the Lord's servant. But I'm fightin' hard to keep down my old salt-water temper. You go! There's the door."

"All right, all right! *I* don't care what you say, so long as it's said so as to stop her from getting him —and said soon."

"It'll be said to-night. Now go! My people are waitin' at the chapel."

"You're not going to that prayer meeting after *this?*"

"Where else should I go? 'Come unto Me all ye that labor and are heavy laden.' And—and "—his voice broke—" He knows that I *am* heavy laden. Lord! Lord! do help me, for this is more'n I can bear alone."

# A CALLER

The lock turned; the door opened and closed. Grace, clinging to the balusters, heard Captain Hammond cross the room, slowly and feebly. She heard him enter the sitting room. Then she heard nothing more, not another sound, though the minutes dragged on and on, endlessly, eternally, and each with a message, a sentence repeated over and over again in her brain. " If she really cares for him, she won't let him ruin his life."

By and by, pale, but more composed, and with her mind made up, she came down into the hall. Drawing a long breath, she turned into the sitting room to face her uncle. By the light shining through the dining-room door she saw him on his knees by the haircloth sofa. She spoke his name. He did not answer nor look up. Alarmed, she touched him on the shoulder. At her touch his arm slid from the couch and he fell gently over upon his side on the carpet.

# CHAPTER XII

## IN WHICH CAPTAIN EBEN MAKES PORT

HALF past eight. In the vestry of the Regular church John Ellery was conducting his prayer meeting. The attendance was as large as usual. Three seats, however, were vacant, and along the settees people were wondering where Captain Elkanah Daniels and his daughter might be. They had not missed a service for many a day. And where was Keziah Coffin?

At the Come-Outer chapel the testifying and singing were in full blast. But Ezekiel Bassett was leading, for Captain Eben Hammond had not made his appearance. Neither had Grace Van Horne, for that matter, but Captain Eben's absence was the most astonishing.

"Somethin's the matter," whispered Josiah Badger to his right-hand neighbor. "Somethin's wrong d-d-d-down to the tavern, sartin' sure. I'm goin' down there just soon's meetin's over and f-f-f-find out. Eben wouldn't no more miss leadin' his meetin' from choice than I'd go without a meal's v-v-vi-vittles. Somethin's happened and I'm goin' to know what 'tis. You'll go along with me, won't ye, Lot?"

The answer was an affirmative. In fact, almost every worshiper in that chapel had determined to

198

visit the Hammond tavern as soon as the service was at an end.

In the Regular parsonage Keziah sat alone by the sitting-room table. Prayer meeting and supper she had forgotten entirely. The minister had not come home for his evening meal, and food was furthest from the housekeeper's thoughts. What should she do? What ought she to do? How could she avert the disaster so certain to overwhelm those two young people the moment their secret became known?

It was in vain that she tried to encourage herself with the hope that Kyan had exaggerated—that the meetings in the grove had not been as frequent as he said they were, or that they had been merely casual. She knew better. She had seen the pair together and the look in John Ellery's eyes. No, the mischief was done, they loved each other; or, at least, he loved her. There was the great trouble.

Keziah, in spite of her worldly common sense, was an idealist at heart. Love matches she believed in thoroughly. If the man had not been a Regular minister, or if he had been a minister in any other town than narrow, gossiping, squabbling Trumet, where families were divided on " religious " grounds, neighbors did not speak because their creeds were different, and even after death were buried in cemeteries three miles apart; if the girl had been other than the ward of bigoted old Eben Hammond— then, though they were poor as poverty itself, Keziah would have joined their hands and rejoiced. Even as it was, she was strongly tempted to do it. Her sense of right and her every inclination urged her toward that course. "Face the world together and fight it out," that was the advice she would like to give them. But no, the battle was too uneven. The odds were too great. They must not think of marriage, for the present, and they must cease to meet. Perhaps some day—she tried to comfort herself with the thought—perhaps some day, years afterwards and under different circumstances, they might——

With Ellery she felt certain she could accomplish nothing by argument or persuasion. She knew him well enough by this time to realize that, if his mind was made up, all Trumet and all creation could not change it. He would keep on his course, and, if wrecked, would go down with colors set and helm lashed. But Grace, perhaps she did not fully realize the situation. She might be made to see, to listen to reason. And, perhaps, it was possible—perhaps, on her part, matters were not as serious. The minister had not acted like a triumphant lover, assured of success; he had seemed, now that she thought of it, more like a pleader, a supplicant. Perhaps, if she could see Grace and talk plainly with the girl, it might not be too late. She determined to try that very night.

She rose and again donned her bonnet and shawl. She was about to blow out the lamp when she heard rapid footsteps, the sound of some one running along the sidewalk in front of the house. As she listened, the footsteps sounded on the path. Whoever the runner was he was coming to the parsonage. She stepped to the door and opened it.

The runner was a boy, Maria Higgins's boy Isaac, whose widowed mother lived down by the shore. He did the chores at the Hammond tavern. His freckled face was dripping with perspiration and he puffed and blew like a stranded whale.

"What's the matter, Ike?" demanded Keziah. "What is it?"

"Have ye—have ye," panted Ike, "have ye seen the doctor anywheres, Mis Coffin?"

"Who? Dr. Parker? Have I seen—what in the world are you comin' *here* after the doctor for?"

"'Cause—'cause I didn't know where else to come. I been to his house and he ain't to home. Nobody ain't to home. His wife, Mis Parker, she's gone up to Boston yes'day on the coach, and—and it's all dark and the house door's open and the shay's gone, so——"

"Who's sick? Who wants him?"

"And—and—all the rest of the houses round here was shut up 'cause everybody's to meetin'. I peeked in at the meetin' house and he ain't there, and I see your light and——"

"Who's sick? Tell me that, won't you?"

"Cap'n Eben. He's awful sick. I cal'late he's goin' to die, and Gracie, she——"

"Cap'n Eben? Eben Hammond! Dyin'? What are you talkin' about?"

"Huh! huh!" puffed the messenger impatiently. "Didn't I tell ye? Cap'n Eben's adyin'. I seen him. All white and still and—and awful. And Gracie, she's all alone and——"

"Alone? Where's Nat?"

"She don't know. He ain't to home. But I got to find Dr. Parker."

"Hold on! Stop! I'll tell you where the doctor is most likely. Up to Mrs. Prince's. She's been poorly and he's prob'ly been called there. Run! run fast as ever you can and get him and I'll go to Grace this minute. The poor thing! Have you told anybody else?"

"No, no! ain't seen nobody but you to tell. They was prayin' over to meetin', and the fellers that waits outside to keep comp'ny with the girls ain't got there yet. And I never met nobody. And 'twas so blasted dark I fell down four times and tore my best pants and——"

"S-sh-sh! Listen to me! Don't tell anybody. Not a soul but the doctor. Half this town'll be runnin' to find out if you do, and that poor girl must be distracted already. I'll go to her. You get Dr. Parker and tell him to hurry."

"I'll tell him; don't you fret."

He was gone, running harder than ever. A moment later Keziah followed him, running also.

It was a misty, black night, and Trumet sidewalks were uneven and hard to navigate. But she stumbled on, up the main road to the Corners, down the "Turn-off," past the chapel of the Come-Outers, from the open window of which sounded the drone of a high, nasal voice. Josiah Badger was "testifying," and Keziah caught a fragment of the testimony as she hurried by.

"I says to 'em, says I, I says to 'em, 'I don't care about your smart mum-mum-minister and what fine sermons he preaches. Let him *be* smart,' I says. Says I, 'Smartness won't g-g-g-git ye into heaven.' (*"Amen!"*) 'No, sirree! it takes more'n that. I've seen smart folks afore and they got c-c-cuk-catched up with sooner or later. Pride goes ahead of a tumble, I've heard tell, and——"

This was all that Keziah heard of Mr. Badger's testimony, for, as she ran on, a rattle of wheels and the thud of hoofs came from behind her. Then a rocking chaise, drawn by a galloping horse, shot by. Dr. Parker's carriage, she was sure. The Higgins boy must have met the doctor and delivered his message.

The horse and chaise were standing by the front gate of the tavern as she pantingly drew near it. The side door of the house was ajar and she opened it softly and entered. The dining room was empty. There was a light on the sitting-room table and low voices came from the little bedroom adjoining. Then, from the bedroom, emerged Dr. Parker and Grace Van Horne. The girl was white and there were dark circles under her eyes. The doctor was very grave.

Keziah stepped forward and held out both hands. Grace looked, recognized her, and with a cry ran toward her. Keziah took her in her arms and soothed her as if she were a child.

"There! there! deary," she said, stroking her hair. "There! there! deary, don't take it so hard. Poor thing! you're worn out. If I'd only known sooner."

"O Aunt Keziah!" sobbed the girl. "I'm so glad you've come. It was so good of you."

"Good! Land of mercy! If I hadn't come, I'd have been worse than the beasts that perish. Don't cry, don't. How is he now? Some better?"

She looked at the doctor as she asked it. He shook his head emphatically.

"Well, well, dear," went on Mrs. Coffin hurriedly. "He will be pretty soon, we'll hope. You mustn't give up the ship, you know. Now you go and lay down somewheres and I'll get my things off and see what there is to do. Some good strong tea might be good for all hands, I guess likely. Where's Hannah Poundberry?"

"She's gone to her cousin's to stay all night. I suppose I ought to send for her, but I——"

"No, no, you hadn't. Might's well send for a poll parrot, the critter would be just as much good and talk less. I'll look out for things, me and the doctor. Where's—where's Nat?"

"He came in just after I sent the boy for the doctor. He's in there with—with him," indicating the bedroom. "Poor Nat!"

Keziah looked longingly toward the door.

"Yes," she said slowly. "Poor fellow, it's an awful shock to him. He and his father are— But there! you lay down on that lounge."

"I can't lie down. I can't do anything but think. Oh, what a dreadful day this has been! And I thought it was going to be such a happy one!"

"Yes, yes, deary, I know."

Grace raised her head.

"You know?" she repeated, looking up into the housekeeper's face.

"I mean I know it's been a dreadful day," explained Keziah quickly. "Yes, indeed it has," with a sigh. "But there! our moanin' over it don't cheer it up any. Will you lay down? No? Well, then, *set* down, there's a good girl."

Grace, protesting that she couldn't sit down, she couldn't leave uncle, and there were so many things to do, was at last persuaded by Keziah and the doctor to rest for a few moments in the big rocker.

Then Mrs. Coffin went into the kitchen to prepare the tea. As she went, she beckoned to Dr. Parker, who joined her a moment later.

" Well, doctor? " she asked anxiously.

The stout, gray-haired old physician—he had practiced in Trumet for nearly thirty years—shook his head.

" Not a single chance," he whispered. " He may possibly live till morning, but I doubt if he lasts an hour. It's his heart. I've expected it at any time. Ever since he had that shock, I've been at him to take things easy; but you might as well talk to a graven image. That Come-Outer foolishness is what really killed him, though just what brought on this attack I can't make out. Grace says she found him lying on the floor by the sofa. He was unconscious then. I'm rather worried about her. She was very near to fainting when I got here."

" No wonder. All alone in this ark of a house and nobody to help or to send. Lucky she found that Ike Higgins. Say, I wonder if the young one's around here now? If he is, he must stand at the gate and scare off Come-Outers. The whole chapel, mates, crew, and cabin boy, 'll be down here soon's meetin's over to see what kept Eben. And they mustn't get in."

" I should say not. I'll hunt up Ike. If a Come-Outer gets into this house to-night I'll eat him, that's all."

" Some of 'em would give you dyspepsy, I guess. Yes, Grace, I'll be there in a jiffy."

The doctor left the house to find young Higgins and post him at the gate. The boy, who had been listening under the window, was proud of his new responsibility.

"I'll fix 'em, doctor," he declared. "I only hope old Zeke Bassett comes. He lammed me with a horsewhip t'other day, 'cause I was ridin' behind his ox cart. If he tried to git by me, I'll bounce a rock off'n his Sunday hat."

"Doctor," whispered Keziah from the kitchen window. "Doctor, come quick. Nat wants you."

Captain Nat was standing at the door of the bedroom. His face was drawn and he had seemingly grown years older since noon.

"He's come to himself, doc," he whispered. "He don't remember how it happened or anything. And he wants us all. Why! why, Keziah! are you here?"

"Yes, Nat. I've been here a little while."

He looked at her steadily and his eyes brightened just a trifle.

"Did you come to see me?" he asked. "Was it about what I said this——"

"No, no, Nat; no. I heard the news and that Grace was alone; so I come right down."

He nodded wearily.

"You can come in, too," he said. "I know dad likes you and I guess— Wait a minute; I'll ask him." He stepped back into the bedroom. "Yes," he nodded, returning, "you come, too. He wants you."

The little room, Captain Eben's own, was more like a skipper's cabin than a chamber on land. A narrow, single bed, a plain washstand, a battered, painted bureau and a single chair—these made up the list of furniture. Two pictures, both of schooners under full sail, hung on the walls. Beside them hung a ship's barometer, a sextant, and a clock that struck the " bells," instead of the hours as the landsman understands them. In the corner stood the captain's big boots and his oilskins hung above them. His Sunday cane was there also. And on the bureau was a worn, heavy Bible.

Dr. Parker brushed by the others and bent over the bed.

" Well, cap'n," he said cheerily, " how's she headed? How are you feeling now?"

The old face on the pillow smiled feebly.

" She's headed for home, I guess, doc," said Captain Eben. " Bound for home, and the harbor light broad abeam, I cal'late."

" Oh, no! you'll make a good many voyages yet."

" Not in this hulk, I won't, doctor. I hope I'll have a new command pretty soon. I'm trustin' in my owners and I guess they'll do the fair thing by me. Halloo, Gracie, girl! Well, your old uncle's on his beam ends, ain't he?"

Grace glanced fearfully at his face. When he spoke her name she shrank back, as if she feared what he might say. But he only smiled as, with the tears streaming down her face, she bent over and kissed him.

" There! there!" he protested. " You mustn't cry. What are you cryin' about me for? We know, you and me, who's been lookin' out for us and keepin' us on the course all these years. We ain't got anything to cry for. You just keep on bein' a good girl, Gracie, and goin' to the right church and— I s'pose Ezekiel'll lead in meetin' now," he added. "I do wish he was a stronger man."

The doctor, whose fingers had been upon the old man's wrist, looked up at Nat significantly.

"There, dad," said the latter, "don't you worry about Zeke Bassett, nor anything else. You just lay in dry dock and let Parker here overhaul your runnin' riggin' and get you fit for sea. That's what you've got to do."

"I'm fit and ready for the sea I'm goin' to sail," was the answer. His eyes wandered from his son to Mrs. Coffin. For an instant he seemed puzzled. Then he said:

"'Evenin', Keziah. I don't know why you're here, but——"

"I heard that Grace was alone and that you was sick, Eben. So I come right down, to help if I could."

"Thank ye. You're a good-hearted woman, Keziah, even though you ain't seen the true light yet. And you're housekeeper for that hired priest—a—a—" He paused, and a troubled look came over his face.

"What is it, dad?" asked Nat.

"I—I— Where's Gracie? She's here, ain't she?"

"Yes, uncle, I'm here. Here I am," said the girl. His fingers groped for her hand and seized it.

"Yes, yes, you're here," murmured Captain Eben. "I—I—for a minute or so, I—I had an awful dream about you, Gracie. I dreamed— Never mind. Doc, answer me this now, true and honest, man to man: Can you keep me here for

208

just a little spell longer? Can you? Try! Ten minutes, say. Can you?"

"Of course I can. Cap'n Hammond, what are you——"

"I know. That's all right. But I ain't a young one to be petted and lied to. I'm a man. I've sailed ships. I've been on blue water. I'm goin' to make port pretty soon, and I know it, but I want to get my decks clear fust, if I can. Gracie, stand still. Nat, run alongside where I can see you plainer. Keziah, you and the doctor stay where you be. I want you to witness this."

"Cap'n," protested Dr. Parker, "if I were you I wouldn't——"

"Belay! Silence there, for'ard! Nat, you're my boy, ain't you? You set some store by the old man, hey?"

"I—I guess I do, dad."

"Yes, I guess you do, too. You've been a pretty good boy; stubborn and pig-headed sometimes, but, take you by and large, pretty good. And Gracie, you've been a mighty good girl. Never done nothin' I wouldn't like, nothin' mean nor underhand nor——"

"Hush, uncle! Hush! Please hush!"

"Well, you ain't; so why should I hush? In this —this dream I had, seems 'sif you—seems as if a man come to me and said that you was— It *was* a dream, wa'n't it?"

He tried to rise. Nat and the doctor started forward. Grace shrank back.

"Of course it was, cap'n," said the doctor briskly. "Now you mustn't fret yourself in this way. Just lie still and——"

"Belay, I tell you. Yes, I guess 'twas a dream. It had to be, but 'twas so sort of real that I— How long have I been this way?"

"Oh, a little while! Now just——"

"Hush! Don't pull your hand away, Gracie. Nat, give me yours. That's it. Now I put them two hands together. See, doctor? See, Keziah?"

"He's wandering. We must stop this," muttered Parker. Mrs. Coffin, who began to comprehend what was coming, looked fearfully at Nat and the girl.

"No, I ain't wanderin', neither," declared the old Come-Outer fretfully. "I'm sane as ever I was and if you try to stop me I'll—Gracie, your Uncle Eben's v'yage is 'most over. He's almost to his moorin's and they're waitin' for him on the pier. I —I won't be long now. Just a little while, Lord! Give me just a little while to get my house in order. Gracie, I don't want to go till I know you'll be looked out for. I've spoke to Nat about this, but I ain't said much to you. Seems if I hadn't, anyhow; I ain't real sartin; my head's all full of bells ringin' and— and things."

"Don't, uncle, don't!" pleaded Grace. "Don't worry about me. Think of yourself, please."

"S-sh-sh! Don't put me off. Just listen. I want you to marry my boy, after I'm gone. I want you to say you will—say it now, so's I can hear it. Will you, Gracie?"

Grace would have withdrawn her hand, but he would not let her. He clung to it and to that of his son with all his failing strength.

"Will you, Gracie?" he begged. "It's the last

thing I'm goin' to ask of you. I've tried to be sort of good to you, in my way, and——"

"Don't, don't!" she sobbed. "Let me think a minute, uncle, dear. Oh, do let me think!"

"I ain't got time, Gracie. You'll have to say it now, or else—— All right, then, think; but think quick."

Grace was thinking. "If she really cares for him, she won't let him ruin his life." That was what Captain Elkanah had said. And here was a way to save him from ruin.

"Won't you say it for me, Gracie?" pleaded Captain Eben. She hesitated no longer.

"Yes, uncle," she answered through tears, "if Nat wants me he can have me."

Keziah clasped her hands. Captain Eben's face lit up with a great joy.

"Thank the Almighty!" he exclaimed. "Lord, I do thank you. Nat, boy, you're consider'ble older than she is and you'll have to plan for her. You be a good husband to her all her days, won't ye? Why, what are you waitin' for? Why don't you answer me?"

Nat groaned aloud.

"A minute, dad," he stammered. "Just give me a minute, for Heaven sakes! Keziah——"

"Keziah!" repeated Eben. "Keziah? What are you talkin' to *her* for? She knows there couldn't be no better match in the world. You do know it, don't ye, Keziah?"

"Yes," said Keziah slowly. "I guess—I guess you're right, Eben."

"Keziah Coffin," cried Nat Hammond, "do you tell me to marry Grace?"

"Yes, Nat, I—I think your father's right."

"Then—then—what difference does— All right, dad. Just as Grace says."

"Thank God!" cried Captain Eben. "Doctor, you and Mrs. Coffin are witnesses to this. There! now my decks are clear and I'd better get ready to land. Gracie, girl, the Good Book's over there on the bureau. Read me a chapter, won't you?"

An hour later Keziah sat alone in the dining room. She had stolen away when the reading began. Dr. Parker, walking very softly, came to her and laid his hand on her shoulder.

"He's gone," he said simply.

# CHAPTER XIII

## IN WHICH KEZIAH BREAKS THE NEWS

IT was nearly five o'clock, gray dawn of what was to be a clear, beautiful summer morning, when Keziah softly lifted the latch and entered the parsonage. All night she had been busy at the Hammond tavern. Busy with the doctor and the undertaker, who had been called from his bed by young Higgins; busy with Grace, soothing her, comforting her as best she could, and petting her as a mother might pet a stricken child. The poor girl was on the verge of prostration, and from hysterical spasms of sobs and weeping passed to stretches of silent, dry-eyed agony which were harder to witness and much more to be feared.

"It is all my fault," she repeated over and over again. "All my fault! I killed him! I killed him, Aunt Keziah! What shall I do? Oh, why couldn't I have died instead? It would have been so much better, better for everybody."

"Ss-sh! ss-sh! deary," murmured the older woman. "Don't talk so; you mustn't talk so. Your uncle was ready to go. He's been ready for ever so long, and those of us who knew how feeble he was expected it any time. 'Twa'n't your fault at all and he'd say so if he was here now."

"No, he wouldn't. He'd say just as I do, that

I was to blame. You don't know, Aunt Keziah. Nobody knows but me."

"Maybe I do, Gracie, dear; maybe I do. Maybe I understand better'n you think I do. And it's all been for the best. You'll think so, too, one of these days. It seems hard now; it is awful hard, you poor thing, but it's all for the best, I'm sure. Best for everyone. It's a mercy he went sudden and rational, same as he did. The doctor says that, if he hadn't, he'd have been helpless and bedridden and, maybe, out of his head for another year. He couldn't have lived longer'n that, at the most."

"But you *don't* know, Aunt Keziah! You don't know what I— I *am* to blame. I'll never forgive myself. And I'll never be happy again."

"Yes, you will. You'll come, some day, to think it was best and right, for you and—and for others. I know you think you'll never get over it, but you will. Somehow or other you will, same as the rest of us have had to do. The Lord tries us mighty hard sometimes, but He gives us the strength to bear it. There! there! don't, deary, don't."

Dr. Parker was very anxious.

"She must rest," he told Mrs. Coffin. "She must, or her brain will give way. I'm going to give her something to make her sleep and you must get her to take it."

So Keziah tried and, at last, Grace did take the drug. In a little while she was sleeping, uneasily and with moans and sobbings, but sleeping, nevertheless.

"Now it's your turn, Keziah," said the doctor. "You go home now and rest, yourself. We don't need you any more just now."

"Where's—where's Cap'n Nat?" asked Keziah.

" He's in there with his father. He bears it well, although he is mighty cut up. Poor chap, he seems to feel that he is to blame, somehow. Says Cap'n Eben and he had disagreed about something or other and he fears that hastened the old man's death. Nonsense, of course. It was bound to come and I told him so. 'Twas those blasted Come-Outers who really did it, although I shan't say so to anyone but you. I'm glad Nat and the girl have agreed to cruise together. It's a mighty good arrangement. She couldn't have a better man to look out for her and he couldn't have a better wife. I suppose I'm at liberty to tell people of the engagement, hey? "

" Yes. Yes, I don't see any reason why not. Yes— I guess likely you'd better tell 'em."

" All right. Now you go home. You've had a hard night, like the rest of us."

How hard he had no idea. And Keziah, as she wearily entered the parsonage, realized that the morning would be perhaps the hardest of all. For upon her rested the responsibility of seeing that the minister's secret was kept. And she, and no other, must break the news to him.

The dining room was dark and gloomy. She lighted the lamp. Then she heard a door open and Ellery's voice, as he called down the stairs.

" Who is it? " he demanded. " Mrs. Coffin? "

She was startled. " Yes," she said softly, after a moment. " Yes, Mr. Ellery, it's me. What are you doin' awake at such an hour's this? "

" Yes, I'm awake. I couldn't sleep well to-night, somehow. Too much to think of, I imagine. But where have you been? Why weren't you at meeting? And where— Why, it's almost morning! "

She did not answer at once. The temptation was to say nothing now, to put off the trying scene as long as possible.

"It's morning," repeated the minister. "Are you sick? Has anything happened?"

"Yes," she answered slowly, "somethin' has happened. Are you dressed? Could you come down?"

He replied that he would be down in a moment. When he came he found her standing by the table waiting for him. The look of her face in the lamplight shocked him.

"Why, Mrs. Coffin!" he exclaimed. "What *is* it? You look as if you had been through some dreadful experience."

"Maybe I have," she replied. "Maybe I have. Experiences like that come to us all in this life, to old folks and young, and we have to bear 'em like men and women. That's the test we're put to, Mr. Ellery, and the way we come through the fire proves the stuff we're made of. Sorrows and disappointments and heartbreaks and sicknesses and death——"

She paused on the word. He interrupted her.

"Death?" he repeated. "Death? Is some one dead, some one I know? Mrs. Coffin, what is it you are trying to tell me?"

Her heart went out to him. She held out both her hands.

"You poor boy," she cried, "I'm trying to tell you one of the hardest things a body can tell. Yes, some one is dead, but that ain't all. Eben Hammond, poor soul, is out of his troubles and gone."

"Eben Hammond! Captain Eben? Dead! Why, why——"

" Yes, Eben's gone. He was took down sudden and died about ten o'clock last night. I was there and——"

" Captain Eben dead! Why, he was as well as—' as— She said— Oh, I must go! I must go at once! "

He was on his way to the door, but she held it shut.

" No," she said gravely, " you mustn't go. You mustn't go, Mr. Ellery. That's the one thing you mustn't do."

" You don't understand. By and by I can tell you why I must be there, but now——"

" I do understand. I understand it all. Lord help us! if I'd only understood sooner, how much of this might have been spared. Why *didn't* you tell me? "

" Mrs. Coffin——"

" John—you won't mind my callin' you John. I'm old enough, pretty nigh, to be your mother, and I've come to feel almost as if I was. John, you've got to stay here with me. You can't go to that house. You can't go to her."

" Mrs. Coffin, what are you saying? Do you know— Have you——"

" Yes, I know all about it. I know about the meetin's in the pines and all. Oh, why didn't you trust me and tell me? If you had, all would have been *so* much better! "

He looked at her in utter amazement. The blood rushed to his face.

" You know *that?* " he whispered.

" Yes, I know."

" Did she tell——"

" No, nobody told. That is, only a little. I got a hint and I suspicioned somethin' afore. The rest I saw with my own eyes."

He was now white, but his jaw shot forward and his teeth closed.

" If you do know," he said, " you must realize that my place is with her. Now, when she is in trouble——"

" Would you want to make that trouble greater? More than she could bear? "

" I think I might help her to bear it. Mrs. Coffin, you have been my truest friend, but one, in Trumet. You *have* been like a mother to me. But I have thought this out to the end and I shall go through with it. It is my affair—and hers. If my own mother were alive and spoke as you do, I should still go through with it. It is right, it is my life. I'm not ashamed of anything I've done. I'm proud. I'm proud of her. And humble only when I think how unworthy I am to be her husband. I suppose you are fearful of what my congregation will say. Well, I've thought of that, too, and thought it through. Whatever they say and whatever they do will make no difference. Do you suppose I will let *them* keep me from her? Please open that door."

He was very tragic and handsome—and young, as he stood there. The tears overflowed the house-keeper's eyes as she looked at him. If her own love story had not been broken off at its beginning, if she had not thrown her life away, she might have had a son like that. She would have given all that the years had in store for her, given it gladly, to have been able to open the door and bid him go. But she was firm.

"It ain't the congregation, John," she said. "Nor Trumet, nor your ministry. That means more'n you think it does, now; but it ain't that. You mustn't go to her because—well, because she don't want you to."

"Doesn't want me? I know better." He laughed in supreme scorn.

"She doesn't want you, John. She wouldn't see you if you went. She would send you away again, sure, sartin sure. She would. And if you didn't go when she sent you, you wouldn't be the man I hope you are. John, you mustn't see Grace again. She ain't yours. She belongs to some one else."

"Some one else!" He repeated the words in a whisper. "Some one *else?* Why, Mrs. Coffin, you must be crazy! If you expect me to——"

"Hush! hush! I ain't crazy, though there's times when I wonder I ain't. John, you and Grace have known each other for a few months, that's all. You've been attracted to her because she was pretty and educated and—and sweet; and she's liked you because you were about the only young person who could understand her and—and all that. And so you've been meetin' and have come to believe—you have, anyway—that 'twas somethin' more than likin'. But you neither of you have stopped to think that a marriage between you two was as impossible as anything could be. And, besides, there's another man. A man she's known all her life and loved and respected——"

"Stop, Mrs. Coffin! stop this wicked nonsense. I won't hear it."

"John, Grace Van Horne is goin' to marry

Cap'n Nat Hammond. There! that's the livin' truth."

In his absolute confidence and faith he had again started for the door. Now he wheeled and stared at her. She nodded solemnly.

"It's the truth," she repeated. "She and Nat are promised to each other. Cap'n Eben, on his deathbed, asked Dr. Parker and me to be witnesses to the engagement. Now you see why you mustn't go nigh her again."

He did not answer. Instead, he stood silently staring. She stepped forward and laid a hand on his shoulder.

"Set down, John," she said. "Set down and let me tell you about it. Yes, yes, you must. If I tell you, you'll understand better. There! there! don't you interrupt me yet and don't you look that way. Do set down."

She led him over to the rocking-chair and gently forced him into it. He obeyed, although with no apparent realization of what he was doing. Still with her hand on his shoulder she went on speaking. She told him of her visit to the Hammond tavern, saying nothing of Mr. Pepper's call nor of her own experience in the grove. She told of Captain Eben's seizure, of what the doctor said, and of the old Come-Outer's return to consciousness. Then she described the scene in the sick room and how Nat and Grace had plighted troth. He listened, at first stunned and stolid, then with growing impatience.

"So you see," she said. "It's settled; they're engaged, and Dr. Parker will tell everybody of the engagement this very mornin'. It wa'n't any great surprise to me. Those two have been brought

"'Mrs. Coffin, stand away from that door.'"

16

up together; 'twas the natural thing that was almost bound to happen. Eben's heart was set on it for years. And she'll have a good husband, John, that I know. And she'll do her best to make him happy. He's a good man and——"

The minister sprang to his feet.

" A good man!" he cried furiously. " A good man! One who will make use of a dying father to drive a girl into— Stand aside, Mrs. Coffin!"

" John, you mustn't speak that way of Nat Hammond. He ain't the kind to drive a girl against her will. And Grace is not one to be driven."

" Are you blind? Can't you see? Why, only yesterday, she— Do you think I shall permit such a wicked crime as that to——"

" Ss-sh! No, it ain't wicked, it's right. Right and best for everybody, for her especial. Yesterday she might have forgot for a minute. But think, just think what would have happened if she cared for you."

" But she does! I know she does. Mrs. Coffin, stand away from that door."

" No, John; if you go out of that door now, to go to her, you'll have to go by main strength. You shan't wreck yourself and that girl if I can help it. Be a man."

The pair looked at each other. Keziah was determined, but so, evidently, was he. She realized, with a sinking heart, that her words had made absolutely no impression. He did not attempt to pass, but he slowly shook his head.

" Mrs. Coffin," he said, " perhaps you believe you're doing right. I hope—yes, I'll give you credit for that belief. But I *know* I am right and I shall go to her. Such a—a *bargain* as that you have just told me of is no more to be regarded than——"

" John, I beg you——"

" *No.*"

" Then go. Go this minute and break her heart and ruin her life and spoil her good name in this village where she's lived since she was eight years old. Go! be selfish. I suppose that's part of a man's make-up. Go! Never mind her. Go!"

" I do 'mind' her, as you call it. I *am* thinking of her."

" No, you're not. It's yourself."

" If it was myself—and God knows it is the only happiness on earth for me—if it was only myself, and I really thought she wished me to stay away, I'd stay, I'd stay, though I'd pray to die before this hour was over."

" I know, I know. I've prayed to die myself afore now, but I'm here yet; and so will you be. We can't die so easy."

" But I know——"

" Do you suppose *she* would come to *you* if she knew it would be your ruin?"

He hesitated. The last time they met, ages before—no, only the previous afternoon—she had told him it was his happiness and his future only that she thought of. He choked and drew his hand across his eyes.

" Mrs. Coffin," he said, " you tell me it will be her ruin. *You* tell me so. You *say* she doesn't want me. I tell you that the only thing that will keep me from her is hearing that from her own lips. When she tells me to leave her I will, and not before."

"She'll tell you, John; she'll tell you. I know you must despise me, pretty nigh. I cal'late you think I'm a worldly old woman, carin' nothin' for your feelin's. Maybe I've talked pretty hard in the last few minutes, but I haven't meant to be hard. To be honest, I didn't think you'd listen to me. I expected you'd insist on seein' her yourself. Well, then, go and see her, if you must, though what will come of it can only be more trouble, for you run the risk of folks knowin' it and beginnin' to wonder. And I know Grace. She's made up her mind and won't change it. But I do ask you this: I ask you not to go now. Wait a little while, do. I left her asleep, worn out by what she's been through and under the effects of the doctor's sleepin' medicine. He said she must rest or he was afraid her brain would give out. For her sake, then, wait a little. Then, if you don't hear from her, maybe I can arrange a meetin' place where you can see her without anyone's knowin' it. I'll try. But do wait a little while, for her sake, won't you?"

At last he was listening and hesitating.

"Won't you?" begged Keziah.

"Yes," he answered slowly. "I'll wait. I'll wait until noon, somehow, if I can. I'll try. But not a minute later. Not one. You don't know what you're asking, Mrs. Coffin."

"Yes, I do. I know well. And I thank you for her sake."

But he did not have to wait until noon. At six o'clock, through the dew-soaked grass of the yard, came the Higgins boy. For the first time in his short life he had been awake all night and he moved slowly.

The housekeeper opened the door. Ike held up an envelope, clutched in a grimy hand.

"It's for you, Mrs. Keziah," he said. "Gracie, she sent it. There ain't no answer."

Keziah took the letter. "How is she? And how's Nat?" she asked.

"They're doin' pretty well, so ma says. Ma's there now and they've sent for Hannah Poundberry. Gee!" he added, yawning, "I ain't slept a wink. Been on the jump, now I tell ye. Didn't none of them Come-Outers git in, not one. I sent 'em on the home tack abilin'. You ought to hear me give old Zeke Bassett Hail Columby! Gosh! I was just ahopin' *he'd* come."

Mrs. Coffin closed the door and tore open the envelope. Within was another addressed, in Grace's handwriting, to Mr. Ellery. The housekeeper entered the study, handed it to him and turned away.

The minister, who had been pacing the floor, seized the note eagerly. It was written in pencil and by a hand that had trembled much. Yet there was no indecision in the written words.

"Dear John," wrote Grace. "I presume Aunt Keziah has told you of uncle's death and of my promise to Nat. It is true. I am going to marry him. I am sure this is right and for the best. Our friendship was a mistake and you must not see me again. Please don't try.

"GRACE VAN HORNE."

Beneath was another paragraph.

"Don't worry about me. I shall be happy, I am

sure. And I shall hope that you may be. I shall pray for that."

The note fell to the floor with a rustle that sounded loud in the stillness. Then Keziah heard the minister's step. She turned. He was moving slowly across the room.

"John," she cried anxiously, "you poor boy!"

He answered without looking back.

"I'm—going—up—to—my—room," he said, a pause between each word. "I want to be alone awhile, Mrs. Coffin."

Wearily Keziah set about preparing breakfast. Not that she expected the meal would be eaten, but it gave her something to do and occupied her mind. The sun had risen and the light streamed in at the parsonage windows. The breeze blew fresh and cool from the ocean. It was a magnificent morning.

She called to him that breakfast was ready, but he did not answer. She could eat nothing herself, and, when the table was cleared, prepared to do the week's washing, for Monday is always washday in Trumet. Noon came, dinner time, but still he did not come down. At last Keziah could stand it no longer. She determined to go to him. She climbed the steep stairs and rapped on the door of his room.

"Yes?" she heard him say.

"It's me," was the reply. "Mr. Ellery, can I come in? I know you want to be alone, but I don't think you'd ought to be, too much. I'd like to talk with you a few minutes; may I?"

A moment passed before he told her to enter. He was sitting in a chair by the window, dressed just as he had been when she returned from the tavern.

She looked sharply at his face as it was turned toward
her. His eyes were dry and in them was an expression so hopeless and dreary that the tears started to
her own.

"John," she said, " I couldn't bear to think of
your facin' it alone up here. I just had to come."

He smiled, and the smile was as hopeless as the
look in his eyes.

"Face it?" he repeated. "Well, Mrs. Coffin,
I must face it, I suppose. I've been facing it ever
since—since I knew. And I find it no easier."

"John, what are you goin' to do?"

He shook his head. "I don't know," he said.
"Go away somewhere, first of all, I guess. Go
somewhere and—and try to live it down. I can't,
of course, but I must try."

"Go away? Leave Trumet and your church and
your congregation?"

"Did you suppose I could stay here?"

"I hoped you would."

"And see the same people and the same places?
And do the same things? See—see *her!* Did you "
—he moved impatiently—" did you expect me to
attend the wedding?"

She put out her hand. "I know it'll be hard,"
she said, "stayin' here, I mean. But your duty to
others——"

"Don't you think we've heard enough about
duty to others? How about my duty to myself?"

"I guess that's the last thing we ought to think
about in the world, if we do try to be fair and square.
Your church thinks a heap of you, John. They build
on you. You've done more in the little while you've
been here than Mr. Langley did in his last fifteen

years. We've grown and we're doin' good—doin' it, not talkin' it in prayer meetin'. The parish commit- tee likes you and the poor folks in the society love you. Old Mrs. Prince was tellin' me, only a little spell ago, that she didn't know how she'd have pulled through this dreadful time if 'twa'n't for you. And there's lots of others. Are you goin' to leave them? And what reason will you give for leavin'?"

He shook his head. "I don't know," he an- swered. "I may not give any. But I shall go."

"I don't believe you will. I don't believe you're that kind. I've watched you pretty sharp since you and I have been livin' together and I have more faith in you than that comes to. You haven't acted to me like a coward and I don't think you'll run away."

"Mrs. Coffin, it is so easy for you to talk. Per- haps if I were in your place I should be giving good advice about duty and not running away and so on. But suppose you were in mine."

"Well, suppose I was."

"Suppose— Oh, but there! it's past supposing."

"I don't know's 'tis. My life hasn't been all sunshine and fair winds, by no means."

"That's true. I beg your pardon. You have had troubles and, from what I hear, you've borne them bravely. But you haven't had to face anything like this."

"Haven't I? Well, what is it you're asked to face? Disappointment? I've faced that. Sorrow and heartbreak? I've faced them."

"You've never been asked to sit quietly by and see the one you love more than all the world marry some one else."

" How do you know I ain't? How do you know I ain't doin' just that now? "

" Mrs. Coffin! "

" John Ellery, you listen to me. You think I'm a homely old woman, probably, set in my ways as an eight-day clock. I guess I look like it and act like it. But I ain't so awful old—on the edge of forty, that's all. And when I was your age I wa'n't so awful homely, either. I had fellers aplenty hangin' round and I could have married any one of a dozen. This ain't boastin'; land knows I'm fur from that. I was brought up in this town and even when I was a girl at school there was only one boy I cared two straws about. He and I went to picnics together and to parties and everywhere. Folks used to laugh and say we was keepin' comp'ny, even then.

" Well, when I was eighteen, after father died, I went up to New Bedford to work in a store there. Wanted to earn my own way. And this young feller I'm tellin' you about went away to sea, but every time he come home from a voyage he come to see me and things went on that way till we was promised to each other. The engagement wa'n't announced, but 'twas so, just the same. We'd have been married in another year. And then we quarreled.

" 'Twas a fool quarrel, same as that kind gen'rally are. As much my fault as his and as much his as mine, I cal'late. Anyhow, we was both proud, or thought we was, and neither would give in. And he says to me, ' You'll be sorry after I'm gone. You'll wish me back then.' And says I, *bein'* a fool, ' I guess not. There's other fish in the sea.' He sailed and I did wish him back, but I wouldn't write fust and neither would he. And then come another man."

She paused, hesitated, and then continued.

"Never mind about the other man. He was handsome then, in a way, and he had money to spend, and he liked me. He wanted me to marry him. If —if the other, the one that went away, had written I never would have thought of such a thing, but he didn't write. And, my pride bein' hurt, and all, I finally said yes to the second chap. My folks did all they could to stop it; they told me he was dissipated, they said he had a bad name, they told me 'twa'n't a fit match. And his people, havin' money, was just as set against his takin' a poor girl. Both sides said ruin would come of it. But I married him.

"Well, for the first year 'twa'n't so bad. Not happiness exactly, but not misery either. That come later. His people was well off and he'd never worked much of any. He did for a little while after we was married, but not for long. Then he begun to drink and carry on and lost his place. Pretty soon he begun to neglect me and at last went off to sea afore the mast. We was poor as poverty, but I could have stood that; I did stand it. I took in sewin' and kept up an appearance, somehow. Never told a soul. His folks come patronizin' around and offered me money, so's I needn't disgrace them. I sent 'em rightabout in a hurry. Once in a while he'd come home, get tipsy and abuse me. Still I said nothin'. Thank God, there was no children; that's the one thing I've been thankful for.

"You can't keep such things quiet always. People are bound to find out. They come to me and said, 'Why don't you leave him?' but I wouldn't. I could have divorced him easy enough, there was reasons plenty, but I wouldn't do that. Then word came that he was dead, drowned off in the East Indies somewheres. I come back here to keep house for Sol, my brother, and I kept house for him till he died and they offered me this place here at the parsonage. There! that's my story, part of it, more'n I ever told a livin' soul afore, except Sol."

She ceased speaking. The minister, who had sat silent by the window, apathetically listening or trying to listen, turned his head.

"I apologize, Mrs. Coffin," he said dully, "you have had trials, hard ones. But——"

"But they ain't as hard as yours, you think? Well, I haven't quite finished yet. After word come of my husband's death, the other man come and wanted me to marry him. And I wanted to—oh, how I wanted to! I cared as much for him as I ever did; more, I guess. But I wouldn't—I wouldn't, though it wrung my heart out to say no. I give him up—why? 'cause I thought I had a duty laid on me."

Ellery sighed. "I can see but one duty," he said. "That is the duty given us by God, to marry the one we love."

Keziah's agitation, which had grown as she told her story, suddenly flashed into flame.

"Is that as fur as you can see?" she asked fiercely. "It's an easy duty, then—or looks easy now. I've got a harder one; it's to stand by the promise I gave and the man I married."

He looked at her as if he thought she had lost her wits.

" The man you married? " he replied. " Why, the man you married is dead."

" No, he ain't. You remember the letter you saw me readin' that night when you come back from Come-Outers' meetin'? Well, that letter was from him. He's alive."

For the first time during the interview the minister rose to his feet, shocked out of his despair and apathy by this astounding revelation.

" Alive? " he repeated. " Your husband *alive?* Why, Mrs. Coffin, this is——"

She waved him to silence. " Don't stop me now," she said. " I've told so much; let me tell the rest. Yes, he's alive. Alive and knockin' round the world somewheres. Every little while he writes me for money and, if I have any, I send it to him. Why? Why 'cause I'm a coward, after all, I guess, and I'm scared he'll do what he says he will and come back. Perhaps you think I'm a fool to put up with it; that's what most folks would say if they knew it. They'd tell me I ought to divorce him. Well, I can't, I *can't*. I walked into the mess blindfold; I married him in spite of warnin's and everything. I took him for better or for worse, and now that he's turned out worse, I must take my medicine. I can't live with him —that I can't do—but while *he* lives I'll stay his wife and give him what money I can spare. That's the duty I told you was laid on me, and it's a hard one, but I don't run away from it."

John Ellery was silent. What could he say? Keziah went on.

" I don't run away from it," she exclaimed, " and you mustn't run away from yours. Your church depends on you, they trust you. Are you goin' to show 'em their trust was misplaced? The girl you wanted is to marry another man, that's true, and it's mighty hard. But she'll marry a good man, and, by and by, she'll be happy."

"Happy!" he said scornfully.

"Yes, happy. I know she'll be happy because I know she's doin' what'll be best for her and because I know him that's to be her husband. I've known him all my life; he's that other one that—that—and I give him up to her; yes, I give him up to her, and try to do it cheerful, because I know it's best for him. Hard for *you?* Great Lord A'mighty! do you think it ain't hard for *me?* I—I——"

She stopped short; then covering her face with her apron, she ran from the room. John Ellery heard her descending the stairs, sobbing as she went.

All that afternoon he remained in his chair by the window. It was six o'clock, supper time, when he entered the kitchen. Keziah, looking up from the ironing board, saw him. He was white and worn and grim, but he held out his hand to her.

"Mrs. Coffin," he said, "I'm not going away. You've shown me what devotion to duty really means. I shall stay here and go on with my work."

Her face lit up. "Will you?" she said. "I thought you would. I was sure you was that kind."

## CHAPTER XIV

### IN WHICH THE SEA MIST SAILS

THEY buried Captain Eben in the little Come-Outer cemetery at the rear of the chapel. A bleak, wind-swept spot was that cemetery, bare of trees and with only a few graves and fewer headstones, for the Come-Outers were a comparatively new sect and their graveyard was new in consequence. The grave was dug in the yellow sand beside that of Mrs. Hammond, Nat's mother, and around it gathered the fifty or sixty friends who had come to pay their last tribute to the old sailor and tavern keeper.

The Come-Outers were there, all of them, and some members of the Regular society, Captain Zeb Mayo, Dr. Parker, Keziah Coffin, Mrs. Higgins, and Ike. Mrs. Didama Rogers was there also, not as a mourner, but because, in her capacity as gatherer of gossip, she made it a point never to miss a funeral. The Rev. Absalom Gott, Come-Outer exhorter at Wellmouth, preached the short sermon, and Ezekiel Bassett added a few remarks. Then a hymn was sung and it was over. The little company filed out of the cemetery, and Captain Eben Hammond was but a memory in Trumet.

Keziah lingered to speak a word with Grace. The girl, looking very white and worn, leaned on the

233

arm of Captain Nat, whose big body acted as a buffer between her and oversympathetic Come-Outers. Mrs. Coffin silently held out both hands and Grace took them eagerly.

"Thank you for coming, Aunt Keziah," she said. "I was sure you would."

"Least I could do, deary," was the older woman's answer. "Your uncle and I was good friends once; we haven't seen each other so often of late years, but that ain't changed my feelin's. Now you must go home and rest. Don't let any of these "— with a rather scornful glance at Josiah Badger and Ezekiel and the Reverend Absalom—"these Job's comforters bother you. Nat, you see that they let her alone, won't you?"

Captain Nat nodded. He, too, looked very grave and worn. "I'll tend to them," he said shortly. "Come, Grace," he added; "let's go."

But the girl hung back. "Just a minute, Nat," she said. "I—I—would you mind if I spoke to Aunt Keziah—alone? I only want to say a word."

Nat strode off to the cemetery gate, where Josiah Badger stood, brandishing a red cotton handkerchief as a not too-clean emblem of mourning. Mr. Badger eagerly sprang forward, but ran into an impossible barrier in the form of the captain's outstretched arm. Josiah protested and the captain replied. Grace leaned forward.

"Auntie," she whispered, "tell me: Did a letter— Did he——"

"Yes, it came. I gave it to him."

"Did—did he tell you? Do you know?"

"Yes, I know, deary."

"Did he—is he——"

" He's well, deary. He'll be all right. I'll look out for him."

" You will, won't you? You won't let him do anything——"

" Not a thing. Don't worry. We've had a long talk and he's going to stay right here and go on with his work. And nobody else'll ever know, Gracie."

" How—  O Aunt Keziah! how he must despise me."

" Despise you! For doin' what was your duty? Nonsense! He'll respect you for it and come to understand 'twas best for both of you, by and by. Don't worry about him, Gracie. I tell you I'll look out for him."

" I guess it will be better if he does despise me. And hate me, too. He can't despise and hate me more than I do myself. But it *is* right—what I'm doing; and the other was wrong and wicked. Auntie, you'll come and see me, won't you? I shall be so lonesome."

" Yes, yes; I'll come. Perhaps not right away. There's reasons why I'd better not come right away. But, by and by, after it's all settled and you and Nat "—she hesitated for an instant in spite of herself—" after you and Nat are married I'll come."

" Don't talk about that *now*. Please don't."

" All right, I won't. You be a good, brave girl and look out for Nat; that's your duty and I'm sure you'll do it. And I'll do my best for John."

" Do you call him John? "

" Yup. We had a sort of—of adoptin' ceremony the other mornin' and I— Well, you see, I've got to have somebody to call by their front name and he's about all I've got left."

"O Aunt Keziah! if I could be one half as patient and brave and sweet as you are——"

"Sssh! here comes Nat. Be kind to him. He's sufferin', too; maybe more'n you imagine. Here she is, Nat. Take her back home and be good to her."

The broad-shouldered skipper led his charge out of the gate and down the "Turn-off." Josiah Badger looked after them disgustedly. As Keziah approached, he turned to her.

"I swan to man!" he exclaimed, in offended indignation, "if I ain't losin' my respect for that Nat Hammond. He's the f-f-fuf-for'ardest critter ever I see. I was just agoin' to hail Gracie and ask her what she thought about my leadin' some of the meetin's now her uncle has been called aloft. I wanted to ask her about it fust, afore Zeke Bassett got ahead of me, but that Nat wouldn't let me. Told me she mustn't be b-b-b-bothered about little things now. *Little* things! Now, what do you think of that, Mrs. Coffin? And I spoke to Lot Taylor, one of our own s-s-sas-sassiety, and asked what he thought of it, and he said for me to go home set d-d-down and let my h-h-h-hah-hair grow. Of all——"

"I tell you what you do, Josiah;" broke in the voice of Captain Zeb Mayo, "you go home or somewhere else and set down and have it cut. That'll take pretty nigh as long, and'll keep it from wearin' out your coat collar. Keziah, I've been waitin' for you. Get in my shay and I'll drive you back to the parsonage."

Mrs. Coffin accepted the invitation and a seat in the chaise beside Captain Zeb. The captain spoke of the dead Come-Outer and of his respect for him

in spite of the difference in creed. He also spoke
of the Rev. John Ellery and of the affection he had
come to feel for the young man.

"I like that young feller, Keziah," he said.
"Like him for a lot of reasons, same as the boy
liked the hash. For one thing, his religion ain't all
starch and no sugar. He's good-hearted and kind
and—and human. He seems to get just as much
satisfaction out of the promise of heaven as he does
out of the sartainty of t'other port. He ain't all the
time bangin' the bulkhead and sniffin' brimstone,
like parsons I have seen. Sulphur's all right for a
spring medicine, maybe, but when June comes I like
to remember that God made roses. Elkanah, he
comes to me a while ago and he says, 'Zebedee,' he
says, 'don't you think Mr. Ellery's sermons might
be more orthodox?' 'Yes,' says I, 'they might be,
but what a mercy 'tis they ain't.' He, he, he! I kind
of like to poke Elkanah in the shirt front once in a
while, just to hear it crackle. Say, Keziah, you don't
think the minister and Annabel are——"

"No," was the emphatic interruption; "I know
they ain't; he ain't, anyway."

"Good! Them Danielses cal'late they own the
most of this town already; if they owned the minister
they'd swell up so the rest of us would have to go
aloft or overboard; we'd be crowded off the decks,
sure."

"No one owns him. Haven't you found that
out?"

"Yup, I cal'late I have and I glory in his
spunk."

"I'm glad to hear you say so. Of course Cap'n
Elkanah is boss of the parish committee and——"

"What? No, he ain't nuther. He's head of it, but his vote counts just one and no more. What makes you say that?"

"Oh, nuthin'. Only I thought maybe, long as Elkanah was feelin' that Mr. Ellery wa'n't orthodox enough, he might be goin' to make a change."

"He might? *He* might! Say, Keziah Coffin, there was Mayos in this town and in this church afore the fust Daniels ever washed ashore; and they'll be here when the last one blows up with his own importance. I'm on that parish committee—you understand?—and I've sailed ships and handled crews. I ain't so old nor feeble but what I can swing a belayin' pin. Boss! I'll have you to know that no livin' man bosses me."

"All right! I didn't mean to stir you up, Zebedee. But from things Cap'n Daniels has said I gathered that he was runnin' the committee. And, as I'm a friend of Mr. Ellery, it——"

"Friend! Well, so'm I, ain't I? If you ever hear of Daniels tryin' any tricks against the minister, you send for me, that's all. *I'll* show him. Boss! Humph!"

The wily Keziah alighted at the parsonage gate with the feeling that she had sown seed in fertile ground. She was quite aware of Captain Zeb's jealousy of the great Daniels. And the time might come when her parson needed an influential friend on the committee and in the Regular society.

The news of the engagement between Captain Nat Hammond and Grace Van Horne, told by Dr. Parker to one or two of his patients, spread through Trumet like measles through a family of small children. Didama Rogers learned it, so did Lavinia Pepper, and after that it might as well have been printed on the walls for all to read. It was talked over and gossiped about in every household from the lighthouse keeper's family to that of George Washington Cash, who lived in the one-room hovel in the woods near the Wellmouth line, and was a person of distinction, in his way, being the sole negro in the county. And whenever it was discussed it was considered a fine thing for both parties concerned. Almost everyone said it was precisely what they expected.

Annabel Daniels and her father had not expected it. They were, however, greatly pleased. In their discussion, which lasted far into the night, Captain Elkanah expressed the opinion that the unexpected dénouement was the result of his interview with Eben. He had told the old Come-Outer what would happen to his ward if she persisted in her impudent and audacious plot to entrap a Regular clergyman. She, being discovered, had yielded, perforce, and had accepted Nat as the next best catch.

Annabel was not satisfied with this explanation. Of course, she said, she did not pretend to believe Grace's statement that she had found her uncle unconscious. No doubt the pair had had an interview and all that. But she believed the minister himself had come to his senses and had dismissed the brazen creature. She did not blame Mr. Ellery so much. He was a young man, with a kind heart, and no doubt the "Van Horne person" had worked upon his sympathies and had taken advantage of his inexperience of feminine wiles.

"*I* think, pa," she said, "that it's our duty, yours

and mine, to treat him just as we always have. He doesn't know that we know, and we will keep the secret. And, as Christians, we should forget and forgive. We'll invite him here as we always have, keep him under our good influence, and be very kind to him, poor innocent. As for Captain Hammond, I'm sorry for him, knowing the kind of wife he is going to have, but no doubt Come-Outers are not particular."

Kyan Pepper was another whom the news of the engagement surprised greatly. When Lavinia told him of it, at the dinner table, he dropped the knife he was holding and the greasy section of fish-ball balanced upon it.

" 'Bishy," said Miss Pepper, "what do you s'pose has happened down to the Hammond tavern?"

"Oh, I know that," was the reply. "I heard that long ago; Cap'n Eben's dead."

" 'Course he's dead; and I knew you knew it. Land sakes! don't be such a ninny. Why, I told you myself."

"Well, I didn't know but you'd forgot. Anybody's li'ble to forget who they've told things to. Why, I've forgot more things——"

"Yes, there ain't no doubt about that. I've told you a million times, if I have once, to tuck your napkin round your neck when you've got your Sunday clothes on. And there you be this minute without a sign of a napkin."

"Why, Laviny! I *must* have it round my neck. I know I——"

"Don't be so foolish! Think I'm blind? Can't I see you ain't got it? Now where is it?"

Kyan began a futile hunt for the missing napkin, in his lap, on the table, and finally under it.

" I don't understand," he stammered, " where that napkin can be. I'm just as sure I had it and now I'm just as sure I ain't got it. What do you s'pose I done with it? "

" Goodness knows! 'Twouldn't surprise me if you'd et it, you're that absent-minded. Here! what's that stickin' out of your breast pocket? "

Her brother put his hand to the pocket indicated and produced the missing napkin, much crumpled.

" There! " he exclaimed, in a tone of relief. " Now I remember. It must have dropped on the floor and I thought 'twas my handkerchief and picked it up and——"

" What did you think you'd be carryin' a white handkerchief for, on a week day? "

" Well, I had on my Sunday suit and——"

" Yes, and for the dear mercy sakes *why* have you got it on? "

Kyan saw an opportunity for self-justification.

" You *told* me to put it on," he declared triumphantly. " You said yourself I'd better rig out in my Sunday clothes 'cause we might go to Eben's funeral. You know you did."

" Hear the man! And then, after you've dressed up to go to his funeral, you pretend to believe I'm goin' to tell you he's dead. I never——"

" Well, what *is* it, then? He ain't come to life, has he? "

" Grace Van Horne's engaged to be married, that's what it is. Look out! Oh, you——"

Just here occurred the accident already described. Knife and fish ball descended upon the waistcoat belonging to the "Sunday suit." Lavinia flew for warm water, ammonia, and a cloth, and the soiled waistcoat was industriously scrubbed. The cleansing process was accompanied by a lively tongue lashing, to which Kyan paid little attention.

"Engaged?" he kept repeating. "Gracie Van Horne engaged? Engaged? En——"

"Be still, you poll parrot! Dear! dear! dear! look at them spots. Yes, yes; don't say it again; she's engaged."

"Who—who—who——"

"Now you've turned to an owl, I do believe. 'Hoo! hoo!' She's engaged to Nat Hammond, that's who. Nothin' very surprisin' about that, is there?"

Kyan made no answer. He rubbed his forehead, while his sister rubbed the grease spots. In jerky sentences she told of the engagement and how the news had reached her.

"I can't believe it," faltered Abishai. "She goin' to marry Nat! Why, I can't understand. I thought——"

"What did you think? See here! you ain't keepin' anything from me, be you?"

The answer was enthusiastically emphatic.

"No, no, no, no!" declared Kyan. "Only I didn't know they was—was——"

"Neither did anybody else, but what of it? Folks don't usually advertise when they're keepin' comp'ny, do they?"

"No—o. But it's gen'rally found out. I know if I was keepin' comp'ny—or you was, Laviny——"

His sister started.

"What makes you say that?" she demanded, looking quickly up from her rubbing.

"Why, nothin'. Only if I was—or you was, somebody'd see somethin' suspicious and kind of drop a hint, and——"

"Better for them if they 'tended to their own affairs," was the sharp answer. "I ain't got any patience with folks that's always talkin' about their neighbor's doin's. There! now you go out and stand alongside the cook stove till that wet place dries. Don't you move till 'tis dry, neither."

So to the kitchen went Kyan, to stand, a sort of living clotheshorse, beside the hot range. But during the drying process he rubbed his forehead many times. Remembering what he had seen in the grove he could not understand; but he also remembered, even more vividly, what Keziah Coffin had promised to do if he ever breathed a word. And he vowed again that that word should not be breathed.

The death and funeral of Captain Eben furnished Trumet with a subject of conversation for a week or more. Then, at the sewing circle and at the store and after prayer meeting, both at the Regular meeting house and the Come-Outer chapel, speculation centered on the marriage of Nat and Grace. When was it to take place? Would the couple live at the old house and "keep packet tavern" or would the captain go to sea again, taking his bride with him? Various opinions, pro and con, were expressed by the speculators, but no one could answer authoritatively, because none knew except those most interested, and the latter would not tell.

John Ellery heard the discussions at the sewing circle when, in company with some of the men of his congregation, he dropped in at these gatherings for tea after the sewing was over. He heard them at church, before and after the morning service, and when he made pastoral calls. People even asked his opinion, and when he changed the subject inferred, some of them, that he did not care about the doings of Come-Outers. Then they switched to inquiries concerning his health.

"You look awful peaked lately, Mr. Ellery," said Didama Rogers. "Ain't you feelin' well?"

The minister answered that he was as well as usual, or thought he was.

"No, no, you ain't nuther," declared Didama. "You look's if you was comin' down with a spell of somethin'. I ain't the only one that's noticed it. Why, Thankful Payne says to me only yesterday, 'Didama,' says she, 'the minister's got somethin' on his mind and it's wearin' of him out.' You ain't got nothin' on your mind, have you, Mr. Ellery?"

"I guess not, Mrs. Rogers. It's a beautiful afternoon, isn't it?"

"There! I knew you wa'n't well. A beautiful afternoon, and it hotter'n furyation and gettin' ready to rain at that! Don't tell me! 'Tain't your mind, Mr. Ellery, it's your blood that's gettin' thin. My husband had a spell just like it a year or two afore he died, and the doctor said he needed rest and a change. Said he'd ought to go away somewheres by himself. I put my foot down on *that* in a hurry. 'The idea!' I says. 'You, a sick man, goin' off all alone by yourself to die of lonesomeness. If you go, I go with you.' So him and me went up to Boston and it rained the whole week we was there, and we set in a little box of a hotel room with a window that looked out at a brick wall, and set and set and set, and that's all. I kept talkin' to him to cheer him up, but he never cheered. I'd talk to him for an hour steady and when I'd stop and ask a question he'd only groan and say yes, when he meant no. Finally, I got disgusted, after I'd asked him somethin' four or five times and he'd never answered, and I told him I believed he was gettin' deef. 'Lordy!' he says, 'I wish I was!' Well, that was enough for *me*. Says I, 'If your mind's goin' to give out we'd better be home.' So home we come. And that's all the good change and rest done *him*. Hey? What did you say, Mr. Ellery?"

"Er—oh, nothing, nothing, Mrs. Rogers."

"Yes. So home we come and I'd had enough of doctors to last. I figgered out that his blood was thinnin' and I knew what was good for that. My great Aunt Hepsy, that lived over to East Well-mouth, she was a great hand for herbs and such and she'd give me a receipt for thickenin' the blood that was somethin' wonderful. It had more kind of healin' herbs in it than you could shake a stick at. I cooked a kittleful and got him to take a dose four times a day. He made more fuss than a young one about takin' it. Said it tasted like the Evil One, and such profane talk, and that it stuck to his mouth so's he couldn't relish his vittles; but I never let up a mite. He had to take it and it done him a world of good. Now I've got that receipt yet, Mr. Ellery, and I'll make some of that medicine for you. I'll fetch it down to-morrow. Yes, yes, I will. I'm agoin' to, so you needn't say no. And perhaps I'll have heard somethin' about Cap'n Nat and Grace by that time."

She brought the medicine, and the minister promptly, on her departure, handed it over to Keziah, who disposed of it just as promptly.

"What did I do with it?" repeated the housekeeper. "Well, I'll tell you. I was kind of curious to see what 'twas like, so I took a teaspoonful. I did intend to pour the rest of it out in the henyard, but after that taste I had too much regard for the hens. So I carried it way down to the pond and threw it in, jug and all. B-r-r-r! Of all the messes that—I used to wonder what made Josh Rogers go moonin' round makin' his lips go as if he was crazy. I thought he was talkin' to himself, but now I know better, he was *tastin'*. B-r-r-r!"

Keziah was the life of the gloomy parsonage. Without her the minister would have broken down. Time and time again he was tempted to give up, in spite of his promise, and leave Trumet, but her pluck and courage made him ashamed of himself and he stayed to fight it out. She watched him and tended him and "babied" him as if he was a spoiled child, pretending to laugh at herself for doing it and at him for permitting it. She cooked the dishes he liked best, she mended his clothes, she acted as a buffer between him and callers who came at inopportune times. She was cheerful always when he was about, and no one would have surmised that she had a sorrow in the world. But Ellery knew and she knew he knew, so the affection and mutual esteem between the two deepened. He called her "Aunt Keziah" at her request and she continued to call him "John." This was in private, of course; in public he was "Mr. Ellery" and she "Mrs. Coffin."

In his walks about town he saw nothing of Grace.

She and Mrs. Poundberry and Captain Nat were still at the old home and no one save themselves knew what their plans might be. Yet, oddly enough, Ellery was the first outsider to learn these plans and that from Nat himself.

He met the captain at the corner of the " Turn-off " one day late in August. He tried to make his bow seem cordial, but was painfully aware that it was not. Nat, however, seemed not to notice, but crossed the road and held out his hand.

"How are you, Mr. Ellery?" he said. "I haven't run across you for sometime. What's the matter? Seems to me you look rather under the weather."

Ellery answered that he was all right and, remembering that he had not met the captain since old Hammond's death, briefly expressed his sympathy. His words were perfunctory and his manner cold. His reason told him that this man was not to blame —was rather to be pitied, if Keziah's tale was true. Yet it is hard to pity the one who is to marry the girl you love. Reason has little to do with such matters.

"Well, Mr. Ellery," said Captain Nat, " I won't keep you. I see you're in a hurry. Just thought I'd run alongside a minute and say good-by. Don't know's I'll see you again afore I sail."

"Before you sail? You—you are going away?"

"Yup. My owners have been after me for a good while, but I wouldn't leave home on account of dad's health. Now he's gone, I've got to be gettin' back on salt water again. My ship's been drydocked and overhauled and she's in New York now loadin' for Manila. It's a long vy'age, even if I come back direct, which ain't likely. So I may not see the old town again for a couple of years. Take care of yourself, won't you? Good men, especially ministers, are scurse, and from what I hear about you I cal'late Trumet needs you."

"When are you going?"

"Last of next week, most likely."

"Will you—shall you go alone? Are you to be —to be——"

"Married? No. Grace and I have talked it over and we've agreed it's best to wait till I come back. You see, dad's been dead such a little while, and all, that—well, we're goin' to wait, anyhow. She'll stay in the old house with Hannah, and I've fixed things so she'll be provided for while I'm gone. I left it pretty much to her. If she'd thought it best for us to marry now, I cal'late I should have—have —well, done what she wanted. But she didn't. Ah, hum!" he added with a sigh; "she's a good girl, a mighty good girl. Well, so long and good luck."

"Good-by, captain."

"Good-by. Er — I say, Mr. Ellery, how's things at the parsonage? All well there, are you?"

"Yes."

"Er—Keziah—Mrs. Coffin, your housekeeper, is she smart?"

"Yes. She's well."

"That's good. Say, you might tell her good-by for me, if you want to. Tell her I wished her all the luck there was. And—and—just say that there ain't any—well, that her friend—say just that, will you? —her *friend* said 'twas all right. She'll understand; it's a—a sort of joke between us."

"Very good, captain; I'll tell her."

"Much obliged. And just ask her to keep an

eye on Grace while I'm gone. Tell her I leave
Gracie under her wing. Keziah and me are old
chums, in a way, you see."

"Yes. I'll tell her that, too."

"And don't forget the ' friend ' part. Well, so
long."

They shook hands and parted.

Didama and her fellow news-venders distributed
the tale of Captain Nat's sailing broadcast during
the next few days. There was much wonderment
at the delayed marriage, but the general verdict was
that Captain Eben's recent death and the proper respect due to it furnished sufficient excuse. Hannah
Poundberry, delighted at being so close to the center
of interest, talked and talked, and thus Grace was
spared the interviews which would have been a
trouble to her. Nat left town, via the packet, on the
following Wednesday. Within another week came
the news that his ship, the *Sea Mist*, had sailed from
New York, bound for Manila. Her topsails sank
beneath the horizon and she vanished upon the wild
waste of tumbling waves and out of Trumet's knowl-
edge, as many another vessel, manned and officered
by Cape Cod men, had done. The village talked of
her and her commander for a few days and then forgot them both. Only at the old home by the landing
and at the parsonage were they remembered.

# CHAPTER XV

## IN WHICH TRUMET TALKS OF CAPTAIN NAT

SUMMER was over, autumn came, passed, and it was winter—John Ellery's first winter in Trumet. Fish weirs were taken up, the bay filled with ice, the packet ceased to run, and the village settled down to hibernate until spring. The stage came through on its regular trips, except when snow or slush rendered the roads impassable, but passengers were very few. Occasionally there were northeast gales, with shrieking winds, driving gusts of sleet and hail and a surf along the ocean side that bellowed and roared and tore the sandy beach into new shapes, washing away shoals and building others, blocking the mouth of the little inlet where the fish boats anchored and opening a new channel a hundred yards farther down. Twice there were wrecks, one of a fishing schooner, the crew of which were fortunate enough to escape by taking to the dories, and another, a British bark, which struck on the farthest bar and was beaten to pieces by the great waves, while the townspeople stood helplessly watching from the shore, for launching a boat in that surf was impossible.

The minister was one of those who watched. News of the disaster had been brought to the village by the lightkeeper's assistant, and Ellery and most of the able-bodied men in town had tramped the three miles to the beach, facing the screaming wind and the cutting blasts of flying sand. As they came over the dunes there were times when they had to dig their heels into the ground and bend forward to stand against the freezing gale. And, as they drew nearer, the thunder of the mighty surf grew ever louder, until they saw the white clouds of spray leap high above the crazily tossing, flapping bunches of beach grass that topped the last knoll.

Three masts and a broken bowsprit sticking slantwise up from a whirl of creamy white, that was all they could see of the bark, at first glance. But occasionally, as the breakers drew back for another cruel blow, they caught glimpses of the tilted deck, smashed bare of houses and rail.

"Those black things on the masts?" asked Ellery, bending to scream the question into the ear of Gaius Winslow, his companion. "Are they—it can't be possible that they're——"

"Yup," shrieked Gaius in reply, "they're men. Crew lashed in the riggin'. Poor fellers! it'll soon be over for 'em. And they're most likely frozen stiff a'ready and won't sense drownin', that's a comfort."

"Men!" repeated the minister in horror. "Men! Great God! and are we to stand by here and see them die without lifting a hand? Why, it's barbarous! It's——"

Winslow seized his arm and pointed.

"Look!" he shouted. "Look at them! How much good would our liftin' hands do against them?"

Ellery looked. The undertow, that second, was sucking the beach dry, sucking with such force that

18                    251

gravel and small stones pattered down the slope in showers. And behind it a wave, its ragged top raveled by the wind into white streamers, was piling up, up, up, sheer and green and mighty, curling over now and descending with a hammer blow that shook the land beneath their feet. And back of it reared another, and another, and another, an eighth of a mile of whirling, surging, terrific breakers, with a yelling hurricane whipping them on.

It was soon over, as Gaius had said it would be. A mighty leap of spray, a section of hull broken off and tossed into view for an instant, then two of the masts went down. The other followed almost at once. Then the watchers, most of them, went back to the village, saying little or nothing and dispersing silently to their homes.

During the next fortnight John Ellery conducted six funeral services, brief prayers beside the graves of unknown men from that wreck. The bodies, as they were washed ashore, were put into plain coffins paid for by the board of selectmen, and buried in the corner of the Regular cemetery beside other waifs thrown up by the sea in other years. It was a sad experience for him, but it was an experience and tended to make him forget his own sorrow just a little. Or, if not to forget, at least to think of and sympathize more keenly with the sorrows of others. Somewhere, in England or Ireland or scattered over the wide world, there were women and children waiting for these men, waiting anxiously for news of their safe arrival in port, praying for them. When he mentioned this thought to the townspeople they nodded philosophically and said yes, they "presumed likely." As Captain Zeb put it, "Most sailors are fools enough to get married, prob'ly this lot wa'n't any exception." It was no new thought to him or to any other dweller in that region. It was almost a fixed certainty that, if you went to sea long enough, you were bound to be wrecked sometime or other. The chances were that, with ordinary luck and good management, you would escape with your life. Luck, good or bad, was the risk of the trade; good management was expected, as a matter of course.

Mr. Pepper made no more calls at the parsonage, and when the minister met him, at church or elsewhere, seemed anxious to avoid an interview.

"Well, Abishai," asked Ellery, on one of these occasions, "how are you getting on at home? Has your sister locked you up again?"

"No, sir, she ain't," replied Kyan. "Laviny, she's sort of diff'rent lately. She ain't nigh so—so down on a feller as she used to be. I can get out once in a while by myself nowadays, when she wants to write a letter or somethin'."

"Oh, she's writing letters, is she?"

"Um—hm. Writes one about every once in a week. I don't know who they're to, nuther, but I have my suspicions. You see, we've got a cousin out West—out Pennsylvany way—and he ain't very well and has got a turrible lot of money. I'm sort of surmisin' that Laviny's writin' to him. We're about his only relations that's left alive and—and so——"

"I see." The minister smiled.

"Yup. Laviny's a pretty good navigator, fur's keepin' an eye to wind'ard is concerned. She was awful down on Phineas—that's his name—'cause he married a Philadelphy woman, but he's a widower man now, so I s'pose she feels better toward him. She's talkin' of goin' up to Sandwich pretty soon."

"She *is?* Alone?"

"So she says."

"To leave you here? Why! well, I'm surprised."

"Godfreys mighty! so be I. But she says she b'lieves she needs a change and there's church conference up there, you know, and she figgers that she ain't been to conference she don't know when. I s'pose you'll go, won't you, Mr. Ellery?"

"Probably."

"Um——hm. I kind of wisht I was goin' myself. 'Twill be kind of lonesome round home without her."

Considering that that variety of lonesomeness had been Abishai's dream of paradise for years, Ellery thought his change of heart a good joke and told Keziah of it when he returned to the parsonage. The housekeeper was greatly surprised.

"Well! well! well!" she exclaimed. "Miracles'll never cease. I don't wonder so much at Laviny wantin' to go to conference, but her darin' to go and leave Kyan at home is past belief. Why, every time she's had a cold her one fear was that she'd die and leave 'Bish behind to be kidnaped by some woman. Kyan himself was sick once, and the story was that his sister set side of the bed night and day and read him over and over again that chapter in the Bible that says there's no marryin' or givin' in marriage in heaven. Dr. Parker told me that he didn't believe 'Bish got ha'f the comfort out of that passage that she did. And now she's goin' to Sandwich and leave him. I can't think it's true."

But it was true, and Lavinia got herself elected a delegate and went, in company with Captain El-kanah, Mrs. Mayo, and others, to the conference. She was a faithful attendant at the meetings and seemed to be having a very good time. She intro-duced the minister to one Caleb Pratt, a resident of Sandwich, whom she said she had known ever since she was a girl.

" Mr. Pratt's a cousin to Thankful Payne over to home," volunteered Lavinia. " You know Thank-ful, Mr. Ellery."

Ellery did know Mrs. Payne and said so. Mr. Pratt, who was dressed in a new suit of black which appeared to hurt him, imparted the information that he'd heard tell consider'ble of Mr. Ellery.

" I enjoyed your sermon to-night fust—rate," he added solemnly. " Fust—rate, sir—yes."

" Did you, indeed? I'm glad."

" Yes, sir. You used words in that sermon that I never heard afore in my life. 'Twas grand."

Lavinia confided to her pastor that Mr. Pratt made the best shoes in Ostable County. He could fit *any* kind of feet, she declared, and the minister ought to try him sometime. She added that he had money in the bank.

The Reverend John rode home in the stage beside Miss Annabel, not from choice, but because the young lady's father insisted upon it. Miss Daniels gushed and enthused as she always did. As they drove by the Corners the minister, who had been replying absently to Annabel's questions, suddenly stopped short in the middle of a sentence. His companion, leaning forward to look out of the win-dow, saw Grace Van Horne entering the store. For an instant Annabel's face wore a very unpleasant expression. Then she smiled and said, in her sweetest manner:

"Why, there's the tavern girl! I haven't seen her for sometime. How old she looks! I suppose her uncle's death has aged her. Well, she'll be married soon, just as soon as Cap'n Nat gets back. They perfectly worship each other, those two. They say she writes him the longest letters. Hannah Poundberry told me. Hannah's a queer creature and common, but devoted to the Hammonds, Mr. Ellery. However, you're not interested in Come-Outers, are you? Ha, ha!"

Ellery made some sort of an answer, but he could not have told what it was. The sight of Grace had brought back all that he was trying so hard to forget. Why couldn't one forget, when it was so painful— and so useless—to remember?

Spring once more; then summer. And now people were again speaking of Captain Nat Hammond. His ship was overdue, long overdue. Even in those days, when there were no cables and the telegraph was still something of a novelty, word of his arrival should have reached Trumet months before this. But it had not come, and did not. Before the summer was over, the wise heads of the retired skippers were shaking dubiously. Something had happened to the *Sea Mist*, something serious.

As the weeks and months went by without news of the missing vessel, this belief became almost a certainty. At the Come-Outer chapel, where Ezekiel Bassett now presided, prayers were offered for the son of their former leader. These prayers were not as fervent as they might have been, for Grace's nonattendance at meetings was causing much comment and a good deal of resentment. She came occasionally, but not often. "I always said she was stuck-up and thought she was too good for the rest of us," remarked "Sukey B." spitefully. "'And, between you and me, pa says he thinks Nat Hammond would be one to uphold her in it. He wa'n't a bit spirituous and never experienced religion. If anything *has* happened to him, it's a punishment sent, that's what pa thinks."

Those were gloomy days at the parsonage. Keziah said little concerning the topic of which all the village was talking, and John Ellery forebore to mention it. The housekeeper was as faithful as ever in the performance of her household duties, but her smile had gone and she was worn and anxious. The minister longed to express his sympathy, but Keziah had not mentioned Nat's name for months, not since he, Ellery, gave her the message intrusted to him by the captain before sailing. He would have liked to ask about Grace, for he knew Mrs. Coffin visited the Hammond home occasionally, but this, too, he hesitated to do. He heard from others that the girl was bearing the suspense bravely, that she refused to give up hope, and was winning the respect of all the thinking class in Trumet by her courage and patience. Even the most bigoted of the Regulars, Captain Daniels and his daughter excepted of course, had come to speak highly of her. "She's a spunky girl," declared Captain Zeb, with emphasis. "There's nothing of the milk-sop and cry-baby about her. Shes fit to be a sailor's wife, and I only hope Nat's alive to come back and marry her. He was a dum good feller, too—savin' your presence,

Mr. Ellery—and if he was forty times a Come-Outer I'd say the same thing. I'm 'fraid he's gone, though, poor chap. As good a seaman as he was would have fetched port afore this if he was atop of water. As for Gracie, she's a brick, and a lady, every inch of her. My old girl went down t'other day to call on her and that's the fust Come-Outer she's been to see sence there was any. Why don't you go see her, too, Mr. Ellery? 'Twould be a welcome change from Zeke Bassett and his tribe. Go ahead! it would be the Almighty's own work and the society'd stand back of you, all them that's wuth considerin', anyhow."

This was surprising advice from a member of the Regular and was indicative of the changed feeling in the community, but the minister, of course, could not take it. He had plunged headlong into his church work, hoping that it and time would dull the pain of his terrible shock and disappointment. It had been dulled somewhat, but it was still there, and every mention of her name revived it.

One afternoon Keziah came into his study, where he was laboring with his next Sunday sermon, and sat down in the rocking-chair. She had been out and still wore her bonnet and shawl.

"John," she said, "I ask your pardon for disturbin' you. I know you're busy."

Ellery laid down his pen. "Never too busy to talk with you, Aunt Keziah," he observed. "What is it?"

"I wanted to ask if you knew Mrs. Prince was sick?"

"No. Is she? I'm awfully sorry. Nothing serious, I hope?"

"No, I guess not. Only she's got a cold and is

kind of under the weather. I thought p'r'aps you'd like to run up and see her. She thinks the world and all of you, 'cause you was so good when she was distressed about her son. Poor old thing! she's had a hard time of it."

"I will go. I ought to go, of course. I'm glad you reminded me of it."

"Yes. I told her you hadn't meant to neglect her, but you'd been busy fussin' with the fair and the like of that."

"That was all. I'll go right away. Have you been there to-day?"

"No. I just heard that she was ailin' from Didama Rogers. Didama said she was all but dyin', so I knew she prob'ly had a little cold, or somethin'. If she was really very bad, Di would have had her buried by this time, so's to be sure her news was ahead of anybody else's. I ain't been up there, but I met her t'other mornin'."

"Didama?"

"No; Mrs. Prince. She'd come down to see Grace."

"Oh."

"Yes. The old lady's been awful kind and sympathizin' since—since this new trouble. It reminds her of the loss of her own boy, I presume likely, and so she feels for Grace. John, what do they say around town about—about *him?*"

"Captain Hammond?"

"Yes."

The minister hesitated. Keziah did not wait for him to answer.

"I see," she said slowly. "Do they all feel that way?"

"Why, if you mean that they've all given up hope, I should hardly say that. Captain Mayo and Captain Daniels were speaking of it in my hearing the other day and they agreed that there was still a chance."

"A pretty slim one, though, they cal'lated, didn't they?"

"Well, they were—were doubtful, of course. There was the possibility that he had been wrecked somewhere and hadn't been picked up. They cited several such cases. The South Pacific is full of islands where vessels seldom touch, and he and his crew may be on one of these."

"Yes. They might, but I'm afraid not. Ah, hum!"

She rose and was turning away. Ellery rose also and laid his hand on her arm.

"Aunt Keziah," he said, "I'm very sorry. I respected Captain Hammond, in spite of—of—in spite of everything. I've tried to realize that he was not to blame. He was a good man and I haven't forgotten that he saved my life that morning on the flats. And I'm so sorry for *you*."

She did not look at him.

"John," she answered, with a sigh, "sometimes I think you'd better get another housekeeper."

"What? Are you going to leave me? *You?*"

"Oh, 'twouldn't be because I wanted to. But it seems almost as if there was a kind of fate hangin' over me and that," she smiled faintly, "as if 'twas sort of catchin', as you might say. Everybody I ever cared for has had somethin' happen to 'em. My brother died; my—the man I married went to the dogs; then you and Grace had to be miserable

and I had to help make you so; I sent Nat away and
he blamed me and———"

"No, no. He didn't blame you. He sent you
word that he didn't."

"Yes, but he did, all the same. He must have.
I should if I'd been in his place. And now he's dead,
and won't ever understand—on this earth, anyhow.
I guess I'd better clear out and leave you afore I
spoil your life."

"Aunt Keziah, you're my anchor to windward,
as they say down here. If I lost you, goodness knows
where I should drift. Don't you ever talk of leaving
me again."

"Thank you, John. I'm glad you want me to
stay. I won't leave yet awhile; never—unless I have
to."

"Why should you ever have to?"

"Well, I don't know. Yes, I do know, too.
John, I had another letter t'other day."

"You did? From—from that man?"

"Yup, from— " For a moment it seemed as if
she were about to pronounce her husband's name,
something she had never done in his presence; but
if she thought of it, she changed her mind.

"From him," she said. "He wanted money, of
course; he always does. But that wa'n't the worst.
The letter was from England, and in it he wrote that
he was gettin' sick of knockin' around and guessed
he'd be for comin' to the States pretty soon and
huntin' me up. Said what was the use of havin' an
able-bodied wife if she couldn't give her husband
a home."

"The scoundrel!"

"Yes, I know what he is, maybe full as well as

you do. That's why I spoke of leavin' you. If that man comes to Trumet, I'll go, sure as death."

"No, no. Aunt Keziah, you must free yourself from him. No power on earth can compel you to longer support such a———"

"None on earth, no. But it's my punishment and I've got to put up with it. I married him with my eyes wide open, done it to spite the—the other, as much as anything, and I must bear the burden. But I tell you this, John: if he comes here, to this town, where I've been respected and considered a decent woman, if he comes here, I go—somewhere, *any*where that'll be out of the sight of them that know me. And wherever I go he shan't be with me. *That* I won't stand! I'd rather die, and I hope I do. Don't talk to me any more now—don't! I can't stand it."

She hurried out of the room. Later, as the minister passed through the dining room on his way to the door, she spoke to him again.

"John," she said, "I didn't say what I meant to when I broke in on you just now. I meant to tell you about Grace. I knew you'd like to know and wouldn't ask. She's bearin' up well, poor girl. She thought the world of Nat, even though she might not have loved him in the way that———"

"What's that? What are you saying, Aunt Keziah?"

"I mean—well, I mean that he'd always been like an own brother to her and she cared a lot for him."

"But you said she didn't love him."

"Did I? That was a slip of the tongue, maybe. But she bears it well and I don't think she gives up hope. I try not to, for her sake, and I try not to show her how I feel."

She sewed vigorously for a few moments. Then she said:

"She's goin' away, Gracie is."

"Going away?"

"Yup. She's goin' to stay with a relation of the Hammonds over in Connecticut for a spell. I coaxed her into it. Stayin' here at home with all this suspense and with Hannah Poundberry's tongue droppin' lamentations like kernels out of a corn sheller, is enough to kill a healthy batch of kittens with nine lives apiece. She didn't want to go; felt that she must stay here and wait for news; but I told her we'd get news to her as soon as it come, and she's goin'."

Ellery took his hat from the peg and opened the door. His foot was on the step when Keziah spoke again.

"She—it don't mean nothin', John, except that she ain't so hard-hearted as maybe you might think —she's asked me about you 'most every time I've been there. She told me to take good care of you."

The door closed. Keziah put down her sewing and listened as the minister's step sounded on the walk. She rose, went to the window and looked after him. She was wondering if she had made a mistake in mentioning Grace's name. She had meant to cheer him with the thought that he was not entirely forgotten, that he was, at least, pitied; but perhaps it would have been better to have remained silent. Her gaze shifted and she looked out over the bay, blue and white in the sun and wind. When she was a girl the sea had been kind to her, it had brought her father home safe, and those home-comings were her pleasantest memories. But she now hated it. It was cruel and cold and wicked. It had taken the man she loved and would have loved till she died, even though he could never have been hers, and she had given him to another; it had taken him, killed him cruelly, perhaps. And now it might be bringing to her the one who was responsible for all her sorrow, the one she could not think of without a shudder. She clung to the window sash and prayed aloud.

"Lord! Lord!" she pleaded, "don't put any more on me now. I couldn't stand it! I couldn't!"

Ellery, too, was thinking deeply as he walked up the main road on his way to Mrs. Prince's. Keziah's words were repeating themselves over and over in his brain. She had asked about him. She had not forgotten him altogether. And what did the house-keeper mean by saying that she had not loved Captain Hammond in the way that— Not that it could make any difference. Nothing could give him back his happiness. But what did it mean?

Mrs. Prince was very glad to see him. He found her in the big armchair with the quilted back and the projecting "wings" at each side of her head. She was wrapped in a "Rising Sun" quilt which was a patchwork glory of red and crimson. A young girl, a neighbor, who was apparently acting in the dual capacity of nurse and housekeeper, admitted him to the old lady's presence.

"Well, well!" she exclaimed delightedly. "Then you ain't forgot me altogether. I'm awful glad to see you. You'll excuse me for not gettin' up;

my back's got more pains in it than there is bones, a good sight. Dr. Parker says it's nothin' serious, and all I had to do was set still and take his medicine. I told him that either the aches or the medicine made settin' still serious enough, and when your only amusement is listenin' to Emeline Berry—she's the girl that's takin' care of me—when your only fun is listenin' to Emeline drop your best dishes in the kitchen sink, it's pretty nigh tragic. There! there! don't mind an old woman, Mr. Ellery. Set down and let's talk. It's a comfort to be able to say somethin' besides ' Don't, Emeline! ' and ' Be sure you pick up all the pieces! ' "

Mrs. Prince's good spirits were of short duration. Her conversation soon shifted to the loss of her son and she wept, using the corner of the quilt to wipe away her tears. " Eddie " had been her idol and, as she said, it was hard to believe what folks kept tellin' her, that it was God's will, and therefore all for the best.

" That's so easy to say," she sobbed. " Maybe it is best for the Lord, but how about me? I needed him more than they did up there, or I think I did. O Mr. Ellery, I don't mean to be irreverent, but *why* was it all for the best? "

Questions like this are hard to answer. The young minister tried, but the answers were unsatisfactory, even to him.

" And there's Nat Hammond," continued Mrs. Prince. " A fine man—no better anywhere, even though his father was a Come-Outer—just goin' to be married and all, now they say he's drowned— why? Why was that necessary? "

Ellery could not reply. The old lady did not

wait for him to do so. The mention of Captain Nat's name reminded her of other things.

"Poor Gracie!" she said. "It's turrible hard on her. I went down to see her two or three times afore I was took with this backache. She's an awful nice girl. And pretty as a pink, too. Don't you think so? Hey? don't you?"

"Yes."

"Yes. I've been kind of expectin' she might get up to see me. Hannah Poundberry told the Berrys that she said she was comin'. I don't care about her bein' a Come-Outer. I ain't proud, Mr. Ellery. And there's Come-Outers and *Come*-Outers. Proud! Lord 'a' mercy! what has an old woman, next door to the poorhouse, got to be proud over? Yes, she told Hannah she was comin', and the Berry folks thought it might be to-day. So I've been watchin' for her. What! you ain't agoin', Mr. Ellery?"

"I think I must, Mrs. Prince."

"Oh, don't! Do stay a spell longer. Gracie might come and I'd like for you to meet her. She needs sympathy and comfort an awful lot, and there's no tellin', you might convert her to bein' a Reg'lar. Oh, yes, you might. You've got the most persuadin' way, everybody says so. And you don't know her very well, do you? Land sakes alive! talk about angels! I snum if she ain't comin' up the road this blessed minute."

John Ellery had risen. Now he seized his hat and moved hastily toward the door. Mrs. Prince called to him to remain, but he would not. However, her good-bys delayed him for a minute, and before he reached the yard gate Grace was opening it.

They were face to face for the first time since they had parted in the grove, so many months before.

She was thinner and paler, he saw that. And dressed very quietly in black. She looked at him, as he stood before her in the path, and her cheeks flushed and her eyes fell. He stepped aside and raised his hat.

She bowed gravely and murmured a "Good afternoon." Then she passed on up the path toward the door. He watched her for an instant and then stepped quickly after her. The black gown and the tired look in her eyes touched him to the heart. He could not let her go without a word.

She turned at the sound of his step behind her.

"Er—Miss Van Horne," he stammered, "I merely wanted to tell you how deeply I—we all feel for you in your trouble. I—I—I am so sorry."

"Thank you," she said simply, and after a moment's hesitation.

"I mean it sincerely. I—I did not know Captain Hammond very well, but I respected and liked him the first time we met. I shall hope that—that—it is not so serious as they fear."

"Thank you," she said again. "We are all hoping."

"Yes. I—I—" It was dreadfully hard to get words together. "I have heard so much of the captain from——"

"From Aunt Keziah? Yes, she was Nat's warmest friend."

"I know. Er—Mrs. Coffin tells me you are going away. I hope you may hear good news and soon. I shall think of you—of him— I want you to understand that I shall."

The door opened and Emeline Berry appeared on the threshold.

"Come right in, Grace," she called. "Mrs. Prince wants you to. She's ahollerin' for you to hurry up."

"Good-by," said the minister.

"Good-by. Thank you again. It was very kind of you to say this."

"No, no. I mean it."

"I know; that was why it was so kind. Good-by."

She held out her hand and he took it. He knew that his was trembling, but so, too, was hers. The hands fell apart. Grace entered the house and John Ellery went out at the gate.

That night Keziah, in the sitting room, trying to read, but finding it hard to keep her mind on the book, heard her parson pacing back and forth over the straw-matted floor of his chamber. She looked at the clock; it was nearly twelve. She shut the book and sighed. Her well-meant words of consolation had been a mistake, after all. She should not have spoken Grace Van Horne's name.

# CHAPTER XVI

"HEY, Mr. Ellery!"

It was Captain Zeb Mayo who was calling. The captain sat in his antique chaise, drawn by the antique white horse, and was hailing the parsonage through a speaking trumpet formed by holding both his big hands before his mouth. The reins he had tucked between the edge of the dashboard and the whip socket. If he had thrown them on the ground he would still have been perfectly safe, with that horse.

"Mr. Ellery, ahoy!" roared Captain Zeb through his hands.

The window of Zoeth Peters's house, next door to the Regular church, was thrown up and Mrs. Peters's head, bound with a blue-and-white handkerchief in lieu of a sweeping cap, was thrust forth into the crisp March air.

"What is it, Cap'n Mayo?" screamed Mrs. Peters. "Hey?"

"Hey?" repeated Captain Zeb, peering round the chaise curtain. "Who's that?"

"It's me. Is somebody dead?"

"Who's me? Oh! No, Hettie, nobody's dead, though I'm likely to bust a blood vessel if I keep on yellin' much longer. Is the parson to home?"

269

" Hey ? "

" Oh, heavens alive! I say is— Ha, there you be, Mr. Ellery. Mornin', Keziah."

The minister and Mrs. Coffin, the former with a napkin in his hand, had emerged from the side door of the parsonage and now came hurrying down to the gate.

"Land of Goshen!" exclaimed the captain, " you don't mean to tell me you ain't done breakfast yet, and it after seven o'clock. Why, we're thinkin' about dinner up to our house."

Keziah answered. "Yes," she said, " I shouldn't wonder. Your wife tells me, Zeb, that the only time you ain't thinkin' about dinner is when you think of breakfast or supper. We ain't so hungry here that we get up to eat in the middle of the night. What's the matter? Hettie Peters is hollerin' at you; did you know it?"

" Did I know it? Tut! tut! tut! I'd known it if I was a mile away, 'less I was paralyzed in my ears. Let her holler; 'twill do her good and keep her in practice for Come-Outer meetin'. Why, Mr. Ellery, I tell you : Em'lous Sparrow, the fish peddler, stepped up to our house a few minutes ago. He's just come down from the shanties over on the shore by the light—where the wreck was, you know—and he says there's a 'morphrodite brig anchored three or four mile off and she's flyin' colors ha'f mast and union down. They're gettin' a boat's crew to-gether to go off to her and see what's the row. I'm goin' to drive over and I thought maybe you'd like to go along. I told the old lady—my wife, I mean —that I thought of pickin' you up and she said 'twas a good idee. Said my likin' to cruise with a parson in my old age was either a sign that I was hopeful or fearful, she didn't know which; and either way it ought to be encouraged. He, he, he! What do you say, Mr. Ellery? Want to go?"

The minister hesitated. "I'd like to," he said. "I'd like to very much. But I ought to work on my sermon this morning."

Keziah cut in here. "Cat's foot!" she sniffed. "Let your sermon go for this once, do. If it ain't long enough as it is, you can begin again when you've got to the end and preach it over again. Didama Rogers said, last circle day, that she could set still and hear you preach right over 'n' over. I'd give her a chance, 'specially if it did keep her still. Keepin' Didama still is good Christian work, ain't it, Zeb?"

Captain Mayo slapped his knee. "He, he, he!" he chuckled. "Cal'late you're right, Keziah."

"Indeed, I am. I believe it would be Christianity and I *know* 'twould be work. There! there! run in and get your coat and hat, Mr. Ellery. I'll step across and ease Hettie's mind and—and lungs."

She went across the road to impart the news of the vessel in distress to the curious Mrs. Peters. A moment later the minister, having donned his hat and coat, ran down the walk and climbed into the chaise beside Captain Zeb. The white horse, stimulated into a creaky jog trot by repeated slappings of the reins and roars to "Get under way!" and "Cast off!" moved along the sandy lane.

During the drive the captain and his passenger discussed various topics of local interest, among them Captain Nat Hammond and the manner in which

271

he might have lost his ship and his life. It was now
taken for granted, in Trumet and elsewhere, that Nat
was dead and would never be heard from again. The
owners had given up, so Captain Zeb said, and went
on to enumerate the various accidents which might
have happened—typhoons, waterspouts, fires, and
even attacks by Malay pirates—though, added the
captain, " Gen'rally speakin', I'd ruther not bet on
any pirate gettin' away with Nat Hammond's ship,
if the skipper was alive and healthy. Then there's
mutiny and fevers and collisions, and land knows
what all. And, speakin' of trouble, what do you
cal'late ails that craft we're goin' to look at now? "

They found a group on the beach discussing
that very question. A few fishermen, one or two
lobstermen and wreckers, and the lightkeeper were
gathered on the knoll by the lighthouse. They had
a spyglass, and a good-sized dory was ready for
launching.

" Where is she, Noah? " asked Captain Zeb of
the lightkeeper. " That her off back of the spar
buoy? Let me have a squint through that glass; my
eyes ain't what they used to be, when I could see a
whale spout two miles t'other side of the sky line
and tell how many barrels of ile he'd try out, fust
look. Takes practice to keep your eyesight so's you
can see round a curve like that," he added, winking
at Ellery.

" She's a brigantine, Zeb," observed the keeper,
handing up the spyglass. " And flyin' the British
colors. Look's if she might be one of them salt
boats from Turk's Islands. But what she's doin'
out there, anchored, with canvas lowered and showin'
distress signals in fair weather like this, is more'n

any of us can make out. She wa'n't there last evenin', though, and she is there now."

"She ain't the only funny thing along shore this mornin', nuther," announced Theophilus Black, one of the fishermen. "Charlie Burgess just come down along and he says there's a ship's longboat hauled up on the beach, 'bout a mile 'n a half t'other side the mouth of the herrin' crick yonder. Oars in her and all. And she ain't no boat that b'longs round here, is she, Charlie?"

"No, Thoph, she ain't," was the reply. "Make anything out of her, cap'n?"

Captain Zeb, who had been inspecting the anchored vessel through the spyglass, lowered the latter and seemed puzzled. "Not much," he answered. "Blessed if she don't look abandoned to me. Can't see a sign of life aboard her."

"We couldn't neither," said Thoph. "We was just cal'latin' to go off to her when Charlie come and told us about the longboat. I guess likely we can go now; it's pretty nigh smooth as a pond. You'll take an oar, won't you, Noah?"

"I can't leave the light very well. My wife went over to the village last night. You and Charlie and Bill go. Want to go, too, Zeb?"

"No, I'll stay here, I guess. The old lady made me promise to keep my feet dry afore I left the house."

"You want to go, Mr. Ellery? Lots of room."

The minister was tempted. The sea always had a fascination for him and the mystery of the strange ship was appealing.

"Sure I won't be in the way?"

"No, no! 'course you won't," said Burgess.

" Come right along. You set in the bow, if you don't mind gettin' sprinkled once in a while. I'll steer and Thoph and Bill'll row. That'll be enough for one dory. If we need more, we'll signal. Heave ahead."

The surf, though low for that season of the year, looked dangerous to Ellery, but his companions launched the dory with the ease which comes of experience. Burgess took the steering oar and Thoph and " Bill," the latter a lobsterman from Wellmouth Neck, bent their broad backs for the long pull. The statement concerning the pondlike smoothness of the sea was something of an exaggeration. The dory climbed wave after wave, long and green and oily, at the top of each she poised, tipped and slid down the slope. The minister, curled up in the bow on a rather uncomfortable cushion of anchor and roding, caught glimpses of the receding shore over the crests behind. One minute he looked down into the face of Burgess, holding the steering oar in place, the next the stern was high above him and he felt that he was reclining on the back of his neck. But always the shoulders of the rowers moved steadily in the short, deep strokes of the rough water oarsman, and the beach, with the white light and red-roofed house of the keeper, the group beside it, and Captain Zeb's horse and chaise, grew smaller and less distinct.

" Humph ! " grunted Charlie.

" What's the matter ? " asked Thoph.

The steersman, who was staring hard in the direction they were going, scowled.

" Humph ! " he grunted again. " I swan to man, fellers, I believe she *is* abandoned ! "

" Rubbish ! " panted Bill, twisting his neck to look over his shoulder. " 'Course she ain't ! Who'd

abandon a craft such weather's this, and Provincetown harbor only three hours' run or so?"

"When it comes to that," commented Burgess,
"why should they anchor off here, 'stead of takin'
her in by the inlet? If there's anybody aboard they
ain't showed themselves yet. She might have been
leakin', but she don't look it. Sets up out of water
pretty well. Well, we'll know in a few minutes.
Hit her up, boys!"

The rowers "hit her up" and the dory moved
faster. Then Burgess, putting his hand to his mouth,
hailed.

"Ship ahoy!" he roared. "Ahoy!"

No reply.

"Ahoy the brig!" bellowed Burgess. "What's
the matter aboard there? All hands asleep?"

Still no answer. Thoph and Bill pulled more
slowly now. Burgess nodded to them.

"Stand by!" he ordered. "Easy! Way
enough! Let her run."

The dory slackened speed, turned in obedience
to the steering oar, and slid under the forequarter of
the anchored vessel. Ellery, looking up, saw her
name in battered gilt letters above his head—the
*San Jose*.

"Stand by, Thoph!" shouted Charlie. "S'pose
you can jump and grab her forechains? Hold her
steady, Bill. Now, Thoph! That's the time!"

Thoph had jumped, seized the chains, and was
scrambling aboard. A moment later he appeared at
the rail amidships, a rope in his hand. The dory was
brought alongside and made fast; then one after the
other the men in the boat climbed to the brig's deck.

"Ahoy!" yelled Burgess. "All hands on deck!

tumble up, you lubbers! Humph! She is abandoned, sure and sartin."

"Yup," assented Bill. "Her boats are gone. See? Guess that explains the longboat on the beach, Charlie."

"Cal'late it does; but it don't explain why they left her. She ain't leakin' none to speak of, that's sure. Rides's light's a feather. Christmas! look at them decks; dirty hogs, whoever they was."

The decks were dirty, and the sails, sloppily furled, were dirty likewise. The brig, as she rolled and jerked at her anchor rope, was dirty and unkempt from stem to stern. To Ellery's mind she made a lonesome picture, even under the clear, winter sky and bright sunshine.

Thoph led the way aft. The cabin companion door was open and they peered down.

"Phew!" sniffed Burgess. "She ain't no cologne bottle, is she? Well, come on below and let's see what'll we see."

The cabin was a "mess," as Bill expressed it. The floor was covered with scattered heaps of riff-raff, oilskins, coats, empty bottles, and papers. On the table a box stood, its hinged lid thrown back.

"Medicine chest," said Burgess, examining it. "And rum bottles aplenty. Somebody's been sick, I shouldn't wonder."

The minister opened the door of one of the little staterooms. The light which shone through the dirty and tightly closed "bull's-eye" window showed a tumbled bunk, the blankets soiled and streaked. The smell was stifling.

"Say, fellers," whispered Thoph, "I don't like

this much myself. I'm for gettin' on deck where the air's better. Somethin's happened aboard this craft, somethin' serious."

Charlie and Bill nodded an emphatic affirmative.

"Hadn't we better look about a little more?" asked Ellery. "There's another stateroom there."

He opened the door of it as he spoke. It was, if possible, in a worse condition than the first. And the odor was even more overpowering.

"Skipper's room," observed Burgess, peeping in. "And that bunk ain't been slept in for weeks. See the mildew on them clothes. Phew! I'm fair sick to my stomach. Come out of this."

On deck, in the sunlight, they held another consultation.

"Queerest business ever I see," observed Charlie. "I never——"

"I see somethin' like it once," interrupted Bill. "Down in the Gulf 'twas. I was on the old *Fishhawk*. Eben Salters's dad from over to Bayport skippered her. We picked up a West Injy schooner, derelict, abandoned same as this one, but not anchored, of course. Yeller jack was the trouble aboard her and—— Where you bound, Thoph?"

"Goin' to take a squint at the fo'castle," replied Theophilus, moving forward. The minister followed him.

The fo'castle hatchway was black and grim. Ellery knelt and peered down. Here there was practically no light at all and the air was fouler than that in the cabin.

"See anything, Mr. Ellery?" asked Thoph, looking over his shoulder.

"No, I don't see anything. But I thought——"

He seemed to be listening.

" What did you think? "

" Nothing. I——"

" Hold on! you ain't goin' down there, be you? I wouldn't. No tellin' what you might find. Well, all right. *I* ain't curious. I'll stay up here and you can report."

He stepped over and leaned against the rail. Bill came across the deck and joined him.

" Where's Charlie? " asked Thoph.

" Gone back to the cabin," was the answer. " Thought likely he might find some of her papers or somethin' to put us on the track. I told him to heave ahead; I didn't want no part of it. Too much like that yeller-jack schooner to suit me. What's become of the parson? "

Thoph pointed to the open hatch.

" Down yonder, explorin' the fo'castle," he replied. " He can have the job, for all me. Phew! Say, Bill, what *is* this we've struck, anyhow? "

Ellery descended the almost perpendicular ladder gingerly, holding on with both hands. At its foot he stopped and tried to accustom his eyes to the darkness.

A room perhaps ten feet long, so much he could make out. The floor strewn, like that of the cabin, with heaps of clothing and odds and ends. More shapes of clothes hanging up and swaying with the roll of the brig. A little window high up at the end, black with dirt. And cavities, bunks in rows, along the walls. A horrible hole.

He took a step toward the center of the room, bending his head to avoid hitting the fo'castle lantern. Then in one of the bunks something stirred, something alive. He started violently, controlled himself with an effort, and stumbled toward the sound.

"What is it?" he whispered. "Who is it? Is anyone there?"

A groan answered him. Then a voice, weak and quavering, said:

"Gimme a drink! Gimme a drink! Can't none of you God-forsaken devils give me a drink?"

He stooped over the bunk. A man was lying in it, crumpled into a dreadful heap. He stooped lower, looked, and saw the man's face.

There was a shout from the deck, or, rather, a yell. Then more yells and the sound of running feet.

"Mr. Ellery!" screamed Burgess, at the hatchway. "Mr. Ellery, for the Almighty's sake, come up here! Come out of that this minute. Quick!"

The minister knew what was coming, was sure of it as he stepped to the foot of the ladder, had known it the instant he saw that face.

"Mr. Ellery!" shrieked Burgess. "Mr. Ellery, are you there?"

"Yes, I'm here," answered the minister, slowly. He was fighting with all his might to keep his nerves under control. His impulse was to leap up those steps, rush across that deck, spring into the dory and row, anywhere to get away from the horror of that forecastle.

"Come up!" called Burgess. "Hurry! It's the smallpox! The darned hooker's rotten with it. For God sakes, come quick!"

He ran to the rail, yelling order to Bill and Thoph, who were frantically busy with the dory. Ellery began to climb the ladder. His head emerged into the clean, sweet air blowing across the deck. He drew a breath to the very bottom of his lungs.

Then from behind and below him came the voice again.

"Gimme a drink!" it wailed. "Gimme a drink of water. Ain't one of you cussed swabs got decency enough to fetch me a drink? I'm dyin' for a drink, I tell you. I'm dyin'!"

The minister stood still, his feet on the ladder. The three men by the rail were working like mad, their faces livid under the sunburn and their hands trembling. They pushed each other about and swore. They were not cowards, either. Ellery knew them well enough to know that. Burgess had, that very winter, pulled a skiff through broken ice in the face of a wicked no'theaster to rescue an old neighbor whose dory had been capsized in the bay while he was hauling lobster pots. But now Burgess was as scared as the rest.

Thoph and Bill sprang over the rail into the boat. Burgess turned and beckoned to Ellery.

"Come on!" he called. "What are you waitin' for?"

The minister remained where he was.

"Are you sure——" he faltered.

"Sure! Blast it all! I found the log. It ain't been kept for a fortni't, but there's enough. It's smallpox, I tell you. Two men died of it three weeks ago. The skipper died right afterwards. The mate—— No wonder them that was left run away as soon as they sighted land. Come on! Do you want to die, too?"

From the poison pit at the foot of the ladder the man in the bunk called once more.

"Water!" he screeched. "Water! Are you goin' to leave me, you d—n cowards?"

"For Heaven sakes!" cried Burgess, clutching the rail, "what's that?"

Ellery answered him. "It's one of them," he said, and his voice sounded odd in his own ears. "It's one of the crew."

"One of the— Down *there?* Has he——"

"Yes, he has."

"Help! help!" screamed the voice shrilly. "Are you goin' to leave me to die all alone? He-elp!"

The minister turned. "Hush!" he called, in answer to the voice, "hush! I'll bring you water in a minute. Burgess," he added, "you and the rest go ashore. I shall stay."

"You'll stay? You'll *stay?* With *that?* You're crazy as a loon. Don't be a fool, man! Come on! We'll send the doctor and somebody else—some one that's had it, maybe, or ain't afraid. I am and I'm goin'. Don't be a fool."

Thoph, from the dory, shouted to know what was the matter. Ellery climbed the ladder to the deck and walked over to the rail. As he approached, Burgess fell back a few feet.

"Thoph," said the minister, addressing the pair in the dory, "there is a sick man down in the forecastle. He has been alone there for hours, I suppose, certainly since his shipmates ran away. If he is left longer without help, he will surely die. Some one must stay with him. You and the rest row ashore and get the doctor and whoever else you can. I'll stay here till they come."

Thoph and his companions set up a storm of protest. It was foolish, it was crazy, the man would die anyhow, and so on. They begged the minister to come with them. But he was firm.

" Don't stop to argue," he urged. " Hurry and get the doctor."

" Come on, Charlie," ordered Bill. " No use talkin' to him, he's set. Come on! I won't stay alongside this craft another minute for nobody. If you be comin', come."

Burgess, still protesting, clambered over the rail. The dory swung clear of the brig. The rowers settled themselves for the stroke.

" Better change your mind, Mr. Ellery," pleaded Charlie. " I hate to leave you this way. It seems mean, but I'm a married man with children, like the rest of us here, and I can't take no risks. Better come, too. No? Well, we'll send help quick as the Lord'll let us. By the Almighty! " he added, in a sudden burst, " you've got more spunk than I have—yes, or anybody I ever come across. I'll say that for you, if you are a parson. Give way, fellers."

The oars dipped, bent, and the dory moved off. The sound of the creaking thole pins shot a chill through Ellery's veins. His knees shook, and involuntarily a cry for them to come back rose to his lips. But he choked it down and waved his hand in farewell. Then, not trusting himself to look longer at the receding boat, he turned on his heel and walked toward the forecastle.

The water butts stood amidships, not far from the open door of the galley. Entering the latter he found an empty saucepan. This he filled from the cask, and then, with it in his hand, turned toward the black hatchway. Here was the greatest test of his courage. To descend that ladder, approach that bunk, and touch the terrible creature in it, these were the tasks he had set himself to do, but could he?

Vaccination in those days was by no means the universal custom that it now is. And smallpox, even now, is a disease the name of which strikes panic to a community. The minister had been vaccinated when he was a child, but that was—so it seemed to him—a very long time ago. And that forecastle was so saturated with the plague that to enter it meant almost certain infection. He had stayed aboard the brig because the pitiful call for help had made leaving a cowardly impossibility. Now, face to face, and in cold blood, with the alternative, it seemed neither so cowardly or impossible. The man would die anyhow, so Thoph had said; was there any good reason why he should risk dying, too, and dying in that way?

He thought of a great many things and of many people as he stood by the hatchway, waiting; among others, he thought of his housekeeper, Keziah Coffin. And, somehow, the thought of her, of her pluck, and her self-sacrifice, were the very inspirations he needed. " It's the duty that's been laid on me," Keziah had said, " and it's a hard one, but I don't run away from it." He began to descend the ladder.

The sick man was raving in delirium when he reached him, but the sound of the water lapping the sides of the saucepan brought him to himself. He seized Ellery by the arm and drank and drank. When at last he desisted, the pan was half empty.

The minister laid him gently back in the bunk and stepped to the foot of the ladder for breath. This made him think of the necessity for air in the place and he remembered the little window. It was tightly closed and rusted fast. He went up to the deck, found a marlin spike, and, returning, broke the glass. A sharp, cold draught swept through the forecastle, stirring the garments hanging on the nails.

An hour later, two dories bumped against the side of the *San Jose*. Men, talking in low tones, climbed over the rail. Burgess was one of them; ashamed of his panic, he had returned to assist the others in bringing the brigantine into a safer anchorage by the inlet.

Dr. Parker, very grave but businesslike, reached the deck among the first.

" Mr. Ellery," he shouted, " where are you? "

The minister's head and shoulders appeared at the forecastle companion. " Here I am, doctor," he said. " Will you come down? "

The doctor made no answer in words, but he hurried briskly across the deck. One man, Ebenezer Capen, an old fisherman and ex-whaler from East Trumet, started to follow him, but he was the only one. The others waited, with scared faces, by the rail.

" Get her under way and inshore as soon as you can," ordered Dr. Parker. " Ebenezer, you can help. If I need you below, I'll call."

The minister backed down the ladder and the doctor followed him. Parker bent over the bunk for a few moments in silence.

" He's pretty bad," he muttered. " Mighty little

chance. Heavens, what a den! Who broke that window?"

"I did," replied Ellery. "The air down here was dreadful."

The doctor nodded approvingly. "I guess so," he said. "It's bad enough now. We've got to get this poor fellow out of here as soon as we can or he'll die before to-morrow. Mr. Ellery," he added sharply, "what made you do this? Don't you realize the risk you've run?"

"Some one had to do it. You are running the same risk."

"Not just the same, and, besides, it's my business. Why didn't you let some one else, some one we could spare— Humph! Confound it, man! didn't you know any better? Weren't you afraid?"

His tone rasped Ellery's shaken nerves.

"Of course I was," he snapped irritably. "I'm not an idiot."

"Humph! Well, all right; I beg your pardon. But you oughtn't to have done it. Now you'll have to be quarantined. And who in thunder I can get to stay with me in this case is more than I know. Just say smallpox to this town and it goes to pieces like a smashed egg. Old Eb Capen will help, for he's had it, but it needs more than one."

"Where are you going to take—him?" pointing to the moaning occupant of the bunk.

"To one of the empty fish shanties on the beach. There are beds there, such as they are, and the place is secluded. We can burn it down when the fuss is over."

"Then why can't I stay? I shall have to be quarantined, I know that. Let me be the other nurse.

Why should anyone else run the risk? I *have* run it. I'll stay."

Dr. Parker looked at him. "Well!" he exclaimed. "Well! I must say, young man, that you've got— Humph! All right, Mr. Ellery; I'm much obliged."

# CHAPTER XVII

## IN WHICH EBENEZER CAPEN IS SURPRISED

BEFORE sunset that afternoon the *San Jose* was anchored behind the point by the inlet. The fishing boats changed moorings and moved farther up, for not a single one of their owners would trust himself within a hundred yards of the stricken brigantine. As soon as the anchors were dropped, the volunteer crew was over side and away, each of its members to receive a scolding from his family for taking such a risk and to have his garments sulphur-smoked or buried. Charlie Burgess, whose wife was something of a Tartar, observed ruefully that he " didn't take no comfort 'round home nowadays; between the smell of brimstone and the jawin's 'twas the hereafter ahead of time."

The largest of the beach shanties, one which stood by itself a quarter of a mile from the light, was hurriedly prepared for use as a pesthouse and the sick sailor was carried there on an improvised stretcher. Dr. Parker and Ellery lifted him from his berth and, assisted by old Ebenezer Capen, got him up to the deck and lowered him into the dory. Ebenezer rowed the trio to the beach and the rest of the journey was comparatively easy.

The shanty had three rooms, one of which was given up to the patient, one used as a living room,

287

and, in the third, Capen and the minister were to sleep. Mattresses were procured, kind-hearted and sympathizing townspeople donated cast-off tables and chairs, and the building was made as comfortable as it could be, under the circumstances. Sign boards, warning strangers to keep away, were erected, and in addition to them, the Trumet selectmen ordered ropes stretched across the lane on both sides of the shanty. But ropes and signs were superfluous. Trumet in general was in a blue funk and had no desire to approach within a mile of the locality. Even the driver of the grocery cart, when he left the day's supply of provisions, pushed the packages under the ropes, yelled a hurried " Here you be! " and, whipping up his horse, departed at a rattling gallop.

The village sat up nights to discuss the affair and every day brought a new sensation. The survivors of the *San Jose's* crew, a wretched, panic-stricken quartette of mulattos and Portuguese, were apprehended on the outskirts of Denboro, the town below Trumet on the bay side, and were promptly sequestered and fumigated, pending shipment to the hospital at Boston. Their story was short but grewsome. The brigantine was not a Turks Islands boat, but a coaster from Jamaica. She had sailed with a small cargo for Savannah. Two days out and the smallpox made its appearance on board. The sufferer, a negro foremast hand, died. Then another sailor was seized and also died. The skipper, who was the owner, was the next victim, and the vessel was in a state of demoralization which the mate, an Englishman named Bradford, could not overcome. Then followed days and nights of calm and terrible heat, of pestilence and all but mutiny. The mate himself died. There was no one left who understood navigation. At last came a southeast gale and the *San Jose* drove before it. Fair weather found her abreast the Cape. The survivors ran her in after dark, anchored, and reached shore in the longboat. The sick man whom they had left in the forecastle was a new hand who had shipped at Kingston. His name was Murphy, they believed. They had left him because he was sure to die, like the others, and, besides, they knew some one would see the distress signals and investigate. That was all, yes. Santa Maria! was it not enough?

This tale was a delicious tidbit for Didama and the " daily advertisers," but, after all, it was a mere side dish compared to Mr. Ellery's astonishing behavior. That he, the minister of the Regular church, should risk his life, risk dying of the smallpox, to help a stranger and a common sailor, was incomprehensible. Didama, at least, could not understand it, and said so. " My soul and body! " she exclaimed, with uplifted hands. " I wouldn't go nigh my own grandfather if he had the smallpox, let alone settin' up with a strange critter that I didn't know from Adam's cat. And a minister doin' it! He ought to consider the congregation, if he done nothin' else. Ain't we more important than a common water rat that, even when he's dyin', swears, so I hear tell, like a ship's poll parrot? I never heard of such foolishness. It beats *me!* "

It " beat " a good many who, like the Widow Rogers, could not understand self-sacrifice. But there were more, and they the majority of Trumet's intelligent people, who understood and appreciated. Dr. Parker, a man with a reputation for dangerously liberal views concerning religious matters and an infrequent attendant at church, was enthusiastic and prodigal of praise.

"By George!" vowed the doctor. "That's *my* kind of Christianity. That's the kind of parson I can tie to. I'm for John Ellery after this, first, last, and all the time. And if he don't get the smallpox and die, and if he does live to preach in the Regular church, you'll see me in one of the front pews every Sunday. That's what I think of him. Everybody else ran away and I don't blame 'em much. But he stayed. Yes, sir, by George! he stayed. 'Somebody had to do it,' says he. I take off my hat to that young fellow."

Captain Zeb Mayo went about cheering for his parson. Mrs. Mayo cooked delicacies to be pushed under the ropes for the minister's consumption. The parish committee, at a special session, voted an increase of salary and ordered a weekly service of prayer for the safe delivery of their young leader from danger. Even Captain Elkanah did not try to oppose the general opinion; "although I cannot but feel," he said, "that Mr. Ellery's course was rash and that he should have considered us and our interest in his welfare before——"

"Dum it all!" roared Captain Zeb, jumping to his feet and interrupting, "he didn't consider himself, did he? and ain't he as important *to* himself as you, Elkanah Daniels, or anybody else in this meetin' house? Bah! don't let's have no more talk like that or I'll say somethin' that won't be fit to put in the minutes."

Even at Come-Outers' meeting, when Ezekiel Bassett hinted at a "just punishment fallin' on the head of the leader of the Pharisees," Thoph Black rose and defended Ellery.

Keziah Coffin was, perhaps, the one person most disturbed by her parson's heroism. She would have gone to the shanty immediately had not Dr. Parker prevented. Even as it was, she did go as far as the ropes, but there she was warded off by Ebenezer until Ellery came running out and bade her come no nearer.

" But you shan't stay here, Mr. Ellery," vowed Keziah. " Or, if you do, I'll stay, too. I ain't afraid of smallpox."

" I am," confessed the minister, " and I'm not going to let anyone I care for expose themselves to it unnecessarily. If you try to come in here I shall "— he smiled—" well, Capen and I will put you off the premises by force. There ! "

Keziah smiled, too, in spite of herself. " Maybe you'd have your hands full," she said. " O John, what in the world made you do this thing? It's dreadful. I shan't sleep a wink, thinkin' of you. I just must come here and help."

" No, you mustn't. You can come as far as the —the dead line once in a while, if Captain Mayo will drive you over, but that's all. I'm all right. Don't worry about me. I'm feeling tiptop and I'm not going to be sick. Now go home and make me some of that—some of those puddings of yours. We can use them to advantage, can't we, Capen ? "

" Bet yer ! " replied Ebenezer with enthusiasm. Keziah, after more expostulation, went back to the parsonage, where the puddings were made and seasoned with tears and fervent prayers. She wrote to Grace and told her the news of the *San Jose*, but she said nothing of the minister's part in it. "Poor thing!" sighed Keziah, "she's bearin' enough already. Her back ain't as strong as mine, maybe, and mine's most crackin'. Well, let it crack for good and all; I don't know but that's the easiest way out."

The sick sailor grew no better. Days and nights passed and he raved and moaned or lay in a stupor. Ebenezer acted as day nurse while Ellery slept, and, at night, the minister, being younger, went on watch. The doctor came frequently, but said there was no hope. A question of time only, and a short time, he said.

Capen occupied his mind with speculations concerning the patient.

"Do you know, parson," he said, "seem's if I'd seen the feller somewheres afore. 'Course I never have, but when I used to go whalin' v'yages I cruised from one end of creation to t'other, pretty nigh, and I *might* have met him. However, his own folks wouldn't know him now, would they? so I cal'late I'm just gettin' foolish in my old age. Said his name's Murphy, them ha'f-breeds did, didn't they? I know better'n that."

"How do you know?" asked Ellery, idly listening.

"'Cause when he's floppin' round on the bed, out of his head, he sings out all kinds of stuff. A good deal of it's plain cussin', but there's times when he talks respectable and once I heard him say ' darn ' and another time ' I cal'late.' Now no Irishman says *that*. That's Yankee, that is."

"Well, he ought to know his own name."

"Prob'ly he does—or used to—but 'most likely

he don't want nobody else to know it. That's why he said 'twas Murphy and, bein' as he *did* say it, I know 'tain't it. See my argument, don't you, Mr. Ellery? "

" Yes, I guess so."

" Um—hm! Why, land sakes, names don't mean nothin' with seafarin' men. I've seen the time when I had more names— Humph! Looks kind of squally off to the east'ard, don't it? "

That night the sick man was much worse. His ravings were incessant. The minister, sitting in his chair in the living room, by the cook stove, could hear the steady stream of shouts, oaths, and muttered fragments of dialogue with imaginary persons. Sympathy for the sufferer he felt, of course, and yet he, as well as Dr. Parker and old Capen, had heard enough to realize that the world would be none the worse for losing this particular specimen of humanity. The fellow had undoubtedly lived a hard life, among the roughest of companions afloat and ashore. Even Ebenezer, who by his own confession, was far from being a saint, exclaimed disgustedly at the close of a day's watching by the sick bed: " Phew! I feel's if I'd been visiting state's prison. Let me set out doors a spell and listen to the surf. It's clean, anyhow, and that critter's talk makes me want to give my brains a bath."

The wooden clock, loaned by Mrs. Parker, the doctor's wife, ticked steadily, although a half hour slow. Ellery, glancing at it to see if the time had come for giving medicine, suddenly noticed how loud its ticking sounded. Wondering at this, he was aware there was no other sound in the house. He rose and looked in at the door of the adjoining room.

The patient had ceased to rave and was lying quiet on the bed.

The minister tiptoed over to look at him. And, as he did so, the man opened his eyes.

" Halloo! " he said faintly. " Who are you? "

Ellery, startled, made no answer.

" Who are you? " demanded the man again. Then, with an oath, he repeated the question, adding: " What place is this? This ain't the fo'castle. Where am I? "

" You're ashore. You've been sick. Don't try to move."

" Sick? Humph! Sick? 'Course I been sick. Don't I know it? The d——n cowards run off and left me; blast their eyes! I'll fix 'em for it one of these days, you hear——"

" Sshh! "

" Hush up yourself. Where am I? "

" You're ashore. On Cape Cod. At Trumet."

" Trumet! *Trumet!* "

He was struggling to raise himself on his elbow. Ellery was obliged to use force to hold him down.

" Hush! hush! " pleaded the minister, " you mustn't try to——"

" Trumet! I ain't. You're lyin'. Trumet! Good God! Who brought me here? Did she— Is she——"

He struggled again. Then his strength and his reason left him simultaneously and the delirium returned. He began to shout a name, a name that caused Ellery to stand upright and step back from the bed, scarcely believing his ears.

All the rest of that night the man on the bed

raved and muttered, but of people and places and happenings which he had not mentioned before. And the minister, listening intently to every word, caught himself wondering if he also was not losing his mind.

When the morning came, Ebenezer Capen was awakened by a shake to find John Ellery standing over him.

"Capen," whispered the minister, "Capen, get up. I must talk with you."

Ebenezer was indignant.

"Judas priest!" he exclaimed; "why don't you scare a feller to death, comin' and yankin' him out of bed by the back hair?" Then, being more wide awake, he added: "What's the row? Worse, is he? He ain't——"

"No. But I've got to talk with you. You used to be a whaler, I know. Were you acquainted in New Bedford?"

"Sartin. Was a time when I could have located every stick in it, pretty nigh, by the smell, if you'd set me down side of 'em blindfold."

"Did you ever know anyone named—" He finished the sentence.

"Sure and sartin, I did. Why?"

"Did you know him well?"

"Well's I wanted to. Pretty decent feller one time, but a fast goer, and went downhill like a young one's sled, when he got started. His folks had money, that was the trouble with him. Why, 'course I knew him! He married——"

"I know. Now, listen."

Ellery went on talking rapidly and with great earnestness. Ebenezer listened, at first silently, then breaking in with ejaculations and grunts of astonishment. He sat up on the edge of the bed.

"Rubbish!" he cried at last. "Why, 'tain't possible! The feller's dead as Methusalem's grandmarm. I remember how it happened and——"

"It wasn't true. That much I know. I *know*, I tell you."

He went on to explain why he knew. Capen's astonishment grew.

"Judas priest!" he exclaimed again. "That would explain why I thought I'd seen— There! heave ahead. I've got to see. But it's a mistake. I don't believe it."

The pair entered the sick room. The sailor lay in a stupor. His breathing was rapid, but faint. Capen bent over him and gently moved the bandage on his face. For a full minute he gazed steadily. Then he stood erect, drew a big red hand across his forehead, and moved slowly back to the living room.

"Well?" asked Ellery eagerly.

Ebenezer sat down in the rocker. "Judas priest!" he said for the third time. "Don't talk to *me!* When it comes my time they'll have to prove I'm dead. I won't believe it till they do. Ju-das *priest!*"

"Then you recognize him?"

The old man nodded solemnly.

"Yup," he said, "it's him. Mr. Ellery, what are you goin' to do about it?"

"I don't know. I don't know. I must go somewhere by myself and think. I don't know *what* to do."

The minister declined to wait for breakfast. He

said he was not hungry. Leaving Ebenezer to put on the coffeepot and take up his duties as day nurse, Ellery walked off along the beach. The "dead line" prevented his going very far, but he sat down in the lee of a high dune and thought until his head ached. What should he do? What was best for him to do?

He heard the rattle of the doctor's chaise and the voices of Ebenezer and Parker in conversation. He did not move, but remained where he was, thinking, thinking. By and by he heard Capen calling his name.

"Mr. Ellery!" shouted Ebenezer. "Mr. Ellery, where be you?"

"Here!" replied the minister.

The old man came scrambling over the sand. He was panting and much excited.

"Mr. Ellery!" he cried, "Mr. Ellery! it's settled for us—one part of it, anyhow. He's slipped his cable."

"What?" The minister sprang up.

"Yup. He must have died just a little while after you left and after I gave him his medicine. I thought he looked kind of queer then. And when the doctor came we went in together and he was dead. Yes, sir, dead."

"Dead!"

"Um—hm. No doubt of it; it's for good this time. Mr. Ellery, what shall we do? Shall I tell Dr. Parker?"

Ellery considered for a moment. "No," he said slowly. "No, Capen, don't tell anyone. I can't see why they need ever know that he hasn't been dead for years, as they supposed. Promise me to keep it a secret. I'll tell — her — myself, later on. Now promise me; I trust you."

"Land sakes, yes! I'll promise, if you want me to. I'm a widower man, so there'll be nobody to coax it out of me. I guess you're right, cal'late you be. What folks don't know they can't lie about, can they? and that's good for your business—meanin' nothin' disreverent. I'll promise, Mr. Ellery; I'll swear to it. Now come on back to the shanty. The doctor wants you."

The next day the body of "Murphy," foremast hand on the *San Jose*, was buried in the corner of the Regular graveyard, near those who were drowned in the wreck of that winter. There was no funeral, of course. The minister said a prayer at the shanty, and that was all. Ebenezer drove the wagon which was used as hearse for the occasion, and filled in the grave himself. So great was the fear of the terrible smallpox that the sexton would not perform even that service for its victim.

Capen remained at the shanty another week. Then, as the minister showed no symptoms of having contracted the disease and insisted that he needed no companion, Ebenezer departed to take up his fishing once more. The old man was provided with a new suit of clothes, those he had worn being burned, and having been, to his huge disgust, fumigated until, as he said, he couldn't smell himself without thinking of a match box, went away. The room which the dead sailor had occupied was emptied and sealed tight. The *San Jose* was to stay at her anchorage a while longer. Then, when all danger was past, she was to be towed to Boston and sold at auction for the benefit of the heirs of her dead skipper and owner.

Ellery himself was most urgent in the decision that he should not go back to the parsonage and his church just yet. Better to wait until he was sure, he said, and Dr. Parker agreed. " I'd be willing to bet that you are all right," declared the latter, " but I know Trumet, and if I *should* let you go and you did develop even the tail end of a case of varioloid— well, 'twould be the everlasting climax for you and me in this county."

Staying alone was not unpleasant, in a way. The " dead line " still remained, of course, and callers did not attempt to pass it, but they came more frequently and held lengthy conversations at a respectful distance. Ellery did his own cooking, what little there was to do, but so many good things were pushed under the ropes that he was in a fair way to develop weight and indigestion. Captain Zeb Mayo drove down at least twice a week and usually brought Mrs. Coffin with him. From them and from the doctor the prisoner learned the village news. Once Captain Elkanah and Annabel came, and the young lady's gushing praise of the minister's " heroism " made its recipient almost sorry he had ever heard of the *San Jose*.

Dr. Parker told him of Grace Van Horne's return to the village. She had come back, so the doctor said, the day before, and was to live at the tavern for a while, at least. Yes, he guessed even she had given up hope of Captain Nat now.

" And say," went on Parker, " how are you feeling? "

" Pretty well, thank you," replied the minister. " I seem to be rather tired and good for nothing. More so than I was during the worst of it."

"No wonder. A chap can't go through what you did and not feel some reaction. I expected that. Don't get cold, that's all. But what I want to know is whether you think I could leave you for a couple of days? The Ostable County Medical Society meets at Hyannis to-morrow and I had promised myself to take it in this year. But I don't want to leave you, if you need me."

Ellery insisted that he did not need anyone, was getting along finely, and would not hear of his friend's missing the medical society's meeting. So the physician went.

"Good-by," he called as he drove off. "I guess your term is pretty nearly over. I shall let you out of jail inside of four or five days, if you behave yourself."

This should have been cheering news, but, somehow, John Ellery did not feel cheerful that afternoon. The tired feeling he had spoken of so lightly was worse than he had described it, and he was despondent, for no particular reason. That night he slept miserably and awoke with a chill to find a cold, pouring rain beating against the windows of the shanty.

He could not eat and he could not keep warm, even with the cook-stove top red hot and a blanket over his shoulders. By noon the chill had gone and he was blazing with fever. Still the rain and the wind, and no visitors at the ropes, not even the light-keeper.

He lay down on his bed and tried to sleep, but though he dozed a bit, woke always with a start and either a chill or fever fit. His head began to ache violently. And then, in the lonesomeness and misery, fear began to take hold of him.

He remembered the symptoms the doctor had warned him against, headache, fever, and all the rest. He felt his wrists and arms and began to imagine that beneath the skin were the little bunches, like small shot, that were the certain indications. Then he remembered how that other man had looked, how he had died. Was he to look that way and die like that? And he was all alone, they had left him alone.

Night came. The rain had ceased and stars were shining clear. Inside the shanty the minister tossed on the bed, or staggered back and forth about the two rooms. He wondered what the time might be; then he did not care. He was alone. The smallpox had him in its grip. He was alone and he was going to die. Why didn't some one come? Where was Mrs. Coffin? And Grace? She was somewhere near him—Parker had said so—and he must see her before he died. He called her name over and over again.

The wind felt cold on his forehead. He stumbled amidst the beach grass. What was this thing across his path? A rope, apparently, but why should there be ropes in that house? There had never been any before. He climbed over it and it was a climb of hundreds of feet and the height made him giddy. That was a house, another house, not the one he had been living in. And there were lights all about. Perhaps one of them was the light at the parsonage. And a big bell was booming. That was his church bell and he would be late for the meeting.

Some one was speaking to him. He knew the voice. He had known it always and would know it forever. It was the voice he wanted to hear.

"Grace!" he called. "Grace! I want you. Don't go! Don't go! Grace! oh, my dear! don't go!"

Then the voice had gone. No, it had not gone. It was still there and he heard it speaking to him, begging him to listen, pleading with him to go somewhere, go back, back to something or other. And there was an arm about his waist and some one was leading him, helping him. He broke down and cried childishly and some one cried with him.

Early the next morning, just as day was breaking, a buggy, the horse which drew it galloping, rocked and bumped down the lighthouse lane. Dr. Parker, his brows drawn together and his lips set with anxiety, was driving. He had been roused from sleep in the hotel at Hyannis by a boy with a telegram. "Come quick," it read. "Mr. Ellery sick." The sender was Noah Ellis, the lightkeeper. The doctor had hired a fast horse, ridden at top speed to Bayport, gotten a fresh horse there and hurried on. He stopped at his own house but a moment, merely to rouse his wife and ask her if there was any fresh news. But she had not even heard of the minister's seizure.

"My soul, Will!" she cried, "you don't think it's the smallpox, do you?"

"Lord knows! I'm afraid so," groaned her husband. "*What* made me leave him? I ought to have known better. If that boy dies, I'll never draw another easy breath."

He rushed out, sprang into the buggy, and drove on. At the ropes, early as it was, he found a small group waiting and gazing at the shanty. The lightkeeper was there and two or three other men. They were talking earnestly.

"How is he, Noah?" demanded the doctor, jumping to the ground.

"I don't know, doc," replied Ellis. "I ain't heard sence last night when I telegraphed you."

"Haven't heard? What do you mean by that? Haven't you been with him?"

"No-o," was the rather sheepish reply. "You see, I—I wanted to, but my wife's awful scart I'll catch it and——"

"The devil!" Dr. Parker swore impatiently. "Who is with him then? You haven't left him alone, have you?"

"No-o," Noah hesitated once more. "No-o, he ain't alone. She's there."

"She? Who? Keziah Coffin?"

"I don't cal'late Keziah's heard it yet. We was waitin' for you 'fore we said much to anybody. But she's there—the—the one that found him. You see, he was out of his head and wanderin' up the lane 'most to the main road and she'd been callin' on Keziah and when she come away from the parsonage she heard him hollerin' and goin' on and——"

"Who did?"

"Why"—the lightkeeper glanced at his companions—"why, doc, 'twas Grace Van Horne. And she fetched him back to the shanty and then come and got me to telegraph you."

"Grace Van Horne! Grace Van— Do you mean to say she is there with him *now?*"

"Yes. She wouldn't leave him. She seemed 'most as crazy's he was. My wife and me, we——"

But Parker did not wait to hear the rest. He ran

at full speed to the door of the shanty. Grace herself opened it.

"How is he?" demanded the doctor.

"I think he seems a little easier; at any rate, he's not delirious. He's in there. Oh, I'm so thankful you've come."

"Is that the doctor?" called Ellery weakly from the next room. "Is it?"

"Yes," replied Parker, throwing off his coat and hat. "Coming, Mr. Ellery."

"For God's sake, doctor, send her away. Don't let her stay. Make her go. Make her *go!* I've got the smallpox and if she stays she will die. Don't you understand? she *must* go."

"Hush, John," said Grace soothingly. "Hush, dear."

Dr. Parker stopped short and looked at her. She returned the look, but without the slightest semblance of self-consciousness or embarrassment. She did not realize that she had said anything unusual, which must sound inexplicably strange to him. Her thoughts were centered in that adjoining room and she wondered why he delayed.

"Well?" she asked impatiently. "What is it? Why do you wait?"

The doctor did not answer. However, he waited no longer, but hurried in to his new patient.

# CHAPTER XVIII

## IN WHICH KEZIAH DECIDES TO FIGHT

THE news was flying from house to house along the main road. Breakfasts were interrupted as some neighbor rushed in to tell the story which another neighbor had brought to him or her. Mr. Ellery was very sick and it was feared he had the smallpox, that was what Mrs. Parker, the doctor's wife, told those who lived near her. By the time the Corners heard of it the tale had grown until the minister was said to be dying. And when it reached Gaius Winslow's home at the upper end of the town he was reported dead. This was denied, upon investigation, but soon another rumor grew and spread; Grace Van Horne was with him, had taken him back to the shanty, and insisted upon staying there until the doctor came. Facing that dreadful disease and— It was wonderful— and queer.

At the Danielses' house the servant girl rushed into the dining room to serve the toast and the story at one swoop. Captain Elkanah's dignity deserted him for an instant and his egg spoon jingled to the floor. Annabel's face turned a dull red. Her eyes flashed sparks.

" Pa ! " she cried, " I—I—if you don't do something now I'll never——"

Her father shook his head warningly. "Debby," he said to the maid, "you needn't wait."

Debby departed reluctantly. After the kitchen door had closed, Captain Elkanah said: "My dear, we mustn't be too hasty in this matter. Remember, Mr. Ellery is very sick. As for—for the Van Horne girl, we haven't heard the whole truth yet. She may not be there at all, or it may be just an accident——"

"Accident! Pa, you make me boil. Accident! Accidents like that don't happen. If you let her stay there, or if— Oh, to think of it! And we were calling him a hero and—and everything! Hero! he stayed there just so she might——"

"Hush! hush, child!"

"I shan't hush. Pa, are you going to let him disgrace himself with *her?*"

"No, no. Probably there ain't any idea of his marrying her. If there is——"

"If there is you put him out of the church and out of this town. And as for *her*— O-oh! And we've been having him here at dinner and—and I have— Oh, I shall die! I wish I *was* dead!"

Then followed hysterics and agony, greedily listened to by Debby, whose ear was at the crack of the door. Captain Elkanah soothed and pleaded and tried to pacify. It ended by his promising to investigate and, if necessary, take steps 'immejitly."

Lavinia Pepper sprung the mine on her brother. Kyan was horrified. He had grown to be one of Ellery's most devoted worshipers.

"Smallpox!" he groaned. "The minister got the smallpox. Oh! that's turrible."

"Ain't it?" observed his sister, also horrified,

but rather relishing the horror. " And if it hadn't been for Gracie Van Horne——"

" *What?* "

" What's the matter with you? I say, if Gracie Van Horne hadn't happened to meet him, wanderin' around, crazy as a coot, and toted him back——"

" Gracie — Van — Horne! Godfreys mighty! She—she met him? Where? Down to Peters's grove, was it? "

" Peters's grove! No. What on earth made you think 'twas there? She'd been visitin' Keziah Coffin at the parsonage, and when she come out on the main road she heard him aravin' down the lane. Must have passed right by this house and we never heard him. I never see such a dead man as you be when you're asleep. You don't *sound* dead, I'll say that for you, but nothin' wakes you up."

" Why, Laviny! you never woke up yourself."

" That's right, lay it onto me. I expected you would; it's just like you. But why in time did you think Grace met the minister way down to Peters's grove? That's the most loony notion ever I heard, even from you. What made you think of it? "

" Nothin', nothin'. I guess I *was* loony, maybe. Dear! dear! dear! have you heard how's he's gettin' on? Is he took bad? "

" I ain't heard nothin' yet, nobody has. But see here, 'Bish Pepper, you act funny to me. I want to know more about that Peters's grove notion. *Why* did you say it? "

Kyan wriggled upon the rack and dodged and squirmed for the next twenty minutes. He tried his best to keep the fateful secret, but he admitted too much, or not enough, and his sister kept up the cross-examination. At the end of the session she was still unsatisfied, but she was on the scent and her brother knew it. He fled to the woodshed and there punctuated his morning task of kindling chopping with groans and awful forebodings.

One of the very first to hear of the minister's illness was Keziah Coffin. Mrs. Parker told her and Keziah started for the beach before the tale of Grace's part in the night's happenings reached the village. She did not wait for a conveyance, hardly waited to throw a shawl over her shoulders, but began to cover the three miles on foot. She had walked nearly two thirds of the distance when Captain Zeb Mayo overtook her and gave her a seat in his chaise.

They said little during the drive, the shock and anxiety forbidding conversation. At the ropes was the same group, larger now, and Dr. Parker's horse was hitched to one of the posts.

"You can't go in, Mrs. Coffin," said Thoph Black. "The doctor give us his orders not to let nobody get by. I guess nobody wants to, but all the same——"

Keziah paid not the slightest attention to Mr. Black. She stooped beneath his arm, under the rope and was on her way to the shanty before they realized her intention. Captain Zeb roared a command for her to return, but she kept on. No one followed, not even the captain. Mrs. Mayo had strictly forbidden his passing the dead line.

Keziah opened the door and entered the little building. The living room was empty, but at the sound of her step some one came from the room adjoining. That some one was Grace.

"You can't go in, Mrs. Coffin," said Thoph Black.

"Aunt Keziah!" she cried. "What did you come here for? Why did you?"

"Gracie!" exclaimed the housekeeper. "You? —*you?*"

Dr. Parker appeared, holding up a hand for silence.

"Hush!" he cried. "He's quiet now and I think he will sleep. Don't talk here. Go outside, if you must talk—and I suppose you must."

Grace led the way. Fortunately, the door was on the side not visible from the spot where Captain Zeb and the rest were standing. Keziah, bewildered and amazed at the girl's presence, followed dumbly.

"Now, auntie," whispered Grace, turning to her, "you want to know how he is, of course. Well, I think he is better. The doctor thinks so, too. But why did you come here?"

"Why did I come? I? Why, because my place was here. I belonged here. For the love of mercy's sakes what are *you* doin' here? With *him?* And the smallpox!"

"Hush. I can't help it. I don't care. I don't care for anything any more. I'm glad I came. I'm glad I was the one to find him and help him. No matter what happens—to me—I'm glad. I never was so glad before. I love him, Aunt Keziah. I can say it to you, for you know it—you must know it. I *love* him and he needed me and I came. He was calling my name when I found him. He might have died there, alone in the wet and cold, and I saved him. Think what that means to me."

The girl was in a sort of frenzy of excitement and hysterical exaltation. All the night she had been calm and quiet, repressing her feelings, and tending the man she loved. Now, with some one to whom she could confide, she was calm no longer. Keziah answered her soothingly, questioning her from time to time, until, at last, she learned the whole story.

The door opened softly and Dr. Parker came out.

"He's asleep," he said. "And he's better, much better. And I'll tell you something else, if you won't make too much noise about it—he hasn't got the smallpox."

The two women looked at him.

"Fact," he said, with an emphatic nod. "Not a symptom of it. I'd have bet my best hat that he wasn't going to have it and I won't have to go bareheaded yet awhile. He is pretty close to brain fever, though, but I guess he'll dodge that this time, with care. On the whole, Keziah, I'm glad you came. This young lady," with a movement of the head toward Grace, "has done her part. She really saved his life, if I'm not mistaken. Now, I think she can go away and leave him to you and me. I'll pretty nearly guarantee to have him up and out of this—this pesthole in a fortnight."

Here was joyful tidings, the better for being so unexpected. Keziah leaned against the boards and drew a long breath. Grace said nothing, but, after a moment, she went into the house.

"That's a good thing, too," commented Parker, watching her as she went. "I wanted to talk with you, Keziah Coffin, and right away. Now, then, there's something up, something that I don't know about, and I rather guess you do. Young women—even when they're her kind and that's as good a kind as there is—don't risk smallpox for any young man

they pick up casually. They don't carry—I guess
it was pretty nearly carrying—him home and put
him to bed and care for him and cry over him and
call him ' dear.' And he doesn't beg them to run
away and let him die rather than to stay there and
risk dying, too. No, not to any great extent. Now,
Keziah, you and I are fairly good friends and we
ought to know each other by this time. I see a light
—a little one. Now, then, if you turn up the lamp,
so that I can see the whole blaze, maybe I can help
those two in yonder."

Keziah considered. " All right, doctor," she
said, when she reached a decision, " all right; I'll tell
you the whole thing, and you can see one of the
reasons why my hair is gettin' grayer. This thing
has reached the point now where there's no keepin'
it quiet. Folk'll know—I s'pose they know already
—that she's been here with him. They'll suspect a
lot more and the truth is better than suspicion—that
is, it can't be worse than the suspicions that come
natural to a good many minds in this town. I am
glad I can tell you, for I guess the time's come to
step out in broad daylight and h'ist our colors. Now,
you listen. Here 'tis, from beginnin' to end."

She went on to tell all she knew of her parson's
love story.

Dr. Parker listened.

" Hum! " he said thoughtfully, " I see. What
made her change her mind so suddenly? You say,
or you gather from what Mr. Ellery told you, that
she had all but agreed to marry him. She cares
for him, that's sure. Then, all at once, she throws
him over and accepts Nat. Of course her uncle's
sudden seizure was a shock and he wanted Nat to

have her, but she isn't the kind of girl to be easily swayed. Why did she do it?"

"Well, doctor, that's kind of a puzzle to me. All I can think is that she come to realize what it might mean to him, the minister, if he married a Come-Outer. I think she done it for his sake, to save him, though what made her realize it all at once I don't know. There's the part we ain't heard."

"I guess you're right. Something happened between the time she left Ellery and when you and I reached the tavern. But never mind that, that doesn't count now. Let's look at things as they are this minute. She's here and folks know it. As they do know it they'll begin to talk, and the more they talk the farther from the truth they'll get—most of 'em. Nat, poor chap, is dead, so her promise to him is canceled. Ellery will get well if he isn't troubled, and her being with him will help more than anything else. I can understand now why he broke down."

"Yes, he ain't been himself since it happened."

"Of course, and the last few weeks of worry and night work have helped to wreck his nerves. Well, as I see it, there's only one thing to do. If she leaves him he'll go to pieces again, so she mustn't leave. And she can't stay without an explanation. I say let's give the explanation; let's come right out with the announcement that they're engaged."

"Whew! that'll stir things up."

"You bet! But let it stir. I like that parson of yours; he's a trump. And I always liked her, although, generally speaking, I don't love Come-Outers. And I like her more than ever now, when she risked what she thought was smallpox to care for him. As I said, she saved his life, and she ought to have him. She *shall* have him."

" But she's a Come-Outer and — there's the church."

" Well, I know it. But he never was so popular as he is now. And she isn't by any means a steady-going Come-Outer. Why, Zeke Bassett and the rest have been finding fault with her and calling her a backslider. That'll help. Then you trust me to whoop up her heroism and the fact that without her he would have died. We can do it, Keziah. Come on! I've tackled a good many jobs, but matchmaking isn't one of 'em. Here goes to tackle that."

Keziah was delighted; here was work after her own heart. But she still hesitated.

" Doctor," she said, " you've forgot one thing, that's Gracie herself. Would she marry him now, knowing it may mean the loss of his ministry and all, any more than she would at first? I don't believe it."

" That's your part, Keziah. You've got to show her she *must* marry him or he'll die; see? Call on me to back you up in any fairy yarn you spin. You prove to her it's her duty to marry him. You'll have to stay here and help nurse, of course, and that's easy because his disease isn't contagious. You convince her and I'll take care of the congregation. He'll live to be minister here for the rest of his life, if he wants to, and she'll be a minister's wife and sit in the front pew. I'll guarantee the church if you'll guarantee the girl. Why, it's your duty! Come, now, what do you say? "

Keziah's hesitation was at an end. Her face lit up.

" I say good ! " she cried. " And I'll be thankful to you all the rest of my life. But for the dear mercy sakes, don't say ' duty ' to me again. Oh, doctor, if you only knew what it means to me to be fightin' at last for somethin' that ain't just duty, but what I really want ! I do honestly believe we can win. Glory, hallelujah ! And now I want to give you a piece of advice, your course for the first leg, as you might say : you see Cap'n Zebedee Mayo."

" Humph ! Cap'n Zeb is the first man I mean to see."

Captain Zeb listened with his mouth and eyes and ears open. Mrs. Mayo was with him when the doctor called, and she, too, listened.

" Well ! " exclaimed the captain, when the plea for support was ended. " Well, by the flukes of Jonah's whale ! Talk about surprises ! Old lady, what do you say ? "

" I say go ahead, Zebedee. Go ahead ! If Mr. Ellery wanted to marry Jezebel's sister, and I knew he really wanted to, I'd—I do believe I'd help him get her. And Grace Van Horne is a good girl. Go ahead."

" Of course," put in Parker, profiting by a hint of Mrs. Coffin's, " of course Daniels will fight tooth and nail against us. He'll be for discharging Ellery at once. And he really runs the parish committee."

" He does, hey ? Well, I cal'late he don't. Not if I'm on deck, he don't. All right, doctor, I'm with you. He, he, he ! " he chuckled. " Say, doc, do you know I sort of love a good lively row. That's been the only trouble with our society sence Mr. Ellery took command of it—there ain't been any rows. He, he, he ! Well, there'll be one now."

There was, and it was lively enough to suit even Captain Zeb. Dr. Parker, on his calls that day, was assailed with a multitude of questions concerning Grace's presence at the shanty. He answered them cheerfully, dilating upon the girl's bravery, her good sense, and the fact that she had saved Mr. Ellery's life. Then he confided, as a strict secret, the fact that the two were engaged. Before his hearers had recovered from the shock of this explosion, he was justifying the engagement. Why shouldn't they marry if they wanted to? It was a free country. The girl wasn't a Come-Outer any longer, and, besides—and this carried weight in a good many households—what a black eye the marriage would be for that no-account crowd at the chapel.

Captain Zebedee, having shipped with the insurgents, worked for them from sunrise to sunset and after. Zeb was something of a politician and knew whom to " get at." He sought his fellows on the parish committee and labored with them. Mrs. Mayo and the doctor's wife championed the cause at sewing circle. They were lively, those sewing meetings, and the fur flew. Didama Rogers and Lavinia Pepper were everywhere and ready to agree with whichever side seemed likely to win. Lavinia was so deeply interested that she forgot to catechise Abishai further about his untimely reference to Peters's grove. And Kyan, puzzled but thankful, kept silence.

It was by no means a one-sided struggle. Captain Elkanah, spurred on by the furious Annabel, marshaled his forces and proclaimed that Ellery, having disgraced the Regular Society, should no longer occupy its pulpit.

" If he does," thundered Elkanah, " I shall never cross the threshold of that church. And I've worshiped there for fifty years. Hum—ha! I should like to know whose money has gone more liberal for that meeting house than mine! But not another cent —no, sir! not one—if that licentious young scamp continues to blaspheme there."

He hinted concerning a good-sized contribution toward a parish house, something the society needed. If Ellery was discharged, the contribution would probably be made, not otherwise. And this was a point worth considering.

Daniels also wrote to his influential friends of the National Regular Society. But Captain Zebedee had forestalled him there and both letters were laid on the table to await further developments. As for the Come-Outers, they were wild with rage and Grace was formally read out of their communion.

" I wonder," shrieked Ezekiel Bassett, in prayer meeting, " what the sperrit of the good and great man who used to lead us from this 'ere platform would say if he was here now? Hey? what would he say? "

Josiah Badger upreared his lanky person. " I dreamed about Cap'n Eben t'other n-nin-nun-night," he stammered. " I see him just as—p-pup-pup-plain as you hear me n-n-now. And he says to me, he says, Josiah,' he says, ' I-I-I-I——' "

" Ki yi! " broke in Thoph Baker, from the shadow of the rear seat. Josiah turned to berate Thoph, who, being in disgrace because of his defense of Ellery, was reckless, and the communication from the dead leader of the Come-Outers was lost in the squabble which followed.

Meantime Keziah, installed as head nurse at the shanty, was having her troubles. The minister was getting better, slowly but surely getting better. The danger of brain fever was at an end, but he was very weak and must not be excited, so the doctor said. He knew nothing of the struggle for and against him which was splitting Trumet in twain, and care was taken that he should not know it. He was not allowed to talk, and, for the most part, was quite contented to be silent, watching Grace as she moved about the room. If he wondered why she was still with him, he said nothing, and the thought of what his congregation might say did not vex him in the least. She was there, he saw her every day, that was enough.

He had expressed a wish to talk with his housekeeper. " I've got something to tell you, Aunt Keziah," he said weakly. " Some news for you and —and——"

" Cat's foot! " snapped Keziah briskly, " don't start in tellin' me news now. I've got my hands full as 'tis. News'll keep and you won't, if you talk another minute."

" But this is important."

" So are you, though you may not think so. If you don't believe it ask Grace."

" Well," the minister sighed. " Well, perhaps I won't tell it now. I'd rather wait until I feel stronger. You won't care, will you? It will be hard to tell and I——"

" No, no! Care? No. If it's bad news I don't want to hear it, and if it's good I can wait, I cal'late. You turn over and take a nap."

She could manage him; it was with Grace that

she had her struggle. John was safe now; he would be himself again before very long, and the girl had begun to think of his future and his reputation. She knew that gossip must be busy in the village, and, much as she wished to remain by his side, she decided that she should not do so. And then Keziah began to fulfill her agreement with Dr. Parker.

First, and bluntly, she told the girl that her leaving now was useless. The secret was out; it had been made public. Everyone knew she was in love with John and he with her. Their engagement was considered an established certainty. Grace was greatly agitated and very indignant.

"Who dared say so?" she demanded. "Who dared say we were engaged? It's not true. It's a wicked lie and— Who is responsible, Aunt Keziah?"

"Well, I suppose likely I am, much as anybody, deary."

"You? You, Aunt Keziah?"

"Yup; me. You are in love with him; at any rate, you said so. And you're here with him, ain't you? If you two ain't engaged you ought to be."

"Aunt Keziah, how can you speak so? Don't you realize——"

"Look here. Don't you want to marry him?"

"*Want* to? Oh, please— How can you? I——"

"S-s-sh! There! there! I am a bull-headed old thing, for sure. But I'm like the dog that chased the rat across the shelf where they kept the best china, my intentions are good. Don't cry, deary. Let's get to the bottom of this thing, as the man said when he tumbled into the well. When I first

318

knew that you and John were in love with each other, I felt dreadful. I knew your uncle and I knew Trumet. If you had married then, or let people know that you thought of it, 'twould have been the end, and ruin for John and you. But things are diff'rent now, a good deal diff'rent. John is worshiped pretty nigh, since his pluck with that smallpox man. He could go into church and dance a jig in the pulpit and nobody—or precious few, at least —would find fault. And you've stood by him. If it wa'n't for you he wouldn't be here to-day, and people know that. Dr. Parker and Captain Zebedee and Gaius Winslow and dozens more are fighting for him and for you. And the doctor says they are going to win. Do you want to spoil it all?"

"Aunt Keziah, that night before uncle died I was upstairs in my room and I heard uncle and Captain Elkanah Daniels talking."

"Elkanah? Was he there at your house?"

"Yes. Somehow or other—I don't know how —he had learned about—about John and me. And he was furious. Aunt Keziah, I heard him say that unless I broke off with John he would drive him from the ministry and from Trumet and disgrace him forever. He said that if I really cared for him I would not ruin his life. That brought me to myself. I realized how wicked I had been and what I was doing. That was why I—I——"

"There! there! Tut! tut! tut! Hum! Now I see. But, Gracie, you ain't goin' to ruin his life. No, nor Elkanah ain't goin' to do it, either. He can't, no matter how hard he tries. I've lived to see the day when there's a bigger man in the Reg'lar church than Elkanah Daniels, and I thank the good Lord for it."

"I never should have come here. I know it. But he needed me. Aunt Keziah, he was sick and dying almost, and I couldn't leave him. I came, and now he will be ruined and disgraced."

"He won't, I tell you; he won't. Listen to me. I ain't talkin' for my health. Listen!"

She argued and pleaded and coaxed, and, at last, when she began to think she had prevailed, Grace brought forward another objection. She had given her word to her uncle. How could she break that promise made to a dying man? She would feel like a traitor.

"Traitor to who?" demanded the housekeeper, losing patience. "Not to poor Nat, for he's gone. And don't you suppose that he and Eben understand things better now, where they are? Do you suppose that Nat wouldn't want you to be happy? I know he would, for I knew him."

It was still unsettled when the long talk was over, but Grace agreed not to leave the minister at present. She would stay where she was until he was himself again, at least. Keziah was satisfied with the preliminary skirmish. She felt confident of winning the victory, and in the prospect of happiness for others, she was almost happy herself. Yet each time the mail was brought to the shanty she dreaded to look at it, and the sight of a stranger made her shake with fear. Ansel Coffin had threatened to come to Trumet. If he came, she had made up her mind what to do.

The parish committee was to meet. Captain Elkanah had announced his intention of moving that

"'He may be minister of the Regular church . . . but he'll
never marry her, now.'"

John Ellery be expelled from the Regular church. There was to be no compromise, no asking for a resignation; he must be discharged, thrown out in disgrace. The county papers were full of the squabble, but they merely reported the news and did not take sides. The fight was too even for that.

Captain Zeb chuckled. " It's all right, Keziah," he said. " We know what's what and who's who. The Rev. Mr. Ellery can preach here for the next hundred year, if he lives that long and wants to, and he can marry whoever he darn pleases, besides. El-kanah's licked and he knows it. He ain't got enough backers to man a lobster dory. Let him holler; noise don't scare grown folks."

One afternoon a few days before the date set for the meeting Elkanah and two or three of his hench-men were on the piazza of the Daniels home, dis-cussing the situation. They were blue and downcast. Annabel was in the sitting room, shedding tears of humiliation and jealous rage on the haircloth sofa.

" Well," observed her father, " there's one thing we can do. If the vote in committee goes against us, I shall insist on the calling of a congregational meeting. Hum—ha! Yes, I shall insist on that."

" Won't be no good, cap'n," sniffed Beriah Sal-ters dolefully. " The biggest part of the congre-gation's for Ellery, and you know it. They're as sot on him as if he was the angel Gabriel. If you'd only told what you knew afore this smallpox busi-ness, we'd have been able to give him and his Come-Outer woman what b'longs to 'em. But not now."

Captain Daniels shifted uneasily in his chair.

" Hum—ha! " he barked, to cover confusion. " Hum—ha! It seemed to me more—er—charitable to give the misguided young man another chance, and I did it. But— What's that?"

Some one was talking excitedly on the sidewalk beyond the lilac bushes at the border of the Daniels property. Voices answered. Didama Rogers darted out of her yard and past the house in the direction of the sounds. Salters rose and walked down to the gate.

"Hey!" he shouted. "Halloo! Ahoy there! You, Em'lous, what is it?"

Emulous Sparrow, the fish peddler, was seated in his cart, which was surrounded by men and women, neighbors of the Danielses. There was a perfect storm of questionings and ejaculations. Salters opened the gate and joined the group. A moment later he came running back, up the walk toward the piazza.

"Cap'n," he shouted. "Cap'n Elkanah, here's news! What do you think? A telegram's just come from Nat Hammond. He's safe and sound in New York, and he'll be here day after to-morrow."

They could not believe it and rushed out to hear more. Emulous, glowing with importance, affirmed that it was so. He had seen the telegram at the store. It was for Grace Van Horne and they were just going to send a boy over to the shanty with it.

"No details nor nothin'," he declared. "Just said 'Am all right. Arrived to-day. Will be in Trumet Thursday.' And 'twas signed 'Nathaniel Hammond.' There!"

"Well, by thunder!" exclaimed Salters. "If that don't beat all. I wonder what's happened to him? Two year gone and give up for dead, and now— What do you cal'late it means?"

Captain Elkanah seized him by the arm and led him out of the group. The old man's face was alight with savage joy and his voice shook with exultation.

"I'll tell you one thing it means," he whispered. "It means the end of Ellery, so far as his marrying her is concerned. She gave her word to Hammond and she'll keep it. She's no liar, whatever else she is. He may be minister of the Regular church, though *I'll* never set under him, but he'll never marry her, now."

# CHAPTER XIX

## IN WHICH A RECEPTION IS CALLED OFF

FAR out on the Pacific coast there are two small islands, perhaps a hundred miles distant from one another. The first of these is uninhabited. On the other is a little colony of English-speaking people, half-breed descendants of native women and the survivors of a crew from a British vessel cast away there in the latter part of the eighteenth century.

On the first of these islands, the smaller one, the *Sea Mist* had been wrecked. Driven out of her course by a typhoon, she staggered through day after day and night after night of terrific wind and storm until, at last, there was promise of fair weather. Captain Nat, nearly worn out from anxiety, care, and the loss of sleep, had gone to his state-room and the first mate was in charge. It was three o'clock, the wind still blowing and the darkness pitchy, when the forward lookout shrieked a warning, " Breakers under the lee! " Almost the next instant the ship was on a coral reef, full of water, and the seas breaking over her from stem to stern.

Morning came and showed a little patch of land, with palm trees and tropical vegetation waving in the gusts and green in the sunshine. Captain Nat ordered the boats to be lowered. Much as he hated the thought, he saw that the *Sea Mist* had made her last voyage and must be abandoned. He went to the cabin, collected papers and charts and prepared to leave. The ship's money, over ten thousand dollars in gold belonging to the owner and to be used in trade and speculation among the East Indies, he took with him. Then the difficult and dangerous passage through the opening in the reef was begun.

Only the captain's boat reached the shore. The mate's was caught by a huge breaker, dashed against the reef and sunk. Captain Nat, his second mate and five of his men were all that was left of the *Sea Mist's* company. And on that island they remained for nearly two weeks. Provisions they had brought ashore with them. Water they found by digging. Nat hid the gold at night, burying it on the beach below high-water mark.

Then, having made sure of his location by consulting the chart, he determined to attempt a voyage to the second island, where he knew the English colony to be. Provisions were getting short, and to remain longer where they were was to risk starvation and all its horrors. So, in the longboat, which was provided with a sail, they started. Charts and papers and the gold the skipper took with them. None of the crew knew of the existence of the money; it was a secret which the captain kept to himself.

A hundred miles they sailed in the longboat and, at last, the second island was sighted. They landed and found, to their consternation and surprise, that it, too, was uninhabited. The former residents had grown tired of their isolation and, a trading vessel having touched there, had seized the opportunity to depart for Tahiti. Their houses were

empty, their cattle, sheep, goats, and fowl roamed
wild in the woods, and the fruit was rotting on the
trees. In its way the little island was an Eveless
Eden, flowing with milk and honey; but to Captain
Nat, a conscientious skipper with responsibilities to
his owners, it was a prison from which he determined
to escape. Then, as if to make escape impossible, a
sudden gale came up and the longboat was smashed
by the surf.

"I guess that settles it," ruefully observed the
second mate, another Cape Codder, from Hyannis.
"Cal'late we'll stay here for a spell now, hey,
Cap'n."

"For a spell, yes," replied Nat. "We'll stay
here until we get another craft to set sail in, and no
longer."

"Another craft? *Another* one? Where in time
you goin' to get her?"

"Build her," said Captain Nat cheerfully.
Then, pointing to the row of empty houses and the
little deserted church, he added, "There's timber
and nails—yes, and cloth, such as 'tis. If I can't
build a boat out of them I'll agree to eat the whole
settlement."

He did not have to eat it, for the boat was
built. It took them six months to build her, and
she was a curious-looking vessel when done, but, as
the skipper said, "She may not be a clipper, but she'll
sail anywhere, if you give her time enough." He
had been the guiding spirit of the whole enterprise,
planning it, laying the keel, burning buildings to
obtain nails and iron, hewing trees for the largest
beams, showing them how to spin ropes from cocoa-
nut fiber, improvising sails from the longboat's can-

vas pieced out with blankets and odd bits of cloth from the abandoned houses. Even a strip of carpet from the church floor went into the making of those sails.

At last she was done, but Nat was not satisfied.

" I never commanded a ship where I couldn't h'ist Yankee colors," he said, " and, by the ever-lastin'! I won't now. We've got to have a flag."

So, from an old pair of blue overalls, a white cotton shirt, and the red hangings of the church pulpit, he made a flag and hoisted it to the truck of his queer command. They provisioned her, gave her a liberal supply of fresh water, and, one morn-ing, she passed through the opening of the lagoon out to the deep blue of the Pacific. And, hidden in her captain's stateroom under the head of his bunk, was the ten thousand dollars in gold. For Nat had sworn to himself, by " the everlasting " and other oaths, to deliver that money to his New York owners safe and, necessary expenses deducted of course, untouched.

For seven weeks the crazy nondescript slopped across the ocean. Fair winds helped her and, at last, she entered the harbor of Nukahiva, over twelve hundred miles away. And there—" Hammond's luck," the sailors called it—was a United States man-of-war lying at anchor, the first American vessel to touch at that little French settlement for five years. The boat they built was abandoned and the survivors of the *Sea Mist* were taken on board the man-of-war and carried to Tahiti.

From Tahiti Captain Nat took passage on a French bark for Honolulu. Here, after a month's wait, he found opportunity to leave for New York on

23  327

an American ship, the *Stars and Stripes*. And finally, after being away from home for two years, he walked into the office of his New York owners, deposited their gold on a table, and cheerfully observed, " Well, here I am."

That was the yarn which Trumet was to hear later on. It filled columns of the city papers at the time, and those interested may read it, in all its details, in a book written by an eminent author. The tale of a Cape Cod sea captain, plucky and resourceful and adequate, as Yankee sea captains were expected to be, and were, in those days.

But Trumet did not hear the yarn immediately. All that it heard and all that it knew was contained in Captain Nat's brief telegram. " Arrived to-day. Will be home Thursday." That was all, but it was enough, for in that dispatch was explosive sufficient to blow to atoms the doctor's plans and Keziah's, the great scheme which was to bring happiness to John Ellery and Grace Van Horne.

Dr. Parker heard it, while on his way to Mrs. Prince's, and, neglecting that old lady for the once, he turned his horse and drove as fast as possible to the shanty on the beach. Fast as he drove, Captain Zebedee Mayo got there ahead of him. Captain Zeb was hitching his white and ancient steed to the post as the doctor hove in sight.

" By mighty! " the captain exclaimed, with a sigh of relief, " I'm glad enough you've come, doctor. I hated to go in there alone. You've heard, of course."

" Yes, I've heard."

" Say, ain't it wonderful! I'm tickled all up one side and sorry all down t'other. Nat's a true-blue feller, and I'm glad enough that he ain't shark bait; but what about the minister and her? She's promised to Nat, you know, and——"

"I know. Don't I know! I've been going over the affair and trying to see a way out ever since I heard of the telegram. Tut! tut! I'm like you, mighty glad Hammond is safe, but it would have spared complications if he had stayed wherever he's been for a few months longer. We would have married those two in there by that time."

"Sartin we would. But he didn't stay. Are you goin' to tell Mr. Ellery?"

"Certainly not. And I hope he hasn't been told. He's getting well fast now, but he mustn't be worried, or back he'll go again. We must see Mrs. Coffin. Keziah is our main hold. That woman has got more sense than all the rest of us put together."

But it was Grace, not Keziah, who opened the shanty door in answer to their knock. She was pale and greeted them calmly, but it was evident that her calmness was the result of sheer will power.

"Won't you come in, doctor?" she asked. "Good afternoon, Captain Mayo."

Dr. Parker entered the building, but Captain Zeb remained outside, stammering that he cal'lated he'd better stay where he could keep an eye on his horse. This was such a transparent excuse that it would have been funny at any other time. No one smiled now, however.

"Is—is Mrs. Coffin—er—Keziah aboard?" the captain asked.

"No, she isn't. She went to the parsonage a few hours ago. Mr. Ellis brought the mail and there was a letter in it for her. She said it was important and that she must go home to see about some things. She'll be back pretty soon, I suppose."

The doctor whispered her name then and she went inside, closing the door after her. Captain Zebedee sat down on the step to ponder over the new and apparently insurmountable difficulty which had arisen. As he said afterwards, "The more I tried to get an observation, the thicker it got. Blamed if I could see anything but fog, but I could hear—I could hear Elkanah and his gang gigglin', ahead, astern and off both bows."

Parker found his patient sleeping soundly and had not disturbed him. Returning to the living room he spoke to Grace.

"Humph!" he grunted, watching her from under his brows, "everything seems to be all right in there. He hasn't been excited or anything like that?"

"No."

"That's good. He mustn't be. You understand that? He mustn't be told anything that will upset him. He's getting well fast and I want it to continue."

"Yes, I understand."

"Hum! Er—have you heard— Has anyone been here?"

"Yes. I have heard. The telegram came and I answered it."

"You did? Well, it's a miracle and we're all thankful, of course. Did you—er—er——"

"Doctor, I must go home. I mustn't stay here any longer."

"Why not?"

"You know why not. I must be at home when

he comes. You must get some one to take my place. Aunt Keziah will stay, of course, and perhaps Mrs. Higgins would come, or Hannah Poundberry. She——"

"Not if I know it. I'd as soon have a hay-cutter running in here as Hannah's tongue. I could stop a hay-cutter when it got too noisy. Well, if you must go, you must, I suppose. But stay through to-morrow, at any rate. Nat won't get here until Thursday, and I may be able to find another nurse by that time. And what I shall say to him," motion-ing toward the other room, "I don't know."

"Must you say anything? Just say that I have been called away for a few days on——on some busi-ness. Don't tell him. Don't tell him the truth, doctor, now. He is too weak and I am afraid——"

She stopped and turned away. The doctor watched her pityingly.

"Cheer up," he said. "At any rate, this is only for a little while. When the captain knows, if he's the man I take him for, he'll——"

She whirled like a flash. "You're not going to tell him?" she cried. "No, no! You mustn't. You must promise me you won't. Promise."

"Somebody'll tell him. Telling things is Tru-met's specialty."

"Then you must stop it. No one must tell him —no one except me. I shall tell him, of course. He must hear it from me and not from anyone else. He would think I was disloyal and ungrateful—and I am! I have been! But I was—I *couldn't* help it. You know, doctor, you know——"

"Yes, yes, I know. Well, I'll promise, but it will all come out right, you see. You mustn't think

331

I—we—have been interfering in your affairs, Grace. But we've all come to think a whole lot of that parson of ours and what he wanted we wanted him to have, that's all."

"I know. Thank you very much for all your kindness, and for your promise."

He would have liked to say much more, but he could not, under the circumstances. He stammered a good-by and, with a question concerning Mrs. Coffin's whereabouts, went out to join Captain Zeb.

"Well?" queried the latter anxiously. "How is it? What's up? What's the next tack?"

"We'll go to the parsonage," was the gloomy answer. "If anybody can see a glimmer in this cussed muddle Keziah Coffin can."

Keziah was on her knees in her room, beside a trunk, the same trunk she had been packing the day of the minister's arrival in Trumet. She was working frantically, sorting garments from a pile, rejecting some and keeping others. She heard voices on the walk below and went down to admit the callers.

"What's the matter, Keziah?" asked Dr. Parker sharply, after a look at her face. "You look as if you'd been through the war. Humph! I suppose you've heard the news?"

Keziah brushed back the hair from her forehead. "Yes," she answered slowly. "I've heard it."

"Well, it's great news, and if it wasn't for—if things weren't as they are, I'd be crowing hallelujahs this minute. Trumet has got a good man safe and sound again, and the Lord knows it needs all of that kind it can get."

"Yes."

"Yes. But there's the other matter. I've been to see Grace. She didn't say so, but it was easy enough to see; the man she promised to marry and thought was dead, is alive. She's a girl of her word —she promised him and she promised her dying uncle —and she'll marry him. And then what will become of John Ellery? He'll go downhill so fast that a ship's anchor wouldn't hold him. If he doesn't die I'll have to send him away somewhere, and the Regular church will lose the minister we've fought so hard for."

"Yes," concurred Zebedee, "and them blasted Danielses'll run the shebang and the rest of us'll have to sing small, I tell you."

"So we've come to you, Keziah," went on the doctor. "Do you see any salvation?"

"Yes, I do."

"You do? Where?"

"In Nat Hammond. If he knows Grace doesn't want to marry him, do you suppose he'll hold her to her promise?"

"I don't know. I'm not so sure. Men don't give up girls like that so easy. *I* wouldn't—by George, I wouldn't! And she won't tell him the whole truth, I'm afraid. She'll pretend to be glad— hang it! she *is* glad—to have him home again and——"

"Of course she's glad. Ain't we all glad and happy and thankful? We ought to be. But "—she hesitated—" doctor, you leave this to me. So far as John and Grace are concerned you needn't worry. I'll take it on myself to see that they have each other, as the Almighty meant 'em to. Leave it to me. Just leave it to me. I *know* I can do it."

She would not say more, nor tell on what grounds she based her optimism. She would go back to the shanty that evening, she said, and stay until the following afternoon. Grace would undoubtedly go to the old tavern to prepare for the homecoming. Let Mrs. Higgins take her place as nurse.

"I shall have to leave, myself," she added, "for a little while; so perhaps you'd better try to get somebody else to help the Higgins woman. Don't ask me any questions, please don't, and be sure not to say a word to anybody—most of all to Grace. Just do as I tell you and leave it to me. And don't come and see me again until after—after he comes home. Good-by, doctor. Good-by, Cap'n Zeb."

She shook hands with each of them, a rather unusual proceeding as they thought of it afterwards. Then they went away and left her.

"Humph!" mused Parker, as they came out at the gate. "Humph! She seems sure, doesn't she. And yet she doesn't act like herself. Did you notice that?"

"Yup. I noticed it. But I expect Nat's droppin' out of the clouds shook her up, same as it done the rest of us. Well, never mind. She's a bully good, capable woman and what she says she'll do she gen'rally does. I'm bettin' on her. By time! I feel better."

Captain Elkanah Daniels and his friends were feeling better also, and they were busy. Trumet had a new hero now. On Wednesday the Boston papers printed excerpts from Captain Hammond's story, and these brief preliminary accounts aroused the admiration of every citizen. It was proposed to give him a reception. Elkanah was the moving spirit

334

in the preparations. Captain Nat, so they learned by telegraphing, would arrive on the noon train Thursday. His was not to be a prosaic progress by stage all the way from Sandwich. A special carriage, drawn by the Daniels span and escorted by other vehicles, was to meet the coach at Bayport and bring him to Trumet in triumphant procession. All this was to be a surprise, of course.

Wednesday afternoon the Daniels following was cheered by the tidings that Grace Van Horne had left the beach and was at her old home, the Hammond tavern. And Mrs. Poundberry reported her busy as a bee " gettin' things ready." This was encouraging and indicated that the minister had been thrown over, as he deserved to be, and that Nat would find his *fiancée* waiting and ready to fulfill her contract. " Reg'lar whirligig, that girl," sniffed Didama Rogers. " If she can't have one man she'll take the next, and then switch back soon's the wind changes. However, most likely she never was engaged to Mr. Ellery, anyhow. He's been out of his head and might have said some fool things that let Dr. Parker and the rest b'lieve he was in love with her. As for pickin' of him up and totin' him back to the shanty that night, that wa'n't nothin' but common humanity. She couldn't let him die in the middle of the lighthouse lane, could she ? "

Thursday was a perfect day, and the reception committee was on hand and waiting in front of the Bayport post office. The special carriage, the span brushed and curried until their coats glistened in the sunshine, was drawn up beside the platform. The horses had little flags fastened to their bridles, and there were other and larger flags on each side of the dashboard. Captain Daniels, imposing in his Sunday raiment, high-collared coat, stock, silk hat and gold-headed cane, sat stiffly erect on the seat in the rear. The other carriages were alongside, among them Captain Zebedee Mayo's ancient chaise, the white horse sound asleep between the shafts. Captain Zeb had not been invited to join the escort, but had joined it without an invitation.

"I guess likely I'd better be on hand," the captain confided to Dr. Parker. "Maybe I can stop Elkanah from talkin' too much about—well, about what we don't want him to talk about, and besides, I'm just as anxious to give Nat a welcome home as the next feller. He's a brick and we're all proud of him. By mighty! I'd like to have seen that craft he built out of cocoanuts and churches—I would so."

Kyan Pepper was there also, not yet fully recovered from the surprise which Lavinia's gracious permission had given him. Abishai had been leaning disconsolately over his front gate early that morning when Noah Ellis, the lightkeeper, jogged down the lane.

"'Mornin', 'Bish," hailed Noah, pulling up his horse. "What's the matter? You look bluer'n a spiled mack'rel. What's the row? Breakfast disagree with you?"

"Naw," replied Kyan shortly. "Where you bound, all rigged up in your shore duds?"

"Bound to Bayport, to see Nat Hammond land," was the cheerful answer. "I ain't had a day off I don't know when, and I thought I'd take one. Be great doin's over there, they tell me. Elkanah's goin' to make a speech and there's eighteen teams of folks goin'."

"I know it. I wisht I was goin', too, but I never have no fun. Have to stay to home and work and slave over them consarned tax papers. Sometimes I wish there wa'n't no taxes."

"Humph! I've wished that, myself, more'n once. Why don't you go, if you want to? Climb right aboard here with me. Plenty of room."

"Hey? You mean that? By godfreys mighty! I'd like to."

"Sartin, I mean it. Come ahead."

Mr. Pepper sadly shook his head. "I guess likely I'd better not," he sighed. "Laviny might not like to have me leave her."

"Oh, fiddlesticks! she won't mind. I'll take care of you. It's perfectly safe. There ain't goin' to be no women around. Haw! haw! haw!"

He was still laughing at his own joke when through the slats of the closed blinds shading the Pepper house parlor a shrill voice was heard speaking.

"Go ahead, 'Bishy dear," called Lavinia. "Go ahead and go. A change of air'll do you good."

Kyan whirled and clutched at the gate.

"*Hey?*" he shouted in amazement.

"Are you deaf? Or is Mr. Ellis laughin' so hard that you can't hear? What is it that's so funny, Mr. Ellis?"

The light-keeper shut off his laughter by a sudden and rather frightened gulp.

"Oh, nothin', nothin', Miss Pepper. Nice day, ain't it?"

"I guess so. I ain't had time to look at it yet.

*I* have to work. I can't let my wife do it for me, like some folks, and take ' days off.' What was it you was laughin' at, Mr. Ellis?"

" Nothin', nothin' at all."

" Hum! They used to tell me there was only one kind of person who laughed at nothin'. Well, 'Bish Pepper, what are you standin' there for? If you're goin', come right into the house and change your clothes this minute."

Kyan obeyed. Shortly he reappeared, clothed like a lily of the field, one that had long since gone to seed. He clambered up beside Noah and they drove off.

" Jerushy!" exclaimed the lightkeeper. " This is kind of unexpected, ain't it? What's got into her to make her so accommodatin'?"

" Godfreys mighty!" was the dazed reply, "*I* don't know. This as fast as you can drive? Hurry up, afore she changes her mind."

So it happened that Mr. Pepper was in Bayport with the rest, awaiting the stage which was bringing Trumet's latest celebrity from Sandwich.

" Here she comes!" shouted Ezra Simmons, the postmaster. " Right on time, too."

Sure enough! A cloud of dust in the distance, rising on the spring wind, and the rattle of rapidly turning wheels. The reception committee prepared for action. Captain Elkanah descended from the carriage and moved in stately dignity to the front of the post-office platform.

" Hum—ha!" he barked, turning to his followers. " Be ready now. Give him a good cheer, when I say the word. Let it be hearty— hearty, yes."

The stage, its four horses at a trot, swung up to the platform.

"Whoa!" roared the driver.

"Now!" ordered Elkanah. "One—two—Hurrah!"

"Hurrah!" shouted the committee, its uninvited guests and the accompanying crowd of Bayport men and boys which had gathered to assist in the welcome. "Hurrah!"

"Hooray!" yelled Kyan, a little behind, as usual.

A passenger or two peered from the coach window. The stage driver ironically touched his cap.

"Thank ye," he said. "Thank ye very much. I've been hopin' for this for a long time, though I'd about given up expectin' it. I'm very much obliged. Won't somebody please ask me to make a speech?"

Captain Elkanah frowned his disapproval.

"We are cheering Cap'n Nathaniel Hammond of Trumet," he explained haughtily. "We are here to meet him and escort him home."

The driver sighed. "You don't say," he said. "And I thought my merits had been recognized at last. And 'twas all for Cap'n Hammond? Dear! dear!"

He winked at Simmons, who wanted to laugh, but did not dare.

"Come! come!" said Captain Elkanah. "Where is he? Where's Cap'n Hammond?"

"Well, now, I'll tell ye; I don't know where he is."

"You *don't?* Isn't he with you?"

"No, he ain't. And he didn't come on the train, nuther. He *was* on it. The conductor told me he see him and set along with him between stations as fur as Cohasset Narrows. But after that he never see hide nor hair of him. Oh, that's so! Here's the mail bag, Ezry."

Captain Elkanah looked at the reception committee and it looked at him. Here was a most disconcerting setback for all the plans. The committee, after asking more, and fruitless questions, went into executive session.

Captain Zeb stepped beside the stage and put one foot on the wheel.

"Say, Thad," he whispered, "is that all you know? Where did he go to?"

"Can't tell you, cap'n. The conductor says he see him afore they got to Cohasset Narrows and not after. Naturally, we s'pose he got off there. Pretty good joke on old Daniels, I call it. Serve him right, figgerin' to take a passenger away from me. He, he!"

"But you do know more, now don't you? Tell a feller—come! I don't like Elkanah any better'n you do."

"Well," the driver's voice dropped still lower. "Well," he whispered, "I did hear this much, though don't you tell none of them: A chap I know was on the train and he said he see Cap'n Nat get off the cars at the Cohasset Narrows depot and there was a woman with him."

"A woman? A *woman?* What woman?"

"Blessed if I know! And he didn't nuther. So long! Git dap!"

The reception committee and its escort drove slowly back to Trumet. The Daniels following was disgusted and disappointed. Captain Elkanah had

340

figured upon keeping Hammond under his own wing until he was safely deposited at the old tavern. Grace was there and Elkanah meant that these two should meet before any inkling of Ellery's story reached Nat's ears. Incidentally, he could drop a few damaging hints concerning the minister's character. To hurt Ellery all he could and prejudice Hammond against him—that was the plan, and now it was frustrated. The captain had not put in an appearance and no one knew where he was or when he would come home. Obviously, there was nothing to do except give up the reception and await further news from the missing man.

Some of those present wished to remain in Bayport until night. Another train was due in Sandwich and, possibly, Nat might come on that. They could telegraph and find out whether or not he did come, and if he did, could send a carriage for him. But this suggestion was overruled. The reception was off.

The homeward journey had some unpleasant incidents. Several Come-Outers had driven over. Nat belonged to them, so they felt—he was the son of their dead founder and leader—and they determined the Regulars should not have him all to themselves. They had come to bid him welcome on behalf of the worshipers at the chapel. Now they took advantage of the general disappointment to make sarcastic and would - be - humorous remarks loud enough for the majestic occupant of the decorated carriage to hear.

" Seems to me," said Thoph Black, " that them flags ought to be ha'f mast. That craft's in distress."

" S-sh-h ! " counciled his companion, another

Come-Outer. "Don't be irreverent. Look who's cruisin' under 'em. That's the King of Trumet. Let's you and me go ahead and fire salutes, Thoph."

Captain Elkanah wrathfully ordered the flags to be removed from the horses' heads and from the dashboard.

As Noah Ellis and his passenger turned into the lighthouse lane another vehicle turned out of it.

"Who was that?" queried Kyan. "Looked like one of the livery stable horses to me."

"'Twa'n't. 'Twas Thankful Payne's and that was her carriage, too. It's gettin' so dark I couldn't see who was drivin' it, but 'twas a man, anyhow."

Kyan seemed to be pondering. "I wonder," he said slowly, "I wonder if that cousin of hers from Sandwich is here visitin'. That Caleb Pratt, seems to me his name is."

"Don't know. Why?"

"Nothin', nothin'. I just wondered, that was all. That might explain why she let me——"

"Hey?"

"Nothin'. Good night, Noah. I'm much obliged to you for takin' me over, even if there wa'n't no reception."

Trumet spent that evening wondering what had become of Nat Hammond. Captain Zeb Mayo wondered most of all. Yet his wonderment was accompanied by vague suspicions of the truth. And, at eleven o'clock, when the village was in bed, a horse and buggy moved down the Turn-off and stopped before the Hammond gate. A man alighted from the buggy and walked briskly up to the side door. There he knocked and then whistled shrilly.

A window overhead was opened.

" Who is it ? " asked a feminine voice.

" Don't be frightened, Gracie," replied the man at the door. " It's me—Nat. I've come home again."

# CHAPTER XX

## IN WHICH THE MINISTER RECEIVES A LETTER

JOHN ELLERY was uneasy. Physically he was very much better, so much better that he was permitted to sit up a while each day. But mentally he was disturbed and excited, exactly the condition which the doctor said he must not be in. Keziah and Grace had gone away and left him, and he could not understand why.

Mrs. Higgins, Ike's mother, was at the shanty and she did her best to soothe and quiet him. She was a kind soul and capable, in her way, but she could not answer his questions satisfactorily.

"Where are they?" he demanded. "Why did they go? Has anything happened? When are they coming back?"

"I can't tell you just when, Mr. Ellery," replied Mrs. Higgins. "Grace had to go home for a—a day or so and Keziah had things to attend to at the parsonage. Don't you fret yourself about them."

"I'm not fretting, but it does seem strange. I could understand why one should go, perhaps, but not both. Didn't Gra— Miss Van Horne tell you why she went?"

"Well, now, Mr. Ellery, don't let's worry about Gracie. She's a good girl with lots of common sense and——"

344

"I know that. But that doesn't answer me. Why did she go?"

"Keziah hadn't been to the parsonage sence that day when you was fust took sick, and I expect likely she felt that she'd ought to——"

"Please, Mrs. Higgins, tell me the truth. I'm not asking about Mrs. Coffin. Didn't Miss Van Horne tell you her reason for leaving?"

"No, she didn't."

"But you know the reason? You're keeping something from me. Did she say when she would come back?"

"No, not exactly, but, of course——"

"I know you're keeping something from me. What has happened?"

"Happened? Land sakes! does anything ever happen in Trumet?"

"I think a good many things have happened lately. And the longer you keep the truth from me the more I shall suspect."

"Mr. Ellery, you set still in that chair, or, when the doctor comes, he'll put you to bed. I've got some cookin' to do and I can't set here gossipin' no longer. You behave yourself and stop frettin'. I'm skipper here now—er—for a while, anyhow—and you've got to take orders from me. There! now I cal'late you're scared, ain't you?"

He did not seem greatly frightened, nor in awe of his new skipper. Instead, he was evidently preparing to ask more questions. Mrs. Higgins hurriedly fled to the living room and closed the door behind her.

The minister heard her rattling pans and dishes at a great rate. The noise made him nervous and he wished she might be more quiet. He moved to the chair nearest the window and looked out over the dunes and the wide stretch of tumbling blue sea. The surf was rolling up the shore, the mackerel gulls were swooping and dipping along the strand, the beach grass was waving in the wind. A solitary fish boat was beating out past the spar buoy. She was almost over the spot when the *San Jose* had first anchored.

The view was a familiar one. He had seen it in all weathers, during a storm, at morning when the sun was rising, at evening when the moon came up to tip the watery ridges with frosted silver. He had liked it, tolerated it, hated it, and then, after she came, loved it. He had thought it the most beautiful scene in all the world and one never to be forgotten. The dingy old building, with its bare wooden walls, had been first a horror, then a prison, and at last a palace of contentment. With the two women, one a second mother to him, and the other dearest of all on earth, he could have lived there forever. But now the old prison feeling was coming back. He was tired of the view and of the mean little room. He felt lonely and deserted and despairing.

His nerves were still weak and it was easy, in his childish condition, to become despondent. He went over the whole situation and felt more and more sure that his hopes had been false ones and that he had builded a fool's paradise. After all, he remembered, she had given him no promise; she had found him ill and delirious and had brought him there. She had been kind and thoughtful and gracious, but that she would be to anyone, it was her nature. And he had been content, weak as he was, to have her near him, where he would see her and hear her speak. Her mere presence was so wonderful that he had been satisfied with that and had not asked for more. And now she had gone. Mrs. Higgins had said "for a day or two," but that was indefinite, and she had not said she would return when those two days had passed. He was better now, almost well. Would she come back to him? After all, conditions in the village had not changed. He was still pastor of the Regular church and she was a Come-Outer. The man she had promised to marry was dead—yes. But the other conditions were the same. And Mrs. Higgins had refused to tell him the whole truth; he was certain of that. She had run away when he questioned her.

He rose from the chair and started toward the living room. He would not be put off again. He would be answered. His hand was on the latch of the door when that door was opened. Dr. Parker came in.

The doctor was smiling broadly. His ruddy face was actually beaming. He held out his hand, seized the minister's, and shook it.

"Good morning, Mr. Ellery," he said. "It's a glorious day. Yes, sir, a bully day. Hey? isn't it?"

Ellery's answer was a question.

"Doctor," he said, "why have Mrs. Coffin and —and Miss Van Horne gone? Has anything happened? I know something has, and you must tell me what. Don't try to put me off or give me evasive answers. I want to know why they have gone."

Parker looked at him keenly. "Humph!" he grunted. "I'll have to get into Mrs. Higgins's wig.

347

I told her not to let you worry, and you have worried. You're all of a shake."

"Never mind that. I asked you a question."

"I know you did. Now, Mr. Ellery, I'm disappointed in you. I thought you were a sensible man who would take care of his health, now that he'd got the most of it back again. I've got news for you— good news—but I'm not sure that I shall tell it to you."

"Good news! Dr. Parker, if you've got news for me that is good, for Heaven's sake tell it. I've been imagining everything bad that could possibly happen. Tell me, quick. My health can stand that."

"Ye-es, yes, I guess it can. They say joy doesn't kill, and that's one of the few medical proverbs made by unmedical men that are true. You come with me and sit down in that chair. Yes, you will. Sit down."

He led his patient back to the chair by the window and forced him into it.

"There!" he said. "Now, Mr. Ellery, if you think you are a man, a sensible man, who won't go to pieces like a ten-year-old youngster, I'll—I'll let you sit here for a while."

"Doctor?"

"You sit still. No, I'm not going to tell you anything. You sit where you are and maybe the news'll come to you. If you move it won't. Going to obey orders? Good! I'll see you by and by, Mr. Ellery."

He walked out of the room. It seemed to Ellery that he sat in that chair for ten thousand years before the door again opened. And then——

348

"Grace!" he cried. "O Grace! you—you've come back."

She was blushing red, her face was radiant with quiet happiness, but her eyes were moist. She crossed the room, bent over and kissed him on the forehead.

"Yes, John," she said; "I've come back. Yes, dear, I've come back to—to you."

Outside the shanty, on the side farthest from the light and its group of buildings, the doctor and Captain Nat Hammond were talking with Mrs. Higgins. The latter was wildly excited and bubbling with joy.

"It's splendid!" she exclaimed. "It's almost too fine to believe. Now we'll keep our minister, won't we?"

"I don't see why not," observed the doctor, with quiet satisfaction. "Zeb and I had the Daniels crowd licked to a shoestring and now they'll stay licked. The parish committee is three to one for Mr. Ellery and the congregation more than that. Keep him? You bet we'll keep him! And I'll dance at his wedding—that is, unless he's got religious scruples against it."

Mrs. Higgins turned to Captain Nat.

"It's kind of hard for you, Nat," she said. "But it's awful noble and self-sacrificin' and everybody'll say so. Of course there wouldn't be much satisfaction in havin' a wife you knew cared more for another man. But still it's awful noble of you to give her up."

The captain looked at the doctor and laughed quietly.

"Don't let my nobility weigh on your mind, Mrs. Higgins," he said. "I'd made up my mind to

349

do this very thing afore ever I got back to Trumet. That is, if Gracie was willin'. And when I found she was not only willin' but joyful, I—well, I decided to offer up the sacrifice right off."

"You did? You *did?* Why, how you talk! I never heard of such a thing in my born days."

"Nor I neither, not exactly. But there!" with a wink at Parker, "you see I've been off amongst all them Kanaka women and how do you know but I've fell in love?"

"Nat *Hammond!*"

"Oh, well, I— What is it, Grace?"

She was standing in the doorway and beckoning to him. Her cheeks were crimson, the breeze was tossing her hair about her forehead, and she made a picture that even the practical, unromantic doctor appreciated.

"By George, Nat!" he muttered, "you've got more courage than I have. If 'twas my job to give her up to somebody else I'd think twice, I'll bet."

The captain went to meet her.

"What is it?" he asked.

"Nat," she whispered, "will you come in? He wants to see you."

John Ellery was still seated in the chair by the window, but he no longer looked like an invalid. There was no worry or care in his countenance now, merely a wondrous joy and serene happiness.

He held out his hands and the captain shook them heartily.

"Mr. Ellery," he said, "as they used to say at the circus, 'Here we are again.' And you and I have been doing all kinds of circus acrobatics since we shook last, hey? I'm glad you're pretty nigh out of the sick bay—and the doctor says you are."

"Captain," began Ellery. Hammond interrupted him.

"Hold on!" he said. "Belay right there. If you and I are to cruise in the same family—and that's what I hear is likely to happen—I cal'late we'll heave overboard the cap'ns and Misters. My name's 'Nathaniel'—'Nat' for short."

"All right. And mine is 'John.' Captain—Nat, I mean—how can I ever thank you?"

"Thank me? What do you want to thank me for? I only handed over somethin' that wasn't mine in the first place and belonged to you all along. I didn't know it, that was the only trouble."

"But your promise to your father. I feel——"

"You needn't. I told dad that it was just as Grace said. She says she's got a better man, or words to that effect. And—I don't know how you feel about such things, John—but I b'lieve there's a broader outlook up aloft than there is down here and that dad would want me to do just what I have done. Don't worry about me. I'm doin' the right thing and I know it. And don't pity me, neither. I made up my mind not to marry Grace—unless, of course, she was set on it—months ago. I'm tickled to death to know she's goin' to have as good a man as you are. She'll tell you so. Grace! Hello! she's gone."

"Yes. I told her I wanted to talk with you alone, for a few minutes. Nat, Grace tells me that Aunt Keziah was the one who——"

"She was. She met me at the Cohasset Narrows depot. I was settin' in the car, lookin' out of the window at the sand and sniffin' the Cape air. By the everlastin'! there ain't any air or sand like 'em any-wheres else. I feel as if I never wanted to see a palm tree again as long as I live. I'd swap the whole of the South Pacific for one Trumet sandhill with a huckleberry bush on it. Well, as I started to say, I was settin' there lookin' out of the window when somebody tapped me on the shoulder. I looked up and 'twas her.

"You could have blown me over with a fan. By the jumpin' Moses, you could! You see, I'd been thinkin' about her—that is, I was——"

He hesitated, turned red, coughed, and went on.

"I was surprised enough to see her, I tell you. Way up there at the Narrows! I couldn't have said a word, anyway, and she never gave me a chance. 'Nat,' she says, 'don't talk now. Come with me, quick, afore the train starts.'

"Still I didn't say anything, nothin' sane any-how. 'Keziah!' I managed to stutter. '*Keziah!*'

"'Come!' says she. 'Hurry! I want you to get off here. I've come here on purpose to meet you. I must talk with you; it's important. You can go to Trumet on the next train, to-night. But now I must talk with you. I *must*. Won't you please come, Nat?'

"Well, I went. The engine bell was beginnin' to ring and we had to move lively, I tell you. I swung her off the step just as the car begun to move. After the smoke had faded away around the next bend I realized that my hat had faded away along with it. Yes, sir! I'd left it on the seat. Ha! ha! ha!"

He laughed uproariously. Ellery laughed in sympathy.

"However, I wa'n't worryin' about hats, just then. All I wanted to do was stand still, like a frozen image, and stare at her. You see, John, I hadn't laid eyes on a friend, one of the real home-made kind, for more days than I wanted to count; and here was one of 'em, one of the best, passed out to me unexpected and ahead of time, like a surprise party present. So I just pumped her hand up and down and stared. I didn't have any exclusive mort-gage on the starin' by no means, for the depot mas-ter and a dozen or so loafers was lookin' at us with their mouths wide open.

"I guess she noticed it, for she says, 'Don't stay here, Nat. Come in the waitin' room or somewheres where we can talk.'

"So into the waitin' room we went and come to anchor on the settee. Six or eight of the loafers set-tled themselves handy to the door, so's they could peek in occasionally. I remember I told one of them not to stretch his neck that way 'cause he might never get it back into shape again and in the gunnin' season that would be dangerous. 'Some nearsighted feller might take you for a goose,' I says. Ho! ho!

"And then, John, we had our talk. Seems she left Trumet Wednesday afternoon. Got the livery stable man to drive her as fur as Bayport, hired an-other team there and come on to Sandwich. Stayed overnight there and took the mornin' train which got to Cohasset Narrows just ahead of the one I was comin' on. She'd been so afraid of bein' late, she said. She must see me afore I got to Trumet.

"Well, she saw me and told me the whole yarn about you and Grace. She tried to break it to me gently, so I wouldn't feel too bad. She knew it would be a shock to me, she said. It was a shock, in a way, but as for feelin' bad, I didn't. I think the world of Grace. I'd do anything she wanted me to do; but most the way down on the train—yes, and long afore that—I'd been dreadin' my comin' home on one account. I dreaded tellin' her that, unless she was real set on it, she'd better not marry me.

"You see, John, I've thought a lot sence I've been away. Had consider'ble time to do it in. And the more I thought the less that promise to dad seemed right. I'd have bet my sou-wester Gracie never cared for me in the way a girl ought to care for a chap she's goin' to ship as pilot for the rest of her days. And, as for me—well, I—I had my reasons for not wantin' to marry her."

He paused again, sighed, started to speak, and then sat silent, looking out of the window. Ellery laid a hand on his knee.

"Nat," said the minister, "you saved my life once, do you remember that? I do, if you don't."

"Saved your life? What are you talkin' about? Oh! that time on the flats? That wasn't savin' your life, 'twas savin' your clothes from gettin' a wettin'."

"No, it was more than that. And now I guess you've saved it again, you and Grace between you. Yes, and Aunt Keziah. Bless her! to think of her going way up there to meet you and help us!"

"Yes. 'Twas like her, wasn't it? She said she knew I'd hear the yarn when I got to Trumet, but she wanted me to hear it just as it was, and nobody but she and Grace and you knew the whole truth about it. So she come. I'm glad she did; not that I shouldn't have done the same, whoever told me, but——"

"Nat, I want to tell you something. Something that only one other person knows. Grace doesn't know it yet. Neither does Aunt Keziah—the whole of it. And if she knew I told you even a part I'm afraid she would, as she would say, 'skin me alive.' But I owe her—and you—more than I could repay if I lived a thousand years. So I'm going to tell and take the consequences."

The captain looked at him. "Well!" he exclaimed. "What's comin' now? More secrets? Blessed if this ain't gettin' more excitin' than the South Seas. I used to think excitement in Trumet was scurcer than cream in poorhouse coffee, but I'll have to change my mind."

"Nat, when—that morning after your father died and after you and Grace had agreed to—to——"

"To do somethin' neither of us wanted to do? Yes, I know. Go ahead."

"That morning Aunt Keziah came home to the parsonage and broke the news to me. She did it as only she could do such a thing, kindly and pityingly and——"

"Of course. That's Keziah."

"Yes. Well, as you can imagine, I was almost crazy. I made a fool of myself, I expect; refused to believe her, behaved disgracefully, and at last, when I had to believe it, threatened to run away and leave my work and Trumet forever, like a coward. She made me stay."

"Did, hey?"

"Yes. She showed me it was my duty to face the music. When I whimpered about my troubles she told me her own story. Then I learned what trouble was and what pluck was, too. She told me about her marriage and—excuse me for speaking of what isn't my business; yet it is mine, in a way—she told me about you."

Captain Hammond did not answer. His good-natured face clouded and he shifted in his chair.

"She told me of you, Nat, all about you—and herself. And she told me something else, which explains why she felt she must send you away, why she thought your marriage to Grace would be a good thing."

"I know. She told you that that darn scamp Anse Coffin was alive."

The minister started violently. He gasped in surprise.

"You knew it? You *knew* it?" he stammered.

"I know it now. Have known it for over a year. My findin' it out was one of the special Providences that's been helpin' along this last voyage of mine. My second mate was a Hyannis man, name of Cahoon. One day, on that pesky island, when we was eatin' dinner together, he says to me, 'Cap'n,' he says, 'you're from Trumet, ain't you?' I owned up. 'Know anybody named Coffin there?' says he. I owned up to that, too. 'Well,' he says, 'I met her husband last trip I was in the *Glory of the Wave*.' I stared at him. 'Met his ghost, you mean,' I says. 'He's been dead for years, and a good thing, too. Fell overboard and, not bein' used to water, it killed him.'

"But he wouldn't have it so. 'I used to know Anse Coffin in New Bedford,' he says. 'Knew him well's I know you. And when we was in port at Havre I dropped in at a gin mill down by the water front and he come up and touched me on the arm. I thought same as you, that he was dead, but he wa'n't. He was three sheets in the wind and a reg'lar dock rat to look at, but 'twas him sure enough. We had a long talk. He said he was comin' back to Trumet some day. Had a wife there, he said. I told him, sarcastic, that she'd be glad to see him. He laughed and said maybe not, but that she knew he was alive and sent him money when he was hard up. Wanted me to promise not to tell any Cape folks that I'd seen him, and I ain't till now.'

" Well, you can imagine how I felt when Cahoon spun me that yarn. First I wouldn't b'lieve it and then I did. It explained things, just as you say, John. I could see now why Keziah gave me my walkin' papers. I could see how she'd been sacrificin' her life for that scum."

" Yes. She wouldn't divorce him. She said she had taken him for better or worse, and must stand by him. I tried to show her she was wrong, but it was no use. She did say she would never live with him again."

" I should say not. *Live* with him! By the everlastin'! if he ever comes within reach of my hands then—there's times when good honest murder is justifiable and righteous, and it'll be done. It'll be done, you hear me! "

He looked as if he meant it. Ellery asked another question.

" Did you tell her—Aunt Keziah—when you met her at the Narrows? " he asked.

" No. But I shall tell her when I see her again. She shan't spoil her life—a woman like that! by the Lord! *what* a woman!—for any such crazy notion.

I swore it when I heard the story and I've sworn it every day since. That's what settled my mind about Grace. Keziah Coffin belongs to me. She always has belonged to me, even though my own pig-headedness lost her in the old days."

"She cares for you, Nat. I know that. She as much as told me so."

"Thank you, John. Thank you. Well, I can wait now. I can wait, for I've got something sure to wait for. I tell you, Ellery, I ain't a church-goin' man—not as dad was, anyway—but I truly believe that this thing is goin' to come out right. God won't let that cussed rascal live much longer. He won't! I know it. But if he does, if he lives a thousand years, I'll take her from him."

He was pacing the floor now, his face set like granite. Ellery rose, his own face beaming. Here was his chance. At last he could pay to this man and Keziah a part of the debt he owed.

Nat stopped in his stride. "Well!" he exclaimed. "I almost forgot, after all. Keziah sent a note to you. I've got it in my pocket. She gave it to me when she left me at Cohasset."

"Left you? Why! didn't she come back with you on the night train?"

"No. That's funny, too, and I don't understand it yet. We was together all the afternoon. I was feelin' so good at seein' her that I took her under my wing and we cruised all over that town together. Got dinner at the tavern and she went with me to buy myself a new hat, and all that. At first she didn't seem to want to, but then, after I'd coaxed a while, she did. She was lookin' pretty sad and worn out, when I first met her, I thought; but she seemed to get over it and we had a fine time. It reminded me of the days when I used to get home from a voyage and we were together. Then, when 'twas time for the night train we went down to the depot. She gave me this note and told me to hand it to you to-day.

"'Good-by, Nat,' she says. 'We've had a nice day, haven't we?'

"'We have, for a fact,' I says. 'But what are you sayin' good-by for?'

"'Because I'm not goin' to Trumet with you,' says she. 'I'm goin' to the city. I've got some business to see to there. Good-by.'

"I was set back, with all my canvas flappin'. I told her I'd go to Boston with her and we'd come home to Trumet together to-morrow, that's to-day. But she said no. I must come here and ease your mind and Grace's. I must do it. So at last I agreed to, sayin' I'd see her in a little while. She went on the up train and I took the down one. Hired a team in Sandwich and another in Bayport and got to the tavern about eleven. That's the yarn. And here's your note. Maybe it tells where she's gone and why."

The minister took the note and tore open the envelope. Within was a single sheet of paper. He read a few lines, stopped, and uttered an exclamation.

"What's the matter?" asked the captain.

Ellery did not answer. He read the note through and then, without a word, handed it to his friend.

The note was as follows:

"DEAR JOHN:

"I am going away, as I told you I would if he

came. He is coming. Tuesday I got a letter from him. It was written at Kingston, Jamaica, almost three months ago. I can't think why I haven't got it sooner, but suppose it was given to some one to mail and forgotten. In it he said he was tired of going to sea and was coming home to me. I had money, he said, and we could get along. He had shipped aboard a brig bound for Savannah, and from there he was going to try for a berth on a Boston-bound vessel. So I am going away and not coming back. I could not stand the disgrace and I could not see him. You and Grace won't need me any more now. Don't worry about me. I can always earn a living while I have my strength. Please don't worry. If he comes tell him I have gone you do not know where. That will be true, for you don't. I hope you will be very happy. I do hope so. Oh, John, you don't know how I hate to do this, but I must. Don't tell Nat. He would do something terrible to him if he came, and Nat knew. Just say I have been called away and may be back some time. Perhaps I may. Love to you all. Good-by.

"Yours truly,

"Keziah Coffin."

The captain stared at the note. Then he threw it to the floor and started for the door. The minister sprang from his chair and called to him.

"Nat," he cried. "Nat! Stop! where are you going?"

Hammond turned.

"Goin'?" he growled. "Goin'? I'm goin' to find her, first of all. Then I'm comin' back to wait for him."

"But you won't have to wait. He'll never come. He's dead."

"Dead? *Dead?* By the everlastin'! this has been too much for you, I ought to have known it. I'll send the doctor here right off. I can't stay myself. I've got to go. But——"

"Listen! listen to me! Ansel Coffin is dead, I tell you. I know it. I know all about it. That was what I wanted to see you about. Did Keziah tell you of the *San Jose* and the sailor who died of smallpox in this very building? In that room there?"

"Yes. John, you——"

"I'm not raving. It's the truth. That sailor was Ansel Coffin. I watched with him and one night, the night before he died, he spoke Keziah's name. He spoke of New Bedford and of Trumet and of her, over and over again. I was sure who he was then, but I called in Ebenezer Capen, who used to know Coffin in New Bedford. And he recognized him. Nat, as sure as you and I are here this minute, Ansel Coffin, Aunt Keziah's husband, is buried in the Trumet cemetery."

# CHAPTER XXI

## IN WHICH MR. STONE WASHES HIS HANDS

MR. ABNER STONE, of Stone & Barker, marine outfitters and ship chandlers, with a place of business on Commercial Street in Boston, and a bank account which commanded respect throughout the city, was feeling rather irritable and out of sorts. Poor relations are always a nuisance. They are forever expecting something, either money—in Mr. Stone's case this particular expectation was usually fruitless—or employment or influence or something. Mr. Stone was rich, he had become so by his own ability and unaided effort. He was sure of that—often mentioned it, with more or less modesty, in the speeches which he delivered to his Sunday-school class and at the dinners of various societies to which he belonged. He was a self-made man and was conscious that he had done a good job.

Therefore, being self-made, he saw no particular reason why he should aid in the making of others. If people were poor they ought to get over it. Poverty was a disease and he was no doctor. He had been poor once himself, and no one had helped him. "I helped myself," he was wont to say, with pride. Some of his rivals in business, repeating this remark, smiled and added that he had been "helping himself" ever since.

Mr. Stone had "washed his hands" of his

cousin, Keziah Coffin, or thought he had. After her brother Solomon died she had written to him, as ing him to find her a position of some kind in Boston. "I don't want money, I don't want charity," wrote Keziah. "What I want is work. Can you get it for me, Abner? I write to you because father used to tell of what you said to him about gratitude and how you would never rest until you had done something in return for what he did for you."

Captain Ben Hall's kindness was the one thing Mr. Stone forgot when he said no one had ever helped him. He disliked to be reminded of it. It was a long while ago and the captain was dead. However, being reminded, he had called upon a friend in the tailoring line and had obtained for Keziah the place of sewing woman. She decided to become housekeeper at the Trumet parsonage and so notified him. Then he washed his hands of her.

But now he was compelled to soil them again. Keziah had appeared at his office, without warning, and demanded that he find her a position. "Demanded" was the proper word. Certainly she had not begged. She seemed to feel that her demand was right and proper, and his acceding to it the least he could do.

"What a fine place you've got here, Abner!" she said, inspecting the office and the store. "I declare it's finer than the one you had when you first went into business, afore you failed. I wish father could have lived to see it. He'd have realized that his judgment was good, even though his investment wasn't."

Captain Hall had invested largely in that first business, the one which failed. Mr. Stone changed the subject. Later in the day he again sought his friend, the tailor, and Keziah was installed in the loft of the latter's Washington Street shop, beside the other women and girls who sewed and sewed from seven in the morning until six at night. Mr. Stone had left her there and come away, feeling that an unpleasant matter was disposed of. He had made some inquiries as to where she intended staying, even added a half-hearted invitation to dinner that evening at his home. But she declined.

"No, thank you, Abner," she said, "I'm goin' to find a boardin' place and I'd just as soon nobody knew where I was stayin', for the present. And there's one thing I want to ask you: don't tell a soul I am here. Not a soul. If anyone should come askin' for me, don't give 'em any satisfaction. I'll tell you why some day, perhaps. I can't now."

This was what troubled Mr. Stone as he sat in his office. Why should this woman wish to have her whereabouts kept a secret? There was a reason for this, of course. Was it a respectable reason, or the other kind? If the latter, his own name might be associated with the scandal. He wished, for the fiftieth time, that there were no poor relations.

A boy came into the office. "There is some one here to see you, Mr. Stone," he said.

"Who is it?"

"I don't know, sir. Looks like a seafaring man, a sea captain, I should say — but he won't give his name. Says it's important and nobody but you'll do."

"Humph! All right. Tell him to wait. I'll be out in a minute."

Sea captains and ship owners were Stone &

Barker's best customers. The senior partner emerged from the office with a smile on his face.

"Ah!" he said, extending his hand. "Glad to see you, Captain—er——"

"Hammond," replied the visitor. "Same to you, Mr. Stone."

"Fine weather for this time of year."

"Fine enough, Mr. Stone."

"Well, Captain Hammond, what can we do for you? Going to sail soon?"

"Not right away. Just made port, less'n a week ago. Home looks good to me, for a spell, anyhow."

"So? Yes, I have no doubt. Let me see—where is your home, captain? I should remember, of course, but——"

"Don't know why you should. This is my first trip in your latitude, I guess. My home's at Trumet."

"Trumet?" Mr. Stone's tone changed.

"Yes. Trumet, down on the Cape. Ever been there? We think it's about as good a place as there is."

"Hu-u-m! Trumet? Well, Captain Hammond, you wished to see me, I understand."

"Yes. Fact is, Mr. Stone, I want to ask you where I can find Mrs. Keziah Coffin. She's a relation of yours, I b'lieve, and she's come to Boston lately. Only yesterday or the day afore. Can you tell me where she is?"

"Why do you wish to see her?"

"Oh, for reasons, personal ones. She's a friend of mine."

"I see. No, captain, I can't tell you where she is. Good morning."

Captain Nat was greatly disappointed.

"Hold on there, just a minute," he begged. "This is important, you understand, Mr. Stone. I'm mighty anxious to find Kezi—Mrs. Coffin. We thought, some of her friends and I, that most likely you'd know where she was. Can't you give us any help at all? Hasn't she been here?"

"Good morning, Captain Hammond. You must excuse me, I'm busy."

He went into the office and closed the door. Captain Nat rubbed his forehead desperately. He had been almost sure that Abner Stone would put him on Keziah's track. Grace had thought so, too. She remembered what the housekeeper had told concerning her Boston cousin and how the latter had found employment for her when she contemplated leaving Trumet, after her brother's death. Grace believed that Keziah would go to him at once.

Nat walked to the door and stood there, trying to think what to do next. A smart young person, wearing a conspicuous suit of clothes, aided and abetted by a vivid waistcoat and a pair of youthful but promising side whiskers, came briskly along the sidewalk and stopped in front of him.

"Well, sir?" observed this person, with cheerful condescension. "Anything I can do for you?"

Captain Nat turned his gaze upon the side whiskers and the waistcoat.

"Hey?" he queried.

"I say, is there anything I can do for you?"

The captain shook his head. "No-o," he drawled dryly, "I'm afraid not, son. I admit that don't seem scarcely possible, but I am afraid it's so."

"Looking for something in our line, was you?"

" Well, I don't know. What might be on your line—clothes? "

The bewhiskered one drew himself up. " I am connected with Stone & Barker," he said sharply. " And, seeing you standing in our doorway, I thought possibly——"

" Yes, yes. Beg your pardon, I'm sure. No, I don't want to buy anything. I come to see Mr. Stone on a personal matter."

" He's busy, I suppose."

" So he says."

The young man smiled with serene satisfaction. " I'm not surprised," he observed complacently. " We *are* a busy house, Mr—er——"

" Hammond's my name. Are you Mr. Barker? "

" No-o, my name is Prince."

" So? Silent partner in the firm, hey? "

" No-o, not exactly. Mr. Prince was slightly embarrassed. " No, I am a—a salesman—at present. Was the matter you wished to see Mr. Stone about a very private one? "

" Middlin'.'"

" Well, I asked because Mr. Stone is a busy man and we like to save him all the—the——"

" Trouble you can, hey? That's nice of you, you must save him a lot, Mr—er—King, was it? "

" No, Prince."

" Sure and sartin', Prince, of course. I knew 'twas connected with the royal family. Well, Mr. Prince, I'm afraid even you can't help me nor him out this time. I'm lookin' up a friend of mine, a widow lady from down the Cape. She's a relation of Mr. Stone's, and she's come to Boston durin' the last day or so. I thought likely he might know where she was, that's all. That would be a little out of your latitude, hey?"

"I don't know. Her name wasn't Coffin, was it?"

Captain Nat started. "It certainly was," he answered eagerly. "How'd you know that?"

Mr. Prince's complacence was superb. "Oh," he answered with condescension, "Mr. Stone trusts me with a good many of his personal affairs."

"I should think likely he would. But about Mrs. Coffin? You was goin' to say?"

"She is with James Hallett & Co., the tailors, on Washington Street. Mr. Stone found a place for her there, I believe. I—er—er—superintended the carrying of her valise and— What?"

"Nothin', nothin'. Hum! Hallett & Co., tailors? What number Washin'ton Street did you say?"

Mr. Prince gave the number.

"Thank you a lot," said Captain Nat, with fervor. "Good-by, Mr. Prince. Hope the next time I come you'll be in the firm. Good day, sir."

"Good day. Nothing else I can do? And you won't wait for Mr. Stone? Very good. Is there any message for him that you would like to leave?"

"Hey?" Nat had started to go, but now he paused and turned. There was a grim twinkle in his eye. "Message?" he repeated. "Why, ye-es, I don't know but there is. You just give Mr. Stone Cap'n Hammond's compliments and tell him I'm lookin' forward to interviewin' him some time. Just tell him that, will you?"

" I'll tell him. Glad to have met you, Captain Hammond."

The captain nodded solemnly. " Say, Mr. King," he said, " you ain't half so glad as I am."

Mr. Prince strutted into the store.

" Who was that chap you were talking with? " asked a fellow-clerk.

" Oh, a hayseed who wanted to see the old man. Poor relation, I guess. I headed him off. Stone is always telling us that time is money, so I saved both of 'em for him. He ought to thank me. Wouldn't be surprised if I got the raise I've been asking for."

Mr. Prince did not get the raise, nor the thanks. But he was surprised.

In the workshop of Hallett & Co., Keziah sat sewing busily. The window near her was closed, stuck fast, and through the dingy panes she could see only roofs and chimneys. The other women and girls near her chatted and laughed, but she was silent. She did not feel like talking, certainly not like laughing. The garment she was at work on was a coat, a wedding coat, so the foreman had told her, with a smile; therefore she must be very particular.

She wondered idly whose coat it might be and who its future wearer was to marry. This reminded her of the minister and Grace. They would be happy now, her talk with Nat had assured her of that, and they, too, would be married one of these days. But she would not attend the wedding. She wondered what John had said when he read her note. He and Grace would be sorry for her, of course; but there was nothing they could do to help. No one could help her, no one. Perhaps by this time the man she had run away from had reached Trumet and her secret was known. How Didama and the rest would spread the tale! How Captain Elkanah and Annabel would sneer and exult! They hated her because she was the minister's friend. And Nat, poor fellow, what would he do? Well, at least he would understand now.

The narrow stairway leading up to the workshop ended in a little boxed-in room where the finished garments were hung to await the final pressing. From behind the closed door of this room came the sound of voices, apparently in heated argument. One of these voices was that of Larry, the errand boy. Larry was speaking shrilly and with emphasis. The other voice was lower in key and the words were inaudible.

"No, sir, you can't," declared Larry. "You can't, I tell you. The boss don't let nobody in there and— Hold on! Hold on!"

The other voice made a short but evidently earnest answer. Larry again expostulated. The workers looked up from their sewing. The door opened and Larry appeared, flushed and excited.

"Where's Mr. Upham?" he demanded. "Mr. Upham!"

Upham was the foreman of the workroom. At the moment he was downstairs in conversation with the head of the house. A half dozen gave this information.

"What's the matter? Who is it?" asked several.

"I don't know who 'tis. It's a man and he's crazy, I think. I told him he couldn't come in here,

but he just keeps a'comin'. He wants to see somebody named Coffin and there ain't no Coffins
here."

Keziah bent lower over the wedding coat. Her
hand shook and she dropped the needle.

"I told him we didn't keep coffins," declared
Larry. "This ain't no undertaker's. Where's Mr.
Upham?"

Keziah's nearest neighbor leaned toward her.

"I guess it's somebody to see you," she said.
"Your name is Coffin, ain't it?"

"No, no. That is, it can't be anybody to see me.
I don't want to see anybody. Tell him so, whoever
it is. I can't see anybody. I—*Nat!*"

He stood in the doorway, beckoning to her.

"Keziah," he said, "come here. I want you.
I'll tell you why in a minute. Come!"

She hesitated. In a measure she was relieved,
for she had feared the man at the door might be her
husband. But she was greatly agitated and troubled.
Everyone in the place was looking at her.

"Nat," she said, trying to speak firmly, "I can't
see you now. I'm very busy. Please go away."

"Come!"

"I can't come. Go away. Please!"

"Keziah, I'm waitin'. And I'm goin' to wait if
I stay here all night. Come!"

She obeyed then. She could not have a scene
there, before all those strangers. She stepped past
him into the little room. He followed and closed the
door.

"Nat," she said, turning to him, "why did you
come? How could you be so cruel? I——"

He interrupted her, but not with words. The

next moment his arms were about her and she was pressed tight against the breast of his blue jacket.

"Keziah," he whispered, "I've come to take you home. Home for good. No, stay where you are and I'll tell you all about it. Praise be to God! we're off the rocks at last. All that's left is to tow you into port, and, by the everlastin', that's what I'm here for!"

When Upham came up the stairs after his long interview with "the boss," he found the door at the top closed. When he rattled the latch that door was opened by a stranger.

"Are you Mr. Hallett?" asked Captain Nat briskly.

"No, I'm not. Mr. Hallett is in his office on the first floor. But what——"

"On the main deck, hey? Well, all right; we won't trouble him. You'll do just as well; I judge you're one of the mates of this craft. You tell Mr. Hallett that this lady here has decided not to cruise with him any longer. No fault to find, you understand, but she's got a better berth. She's goin' to ship along with me. Ain't that so, Keziah?"

Keziah, pale, trembling, scarcely realizing the situation even yet, did not speak. But Captain Nat Hammond seemed to find his answer in her silence. A few minutes later, her arm in his, they descended the gloomy, dusty stairs, and emerged into the sunshine together.

That afternoon Mr. Abner Stone again "washed his hands" of his poor relation—this time, as he indignantly declared, "for good and all."

# CHAPTER XXII

IN WHICH KEZIAH'S PARSON PREACHES ONCE MORE

TIME has wrought many changes in Trumet. The packet long since ceased to ply between the village and Boston, the stage has been superseded by the locomotive, the old "square-riggers," commanded by Cape Cod men, no longer sail the seas. Along the main road the houses have changed hands. Didama Rogers peers no more from her parlor window; that parlor is now profaned by the frivolous and irreverent summer boarder. But the old residents love to talk of the days that are gone and if you happen to catch Mr. Isaac Higgins, now postmaster and a dignified member of the board of selectmen, in a reminiscent mood he will very likely tell you of the meeting of the parish committee called by its chairman, Elkanah Daniels, to oust the Rev. John Ellery from the pulpit of the Regular church.

"I'll never forget," says Mr. Higgins, "that parish committee meetin' if I live a thousand year. I, and two or three other young shavers, was hid in the little room off the vestry—the room where they kept the dishes they used for church suppers—and we heard the whole business. Of course nobody knew that Nat was goin' to marry Keziah then, but they did know that he wa'n't goin' to marry Grace

373

Van Horne, and had given her up to the minister of his own accord. So Daniels's guns was spiked and he didn't stand no chance at all. However, you'd never have guessed it to look at him. He marched into that meetin' and up to the platform as stiff and dignified as if he'd swallered a peck of starch. He called the meetin' to order—'twas a full one, for all hands and the cook was there—and then got up to speak.

"He opened fire right off. He raked John Ellery fore and aft. The parson, he said, had disgraced the society and his sacred profession and should be hove overboard immediate. 'Twas an open secret, he said. Everybody knew how he, minister of a Reg'lar church, had been carryin' on with a Come-Outer girl, meetin' her unbeknownst to anyone, and so on. As he got warmed up on this subject he got more bitter and, though he didn't come out open and say slanderous things, his hints was as nigh that as a pig's snout is to his squeal. Even through the crack of the dish-closet door I could see the bristles risin' on the back of Cap'n Zeb Mayo's neck.

"At last Cap'n Zeb couldn't stand it no longer.

"'Belay there!' he sings out, jumpin' to his feet. 'I want to ask you one question, Elkanah Daniels: Are you tryin' to say somethin' against Grace Van Horne's character?'

"Well, that was a sort of sticker, in a way, and I cal'late Daniels realized it. He 'hum-ha'd' and barked a little and then give in that he couldn't swear the Van Horne person's character wa'n't all right, but——

"'Couldn't swear!' snorts Zeb. 'You better not try to, not when the minister or Nat's around.

374

Aw, belay! you want us to fire John Ellery out of this society—the best minister it ever had or ever will have—because he had the sense to get sweet on a good clean girl and the spunk to ask her to marry him. And you're down on her because she's been brought up in a Come-Outer family—at least, that's the reason you give out, though some of us have suspicions 'tain't the real one. Why! she risked what she thought was smallpox to keep him from dyin' that night she picked him up, ravin' distracted, in the middle of the lighthouse lane, and if he hadn't married her after that I, for one, would have been willin' to vote to give him his walkin' papers, Come-Outer she may have been, but, by time, she's got religion that's good enough for me and I'll be proud to see her the wife of my minister. Don't let's have no more chin music. We know what you want and what you called this meetin' for; now let's vote on it.'

" Three or four sung out ' Question ' and ' Vote.' But Elkanah held up his hand.

" ' Gentlemen,' says he, ' before I ask for the vote I want to say just one word. I've worshiped in this meetin' house ever sence I was a child. I was christened in it; my father worshiped here afore me; I've presided over the meetin's of this body for years. But I tell you now that if you vote to keep that rascally hypocrite in your pulpit I shall resign from the committee and from the society. It'll be like cuttin' off my right hand, but I shall do it. Are you ready for the vote? Those in favor of retaining the present minister of this parish will rise. Those opposed will remain seated.'

" Every man on the floor stood up. Daniels himself was the only one that stayed settin' down.

"'It is a vote,' says he, white as a sheet, and his voice trembling. 'Gentlemen, I bid you good day.'

"He took up his hat and cane, give one look around the vestry, as if he was sayin' good-by to it, and marched down the aisle as straight and starchy as he'd come into it. Only, when he reached the door, he put up one hand as if he was steadyin' himself. There was precious few in that vestry that liked Elkanah Daniels, but I'm bettin' high there wa'n't a one who didn't feel sorry for him then.

"'Twas quiet as could be for a minute or so after he'd gone. Then Cap'n Zeb draws a big breath and flings up his hand.

"'Shipmates,' says he, 'this is the Almighty's house and we've got to do it quiet, but I propose three whisperin' cheers for the Rev. John Ellery and the lady that's goin' to be his wife.'

"So they give 'em—hearty, too, if they was whispered—and that's all there is to that meetin' worth tellin' about."

Captain Daniels and his daughter moved to Boston that summer. They never came back to Trumet to live. Annabel remained single until after her father's death; then she married a man very much younger and poorer than she was. It was remarked by acquaintances of the couple that the difference in age became less and less apparent as their married life continued.

"Humph!" observed Captain Zeb, summing up the situation, "he started about ten year astern, but he'll beat her on the run into the cemetery, now you mark my words. Annabel's temper's cal'lated to keep any average chap drivin' on that course, bows under. There's a three-reef breeze blowin' off her tongue, day and night."

On a Sunday morning, a few weeks after the committee meeting, the Regular church was crowded. John Ellery was to preach his first sermon since the *San Jose* came ashore. Every member of the congregation was present. Even Mrs. Prince, feeble but garrulous, was there. Gaius Winslow, having delivered his brood of children at the church door, made a special trip in his carryall to fetch the old lady. Captain Zebedee and Mrs. Mayo beamed from their pew. Dr Parker and his wife smiled at them across the aisle. Didama Rogers's new bonnet was a work of art and her neck threatened to twist itself off as she turned to see each one who came in.

Lavinia Pepper sailed to the front. She was dressed in a new black alpaca which rustled so very much like silk that nearsighted people might have been deceived by it. With her was a man, apparently suffering from strangulation because of the height and tightness of his collar. " It's Caleb Pratt, from Sandwich," whispered Didama. " Thankful Payne's relation, you know. Have you heard what folks are sayin'? I guess it's true, because— Look at Kyan! you'd think he was goin' to his own funeral."

Abishai's expression was not cheerful, certainly. He followed Mr. Pratt and his sister to the Pepper pew and subsided sadly in the corner next the wall. Occasionally he was observed to wipe his forehead and once—it was during the prayer—he groaned audibly. Lavinia's dig in the ribs prevented his repeating the sound, but, judging by his looks, he continued to groan in spirit.

There was a stir at the door. All heads swung in that direction—all but Mr. Pepper's, that is. The minister and Grace were coming up the aisle and behind them came Captain Nat Hammond and Keziah Coffin. Nat was smiling and self-possessed. Never before in his life had he entered the Regular meeting house as a worshiper, but he seemed to be bearing the ordeal bravely. It was Grace's first visit to the church, also, and she was plainly embarrassed. To be stared at by eighty-odd pairs of eyes, and to catch whispered comments from the starers' tongues, is likely to embarrass one.

Yet the comments were all friendly.

"I declare!" whispered Mrs. Prince, "I never see her look so pretty afore. I knew she was the best lookin' girl in this town, but I never realized she was *such* a beauty. Well, there's one thing sartin'—we've got the handsomest parson and parson's wife in *this* county, by about ten mile and four rows of apple trees. And there's the other bride that's goin' to be. I never see Keziah look so well, neither."

Keziah did look well. Her parson had emerged triumphant from his battle with disease and adverse fate and was more than ever the idol of his congregation. He was to marry the girl of his choice—and hers. The housekeeper's ears were still ringing with the thanks of John and Grace. Both seemed to feel that to her, Keziah Coffin, more than anyone else, they owed their great joy. Some of the things they said she would never forget. And her own life, too, was freed forever of its burden, the secret which had hung over her for so many years. Only a very few knew that secret, and they would not disclose it.

Toward the memory of the man buried in the stranger's lot at the cemetery she felt almost kindly now. While he lived she had feared and dreaded him, now she was beginning to forgive. For he had paid his debt with his life, and with her, beside her, was the other, the one whom she had loved, had given up, had mourned for, and who was now to be hers always. No wonder Keziah looked well. She was happy, and happiness is a wondrous beautifier.

The minister went up the stairs to the pulpit. He was still white and thin, but his eyes were bright and his voice clear. He gave out the opening hymn and the service began.

They said it was the finest sermon ever preached in that church, and perhaps it was. When it was over, before the benediction was pronounced, Ellery stepped out from behind the pulpit to the edge of the platform. He looked over the friendly faces upturned to his and, for an instant, it seemed that he could not trust himself to speak.

"My friends," he said, "I cannot let you go without a personal word. I owe you so much, all of you, that nothing I can say will convey to you my feeling of gratitude and love for this congregation and this church. You have stood by me all through. You trusted me and believed in me. I came to Trumet a stranger. I have found here the truest friends a man could hope to find—yes, and more than friends. If I live, and while I live, I shall hope to prove by the best effort that is in me my realization of the great debt I owe you and my desire to repay it, even though the payment must, of necessity, be so inadequate. God bless you all—and thank you."

"Wa'n't it lovely!" gushed Didama. "And when he said that about true friends he was lookin' straight at Gracie all the time."

"Didn't seem to me so," declared Gaius Winslow. "I thought he was lookin' at Cap'n Hammond."

"Well, now, that's queer," put in Mrs. Parker, the doctor's wife. "I would have sworn he was looking at Keziah Coffin."

Captain Zebedee grinned. "I cal'late you're all right," he observed. "I wouldn't wonder if he was lookin' at all of 'em."

There was much hand shaking and congratulation and the church emptied slowly. Among the last to leave were the Peppers and Mr. Pratt. Lavinia took the minister aside.

"Mr. Ellery," she simpered, "I've—that is, Caleb and me—will prob'ly want you to— That is, we want you to be the one——"

"Yes, Miss Pepper?"

"Oh, my sakes! you see— 'Bishy dear, come here a minute, won't you?"

Kyan approached, the picture of desolation.

"What do you want?" he asked gruffly.

"Heavens to Betsy! Don't look so sour. A body'd think you was goin' to be hung, to look at you. 'Bishy, you tell Mr. Ellery all about it, there's a dear. He'll tell you, Mr. Ellery; and remember we count on you. Neither me nor Caleb wont have nobody else."

She seized Mr. Pratt by the arm and led him hastily away. Kyan looked after them.

"Hung?" he muttered. "I wish, by godfreys mighty, I had the hangin' of *some* folks! I'd put a tighter collar on 'em than they've got now, *I* bet you!"

The minister's lips twitched. He knew what was coming. Hints of a surprising nature had been circulating about Trumet.

"What's the matter, Mr. Pepper?" he asked.

"Matter? Matter enough! You know what she's goin' to do? She's goin' to marry *that!*"

The last word was emphasized by a furious gesticulation toward the back of the gentleman from Sandwich.

"Who? Mr. Pratt? Is your sister to marry him? Indeed! I congratulate them both — and you."

"Me? What in tunket—I ask your pardon, Mr. Ellery, for talkin' so in the meetin' house—but what are you congratulatin' me for?"

"Why, because your sister is to have a good husband; at least people speak highly of him."

"Ugh!"

"And because—well, Mr. Pepper, you have been quite confidential with me; we have shared secrets, you know; and I thought possibly the new arrangement might make it a bit more pleasant for you."

"Pleasant? How?"

"I suppose Mr. Pratt will take his bride home to Sandwich, and you, being here alone, will be more free."

"Free?" Kyan repeated the word wrathfully. "Free! I'll be about as free as a settin' hen under a barrel, I will. Is a feller free when he's got two pickin' at him instead of one? I thought I was goin' to have a little peace and comfort; I thought that same as you, Mr. Ellery. I've had my suspicions as to her and him for some time. That day when I cal'lated I'd locked her up and come back to find she'd gone buggy ridin', I thought 'twas queer. When she went to conference and left me alone I smelt a rat. When she took to letter writin' the smell got stronger; until the last few weeks I've been sartin of the game she was up to. And I never complained, no sir! Some brothers would have ripped up the eternal foundations afore they'd have let their sister break up their home and desert 'em for a stiff-necked, bald-headed old shoe peddler like——"

"Hush! hush! Mr. Pepper. You forget——"

"No, I don't forget, nuther. Mr. Ellery, you don't know it all. When Laviny come to me and told me what she was goin' to do, was I obstinate? Did I stand on my rights as head of the family and tell her she couldn't do it? No, sir-ee, I didn't! I was resigned. I says to her, 'Laviny,' I says, 'I won't say that I shan't be turrible lonesome without you. I won't say that I ain't sort of shocked and grieved at our partin' after all these years. But what's my personal feelin's when I compare 'em with your happiness? Nothin', nothin' at all!' I says. 'Bless you, Laviny,' says I. 'When you goin' to go away?' And what do you s'pose she says to me? Why, that she wa'n't goin' away at all. That—that Pratt thing has sold out his shoe store up to Sandwich and is comin' here to live. Comin' to live at our *house*, mind you, with her and with *me!* ''Twill be so nice for you, 'Bishy dear,' she says, ' to have a man in the house to keep you comp'ny and look out for you when I ain't round.' Godfreys mighty!"

This portion of Kyan's disclosure was surprising,

if the announcement of his sister's engagement was not.

" Mr. Pratt is coming to Trumet? " the minister repeated. " What for? What is he going to do here? "

" Keep shoe store, I s'pose likely. Laviny says there's a good openin' for one in this town. I told her the best openin' I could think of for him was the well and I hoped to the nation he'd fall into it. Then she went for me like a dogfish after a herrin' and I never had a taste of vittles till I'd took it all back and said I was glad he was goin' to live with us. Free! Don't talk to me about freedom! Godfreys mighty! "

Ellery smothered his desire to laugh and expressed sympathy. Abishai listened in sullen silence.

" Well," he said, turning to go, " I ain't goin' to stand it, if I can help it. I've been doin' some thinkin' on my own account and there's two ways of gettin' even. That Caleb critter is marryin' into our family 'cause he knows I'm well off. I'll cheat him, by godfreys! I'll will every cent of my fifteen hundred dollars to the poor or the heathen or somethin'. I will, sure's taxes."

The minister was obliged to laugh, then.

" I wouldn't do that," he said. " From what I hear, Mr. Pratt is worth several times fifteen hundred."

" I know it; but he's so dum mean that 'twould break his heart to see even ten cents gettin' away from him. However, that ain't my only plan. He and Laviny ain't got any mortgage on the marryin' business. Other folks can do it as well as them. What do you think of Hannah Poundberry? "

"What do I think of her? What do you mean?"

"Never mind what I mean. Just you keep that in your head, Mr. Ellery. You remember that I asked you, as man to man, 'What do you think of Hannah Poundberry?'—Yes, yes, Laviny, I'm a-comin'. They want me to ask you to marry 'em," he added. "I s'pose you'll have to. But say, Mr. Ellery, when you do, just tell Pratt that your usual price for the job is ten dollars. That'll spile his honeymoon for him, or I miss my guess."

He turned away and moved sulkily toward his beckoning sister and her escort; but wheeled once more to add, in a mysterious whisper, "Don't you forget now, Mr. Ellery. Remember that question I put to you: 'What do you think of'—Yes, yes, Laviny, I hear you!—of you know who?'"

That evening, at the parsonage, Keziah was clearing the table and Captain Nat was helping her. A happy party of four had enjoyed the meal, John and Mrs. Coffin acting as hosts and Grace and the captain being the invited guests. Now the younger couple had gone over to the church, the bell of which was ringing for evening service.

"Hurry up, Keziah," urged Nat. "If you and me don't get decks cleared pretty soon we'll be late for meetin', and I'd hate to do that, considerin' I'm such a brand-new disciple, as you might say. What do we do next, shorten sail? Like this, hey?"

He pulled the cloth from the table, sending the crumbs flying in all directions, and proceeded to fold it, after a fashion.

"There!" he exclaimed with satisfaction;

"there she is, canvas furled and under bare poles. Now we can clear out, can't we? What's the matter?"

Keziah took the cloth from his hands and refolded it.

"Nat Hammond," she said, laughing, "you may be a good sailor, but you're an awful poor housekeeper. Look at the mess you've made of that floor."

Nat looked at the scattered crumbs and shook his head.

"By the everlastin'!" he observed, "I did make dirty weather on that tack, didn't I? Cal'late I ain't much of a housekeeper, same as you say. Maybe that's why I was so dreadful anxious to get a good one to cruise along with me. Well, I've got her. I'm satisfied."

He walked to the back door of the kitchen, threw it open, and stood looking out.

"Keziah," he said, "come here a minute."

She came from the dining room and stood at his side. He put an arm about her.

"Look off there," he said, pointing with his free hand. See that?"

The sun was just setting and all the west was gorgeous with crimson and purple and yellow. The bay was spangled with fire, the high sand bluffs along the shore looked like broken golden ingots. The fields and swamps and salt meadows, rich in their spring glory of bud and new leaf, were tinged with the ruddy glow. The Trumet roofs were bathed in it, the old packet, asleep at her moorings by the breakwater, was silhouetted against the radiance. The church bell had ceased to ring and there was not a sound, except the low music of the distant surf.

" Look at it, Keziah," urged Captain Nat.

" I'm lookin', Nat," she answered. " It's beautiful."

" Ain't it? I love it, you know that, and I never thought I should be anxious for the time to come when I must leave it. But I am. I want to go."

They were to be married in another month. It would be a double wedding, for Grace and the minister were to be married at the same time. Then Nat and his wife were to go to New York, where a new ship, just out of the builders' hands, was to be ready for him. She was a fine one, this successor to the *Sea Mist*. She had been building for more than a year and when Captain Hammond returned, safe and sound, and with their money in his possession, the owners decided at once that he should command the addition to their fleet. She was to sail for Liverpool and Keziah was to be a passenger.

" I can't hardly wait to get to sea," went on Nat. " Think of it! No more lonesome meals in the cabin, thinkin' about you and about home. No, sir! you and home'll be right aboard with me. Think of the fun we'll have in the foreign ports. London, and you and me goin' sightseein' through it! And Havre and Gibraltar and Marseilles and Genoa and —and—by and by, Calcutta and Hong Kong and Singapore. I've seen 'em all, of course, but you haven't. I tell you, Keziah, that time when I first saw a real hope of gettin' you, that time after I'd learned from John that that big trouble of yours was out of the way forever, on my way up to Boston in the cars I made myself a promise—I swore that if

you did say yes to me I'd do my best to make the rest
of your life as smooth and pleasant as the past so
far had been rough. I ain't rich enough to give you
what you deserve, nowhere near; but I'll work hard
and do my best, my girl—you see."

Keziah was looking out over the bay, her eyes
brighter than the sunset. Now she turned to look up
into his face.

" Rich ! " she repeated, with a little catch in her
voice. " Rich ! there never was a woman in this
world so rich as I am this minute. Or so happy,
either."

(2)

THE END

## Cy Whittaker's Place

27 illustrations by Wallace Morgan, colored inlay on cover. 12mo. Cloth, $1.50.

Cape Cod life, as pictured by Joseph C. Lincoln, is delightful in its homeliness, its wholesomeness, its quaint simplicity. The plot of this novel revolves around a little girl whom an old bachelor, Cy Whittaker, adopts. Her education is too stupendous a task for the old man to attempt alone, so he calls in two old cronies and they form a "Board of Strategy." A dramatic story of unusual merit then develops; and through it all runs that rich vein of humor which has won for the author a fixed place in the hearts of thousands of readers. Cy Whittaker is the David Harum of Cape Cod.

"There isn't a dull page in it all. . . . The story is a very attractive one, and has the marks of a book that will have a permanence far beyond the ordinary."—*New Haven Register*.

## Our Village

Illustrated with 4 half-tone and 35 line drawings. Ornamental cover in cream and gold. 12mo. Cloth, gilt top, uncut edges, $1.50 net.

The minute fidelity to life and character of this story of life on Cape Cod thirty years ago is as remarkable as it is delightful. A man needs the quality of a Maupassant to draw life so absolutely as it is, but happily he does not, when writing of our quaint New England folk, find the sordid hopelessness that discounts for many readers the art of the great French master. If you were ever at a school picnic or a clambake, or lived in a country village—and enjoyed it—you will make a mistake if you do not recall those good times in the most vivid possible way by reading this book.

"Anyone who has read any of Lincoln's stories will need no urging to take up this book. He is one of the best humorous writers of the day, and Cy Whittaker and the other characters in his latest novel are as good as anything Mark Twain ever created."—*San Francisco Chronicle*.

D. APPLETON AND COMPANY, PUBLISHERS, NEW YORK